THE *Love* PENALTY

BOOK FOUR
NOLAN
U

Katy ♡ xoxo Archer

KATY ARCHER

THE LOVE PENALTY
Nolan U Hockey #4

Cover Design © Designed with Grace

ISBN: 978-1-991138-19-4 (eBook)
ISBN: 978-1-991138-22-4 (paperback)

Archer Street Romance
www.katyarcher.com

CHAPTER 1
LEILANI

One week ago...

The weather has turned from the hope of spring to the reminder of winter. The gray sky above and the icy drizzle hitting the window make me shiver. Or maybe it's the subzero temperatures in the truck. Seriously, a blast from Antarctica could probably whip through this vehicle and we wouldn't even notice its effects.

I glance into the front seat and frown at the driver. He's gripping the wheel with this stony, pissed-off look.

Well, it's not like I asked him to take me. I was happy to bus back to Nolan, but do you think anyone would let me?

Asher freaking volunteered, so he really shouldn't be looking so annoyed about it.

I cross my legs and shuffle in the back seat, feeling like some rich bitch who's being chauffeured to college by Mommy and Daddy's driver.

That's probably what Asher thinks of me. That I'm a snob or something. That I look down on him like he's my underling driver. That I'm sitting in the back of his pimped-out truck, disgusted that the seats aren't pure leather.

But I'm not like that.

I grew up in a family of ten. The backs of our cars were filled with crumbs and candy bar wrappers and empty juice boxes, lone socks and baseball caps, the odd shoe, and three library books that were due back weeks ago.

It drove me nuts growing up in so much chaos. If anything, being in the back of Asher's truck is luxurious... and if he weren't so annoyed with me, I'd probably be enjoying this ride.

But I couldn't sit in the front with him.

I barely know the guy. Like I'm gonna sit close enough that he can reach over and grope my leg or something. Forget it.

The athletes at my school are all the same—sex-crazed man-sluts who aren't satisfied unless they're pouring sweat on a field, court, or arena... or getting high off drugs or an orgasm. They live for cheap screws and good times.

My best friend is dating one now, and before she managed to take him off the market, the guy was Mr.

One-Night Stand. I mean, I guess Casey's okay. And Ethan and Liam are really nice guys too.

But Asher?

Ugh! He thinks he's God's gift to the world, and women are simply placed on this earth to service him.

Well, not me.

I cross my arms with a little huff and follow the raindrops on the glass, tracking their path from the top of the window down to the bottom.

It's so freaking quiet in here.

It's making me edgy, but I'm not going to break the silence. If I ask him to turn on the radio, he'll probably huff and make me feel like the biggest pain in the ass.

Why did I agree to this?

Why could I not get over myself and stay in Denver for one more night?

But no, I had to have an internal meltdown and then a mild panic attack over an upcoming world history assignment. The thought of not spending all day tomorrow working on it is giving me conniptions, and I have to get back.

I need top marks on this. I can't go slacking off, partying in Denver like exam season isn't just around the corner. I've got a scholarship to maintain. A family to make proud.

My heart thunders as I grip the edges of my sweater and remind myself to breathe.

I should never have come to Denver in the first place.

But Caroline's been worried about me, and she won't let up.

"How are you today?"

"You good?"

"Do you want to talk about it?"

There are only so many ways I can say "I'm fine." She's starting to see right through me, so I said yes to Denver as a way to appease her. She was so freaking happy, and I swear I did my best. I line-danced, I played poker, I smiled and laughed when everyone else did. I tried to distract myself at every turn, but then came the afternoon at the spa—a chance to finally stop and relax... and, well, the opposite happened. My brain had no place to go, and all those thoughts I'd been avoiding came back like a tornado.

I have to get to my dorm, to my desk, to my computer.

I need quiet, space, isolation.

But how do you explain that to someone without sounding like the world's biggest nerd?

How do you tell your effervescent, life-of-the-party friend that you're crumbling, and the only thing to make you feel grounded is diving into someone else's past? That studying the life of a servant boy in Pompeii or a resistance fighter in war-torn France helps you sleep easier at night than having to face the world as it is today?

I went away to college thinking it would be the making of me.

And maybe, in some ways, it has been.

But it's also destroyed a part of myself that I desperately want back. The carefree Lani who was ready to take the world by storm is dying a slow death, bogged down by uncertainty and pressure.

I don't know how to get her back.

And so I sit here staring at raindrops and hoping the guy in the driver's seat will be true to his word and drop me outside my dorm as fast as possible, so that I can run inside and re-edit my essay, poring over each sentence until I have perfection.

Shit, I really have lost it.

It makes me feel pathetic.

I don't want to be some anxious scaredy-cat in the back seat. I want to be the balls-of-steel version of me who would have sat in the front with my chin held high. The one who would have slapped away wandering hands and told Mr. Hot and Handsome that if I wanted him to touch me, I'd let him know.

My throat hurts as I swallow and shrink in on myself a little more.

My gaze darts to his fingers wrapped around the steering wheel. He has nice hands, Asher Bensen. His fingers are long, his nails nicely cut and shaped, like he takes care of himself in the small ways too. They match his handsome, brooding face with his dark hair and chiseled jawline. He has a weekend's worth of stubble on his chin, and it only adds to his sex appeal.

A trembling desire works through me, and I push my arms into my stomach, willing it away.

As if! I am *so* not attracted to that asshole.

I mean, I get why the puck bunnies love him. But they only see him for short amounts of time. I've had to talk to the guy on the phone, sit next to him during a quiz night... and I just spent the entire weekend around him.

It really is such a shame that someone so gorgeous can be so insanely irritating. Sometimes I want to slap that arrogant smirk right off his face. And those eyes of his—they study everything, like he's constantly looking for an opening to be a pain in the ass.

His gaze darts to the rearview mirror, and our eyes connect for the briefest moment.

Shit, did he sense me checking him out?

Kill me now!

Whipping my head to the right, I stare at those raindrops like they're somehow going to save me.

Stupid sexy hockey player with his grumpy-ass frown and piercing blue eyes.

He's not getting the better of me.

No, sir.

Closing my eyes, I force my mind back to world history, mentally revising my notes on the impact of female spies during the Second World War and how their stories affected the feminist movement back then, and today.

CHAPTER 2
ASHER

She was watching me, no doubt hexing the back of my head with some spell that will make my brain melt or turn me into a useless, pussy blob.

Seriously, she reminds me of Narcissa Malfoy with her haughty looks. That gaze of hers could make the president feel like a cockroach.

Darting my eyes back to the front windshield, I turn the headlights on. The sun hasn't set any faster than normal, but the gray clouds are making the world dark. The wipers brush across my windshield, and I focus on their rhythm while I stew in this painful silence.

Why did I agree to this?

She sat in the back.

The fucking *back*.

Like I'm her chauffeur or some shit!

Who does that?

I've given up the rest of my weekend for this chick.

Sure, she could have caught the bus, but like any of us were gonna make her do that. And then I looked around the room and saw all of my favorite people lamenting an end to their awesome time in Denver, and I couldn't let it happen.

So, I took one for the team.

I played the martyr card—wasn't gonna waste that, now was I?

They'll all owe me a little something, and I'll collect when I'm ready. I guess I should at least be grateful for that.

But driving the ice queen home is not exactly fun.

It's such a shame that someone so gorgeous can be so fucking annoying. She's heading back a day early so she can study.

Seriously.

What a way to spend a Sunday. I mean, I should probably study, too, but who gives up Denver for the books?

It's insanity, I tell you. In-san-i-ty!

Clenching my jaw, I battle against the mouthful of words I want to spew at her.

"What is your problem? We were all having a blast, and you had to go and ruin it, didn't you? It's kind of selfish, you know."

But I don't say any of it. If I dare to even speak, she'll probably throw me one of those icy glares. Her luscious lips will pull down in that unimpressed frown, and I'll be dodging metaphorical bug spray while my cockroach ass scuttles into hiding.

But this silence is fucking killing me.

And dammit, it's my truck!

With a soft growl, I punch the console and turn on the radio, forgetting that I drove down here by myself the other day, because I was stopping off to say hi to my aunt and uncle first.

Classical music starts blasting through the speakers, the energetic strings taking up every square inch of my truck.

Yes, shut up, I listen to classical music, okay? I like it. And the only time I ever get to hear it is when I'm by myself, so of course I pumped that shit until I was surrounded with a symphony of sound that made me feel like I could fly.

My eyes bulge as I start jabbing the screen, muttering lies while trying not to look in the rearview mirror. "Who's been messing with my console? Damn radio."

I dart a look at the road before struggling to change my tunes, then giving up with a huff and turning it off.

That's when I hear her soft laughter. It's more mockery than anything, and it gets my back up.

"I don't know who was messing with—"

"I love *The Four Seasons* by Vivaldi. It's inspirational. 'Winter' is my favorite season from that piece."

Checking the rearview mirror, I catch her eye, and wow. She seems to be serious. She raises her eyebrows at me, like she's daring me to call bullshit.

I frown and scratch between my eyebrows. What's she playing at here?

"You… you like classical music?" I finally ask.

"Yeah." She shrugs. "It moves me. I grew up playing the cello. My dad was a double bass man, and… we bonded over it, I guess."

Wow. She's talking to me. She's actually saying words in a civil tone, and there appears to be no venom coming out of her mouth. I check the mirror again, just to be sure. She's looking out the window, and I decide to test the waters with a little truth.

"I played violin in high school. Hated every second of it," I admit with a dry laugh. "But I did love being part of an orchestra. I loved the music."

She snickers. "So, no one was messing with your stereo, then?"

Busted.

Well, shit. May as well own it.

With a little sigh, I turn the music back on and can't help asking, "Any favorite composers?"

Glancing at me, she plays with a little smile before looking out the window again. "I'll always have a thing for Beethoven. His Fifth Symphony is phenomenal. And 'Jupiter' by Holst moves me every time."

Nice taste. She obviously likes the grandiose stuff. Which means she'll probably also like… "'Fanfare for the Common Man' is one of my favorites."

She grins. "They always use that in space movies. It's perfect."

"Just like they use 'O Fortuna' in medieval ones."

She nods, sitting forward and looking right at me. "I

sometimes listen to instrumental movie soundtracks when I'm studying."

"Me too." I can't help smiling. I should be frowning, because I don't like this woman, and having things in common with her is crippling my resolve. But I can't shut up. "*Robin Hood: Prince of Thieves*... I know that movie's really old, but the soundtrack is fucking brilliant."

"It is," she agrees. Holy shit, the woman knows how to agree with something I said! "And Harry Potter, you can't pass up that soundtrack. It's so magical. And don't even get me started on *How to Train Your Dragon*. That one makes my soul soar." She laughs.

It's a pretty sound, carefree, just the way it was when she beat us all at poker last night.

I drink it in, trying not to be mesmerized by it, but damn, I want her to laugh again.

It takes me a second to find my voice while my freaked-out brain adjusts to the fact that Leilani *Ice Queen* Iona is conversing with me in a way that's... well, fuck me... it's civil!

Don't even ask me why, but I want to keep it going, so I scramble for the first question I can find.

"So, you a Potterhead, then, or you just like the music?"

Her lips purse, her freckled nose scrunching as she murmurs, "I am. Like full-blown. I used to dress up as Hermione Granger every Halloween. Although, one year, I went as Professor Trelawny, and that was so fun." She lets out an almost giggle, shaking her head at the window as she obviously looks back through her memory.

No fucking way.

My smile grows a mile wide. There are no Potterheads at Hockey House. In fact, I was beginning to wonder if Nolan U was a Muggle pit, but there she is... sitting in the back seat of my truck. A full-blown Harry Potter fan.

She starts to grin, and I manage to catch her eye in the rearview mirror.

It's a connection. There's no other way to describe it. I feel this jolt of electricity nip me, and I think she does, too, because all of a sudden, her eyes bulge, and then her expression shuts down.

Slumping back in her seat, she looks out the window and is probably reeling the same way I am.

We were just talking like normal people do. No, it was more than that. We were talking like you do with a new friend. Like when you're a kid and you realize the person sitting next to you in class has the same pencil case or you both love the same book series or you're wearing the same sweater. It's that commonality connection.

But I can't share that with Lani.

She's the fucking ice queen of Nolan U.

We can't be friends.

We can't be anything.

So I turn back to my job as driver, clenching my jaw as "The Blue Danube" by Johann Strauss crescendos around us.

CHAPTER 3
LEILANI

So, Asher's a Potterhead just like me. Unbelievable. I wonder how many people actually know that. I can't imagine the Hockey House bros not hassling the life out of him for it. Not that Harry Potter isn't completely cool, I just don't know if it's hockey-jock, caveman cool.

Much to my horror, I'm dying to know which house he's in. It's taking maximum effort not to ask which one is his favorite book and which character he relates to. I bet it's Snape. Although, that guy's like one of the best heroes in the entire series. In fact, he's one of my favorite characters.

So, Asher is not allowed to be Snape.

Maybe he could be... Peter Pettigrew.

I internally snort, thinking about that wretched, two-faced shifter rat who betrayed his friends to Voldemort.

No, Asher's not like that. If there's one thing I noticed

about him this weekend, he seems to be loyal. I get the impression that he'd do anything for his hockey bros; he just acts like he doesn't give a shit, but I bet he'd move heaven and earth for those guys.

So, maybe he's a Gilderoy Lockhart, then. The man who thinks the sun shines out his ass and he's been placed on Earth to save it... when in reality he's a lying coward.

I fight a grin, forcing myself not to look in the rearview mirror in case he's trying to smile at me again. I don't want to connect with him. It's horrifying enough that he's into one of my favorite book series ever. I don't want to find any other connections with the guy.

I don't want him to know that I'm most like Hermione, although he's probably already thinking it. She was my hero when I was growing up. I wanted to be just like her. Although, when I took the quiz, I ended up in Ravenclaw, but you know, I'd argue that Hermione would have been quite happy in Ravenclaw as well.

I'm seconds away from asking Asher if he agrees before I quickly clamp my lips together. What is wrong with me?

Don't you dare start up another conversation with that man.

He's rude, remember?

He called you a shrutebag the first time you spoke on the phone.

And you're allowed to hold that against him forever if you want to!

With a light sniff, I cross my arms, staring out the window with fresh resolve. Asher Bensen is an arrogant, impatient, annoying know-it-all, and I refuse to like him on principle alone.

There. Done.

Easy resolve.

Except that he also sacrificed the last of his weekend to drive you back to Nolan, and he listens to Vivaldi when he's driving alone, and he smiled at you when you admitted you like Harry Potter.

Shit! I need to stop this. I can't get soft around this guy. I can't get soft around any guy. I have to keep my wits about me.

Which is why I tense up when I feel the truck slow down.

"What are you doing?" I sit up and glance out the windshield.

"We need gas," he murmurs, pulling into the station and gliding to a stop next to Pump 11.

I don't say anything as he hops out of the truck and try not to notice how sexy he looks pumping gas.

That's not a sexy thing, Leilani!

So why is my heart hammering in my chest? Why does my tongue feel thick and wet as I watch him doing this inane, simple task?

Clenching my jaw, I force myself to look away, but it only takes moments for my eyes to track back to him. He jiggles the nozzle, then returns it to the pump, dusting his hands on the back of his jeans before striding around the front of the truck.

Crap, even his walk is beautiful.

No, it's not! Stop it!

I'm so riled by my attraction that when he slips back into the truck, I stupidly let out a growl.

He frowns, turning to look at me. "What's your problem now?"

His snippy tone actually helps, and I rise to it with relish. "Nothing. Would you just drive already? Stop messing around."

He rolls his eyes. "Whatever you say, Your Highness."

"I am not—" I growl again, a throaty one that actually makes him snicker. "Oh, shut up. I just want to get back, so start the engine and let's go."

"You're grumpier than you were when we started."

"Yeah, well, I'm having to travel back to Nolan with *you*, so if that's not enough to make me grumpy, I don't know what is."

He pauses before starting the engine, and I suddenly hate myself for being so bitchy.

Spinning yet again, he gives me the driest glare I've ever seen and mutters, "Do you want me to kick you out of this truck? Is that what you're trying to achieve here? You want me to leave your ass stranded at a gas station?"

I narrow my glare even more and seethe, "You wouldn't dare."

"Really? You want to try me?" His grumpy scowl nearly makes me laugh for a second.

I don't even know why, but I'm suddenly fighting this ridiculous giggle. My belly shudders with it as I bite my lips together and battle this stupid smile that's trying to form.

"Just drive," I finally manage.

"You know what your problem is?"

"Here we go," I mutter.

"I think you're hangry. I'm trying to remember if you ate anything for lunch, but I think you were too stressed about trying to get back to Nolan, and now your blood sugar is low and your inner beast is coming out to play. Unfortunately, for the nice guy who's offered to drive you back a day early"—he points at himself—"he's having to suffer your—"

"Okay, fine, I'm hungry!" Now that he's suggested it, I realize that I kind of am.

I only nibbled at lunch because I *was* stressed trying to figure out how I was going to tell everyone that I needed to leave. I knew it would disappoint people, and I didn't want to hurt Caroline's feelings. But I couldn't stay. I need my room. Solitude. Safety.

Which is why I'm desperate to get back, but... you know, maybe I'm also desperate for some steak fries and a meaty burger.

"I knew it." Asher grins. With a laugh that's annoyingly triumphant, he spins and finally starts the engine. "I know a great place that's just off the next exit. Can you last ten minutes, or do I need to grab gas station snacks first?"

"I can last ten minutes," I grit out.

"Excellent." He checks over his shoulder before pulling away from the pump and joining the flow of traffic. "And don't worry, by the way. I turn full-blown Hulk if I don't get fed regularly, so... you know." He grins into the rearview mirror, and it's impossibly hard not to smile back.

My lips start to rise, but I catch them before any teeth can show.

Crap. He's not allowed to be charming!

He's Asher Irritating Bensen.

No, wait, I can do better than that.

He's Asher Drives-Me-Fucking-Crazy Bensen.

Asher Asshat Bensen.

I smirk. Asher Asshat. I like that.

My brain does a playful little giggle as I let that swirl through my head for a while. The streetlights flash past like a swift drumbeat, and we're soon pulling into a parking space just outside Riley's Righteous Bar & Grill.

"This place does the best burgers. I'll buy you whatever you want. Order three if you will. No judgment here."

"I'm paying," I murmur as I grab my purse.

"What?" Asher swivels in his seat to snap at me. "No, I can buy you dinner."

"No way. You paid for gas."

"It's my truck!"

I finally glance up at him, noticing the incredulous look on his face. It's oddly satisfying.

With a cheesy grin, I pop open my door and tell him, "I don't care. I'm paying for dinner or we're not eating."

He rolls his eyes and huffs, muttering his way out of his truck and slapping the door closed.

I stifle another giggle as I meet him at the restaurant door and let him open it for me.

CHAPTER 4
ASHER

I catch a whiff of her perfume as she glides past me. It's intoxicating to say the least. Everything about this woman is. From her brown skin to those freckles on her nose and those big eyes that seem to take in everything. She's a Polynesian princess, and my stupid brain can't help picturing that lush, curvy body in a grass skirt with a coconut bra.

That's probably really bad, but damn, she would look fucking fine in that getup.

Those hips of hers swaying to some Hawaiian beat, her toes sinking into the sand while she danced for me.

Would you shut the fuck up? She's not going to dance for you, you moron.

She may be beautiful, but she's a bitch. An intelligent, bossy, Potterhead, likes-classical-music bitch.

What a mindfuck.

I shake my head, forcing my eyes away from her body

while she walks to a table near the center of the room. It's basically the only one left. This place is packed.

It's only then that I notice the guy at the front getting ready to start up a quiz night.

Lani takes a seat and pulls her phone out of her purse. "Quiz night," she murmurs.

I nod as I sit in the chair beside her. She's already downloading the app displayed on the screen up front, and it's obvious she wants to take part. Truth is, so do I. I love this kinda shit. Competition. Trivia. It's my drug of choice (not that I'll ever admit that to anyone), but being on a team with this woman?

Can I stand it?

You've done it once before.

Yeah, but I had Caroline and Casey as buffers. It's just the two of us tonight and—

"Wanna?" She shows me the app on her phone screen, and I nod before logic has time to stop me.

She starts filling in our team information before I can retract my agreement, and then the waitress comes over to distract me.

"Yeah, can I get the double cheeseburger with a side of fries and a Coke Zero, please." I don't even need to look at the menu to order. I've been to this place a couple times before, and I found my gold. Why bother ordering anything else?

Lani scrambles for the menu, passing me her phone while she quickly scans the selection.

I continue filling in the little intro form because my

brain is stupid and obviously hasn't gotten the message that I don't really want to do this.

"I'll have the buttermilk chicken sandwich, please."

"Any sides or drinks?" The waitress takes the menu from her.

"Just water, and I'll steal some of his fries."

"Oh, will you now?" I mutter.

She fights a grin. "I'm paying."

"So? They're my fries."

With a little eye roll, she shakes her head. "Please tell me you're not one of those guys who doesn't share food."

"If I shared food in Hockey House, I'd never eat anything. You saw Casey inhale that pizza last night, right?"

She snorts and her shoulders shake with laughter as she continues to fight her grin. She really doesn't want that thing to show. Pity. When she lets one of those smiles free, it's seriously stunning.

Which you don't want to see, remember? Stop wishing for stupid shit!

I clear my throat and focus back on the phone screen.

"What should we call our team?" I ask.

She looks thoughtful for a minute, the side of her nose creasing on the left.

"What about Potterheads?" I can't help myself.

For a second, I think she's going to frown and shake her head, tell me I'm lame, and then—

But her shoulder hitches, and she softly agrees. "Okay."

Wow. She agreed! Miracles do happen, people.

Placing her phone down, I sit back in my chair and wait for the first round to start. It's kind of awkward just sitting here not saying anything to this woman, and eventually, I give in with a sigh and ask the question that's been burning my brain since our conversation in the car.

"So, which Hogwarts house are you in?"

She gives me a closed-mouth smile. "Can you guess?"

"I'm gonna have to say Ravenclaw."

She cringes, and I know I got it right. "Am I that transparent?"

I laugh and shake my head. "You're smart and decisive. You don't take bullshit. You're a Ravenclaw through and through."

"Just like you're a Slytherin."

"What?" I bulge my eyes at her, touching my chest and feigning offense until she laughs.

There's that pretty sound again.

"I'll have you know that I am a Gryffindor. I did the test three times to check."

"Because you didn't believe the results." She gives me a pointed look. "Because you're *actually* a Slytherin."

I smirk. "Guess that makes me Harry Potter. He was kind of split between those two. Could have gone in either house."

She makes a face, sticking out her tongue before slaying me. "No way you're a Harry. You've got Gilderoy Lockhart written all over you."

"That coward?" I gape at her, then growl in my throat. "Woman, you don't know me at all."

I'm kind of half joking, but the statement seems to shut her up, and I feel bad for killing what seemed to be a lighthearted moment.

She's going back to her perpetual frowny-face, and I'm trying to decide if I've got the energy, or willpower, to get her smiling again.

Thankfully, the quiz master steps up and gets things going.

We nail the first round with ease. It was history, and I know she's majoring in that, so I let her answer most of the questions, even though I knew them as well.

For the second round, I take charge because it's sports, and she obviously doesn't care too much because she barely knew any of the answers.

Our food arrived in the middle of the geography round, which we were cruising through, and then we only got one wrong for the entertainment round.

She ate ten of my fries while we tried to remember who won the Best Actor Award for the 2014 Oscars. I will never admit this to her, but Matthew McConaughey was a lucky guess on my part. I was tossing up between him and Leonardo DiCaprio and just happened to fall the right way. She was convinced it was Eddie Redmayne for *The Theory of Everything*, but she wasn't holding the phone, so... lucky for us.

She stole my last two fries, and I growled at her, but

she ignored me with a grin, munching away while smearing her greasy fingers on the screen.

"What is the rarest blood type in humans?" She looks to the ceiling.

"AB negative." I wipe my fingers on a napkin.

"Are you sure?"

I roll my eyes. "You don't have to ask me that every single time. Yes, I'm sure."

"Fine." She bulges her eyes like *I'm* the unreasonable one.

Honestly, she drives me fucking nuts!

So, why the hell do I want this night to last?

"And final question of the evening...," the quiz master says while my gut deflates.

Seriously? I should be happy, but...

Lani turns to me with a little grin. "We're gonna win this."

Damn, that look on her face right now.

My brain takes a quick snapshot before she turns back to the front.

"What is the heaviest organ in the human body?"

We both think on that for a second before I snap my fingers and we say in unison, "The liver."

Her lips stretch wide and she flashes those straight white teeth at me before punching in our answer.

"Done." She sits back like she knows she's aced the test, and I can't help snickering.

"You're like the top of your class, always, aren't you?"

"It's the only place to be." She looks at me like I'm dumb for thinking otherwise.

I shake my head with a rueful grin, biting my tongue against any kind of comeback.

"And the final tally shows that the winners are…" The quiz master draws out the words like he's announcing the contenders in a WWE match. "The Potterheads!"

"Yes!" I raise my arms with a loud whoop, soaking in the applause.

Lani laughs, clapping along with the crowd, then actually high-fiving me when I hold my hand up.

Seriously, people. Miracles!

The quiz master's assistant walks over with a friendly grin, gifting us vouchers for a free meal each. Lani passes one of them to me.

"You can keep it." I wave my hand through the air.

"No way. You answered some of the questions. It's only fair."

"Some?" I raise my eyebrows. "Girl, I answered most of them."

"Most?" She mirrors my expression, her eyes heating with a look that's downright sexy.

Fuck, I want to take that pretty face in my hands and lay one on her. It'd be the perfect way to shut up the rant she's just launching into.

And get a slap in the face.

And piss off Caroline.

Which in turn will piss off Casey.

Which will rile Ethan, who'll call me a douche for crossing lines and—

"Kidding." I end her rant like a diplomat and take the voucher from her. If I don't, she'll probably lecture me about equal rights or some shit. It's impossible to be chivalrous these days.

Though she does let me hold the door for her again, so at least that's something.

We reach the top of the steps and both pause, gazing up at the night sky and not saying anything. It's stopped raining, but there's still a damp chill in the air.

"That was fun," she murmurs. "Never tell anyone I said this, but... you're really smart."

I give her a side-eye, fighting a grin as I admit, "Yeah, you're kinda clever too."

"Damn right." She flicks her hair over her shoulder, and I grin at the playful look in her eyes.

So this is what ice looks like when it starts to defrost. Not bad.

Not bad at all.

CHAPTER 5
LEILANI

That smile on his face is way too sexy, and I need to get away from it ASAP.

I can't go letting my guard down now. One quiz win does not suddenly turn Asher into a nice guy. Sure, it makes him a million times sexier than he was before...

Dangerous. Don't go there!

I step forward, suddenly desperate to get away from him, and don't notice how slippery the stairs are until my feet are skidding out from under me.

"Whoa." A strong arm catches me around the waist, helping me down the last two steps until I'm securely on my feet... and in his embrace.

The air puffs between us, little white clouds that give away how fast my heart is racing.

It's just the shock of nearly falling down the stairs. That's all it is.

Except...

He still hasn't let me go, and my hands are still clutching his jacket.

I need to release my grip, thank him, step back—anything!

But I'm just standing here like a moron, breathing.

Breathing and... and wanting.

Wanting to...

My body acts before my brain can stop me, and I don't know if he leaned in first or if my eyes were saying something I didn't realize, but our lips are now suctioned together. His grip around my waist tightens as I tug on his jacket, pulling him that much closer. When his tongue skims my lower lip, I open my mouth without hesitation, inviting him in.

He tastes perfect, remnants of Coke and ketchup and salt. This heady combination of manly awesomeness and my favorite kind of food. I lash my tongue against his, all thought expiring as I'm caught in this uncontrolled moment.

His hand glides up my back, splaying between my shoulder blades while I tip my head, changing the angle of our kiss. I deepen it until I feel like I'm moving into his mouth, finding a happy home there.

He feels so good.

So hot.

My body starts to burn, to yearn, to—

Oh fuck!

Like the screeching of brakes just before an accident, I get hit with—

No, I can't think about that.

Fuck. Shit!

Stop!

I lurch away from him, reeling at what I've just let happen. Reeling at my own weakness.

Breaths punch out of me as I wriggle myself free of his grasp, then crack him across the face with my hand.

His head jerks to the side, and I quickly fist my fingers, tucking them into my chest and wincing while he tries to figure out what just happened.

"What the fuck?" He rubs his cheek, turning back to face me with an indignant frown. "You couldn't just say, '*Stop, please*'?"

"I—"

"What is wrong with you?" He takes another step away from me, flicking up his hand. "You leaned into me."

"I didn't mean to do that." I rush out the words. "I don't want to kiss you."

He goes still, narrowing his eyes at me while he rests his hand on the hood of his truck. "Yes, you do."

"No, I—"

"You do." He points at me. "You just don't want to admit it. But you fucking loved that kiss."

"That's not possible." Crossing my arms, I raise my chin and glare right back at him.

"Why?" He shrugs. "I enjoyed it."

"What?" I frown at his smirk. "No, you didn't. You hate me."

He looks to the sky with a soft groan. "I do not hate you."

"Well, you should," I snap. "I hate you."

And that's when everything playful and good and nice that we'd shared tonight disappears. It evaporates after my three little words and is quickly replaced with the old, familiar stoniness that Asher and I have been building our relationship on.

His eyebrows form a roller coaster as he gives me a skeptical frown. "You hate me?"

I should tell him no. I should admit how much I was enjoying that kiss, until...

No! I can't tell him anything!

I can't let my guard down like this. I have to be strong and in control.

So, despite the burning in my throat, I look him right in the eye and say it like I mean it. "Yes, I hate you. I have no idea what possessed me to kiss you. It was probably the win or something, but I quickly figured that it was the wrong thing to do. Because I hate you. And nothing you ever say or do will make me change my mind about that."

His eyebrows pop high, and I may as well have just kicked him in the balls. A flash of pain darts across his expression before he evens it out to that pissed-off look he was wearing when we left Denver.

"Well, thanks for that shrute-tastic comment. Guess things are back to normal, then." He stomps around his truck while I stay in my spot, still breathing like it's the only thing I'm capable of doing. "Let's go!" he barks, yanking open the back door for me.

I shuffle around to it, refusing to look at him while I slide into my seat and secure the belt around me.

He slams my door shut, then climbs in and slams his door shut, turning on the engine without a word and reversing out of his spot way too fast. "O Fortuna" starts blasting through the stereo. It gives me chills, but not in the inspired way I usually get when listening to this music.

It's like an operatic omen.

My relationship with Asher is doomed. Not that it ever could have been anything.

You sure about that?

I snap my eyes shut against the question.

It's doomed. I can't have it any other way.

I can't let myself go falling for a guy like him.

I can't let myself go falling for anybody.

I'm better off on my own.

CHAPTER 6
ASHER

I let the music play. I have to. It's not like I can speak. If I do, I'll end up spilling some filth that I might regret later.

She hates me?

She fucking hates me.

Well, that's just great.

I experience a kiss that blows my head right off, and she slaps me for it.

I'm still reeling over her sweet taste while she's telling me I'm not worthy of breathing the same air as her.

Fucking fantastic!

I thought she was into it.

Dammit, it felt like she was *so* into it. And then she just pulls away with no warning and cracks me across the face.

Fucking psycho!

She's surprisingly strong, and I can still feel remnants

of her stinging slap on my cheek. I bet I've got little red finger marks on my skin.

Witch.

She should be in Slytherin, for fuck's sake. She's pure evil.

Clenching my jaw, I drive the rest of the way back to her dorm without saying a word. Thankfully, we were over halfway home when we stopped for dinner, so it doesn't take too long.

It's raining again when I pull up outside Huxley Hall, but it's only lightly spitting, so I don't offer her my umbrella from the back.

Maybe that makes me an asshole, but let's not forget that she hates me. She probably wouldn't take the offer anyway.

"You need a hand with your stuff?" The words come out of me before I can stop myself.

Dammit! Curse my parents for raising me to be a gentleman.

"No." She unlatches her belt and nudges the door open.

"Can you get inside safely?" I mutter.

"Yeah, I've got my card." She unzips her purse and pulls it out of her wallet, then reaches across the seat to grab her overnight bag.

My finger taps against the wheel as I fight the urge to carry it for her.

The second her feet hit the curb, I hover my foot over the accelerator. There's no need for pleasantries when you're dropping off someone who doesn't like you, so as soon as the back door is shut, I punch it, rocketing away from her with a screech of my tires.

I don't bother looking in the rearview mirror.

Maybe she's standing on the curb watching me drive off.

Maybe she regrets what she said to me.

Part of me hopes she does.

And then the sensible part of me decides not to give a shit, because there are plenty of gorgeous women at Nolan U, and I don't need one who's gonna give me so much fucking trouble.

My phone starts ringing and I growl, wondering if I should ignore it. It's probably Caroline, checking that Lani got back okay.

But then I see my cousin's name flash across the screen and I punch the console.

"Harvey, how's it going, man?"

"Yeah, cool, cuz." He sounds drunk.

I roll my eyes. He always does this to me. He gets drunk, then gets weird, and I have to talk my way through a bullshit phone call.

"Where you at?" I ask, hoping he's not after a rescue somewhere.

That's another thing he's pretty good at. He gets plastered (or arrested—that happened last year), and I have to sweep in with a pickup so he doesn't have to call his parents.

I'm closer, right?

Lennox is only an hour away for me.

Denver's like a three-hour drive for him, and I doubt Uncle Hayes would be that impressed having to drive all that way because his son was too wasted to even order an Uber.

Although, he would. He'd drive across the country to help his intoxicated son get home safely. Uncle Hayes is the best.

My whole Denver family is, which is why I smile at the phone and try to shake off the frosty chill of my evening.

"I'm at a party. You wanna join me?"

"Nah, man." I shake my head. "Can't be assed driving up to Lennox."

"Come on..." He drags out the words. "I drive to Nolan all the time for you."

"No, you don't," I laugh. "You drive to Nolan for the girls. I just happen to be here too."

His laughter is sloppy and loud. "So right, man. Nolan's got great girls."

"It does." I nod, reminding myself how true that is.

Lots of great girls who aren't mean bitches. Lots of great girls who like me and want to hang with me, because I'm fucking awesome.

The words ring hollow in my head, but I shake them off and mutter them under my breath. It doesn't matter that one chick hates me. That doesn't make me any less than any other guy at this school.

I clench my jaw, wishing it was easier to believe that.

"Well, you're missing out," Harvey slurs. "I've got myself some honeys here, and they are ready to par-tay. You know what I'm sayin'? Party, brah. Par...ty!" His voice pitches, and I end up laughing, then shaking my head.

Glancing at my console, I look at the time. It's only nine thirty, and what kind of loser would I be if I just went back to Hockey House and sulked my ass off?

I should go party with Harvey and his honeys.

"Okay, man." I nod, pressing down a little harder on the gas. "Send me your location, and I'll see you soon."

"That's my man!" Harvey whoops, and I crack up laughing.

I'm feeling better already. Time to put Lani out of my brain and get myself some Lennox sugar... though I can't ignore the thought that it probably won't taste as sweet.

CHAPTER 7
LEILANI

One week after the mind-blowing kiss...

You'd think one little kiss would be easy to forget, but nope.

Every time I let my mind wander for even a second, I track back to the feeling of Asher's tongue gliding against mine. The way his hand splayed across my back, his grip around my waist. His smell. His taste. His—

"Stop it," I whisper under my breath, causing the woman at the table next to mine to glance up and frown at me.

I force a smile, but it's stiff and awkward and... dammit, I have to get out of here.

Slapping my laptop closed, I figure I can keep

studying in my dorm room. Caroline's over at Hockey House anyway, so I have the place to myself.

I usually love that, but I was feeling restless, which is why I came to this café to do some more work. But this place is making me just as edgy, so I may as well be in the privacy of my own frickin' dorm room!

With a huff, I storm out of Java Jeans, nearly knocking a poor girl over in my haste.

"Sorry," I murmur, feeling my face flush as I dip my head and make a beeline for Huxley Hall.

Shoving my hands in my pockets, I feel my laptop thump against my back as I hustle down the sidewalk. My pace is too fast for the crowded pathway, but I swivel and weave through the steady flow of human traffic.

It's a Sunday, and I have no idea why it's so busy.

Probably because spring is in the air and it's mildly warm for a change.

Probably because the sun is shining and people want to be outside enjoying it.

Probably because the average Joe and Jenny know what it means to relax and enjoy life.

Unlike me, who is stuck in this vortex of constantly seeking perfection so I don't have to think about what happened to me.

I don't like this new girl I'm becoming, but I don't know how to get off this train.

A cold sweat prickles the back of my neck, my head spinning as I dodge my darkest memories. My fingers are shaking when I swipe my card and push the Huxley door open. Running up the stairs, I make it obvious that I don't have time for chitchat as I pass open doorways and the common room.

People have stopped calling out hellos and greetings to me.

It took me a couple weeks to notice, but all of a sudden, it dawned on me that pleasantries for Leilani Iona have dried up. Because that cold bitch doesn't respond anyway. She's too busy to talk anymore. She doesn't care how other people are doing...

Because she's drowning, and she doesn't know how to tell anyone the truth.

I unlock my door and quickly slap it closed behind me, leaning against the wood and trying not to wonder what they say about me now. I'm sure *cold bitch* is thrown around a little. Maybe the odd *study freak* or *high and mighty snob.*

They're all probably fair assessments.

They're all wrong.

Well, maybe not the study freak one.

But have any them wondered, *Why the change?*

Why doesn't she stop and chat the way she used to? Why does she never come out to parties anymore? Why does she ignore us all the time?

I couldn't tell them, even if I wanted to.

I can't tell anyone.

With a thick swallow, I turn to my bed, dropping my laptop bag on the quilt and kicking off my shoes.

I'm just about to sit down when the door bursts open and Caroline breezes in with a goopy smile.

"You're not going to believe this!" she squeals.

I wince at the high notes her voice is making while she grabs my hands and forces me into a happy-dance spin.

"What?" I end up laughing the word because crazy-happy Caroline always makes me smile.

"Casey bought us a puppy!"

I pull her to a stop, blinking a couple times, then finally managing to say, "What?"

"I know! Isn't that crazy?"

"Yes. Very." My tone is dry and filled with concern while my brain starts exploding with all the reasons why this is a terrible idea.

"No, come on, it's good crazy!" She pulls her phone out of her jeans pocket. "He's a little Shih Tzu cross, and we've named him Fezzik."

"Isn't that the giant from *The Princess Bride*?"

"Yes!" Caroline cracks up laughing, her red curls dancing as she throws her head back. "The name is supposed to be ironic. Funny, right?"

"Hilarious." I nod, trying to be encouraging, and I do have to admit that my heart melts a little when she shows me the pics.

It's actually the one of Casey holding the little guy against his chest that gets me the most. It's all kinds of adorable, and I kind of want to call the guy and tell him "good job."

But the practical, cynical side of me can only see how illogical it is to buy a puppy for your girlfriend when you don't even live together.

Not to mention the work and effort that goes into raising a puppy. Do they have any idea?

"So, a puppy's a lot of work." I wince. "You're not worried it's too much too soon?"

"Don't." Caroline holds up her finger. The look on her face is stern and unyielding. "You are not allowed to ruin this for me with practicality and sensibleness. I am now the proud mother of the cutest puppy in the world, and you shall be happy for me."

I let out a soft laugh and force my head to bob. "Okay. I'm happy for you."

"Thank you." She jumps on her toes, kissing my cheek before walking into the bathroom. "I'm gonna take a quick shower, then head back to Hockey House for dinner. You wanna come with? Rachel's cooking, and you can meet little Fezz."

Hockey House?

Asher?

Yeah, that can't happen.

"Oh, you know, I would, but... um, this assignment is kicking my ass."

Caroline lets out a dramatic wail. "Lani! You're killing me, kid." Her spray of red curls appears in the bathroom doorway. "It's Sunday. You need to stop working and take a break."

"I would. I really want to, but—"

"Then do it."

"I can't."

Caroline's shoulders slump, her blue eyes filling with that sad concern I hate so much.

I glance away from it, my shoulders tensing as she tries yet again.

"Lei-Lei, what's going on with you?"

A small part of me wants to just blurt it out. Maybe if I tell someone, I'll feel better, but every time I go to open my mouth, my brain freezes. I can't unlock that box in the back of my head. If I open that thing, all the ugly will come out and swallow me whole.

"I'm just stressed about school."

"You never used to be that way." She steps out of the bathroom, moving closer, getting within range.

Panic seizes me, and I scramble for my bag, shoving my shoes back on while I talk. "I know. This year has just been pressure, pressure, pressure and—"

"It didn't start out like that."

"I've got this scholarship, and I really can't afford to let my grades slip."

Caroline laughs. "You work all the time. Your grades aren't going anywhere but up, girl."

I force out a laugh, shaking my head and refusing to look at her. "I'm sorry, I just... I'll relax once the summer hits."

Glancing across at her, I can see she doesn't believe me.

I don't either.

If anything, the summer terrifies me. Long weeks of no intense work to focus on? I'm gonna have to figure out a plan for that. I need a job. Maybe I'll take two, or three, even. That'll get me some decent spending money for the next school year, right?

My heart rate accelerates as my mean old brain has me rushing through solutions I don't even want to take.

"I'm gonna go to the library." I point to the door and make a beeline for it.

"You have no life!" Caroline calls after me.

I close my eyes as the door click shuts behind me, hating that she's right.

About everything.

I didn't used to be like this.

How can one incident change so much about me?

Is this my life from now on?

A heavy feeling spreads through my chest, running down my limbs and turning them to concrete as I slowly shuffle back out of my dorm and try to find another hole on campus that I can crawl into and disappear.

CHAPTER 8
ASHER

I push off the wall and skate like the devil, pumping my arms and gaining as much speed as quickly as I can. Reaching the end, I do a slide and spin in the opposite direction, hauling ass back to the other end of the rink.

It's tiring work, but I don't give a shit right now. I need to burn off steam, build up a sweat—anything to get rid of this angst that's eating me like a fucking parasite.

I've got a lot of shit going on right now.

The Lennox party ended up being a bust. I got there just in time to see Harvey disappearing down the hallway with a honey tucked under his arm. He said a brief "Hi," then pointed at the girl and mouthed, "Sorry, man!"

Lucky bastard. I didn't see him again, and about an hour later, after one beer and some chick's tongue down my throat, I ended up leaving. I couldn't help comparing the make-out session with Lani's searing kiss, and it made it impossible to take things further.

By the time I got home, I was fuming, and even choking the chicken in front of some decent porn didn't do the trick.

I've been restless ever since.

And it doesn't help that I can't find any peace in my own fucking house either.

That stupid puppy doesn't know the meaning of the word *silence*—I'm serious about that one. If he's not yapping, he's snoring in his sleep or making these weird little sounds like he's dreaming.

It doesn't seem to bother anyone but me.

Sure, he's cute. I get it. Puppies are adorable.

But they're not so great when they're peeing on the couch or leaving little stink nuggets in the corner of the kitchen. I nearly stepped on one the other day—and I was in bare feet!

Casey laughed so hard he nearly peed his pants.

It's been less than a day and I'm already over it.

And I'm still worried what Uncle Hayes and Aunt Carla will say if they ever find out. I checked the rental contract last night, and it stipulates that pets are allowed with permission from the owners... which we haven't gotten yet. So yeah, that's gonna be awesome.

Casey says it's easier to ask for forgiveness than permission, but does he get that we could get kicked out of our lush, six-bedroom house if we don't show some respect? We're living there for free while we're studying. Does he not get how fucking amazing that is?

My aunt and uncle could be making bank on that

place, but they're helping us out because they're good people, and I don't want to take advantage of their generosity.

I should probably just call them and let them know about the puppy, but if they tell me "no pets," then what the fuck am I supposed to do?

It's not like I can kick Casey out. He's one of my best friends.

I don't know what I'd do without the Hockey House bros. Sure, I rub them up the wrong way sometimes. They think I'm an arrogant, rich asshole when I say oblivious shit. I don't know what it was like to grow up without everything at my fingertips. That's not actually my fault. I try to understand where they're coming from, but sometimes shit slips out... and I always hate myself when it does. I don't want them seeing me this way, but part of me wonders if it wasn't for Hockey House whether any of them would truly be my friends. Do they just put up with me because I provide free accommodation?

The thought blackens my mood even further, and I skate a little harder until one of the assistant coaches wanders into the arena and barks at me to call it quits.

"Don't go killing yourself during the offseason, man." He leans against the boards and gives me a grin.

I skate over to him and run a hand through my sweaty hair.

"What's eating you?" He lightly nudges my shoulder. "You only skate this hard when you're pissed about something."

"Nothin'," I mutter.

"Well, if you need to chat, you know where my office is." His backhand slap on my arm is friendly, and I force a smile before he walks away, obviously content with his little check-in.

Jumping over the boards, I slump down on the seat and start unlacing my skates. I'm the only guy here at the moment. Mr. Zamboni will start smoothing out the ice soon, and unlacing here gives me a few extra minutes to avoid the guys.

They're all showering up in the locker room, no doubt making plans for tonight, talking about their girlfriends and shit. Connor and Riley will be jumping in with their latest hot dates, and I'll be standing there seething, because the hottest date I had recently hates my guts.

I don't want to admit that to anyone.

What I really want to do is freeze her out of my brain and move the fuck on, but do you think I can forget that kiss? Her smile? How smart she is? The fact that she's a Ravenclaw goddess who's put a fucking spell on me?

Kicking off my boots with a growl, I snatch them up and pad back to the locker room.

Steam is billowing out of the shower stalls as I walk past and dump my stuff next to my locker.

"What took you so long?" Casey asks once his head's popped through his shirt.

"Doing some extra skating," I mutter.

"Why?"

"Because I felt like it!"

He gives me an odd look, then narrows his eyes at me. "Is this about the puppy? You're still pissed, aren't you? Dude, seriously, get over it. I'm gonna train that thing until he's the best-behaved dog on the block, I swear."

I close my eyes, shaking my head and wishing it was just about the puppy.

"I had a dog growing up," Baxter interjects. "I can help train the little guy."

"Thank you." Casey points at him but keeps his eyes on me. "See? It's all gonna be good."

"It takes a while, though. You're gonna have to be consistent and firm. Dogs thrive on routine." Baxter keeps going, droning on about all he knows and making Casey squirm when the man-child idiot starts to realize how much work this is gonna be.

"It'll be great to get your help, Bax. Thanks!" Casey cuts him off, probably putting himself in a bad mood as he thinks about how this is gonna change his life.

That idiot never looks beyond the next fucking hour.

"I've got your back, bro." Baxter gives him a rare grin, then goes quiet. He's spoken more words in the last three minutes than he probably has all day. I'm guessing he's now exhausted.

I roll my eyes and turn back to my locker, stripping off my sweaty gear and heading for the showers.

Taking my time, I soak under the hot spray until I'm just starting to relax.

"Come on, rich boy! Hurry it up!" Casey shouts from the doorway.

I close my eyes, gritting my teeth against any kind of comeback. I hate it when they call me *rich boy*. They only do it when they think I'm acting rich. I didn't realize taking a long shower after a shitty day was a rich thing to do, but Casey obviously does.

Grabbing my towel, I stalk out of the shower, drying off quickly and hurrying to get dressed while Casey and Liam stand there chatting. I tune out their conversation, my mind wandering back to... yep, you guessed it... freakin' Lani!

"Just heard from Mick." Ethan slips his phone into his back pocket as he walks past me. "She and Caroline are going to Offside for dinner before we all head home to hit the books. You guys in?"

I glance over my shoulder as Liam responds. "Nah, man. Rachel's at the diner tonight. Think I'll go eat there and study until she's done."

"Cool." Ethan points to Casey. "You? Or have you got doggy duties?"

Casey's smile fades, his shoulders slumping. "Shit. The dog."

"Got you covered, man." Baxter walks past him, slapping him on the shoulder with a grin. He looks pretty damn excited.

"Seriously?" Casey perks up instantly.

"Of course. I'd much rather hang with a cute puppy than a bunch of weirdos at a sports bar."

"You think *we're* weird?" I mutter under my breath.

Baxter's our team goalie, and I swear he was a hermit crab in a past life.

He seems to be allergic to people and normal conversation. Sure, he shuffles out for dinner sometimes—mostly on the nights Rachel cooks—but he barely says a word. As soon as he's done eating, he disappears back to his room. Most days, he's holed up in there, happy with his own company. I don't know what the hell he does with his time, but the guy's an introvert to the extreme.

But he obviously loves animals, and Fezzik's got him voluntarily starting conversations and offering to help out.

Grinning like he just won the lottery while Baxter heads out the door, Casey turns to me. "You comin'?"

I nearly say no, but do I honestly feel like going back to Hockey House right now? My brain needs food before studying, and although I could go hang in the Athlete's Hall and get a decent meal, the thought of my bros all having fun at Offside without me is too much.

So I say yes.

Because what the hell. A beer and some pizza will hit the spot. I can hang with my crew, flirt with a puck bunny or two. Shit, I might even get laid, and that'll help me relax enough to hit the books when I get home.

It also might have the added effect of tricking my brain into forgetting about a certain Hawaiian beauty with the lips of an angel and the tongue of a sorceress.

CHAPTER 9
LEILANI

My fingers tap away on my keyboard, making a steady stream of clicks that reassure me that I'm gonna nail this assignment. It's my last one for this class, and then my focus will shift to exam prep. I have five exams in total, and this year, they're all clumped together over three days. It's going to be so frickin' stressful. Although, I'm feeling pretty good about two of them. I've been working consistently all year, and I've got excellent recall. I'm confident I can nail the history paper, and I'm actually looking forward to my anthropology one. The others... I'm gonna need to put in some serious study time.

The thought both exhausts and excites me.

Call me a nerd, but I enjoy studying. Learning stuff is interesting. I love building my knowledge base and expanding my awareness of the world. I love being able to contribute intelligent comments to conversations, and yes, raising my hand in class and answering a question correctly always gives me a buzz.

Shit, I really am such a nerd.

But hey, it's me, and I'm gonna own that shit.

If anything, my nerdiness is kind of saving me, because poring over books and escaping into history helps me to avoid the present.

My phone dings, sounding loud in the empty dorm room, and I reach for it with a frown. I don't know why I don't just turn the thing off, but I'm so aware that my parents might try to reach me. They love sending me pics of my younger siblings. The baby of the family—Melika —went to her first dance class yesterday. She's two and the cutest toddler on the planet. Mom took her to something called Wriggle and Rhyme. Basically, the kids sing songs that have been around for decades and jump around, flapping their arms and giggling. They call that dancing, and little Mel looked so freaking happy. The video Mom sent me was adorable. It made me tear up just a little, wishing I could be a carefree two-year-old again.

I seriously don't know how my mother has the energy for all her kids. The doctors told her she was too old to be having another child, but she refused to listen and continued with the pregnancy. She's now a forty-three-year-old woman with a two-year-old... and seven other children. But she seems to thrive on being a parent. I don't know what she's going to do when Melika starts school and she doesn't have babies at home anymore.

Maybe by then my older brother, Noa, will have started having kids. He did get married last summer, so who knows. Mom can shift into kupuna wahine mode and start her grandma duties. She'll love it.

I grin, picturing her surrounded by grandchildren. But then my smile fades when I start to wonder if I'll be able to provide her any. If I even want kids. I thought I did, but now I'm not so sure.

A shudder travels down my spine and I snap my eyes shut, willing that box in my brain to stay sealed up tight. I hate it when it rattles like that, threatening to pop open and flood my brain with ugly memories.

It'll be a tsunami I won't survive.

My phone dings again, reminding me that I totally spaced out and still haven't checked my message. Spinning it over, I read the screen and see Caroline's name.

We're going to Offside for a drink. Please come join us. I miss you!

Why does she keep doing this to me?

Can't she understand that I need to hide away from places like that?

She won't unless you tell her the truth.

My stomach pinches, a breath catching in my chest as I imagine trying to explain why I've been acting like this lately. What will she think? Say?

Ugh. Her reaction.

I can't do it.

So, what do I do instead?

Ignore her?

Keep being a shitty friend?

She's gonna hate me... or stop trying altogether. That fear drove me to Denver, and I did have a few good times there. The poker was fun and—

"Shit," I mutter, quickly typing back.

She responds within seconds.

Yay!!!!!!!!!!!!!!! See you there, wahine!

I swallow, staring at my laptop screen with a fleeting look of longing before closing it and getting ready to go out.

I almost consider changing but decide that my high-waisted flares and simple white T-shirt are fine. Shoving on my boots, I grab my leather jacket and flick my thick hair out, then force myself to put on a little lip gloss.

I'm usually into makeup and doing things to make my eyes pop, but ever since... well, I just don't care as much anymore. I don't want anything that will draw attention to me anyway.

Pausing by the mirror, I check my reflection and give myself a quick pep talk. "You're doing this for your best friend who loves you. And you love her, and you don't want to lose her, so you go, you smile, you laugh." I swallow, gritting my teeth and speaking firmly. "You can do this, Lani. You can do it." My voice cracks and I blink quickly, taking in a fortifying sniff before walking out the door.

I order an Uber, then wait outside the dorm building. Thankfully, it arrives in just a few minutes and I jump in, muttering a soft "Hi" before ignoring the driver. Nibbling my lip in the back seat, I manage to eat off most of my gloss before we pull up outside Offside.

"Thanks for the ride," I murmur as I open the door.

"Have a good night." The driver grins at me. I wonder if his smile would be so broad if he knew the chaos in my chest right now. If he could feel the maelstrom in my stomach.

You're doing this for Caroline. She's your best friend. Step the hell up, Lani!

My pep talk turns into more of a lecture as I fist my fingers and walk toward the bar.

The door swings open before I get to it, and I wait for the group to exit before I slip behind them. The music of the live band envelops me first.

They're one of the local bands, and they're pretty good. I've heard them play before. They've got a pop-rock style that's easy to dance to, and their original stuff is just as good as the covers they play.

The place is vibing for a Monday night. Now that hockey and football seasons have come to an end, I guess people have more time to party? I don't know.

All I know is that my teeth are on edge, and it's taking everything in me not to spin for the door again.

"Lani!"

I hear my name and turn toward the sound.

Caroline's bright curls catch my eye first. She's grinning and waving, obviously happily surprised to see I actually made it.

"Yay! You came!" She wraps me in a hug, pulling me farther into the bar. I'm forced to go with her and am soon stumbling against the table and saying hi to Ethan and Casey.

Two other guys are there as well. I recognize them from the team, but I don't know their names. I give them a polite wave, then ask, "Where's Mikayla?"

"She's gettin' drinks." Ethan points over his shoulder.

I turn to look at the bar and that storm in my stomach turns into a deadly tornado.

Shit.

Asher's here.

CHAPTER 10
ASHER

"Yep, and just the two beers." I hold up two fingers to the bartender.

She gives me a wink and uncaps two bottles of Corona, shoving a lime in each neck before popping them on the tray.

"Thanks."

I double-check the drinks order and am about to take it to the table when Mick snatches my arm.

"Wait, wait, wait! We're gonna need more than two pizzas. Come on, man." She gives me a droll look before going back to scanning the menu.

"But I've already paid," I mutter.

She ignores me, calling the bartender over again. "Yeah, can we add a couple more things to our food order, please? We'll take two large fries and a basket of onion rings, and let's chuck in a plate of those chicken poppers with extra ranch."

"Good God, woman, we're not feeding an army."

"We're feeding a pack of hungry cougars—that's about the same as an army," she argues while I glance over my shoulder and notice another person has joined our table.

Great, another mouth to feed, making Mick even more right.

Who is that, anyway?

I narrow my eyes, about to ask the little shorty beside me, when my stomach pinches into a hard knot.

"Aw, shit," I grumble. "Who invited her?"

"What?" Mick glances up at me, then frowns and turns to see who I'm talking about. "Oh, is that Lani? Cool. I can't believe she came."

"Why did she come? She never even wants to be at these things."

"Maybe she's got a break between assignments or something."

"Whatever." I roll my eyes. "She's probably found some extra work to do. The girl doesn't know how to relax."

"Okay, fine, so maybe she's here for Caroline. Trying to be a good friend or something."

I scoff, turning back to rest my arms on the counter. I'll take the drinks over soon. I just need a minute.

"What is your problem?" Mikayla laughs out the question. "Do you really hate her that much?"

"No." I frown. "I don't hate her. She hates me."

Mikayla's look is downright comical, but I don't hear

myself laughing. If anything, my frown grows that much deeper.

"Stop looking at me like that," I grouse.

"I can't help it. You're twenty-one, dude, and you sound like a fifth grader."

"Shut up. I do not."

"Ah, yeah, you do." She bulges her eyes at me. "We're all grown-ups here. You can handle being around someone you don't like for one evening."

"I don't not like her," I clarify. "She doesn't like me. As soon as I get to the table, she'll probably want to leave."

"Why?"

"I don't know!" I hedge. Like I'm going to admit to our searing kiss or the fact that I can't stop thinking about her.

"Okay." Mick pats my arm. "How do you know she feels this way?"

"Because she told me." I turn to give her an emphatic look. "Right to my face."

Mikayla's mouth pops open. "She said it your face?"

"Yes. She told me she hates me and that nothing I say or do will ever make her change her mind."

Mick's eyes spark. "Well, that's a bit of bullshit right there." She looks back to the table, then up at me. "I know you've got some douchy qualities..."

"Thanks?"

"But"—she holds up her finger—"you're a really lovable guy. So that girl over there is not allowed to hate you." Mikayla clicks her tongue. "She obviously just doesn't know you that well yet."

I sigh, running a hand through my hair. "She doesn't want to get to know me."

"Well, tough shit for her. She's here. You're here. We'll be eating at the same table. She's just gonna have to get over herself."

Rearranging my hair back into place, I steal another glance at the table and mutter, "Maybe I should just go."

"Or..." Mikayla's face lights with a grin. "We could have ourselves some fun."

My eyes narrow as my ears start burning. What is this lil' mouse up to?

"Fun?" My tone is dry and skeptical.

"Yeah." Mick wiggles her eyebrows. "I'm gonna wager ten bucks that you can't make her smile."

Dammit, this woman knows me too well.

A bet? I can never resist one of those!

"Ten bucks." I grab the bottle of beer off the tray and take a swig. "If I can make her smile, I win ten bucks."

"Yep." Mick nods like she's all proud of her smarts.

I snicker and stick out my hand. "Let's make it twenty."

"Deal. I wanna see how much this chick really hates ya." Mick laughs, skipping away from the bar with our table number and leaving the tray of drinks for me.

I slide it off the bar, carefully navigating my way around the crowds of people, making it to the table without spilling a drop.

Mick's already climbing onto a stool next to Ethan while I place the tray down and start doling out drinks. Lani's standing right beside me, stiff as a two-by-four.

I give her a side-eye, then sense Mikayla watching me. She winks before taking a sip of her ginger ale and whispering something to Ethan.

Great. So now he's gonna know, and the pressure will really be on. His eyes dart to mine, and that classic Ethan smirk comes into play.

Ignoring the way his mouth pulls up at the side, I get to work.

I am not losing a twenty to the shortest person at this table!

Clearing my throat, I pull the empty tray toward me and turn to Lani.

"Hi, there." I force a smile.

She gives me a deadpan stare, and there go my cockroach legs, wanting to scuttle away to freedom.

Forcing a charm I'm far from feeling, I remind myself that winning a bet, no matter how small it is, will make me feel better. "Can I get you a drink?"

"No." Lani's dark eyebrows rise. "I can get my own drink."

"Suit yourself." I hold out the tray. "Can you return this for me at the same time?"

"Uch." She lets out a disgusted snort, snatching the tray off me and storming toward the bar.

Caroline cringes while Mick rolls her eyes. "Great start, Casanova."

"Hey." I click my fingers and point at her. "It's twenty for a smile. I'm not trying to win her fuckin' heart."

"Yeah, well, I can guarantee you won't with that kind of attitude." Mick pins me with a pointed glare before her lips break into a triumphant smile. "I'm just stoked that I'll be leaving here twenty bucks richer when you crash and burn tonight."

"You're such a little shit." I shake my head but end up grinning at her.

Ethan gives me an unimpressed glare while Mikayla throws her head back with a laugh and Caroline leans in with a curious frown.

"What the hell are you guys up to?"

CHAPTER 11
LEILANI

While ordering myself a drink, I nearly bailed, but then Caroline skipped over with a happy little smile and I couldn't do it to her.

She seems so pleased to have me here, and I don't want to let her down.

So, I'm back at the table, nibbling on fries and—much to my annoyance—having to work overtime not to laugh or smile at Asher, who seems to be on a roll with his humor tonight. I guess I've seen hints of this side of him before, but usually it's Casey who's being the clown. Not tonight, though. If anything, he's unusually quiet, giving Asher the floor. And Mr. Hot Lips (dammit, I want to taste them again!) seems determined to have everyone in stitches as he regales us with stories from his days at boarding school.

The one about the green army men being hidden around the school and discovered in the most random places for Asher's entire junior year was one of my favorites, but the one I couldn't keep a straight face for was his senior class prank, where they borrowed a thousand chickens from a local farmer (paid him a truckload of money for it) and set them loose in the school during morning assembly. The way he described the teachers running around trying to catch chickens was hilarious, and I had no choice but to start laughing along with everybody else.

Asher turns to spot my grin, and the look on his face can only be described as triumphant. He casts a look across the table at Mikayla, who is smiling from ear to ear. She shakes her head, then glances at me, blushing like she's been busted.

What the hell is going on between those two?

I check Ethan's face, but he doesn't seem fazed by whatever silent conversation is happening between his girlfriend and Asher.

Shifting on my stool, I force my gaze away, deciding not to care about whatever secret little joke they have. Snatching another fry, I shove it in my mouth, then wash away the salty taste with the last of my root beer.

Ugh. Why'd I order a root beer? I basically only drink water but felt like I should get something after making a big deal to Asher that I can buy my own drink. Why didn't I just smile and say, "A water, please"? It wouldn't have cost him anything. But I just couldn't converse nicely with him, could I?

Because I hate him.

Apparently.

Except I don't, because he's smart and funny and handsome and—

Shit!

Swiveling my body away from him, I focus on Caroline's conversation with Casey. They're talking about the dog and someone at Hockey House called Baxter. The name sounds vaguely familiar, but I can't picture the guy's face.

"I'm telling you, babe. We could lose the dog to this guy."

Caroline snorts. "Baxter's adorable, and he's not going to steal our dog. I'm grateful for his help. If he wasn't with Fezz tonight, we'd have to be. It's like having a built-in babysitter. It's awesome."

"True," Casey concedes. "I just don't want the little guy bonding with Bax when he should be bonding with us."

"He'll bond with us." Caroline slides her arm around his shoulders, planting a kiss on his cheek. "It's your bedroom he sleeps in, and you're the one who got the nose licks this morning."

Casey grins, kissing his girl while I try to wrap my head around the fact that Nolan U's man-slut, Casey Pierce, is worried about his puppy bonding with someone else in the house. Caroline has seriously changed his life big-time. The guy was allergic to being attached to anything, and now he's got himself a perma-nent girl *and* a fur baby.

All because of a failed condom.

It's weird how one small thing can have such a massive impact on your life.

The remnants of my smile start to fade, and then my lips fully flatline when a tall blonde with straight white teeth approaches our table.

"Hi." He smiles at me like I'm the only woman in this place.

I tense, knowing exactly what that look means. He wants a dance or my number or name or—

"Nope." I shake my head.

He gives me an odd frown before trying again. "I was just wondering if you wanted to—"

"Nope."

"I—"

"No. Move along." I point behind him and wiggle my fingers. "*Move* along."

The moron takes a good thirty seconds to figure out what the hell I'm saying, like rejecting him is the most bizarre thing in the world. He's obviously not used to getting shot down.

Eventually, his smooth smile turns into a scowl, and he mutters something insulting under his breath as he stalks away from the table.

I straighten my spine, desperate to shake off the encounter. Desperate to hide how disgusting I feel right now.

Mikayla cracks up laughing, which kinda helps, and then goes in for a high five. "Nicely done, Ice Queen!"

I give her a droll look but can't leave her hanging. Our hands slap together while Casey hisses. "You didn't even give the guy a chance to finish his sentence."

"Because she already knew what he was going to ask," Caroline argues.

"And the fact that he got all shitty after he *finally* got the message proves that he was looking for a quick hookup and nothing more." Mikayla gives me an impressed grin. "You read him well, lady. Good job."

I don't how to respond to that, so I just give her a weak smile. I can sense Asher's gaze on me and can tell the other two guys—Riley and something starting with a C— are not impressed by my rude rejection.

Maybe they've been treated like that by girls before and it hurts them more than they're willing to let on.

Shit.

I never would have been so rude to someone before, but—

"I should go," I murmur, reaching for my bag. "I've got to study and—"

"No!" Caroline grabs my wrist. "You studied all weekend. Lani, come on. You deserve a break. Stay here and have fun with us."

"In this dirty bar surrounded by sleazoids and creeps?" I can't help the quip. My shoulders are tingling, and I just want to go home.

"They're not all like that." Caroline's voice goes soft, her blue eyes getting all sad and worried again. She wants to know what's happened to me. What's changed me.

Leaning close, she whispers in my ear, "You used to know how to let loose and have some fun."

"Thanks," I mutter.

"I'm serious. We're out. Let's go dance." She leans back with an excited grin. "You love dancing. You love this song. I know you love this song!"

I do, but... "I don't want to spend my night getting hit on."

"I won't let that happen," Asher pipes up.

I flinch and look over my shoulder to see how serious he is. His gaze is deep and penetrating, and dammit, I believe him.

"Neither will I." Ethan finishes his drink, then places it on the table with a definitive thump. "If you don't want any guys going near you, we'll make sure they stay away."

"Even I won't hit on you. I promise." Asher winks. I give him an unconvinced glare and he laughs, raising both hands. "I swear."

"Come on." Caroline grabs my wrist, the look in her eyes downright pleading. "Dance with me. Dance with your bestie."

I give in with a sigh, letting her drag me off the stool and onto the dance floor. The music is thumping, and my body can't help but respond to it. I love getting lost in a beat, and as soon as the hockey guys form a circle around us, I start to relax and let myself get into it. Mikayla's a great dancer, and I mirror her moves so we're dancing in sync. Caroline joins in, throwing her head back and shouting along to the lyrics. I can't help joining her. I really do love this song. In fact, the entire set has been awesome so far, and as soon as that song comes to an end, the band cranks into another great number.

It's quickly obvious which of the guys can move and which of them wish they were anywhere else. But they're playing bodyguard for me (and probably their girl-friends). It's actually kinda sweet. Riley soon gives up his post and starts dancing with us. He's got some moves... and so does Asher. He can't help himself. Soon he's right up there alongside me, moving his hips and grooving to the beat.

I get caught up in the moment, raising my arms and shifting my feet. I let the music take me and I'm swept away, forgetting about everything and just enjoying a moment of the old me. The girl who could spend a night on the dance floor, singing and acting silly with her friends.

The girl who let the music take her away.

The girl who didn't mind a guy's hand on her hip. Didn't mind his body gliding in behind hers.

I shuffle closer to Asher without thinking, at first not even noticing his hand lightly brushing my side.

He's just moving in time with me, smiling at Caroline as she flicks her hair around and laughs at something Casey just said to her. He wraps his arm around her waist and pulls her close, resting his chin on her shoulder and saying something else against her ear. She's grinning and gyrating against him.

I remember that feeling. A guy's arm securing me

against him, my back tucked into his torso. I used to love that feeling. I'd always look for it at parties. A little flirtation on the dance floor.

It was one of my favorite ways to spend a Friday night.

Until it became something different.

Until one guy ruined everything.

Asher's hand skims my hip again, his body moving in behind mine. My booty wants to back right into him. We could find the rhythm together and sway to the beat...

But something in my brain just clicked.

It's a sound I've been trying to avoid. But I can feel it. The lid of the box I've been desperate to keep shut just flew open, and my body is flooded with ugly reminders of that night.

The one that started out with a little flirtation on the dance floor and turned into something completely different.

My body jerks like I've just been electrocuted, panic sizzling my entire system as I stumble off the dance floor.

"You okay?" Asher reaches for my arm, no doubt trying to steady me.

I flick him off and barely manage to say, "I have to use the bathroom," before careening away like I'm being chased by the devil.

Maybe I am.

Little demon memories flutter around me as I fight the sob in my throat and run for the safety of a lockable stall.

CHAPTER 12
ASHER

I stand there paralyzed for a second, wondering what the hell I'm supposed to do.

I thought that was going so well.

Lani was starting to relax. She was smiling, swaying her hips, singing along with Caroline, and then I took it one step too far.

I got too close.

Dammit!

I should have stayed on the edge like Ethan and Connor, looking like presidential security detail instead of getting into the dancing action with Riley and the girls.

But I couldn't resist the fun. The music is great tonight, and my feet just wouldn't stay still.

"What just happened?" Caroline stops beside me.

"I'm not sure. I just..." I shrug, forcing myself to remember the truth. "She just really hates me."

"She said she needed the bathroom," Riley chips in,

looking awkward as hell. "Maybe she's got the runs or something?"

Caroline's eyebrows dip together.

I give her a hopeless frown. "I think she just wanted to get away from me as fast as she could. I got too close and—"

"I so don't get it. You're just her type." Her lips drop into an unhappy pout. "Ever since I got pregnant, she just hasn't been the same. I don't know why. Was it me?"

"Of course not, baby." Casey holds the back of her neck, giving it a light squeeze and kissing the side of her head.

"She just seems to want to separate herself from everyone these days."

"She loosened up a bit tonight."

"Maybe one of us should go check on her." Ethan's deep voice carries across the music.

"Well, it can't be me," I mutter.

"I'll go." Caroline walks away with Casey following in her wake.

I sigh, watching the mound of red curls disappear into the crowd. Mikayla sidles up beside me. With a sad smile, she pulls a twenty out of her pocket and holds it up for me to grab.

I give her a side-eye, taking the money with another heavy sigh. "Not sure I really deserve this."

"You made her laugh. When she took a few seconds to stop stressing so hard, she thought you were hilarious.

When she lets her guard down, she really is a different chick."

"Yeah." I shake my head, wishing I hadn't found her so damn intoxicating on the dance floor.

But the way her body moved? Holy fuck, she was hot.

The smell of coconut in her hair... and those luscious hips. It took everything in me not to pull her back against me and feel her body curve into mine.

Our kiss sears me all over again, disappointment following swiftly in its wake.

She's got to be the most confusing woman on the planet. And of course she had to capture *my* attention.

If my stupid brain doesn't get over this shit soon, I'm gonna drive myself insane.

I should spin back around and walk straight onto the dance floor again.

I bet there'll be some chick out there who wants to feel my body pressed against hers.

But I don't.

Because my feet can't move.

All I can do is stare at the entrance to the bathrooms and worry about the girl who's locked away inside them.

CHAPTER 13
LEILANI

I grip the edge of the toilet and hurl into the bowl.

It's the same thing I did that night.

Once I found the ability to move. To pull my dress back down. To shuffle out of the bedroom.

I was shaking from head to toe.

I don't even know how I was able to walk, to weave around the myriad of people in the house, but somehow I made it to the bathroom, and by some miracle it was free.

I locked the door behind me, dropped to my knees, and threw up every ounce of alcohol in my body.

That's the last time I tasted beer or wine or anything like that.

I will never drink alcohol again.

I will never put myself in a position where I don't have my full wits about me. Maybe if I hadn't been so tipsy, my brain would have warned me that one-night stands could be dangerous.

My brain would have reminded me that I'm holding out for the real deal.

But I was pissed and angsty and needed to get me some.

I thought it'd make me feel better, but I soon realized that I wasn't after a hot, quick fuck. I wanted to go, but...

Closing my eyes, I try to block out the sound of his grunting, the panic that seized me when he didn't adhere to my request.

"Stop."

We'd only just started, but I'd changed my mind.

So I said, "Stop." Loud and clear.

And I know he heard me because his reply will ring in my head forever.

"I'm not done with you yet."

CHAPTER 14
ASHER

The professor is droning on about something. Usually, I'm pretty engaged in these classes. I love anthropology. I mostly take business studies and shit with numbers, marketing, economics, but I have two classes that are just for me—history and anthropology. I have to take them as extras, but I don't care. Sure, it creates more work for me, and during hockey season, it's intense, but I love the learning, so it's never felt like a drag.

Today, however... it does.

Because my mind is too full with other thoughts.

Thoughts of a brown-skinned beauty who hates me.

Something was off last night.

When I compare the way she acted on the dance floor, just before she escaped to the bathroom, to the slap in the face after our kiss...

I don't know. There was fire in that slap—authority, boss-bitch vibes.

Last night, it was almost like she was scared. I didn't think that at first. We were dancing. She seemed into it. I let my hand brush her hip, and then she took off.

I was half expecting her to storm out of the bathroom with an angry scowl and knee me in the balls for daring to touch her, but she kind of shuffled out looking sick and pale.

Caroline hovered beside her, talking a mile a minute, while Casey walked behind them looking uncomfortable as fuck. He's never done well with emotional women. I'm much better with that kind of thing, and I moved in to say what I could, but Lani walked right past me as if I wasn't even there.

"Lani, wait! Let me just grab my stuff!" Caroline called after her, but Lani didn't seem to notice.

She made a beeline for the exit, and I chased after her, dodging people and making it out the door just as she was running for a car. I didn't know who the hell was driving it, but Lani seemed to. The girl behind the wheel was nodding and waving her over. Maybe it was a friend from Huxley Hall or something.

"Lani!"

She spun around when I shouted her name, and that's when I saw it—this wide-eyed desperation. Fear, stark and obvious.

It made me falter, and I jerked to a stop, all my words stolen by that one look.

Not that I've spent much time with her, but one thing

I know about Leilani Iona is that she's strong and fierce and you don't mess with her.

But that look...

It's not sitting right inside me.

I can't seem to get it out of my head or let it go.

I'm becoming obsessed with wanting to make sure she never looks like that again.

Caroline raced out after us just as the car was pulling away. She let out a soft sigh, then kind of whimpered. I turned to check on her and saw tears spilling free.

"I don't know why she's acting like this. Why is she pushing me away?" Her voice wobbled.

"Did she say anything when she came out of the bathroom?"

Caroline shrugged. "That she wasn't feeling well, but I don't know if I believe her. She just keeps pushing me away. I don't know what to do."

I was about to run my hand down her back, offer her some comfort, but Casey came out of the bar, so I took a step away and let him do it instead. He spoke all soft and sweet, then asked if she wanted to stay the night at Hockey House.

She nodded, and they shuffled off to his beat-up Jeep while I stayed on the curb, looking down the road and wishing I'd never met Leilani.

I'm not trying to be an asshole, but she's consuming me in ways I don't want her to.

I couldn't sleep last night, and it was her fault.

I can't concentrate on this lecture, and it's her fault.

I don't want her eating up so much brain space. I wish I'd never offered to drive her back to Denver. I wish I'd never seen one of her smiles or felt her tongue glide against mine.

I wish I hadn't chased her last night and called her name.

I wish I'd never seen that look on her face, because it's fucking haunting me.

What I should be doing is staying far away from her and getting my fucking life back.

But do you think my stupid-ass brain gets the message when I walk into Java Jeans forty minutes later and spot her lining up to order?

She's standing there in a pair of jeans that hug her fine ass perfectly. Tucked into those is a simple T-shirt with small yellow flowers peppering the fabric, and she looks a combination of sexy and cute. Which is so fucking dangerous.

Her hair is up in a top knot thing, exposing her neck and the small tattoo just beneath her hairline. It's four spirals in the shape of a square. Obviously a symbol that's meaningful, because Lani does not strike me as the kind of woman to get a tattoo on a whim. I wonder if it's got to do with Hawaii or her heritage or something.

Shit, that tattoo only adds another hazard layer.

She's way too sexy for her own good.

Or for my own good.

Fuck. Whatever! I want her with a burn so strong, I feel like my body's about to combust.

"Shit," I mutter under my breath, nearly bailing on my late-morning coffee.

But of course my fucked-up brain misses that memo, and I walk right up to her.

She flinches when I stand beside her, then lets out a derisive snort when she sees it's me.

"Hey." I grin.

She gives me a caustic smile, then crosses her arms and looks up at the menu board on the wall. I bet she already knows exactly what she wants, but anything not to look at me, right?

"Can I buy you a coffee?"

"No," she clips.

"A tea?"

She glances at me like I'm weird. "No."

"A muffin? Bagel? Slice of banana bread?"

"No, no, and ew."

"You don't like banana bread?" I frown.

"Bananas are gross," she mutters.

"Okay." I bulge my eyes. "So, what fruit do you like, then?"

She sucks in a breath as if she's losing her patience, but then she lets out a short sigh and rattles off, "Apples, cherries, and watermelon."

I nod. "So, can I buy you a slice of apple pie, then?"

She huffs and rolls her eyes. And I think her patience is officially up. "No. I don't want you to buy me anything!"

We move forward in the line, and I hold my sigh in

check. "Okay, fine. Maybe you can buy *me* something, then."

She looks up with a horrified frown, and I can't help a soft snicker after I wink at her.

She clicks her tongue and shakes her head.

I should seriously learn when to quit, but I'm a real dumbass sometimes.

"It's a shame they don't serve butter beer," I murmur, squinting at the board like I'm willing the menu to change.

Lani's lips twitch. "You're not a pumpkin juice fan?"

"Ugh." I make a face. "Seriously. Can you think of anything grosser?"

"Banana juice?"

I can't help a soft snort, my lips breaking into a wide grin as we approach the counter.

"Yeah, hi." Lani gives the woman a polite smile. "I'll take a double-shot latte with oat milk, please, and he'll have..." She points her thumb at me.

"Seriously? You're buying me a drink?"

"Don't look so surprised and order something," she grits out.

It's hard not to laugh. For some reason, this feels like a win. "Okay, then, I'll have an Americano and an oatmeal raisin cookie, please."

"All righty." The server taps the computer screen. "Anything else?"

"No, that's it. Thanks." Lani holds her phone over the

machine until it makes a payment ding and then shuffles to the end of the counter to wait for our order.

"Thanks for this." I smile down at her, everything in me rebelling against the fact that I let her pay. Again. I'm gonna have to make it up to her at some point. I can't keep letting this woman buy me food. And I'm not being sexist, I'm being fair. She paid for dinner on that quiz night, and it's really my turn.

But I get the vibe that guys buying her food makes her feel weak or something. I'm seriously gonna have to sort that shit.

Leaning my elbow on the counter, I watch her put her purse back into her bag, then stand tall and try to look anywhere but at my face.

I get that she hates me, but if she really despises me that much, she wouldn't have bought me anything, so I'm gonna go for it.

"Hey, I don't suppose you'd want to drink your latte sitting next to me, would you?"

She gives me a little side-eye, then huffs. "Fine, as long as you don't ask me anything about last night or if I'm okay. Because I'm fine." She gives me a pointed look that tells me she's lying, but... you know what, I'm gonna take what I can get.

"Deal." I nod, then throw in another wink when she eyes me up to check that I'm being serious.

Much to my satisfaction, her lips twitch with a grin that she is failing to hide.

CHAPTER 15
LEILANI

What the hell is my problem?

Why did I agree to this?

I don't want to sit and drink my coffee with Asher, but there's something so freaking irresistible about the guy... and maybe I do want to make up for the fact, just a little bit, that I kind of treated him badly last night.

He didn't do anything wrong.

If anything, he chased me to make sure I was okay, and all I did was stare at him and tell him to fuck off.

Actually, I don't know if I said the fuck off part out loud or not, but I screamed it in my head because I could seriously not handle talking to anyone. Grace Parker drove me back to Huxley Hall, which was really sweet of her. She's one of those girls who will do anything for anyone because her heart is made of pure gold. She rabbited on about... I have no idea the whole trip back to the dorm, and it was exactly what I needed. She didn't once ask me if I was good or who that guy was who shouted my name. And she seemed oblivious to my mood.

Unlike Caroline, who texted me a dozen times throughout the night. I woke up this morning and felt nothing but a heavy dose of guilt. So, I've texted her a big apology.

She didn't come home last night, and I didn't blame her. Who'd want to hang out with me when I'm such a bitch at the moment? But I don't know how else to be. I can't talk about what happened to me, and if people push too hard, my claws seem to come out.

Caroline was really sweet about it, saying it's all good, and we're gonna catch up later, but that thought is an anvil on my chest. She's gonna want to talk, and I need to figure out a way to divert conversation to light, safe topics that I can handle.

"Order for Laney!"

My nose wrinkles as I reach for my cup. "They always say my name wrong."

Asher laughs as he grabs his coffee and heads for a couple of armchairs in the corner. I follow without protest because the coveted armchairs are hardly ever available. We grab the spot before anyone else can, and I sink into the soft cushions with a sigh.

"So, you been in classes all morning?" Asher takes a sip of his coffee before breaking off a bite of his cookie.

"I had one early class, and then I spent the last two

hours in the library." I rub my forehead. "But I started going cross-eyed, so I figured I needed a caffeine kick."

"Good call." He holds out his plate and silently offers me some of his cookie. I should refuse, but for some reason, I take a small chunk. I did pay for it, after all.

I'm surprised he let me, actually. I kind of want to ask why he did, but that could lead to a deeper conversation, and I'm really determined to keep things as light and fluffy as possible today. Instead, I tell him about the assignment I'm working on, and he seems pretty interested. We talk about history for a while, and he gives away how much he loves the subject. Much to my annoyance, I'm impressed by his vast knowledge. He obviously reads big, fat novels and nonfiction books about actual events in history. Or maybe he's more of a documentary man. Whatever, he's fascinated by the same stuff as me, and it's...

I don't know what it is. Half of me loves it, but the other half hates that we have so much in common.

I take another small chunk of cookie, then brush the crumbs off my fingers.

As soon as I've swallowed my mouthful, I ask him, "Why aren't you a history major?"

He shrugs. "It's just a hobby. I'm majoring in business studies."

"Oh, so no pro hockey for you?"

"Nah, I'll no doubt join the family business after I graduate." His eyebrows furrow, and I kind of want to ask him more, but that feels too personal. If he shares something like that, he might expect the same from me, so I quickly change the subject.

"So, violin in high school. Do you play anything else?"

"Piano." He shrugs. "I got it into my head when I was fourteen that I could be the next Billy Joel or John Legend."

His eye roll makes me laugh.

"But I soon figured out that my fingers are not that nimble, and I wanted to be on the ice more than sitting on a piano stool. So, yeah, not exactly the maestro."

Man, he's got a sexy voice. And that smirk, which I use to think was so arrogant, has a playfulness about it. It's almost self-deprecating from this new angle, and it makes me want to sit in this chair for the rest of the freaking day.

"How about you, Miss Cello?"

"Uh, ukulele... and also piano."

"Damn," he mutters, shaking his head. "Yet another thing we have in common. Could you stop that now, please?" His emphatic look contradicts the grin in his eyes, and I end up laughing. Again. Because he does that to me. Makes me smile. Makes me laugh.

It's infuriating!

"I wonder what else we both like..." He bites his lip in thought, then throws a bunch of rapid-fire questions at me.

"Favorite color?"

"The sky on a cloudless day."

His eyes light with appreciation.

"Favorite movie?"

"Which genre?"

"Oh, okay, so it's like that." He wiggles his eyebrows at me. "All right, I'll get specific, then. I already know you love Harry, so I'm guessing you're a fan of Lord of the Rings?"

I nod.

"Narnia?"

I nod again and can't help adding, "I used to read those books every year when I was a kid. My dad would read them to me. Then, when I got old enough, I started reading them to my younger brothers and sisters."

"How many siblings do you have?"

"Seven."

His mouth drops open, and I can't help a soft giggle. "How about you?"

"Two. Twins. Older brothers. Not very close."

I tip my head to study him for a moment, then murmur, "That's sad."

"I've got my cousins. They're more like siblings to me. We're closer in age, and I used to spend holidays with them."

I smile.

"I'm guessing your tribe is all tightknit, then?" He leans back in his chair to study me, and I can't help getting caught in the color of his eyes again. Of course they had to be blue. Like the sky on a cloudless day.

I swallow and look down. "Yes and no. I mean, we love each other a lot, but we're so spread out. My youngest sister is two. She's gonna grow up without me around. And the siblings who are closest to me in age are all boys, and they drove me crazy growing up. There's seven years between me and my next sister, who is extremely close to her younger sister, because there's only two years between them. So..." I snicker and shake my head. "That was a really long explanation for a short answer."

"No, it's interesting. I'm guessing Caroline feels more like a sister to you, then?"

"Yeah, we're really close." The words die in my mouth as I think about the fact that we used to tell each other everything.

But not anymore.

Because I'm tearing us apart with my big, ugly secret.

My skin prickles, and I shift in my seat. Asher's keen gaze narrows, and I feel the weight of it until he sits forward and licks his finger, picking up cookie crumbs off his plate and casually asking, "What do you like to read? Other than Harry and Narnia?"

"Um... biographies about famous people in history, fiction about famous times in history, other fantasy stuff. I just finished *Fourth Wing* a couple weeks ago and really need to get my hands on *Iron Flame*."

He nods but obviously hasn't heard of those books before.

"How about you?" I ask.

"I'm a huge Ken Follett guy."

"Oh, he's amazing!" I sit forward, excitement sizzling

through me. "Please tell me you've read *Pillars of the Earth* and all related books."

"I have." He laughs, licking the crumbs off his finger. "And I recently watched the miniseries as well, but it's not as good as the books."

"Movies often aren't, although... if it gets people enjoying stories that I love, I don't mind so much. I gotta say, the Lord of the Rings movies... superior to the books. The books are great, they're just—" I wince. "—long."

"And boring." He bulges his eyes. "What is it, like fifty pages just for the Council of Elrond?" He slumps back in his seat and starts to snore.

The move cracks me up, and a loud guffaw bursts out of me before I can stop it.

Slapping my hand over my mouth, I try to curb my laughter, but now he's pulling faces and shit! He's not allowed to be this charming and hilarious! And he's not allowed to be so easy to talk to... or like all the same things I do.

This isn't fair!

I don't want to be attracted to this man, but he's making it impossible.

My belly is still rumbling with pent-up giggles when Asher's expression changes. Gone are the silly faces, and instead an aloof kind of cool washes over him.

He raises his chin, acknowledging someone behind me, and I turn to spot a bunch of tall, athletic-looking guys.

Glancing back at Asher, I notice the smirk on his face

has changed again. It's back to the arrogant one I've seen so many times before, and it stays that way as he stretches his arm across the sides of the chair and looks at me like he couldn't care less if I was here or gone.

I lean back, cross my arms, and narrow my eyes at him. "Who are those guys?"

"What guys?"

A pitiful laugh pops out of me. "Come on, you're not that stupid."

He clenches his jaw, smirking at me before casually replying, "Just some of the basketball guys. I go to their games when I can."

"Okay. And, um..." I lick my lips, threading my fingers together. "Are you embarrassed to be seen with me or something?"

"What?" His eyes bulge. "Are you kidding me? You're so fucking hot, of course not. If anything, you're a trophy."

My head jerks back. "Excuse me?"

His face bunches into an immediate cringe. "I didn't mean it like that. You're not an object. You're a human being, and I respect you and—"

"Okay, shut up." I raise my hand at him.

He looks at the tall guys, who are shuffling away from the counter to wait for their orders. When they turn to glance our way, he schools his expression once more. Mr. Cool and Aloof at your service.

I narrow my eyes at him. "If you're not embarrassed to be seen with me, then why are you suddenly acting all weird?"

"I'm not acting weird." He frowns.

"Uh..." My eyes dart from left to right. "Yeah, you are."

"No, I'm—" He smirks again, looking all kinds of cool while raising his chin to acknowledge the towering squad of athletes as they grab their coffees and leave Java Jeans.

As soon as they're out the door, he slumps back in his seat and says, "What were we talking about again?"

My face puckers into a scowl—I can feel it. Crossing my arms and tapping my finger on my elbow, I give him a stern look and ignore my better judgment, venturing into deeper territory, because I have to know...

"Why did you do that?"

CHAPTER 16
ASHER

"Do what?" I have no idea what was in her coffee, but the look she's giving me right now has an x-ray quality that's making me uncomfortable.

I shrug, going for casual and detached, but she's not going to let me get away with it.

I seriously don't know what she's talking about, so this conversation should be fun.

Yes, that was sarcasm.

Bracing myself, I try not to shy away from her pointed look.

"You totally changed the second they walked in the door." She flicks her finger between me and the entrance. "You were being funny and pulling silly faces, and then you just... detached. It was like watching you put on a costume or something."

"I don't know what you're talking about." I shake my

head, not enjoying the way my heart rate just picked up. What the fuck is she going on about? I didn't detach!

"You don't even realize you did it." Her mouth can't decide if it wants to drop open and gape at me or curl into a smile and laugh at me. "I swear, the second those guys walked in, you *changed*. You went all cool and aloof, like talking about the Council of Elrond and Narnia and Ken Follett were these taboo things. Like it's not okay to be an elite athlete who likes classical music and talking about history." Her eyes narrow again, and I can feel the beams shooting out of them, reading me like I'm a fucking open book.

A book *I* obviously haven't read yet!

"You don't need to hide, you know. It's okay to let your geek flag fly. I like you better that way."

I can't help a scoff. "You don't like me at all. You've made that abundantly clear."

She goes quiet, her eyes dipping to the table, before she finally murmurs, "Yet I'm sitting here drinking coffee with you." Her jaw works to the side before she lets out a self-deprecating laugh. "I must be insane—a crazy person, maybe, because..." She shakes her head, pressing her lips together before letting out a sigh. "Because you annoy me, and you're arrogant, and you obviously have these two sides to your personality. I should be running in the opposite direction, but I'm still freaking sitting here!" Her arms flick up, smacking back down on the arms of the chair while I find my voice.

It starts out as more of a croak. "I guess I'm crazy, too,

then." I clear my throat, quickly licking my lips before admitting, "For reasons only the universe will ever understand, I kinda can't stop thinking about you."

Her lips part just a fraction, and I imagine kissing them again. Taking that beautiful face in my hands and pressing my lips to hers.

Would that freak her out?

I curl my fingers and shuffle in my seat. "Look, I don't get it. I mean, that kiss was..." I puff out of my cheeks, then give her an appreciative smile. "But even before that, being around you is..." My eyes soften as I drink her in. "I don't know why I like you so much, but I do. And it's not just because you're sexy as hell. You... talking to you is..." I lick my lips again. "It ignites me."

We stare at each other for a few thick beats, and then when she still doesn't say anything, I give her a hopeless shrug.

She purses her lips, like she's fighting a smile, then softly admits, "I kinda can't stop thinking about you either. Which is super annoying."

"Yeah, it really is." I grin, and her smile grows to match mine.

We get caught in something then. I don't know what it is, but if this were a movie, the camera would be spinning around our heads right now, capturing this chemistry from all these different angles.

It makes it hard to think past my next breath. It makes it easy to forget her accusations about how I'm different around my fellow athletes. Shit, maybe I am. Maybe it's safer that way. Maybe it's just fucking easier to show them what they want to see.

Which means... fuck, I've been showing Lani a side of myself that no one else knows. And I've been doing it without even thinking. Zero hesitation or worry about what she might think of me behind my back.

I didn't give a shit because she didn't mean anything to me.

But she does.

She fucking does.

And the weirdest thing is, I want to show her more. Because she likes me better that way.

The words whistle through my chest, warm and intoxicating.

I have to kiss her again.

I want to take our connection to the next level, so she knows how much I meant what I said.

I like her.

I like her a whole fucking lot.

She blinks and clears her throat, reaching for her bag. For a second, I worry that I said all of that out loud. She had me in some kind of trance; I could have easily opened my mouth and let all that shit tumble free.

"I should probably get going."

"Wait, what did I say?" I reach for her arm, lightly wrapping my fingers into the crook of her elbow.

"Nothing." She smiles, and the light in her eyes tells me it's okay. "I just noticed the time, and I should probably get ready for my next class. Thanks for hanging out with me."

That's too polite.

I don't want that kind of thanks.

She stands and I scramble for my bag, flinging it over my shoulder as I chase her out the door.

"Lani!" I call her to a stop, and by some miracle, she does.

Slowly turning to face me, she waits while I approach... and doesn't step back when I stop mere inches from her.

Staring down into her eyes, I slowly cup her cheek, my thumb gliding along her cheekbone.

She's gazing at my face, her big brown eyes drinking me in as I move in even closer. I'm taking it easy this time, giving her every chance to back away, but she doesn't.

Her breath catches the air between us, and then it's gone as our lips press together for the softest initiation ever...

And it's like a spark to a flame.

A current passes between us. A bolt of energy that seems to fuse our bodies together. The sweet peck quickly turns into a passionate kiss like we're drinking each other's life force and completely unaware of any other human being on the planet.

People are probably gliding past us, double glancing at this couple in a serious lip-lock.

But I don't give a shit.

I'm not even conscious of them.

All I feel is the kiss. Lani's tongue, her taste, her sweet tits pressing against my chest. All I hear is the sweet suction between us just before we pull away for a small puff of air, then dive back for more.

My arm wraps around her waist while my fingers trail into the back of her hair.

She's squeezing my shoulders, pulling me close... then jerking in my arms and shoving me away.

I step back like I've just been electrocuted, and she gapes at me, bug-eyed—just like last time.

"I thought you wanted..." My voice trails off while her head bobs.

"I did." She bites her lips together, her eyes glassing before she closes her eyes and shakes her head.

"Lani, I—"

"I can't," she whimpers, then takes off running.

I don't chase her. I can sense that would 100 percent be the wrong thing to do.

So, as much as it kills me, I stand my ground and watch her disappear.

"Burn, dude," a guy walking past me hisses.

I give him a dry glare, which only makes him snicker, then grip my bag strap and head in the opposite direction.

At least she didn't slap me in the face this time.

I just wish I could figure out what's making her pull away so fast. If she wants to kiss me, then why won't she fucking let herself do it?

CHAPTER 17
LEILANI

It's been four days since I ripped myself away from Asher and fled.

Four days of pure embarrassment.

Four days of torturous guilt.

Four days of deep self-loathing.

I wanted to kiss him. Oh gawd, the second his hand cupped my cheek, I was putty in his arms. His lips were perfect. His arm pinning me to his rock-hard body was all-consuming. I wanted him so badly it hurt.

And that's what freaked me out this time.

I want him.

I want his body on mine. *In* mine. I want those beautiful hands exploring every curve of my body. I want those fingers touching all my sensitive spots and sending me over the edge. And he could do it. He could make me scream his name with barely any effort.

And that terrifies me.

That he could have such a hold on my physical senses.

That he could be weaving his way into my soul so easily.

"It ignites me."

He said those words, and they made something in my chest simultaneously melt and spasm.

How can he undo me so easily?

I've been wound up tight, trying to protect myself against my own weakness. I can't go falling back into a trap of letting some guy control me again. I won't lose my power to a man. I won't ever put myself in a position where I just have to take it.

But Asher wouldn't do that to you, would he?

He's not some stranger at a party.

You're getting to know him.

You're getting to like him.

The air in my lungs goes cold and wispy.

Wiping the steam off the bathroom mirror, I stare at my misty reflection. My skin is still tingling from my piping-hot shower, and the bun on the top of my head has droplets of water clinging to it.

I let it out, and the thick black locks cascade down my bare back.

Is this me now?

Is this my new life?

Where the only person who will ever see me naked again is... me?

If I can't let a guy touch me, then this is what I'm sentencing myself to. I'll be celibate. Forever.

My throat clogs, my lips trembling as I let that thought ride through me.

I've been so busy guarding myself against anyone learning the truth that I haven't taken the time to think through the consequences.

But there they are.

I've met someone I want to be with. Someone who I desperately want to despise but can't.

Someone who sets my body on fire and my heart alight.

Yet I'm denying myself because of some nameless asshole who took what I wasn't willing to give. Who made me feel totally powerless.

And now *I'm* the one convicting myself to a life sentence of no sex and no intimacy.

"Is that really what you want?" I ask my reflection.

The NO resounds through my body. From the edges of my brain to the center of my chest to the tips of my toes.

I'm only twenty years old, and I won't become some nun or hermit cat lady.

I can't let that asshole do this to me.

Tears fill my eyes, a few splashing free as I keep talking to myself in the mirror. "So, what do you have to do, then?" My eyes dip to the sink as I mumble my answer. "I have to put myself back out there. I have to get over this."

I have to make things right with Asher.

I close my eyes, the answer relieving and terrifying me in the same heartbeat.

But I have to do this.

I can't let that stranger from the party destroy my life. He's already taken over two months of it. And I can't let him have another day.

Snatching my hairbrush, I slap it against the sink and suddenly spit, "No more! You can't have one! Minute! More!" I bash my brush on the sink, one hit per word, before throwing it against the wall and heaving. "No more."

Flinging the bathroom door open, I wrestle my clothes off the hangers, shoving my legs into a pair of jeans and throwing on my favorite sweater. This one hugs my body, showing off my curves the way I used to like so much. I refuse to look in the mirror as I tame my waves with my fingers, then shove my feet into my slip-on leather ankle boots.

"No more," I murmur again, forcing air through my nose as I grab my purse and head out the door.

There's a chance Caroline is at Hockey House right now, and that makes me a little hesitant to go there. If I show up and she sees me, will she wonder why I'm there? I could play like I was looking for her, but then I'll have to come up with a reason why. The thought of making up yet another lie exhausts me. All I can hope is that she and Casey are out.

Pulling out my phone, I toy with the idea of ordering

an Uber, then change my mind and figure the walk might do me good. It'll give me a chance to think about what I'm going to say.

I also run the risk of chickening out, but then images of me with scraggly gray hair and fifteen cats meowing in my single-bedroom apartment force my legs forward.

If I don't want that future, then I need to take control. Something I should have done weeks ago.

Fuck that asshole!

May he burn in eternal hell!

I wish I knew his name so I could curse him properly. But I didn't find out any of those essential details, did I? I just let him kiss me and touch me and enter me without knowing a fucking thing.

I will forever hate myself for that.

Clenching my jaw, I grind my teeth together and follow the Maps app on my phone.

It takes me about thirty minutes, but I finally slow to a stop outside Hockey House.

Oh shit.

This is it.

Fisting my hands, I dig my nails into my palms and wonder if I'm capable of doing this. I loiter in the drive-way, spotting Asher's truck and figuring he must be home.

Do it. Do it now! You came all this way!

With a thick swallow, I shuffle to the door. My finger is shaking as I press the doorbell and hope to God Casey or Caroline doesn't answer the door.

In fact, if anyone but Asher swings back this wood, I might just bolt.

The handle clicks and I catch my breath, my lungs starting to burn as I wait for the reveal.

"Hi." The person stares down at me. "Can I help you?"

For a second, I think I might have the wrong house and quickly check my phone app. I don't recognize this man at all, and I—

"Who are you looking for?"

"Um..." I stare back up at the tall guy with his wavy, honey-colored hair and reluctant expression. "I'm sorry. I think I might have the wrong house."

He tips his head to stare at me, looking ready to shut the door in my face, when he suddenly sighs like I'm a pain in the ass and mutters, "This is Hockey House."

"Oh." I blink. "Well, then... who are you?"

He raises his eyebrows like this is no great surprise. "Baxter. I usually don't answer the door."

Baxter. The name sounds familiar. Caroline must have mentioned him. "Are you on the team?"

"I'm the goalie."

"Oh wait!" I click my fingers, feeling like an idiot for not remembering faster. "You love the dog, right? Caroline says you're really great with him."

A shy smile curves his lips. "Fezz is a cutie. And he's the only guy in this place who isn't a smartass, so yeah, I like him."

I can't help a grin.

"So." He raises his eyebrows. "Who are you looking for?"

"Oh, um... Asher. Is he around?"

"Yep." Baxter pulls the door open wide and I slink past him, then wait for some direction.

He points to the hallway left of the stairs. "He's in his man cave. The door straight ahead there."

"Okay, thanks."

"Uh-huh." Baxter nods, then wanders off in the opposite direction.

I swallow, my pulse quickening as I inch my way toward that door. I capture strains of guitar as I draw near and wonder for a moment if he's playing, but then the bass and drums kick in and I recognize the band. I listen to this album sometimes too.

Of course you do.

I roll my eyes at yet another thing we both like. This is insane! I bet the universe is having a big ol' laugh over this one. *I know! I'll find the most annoying person on the planet and then make you so attracted to him that you can barely stand it... oh, and let's give you two a bunch of stuff in common as well. This is gonna be hilarious!*

The thought nearly makes me bail, but then my fingers curl into a fist and I tap my knuckles on the wood. My knock is so quiet, it's barely audible, but it pushes the door open, and I'm soon staring at the back of Asher's mussed-up hair.

He must be having a sloth day. I can't remember the

last time I had one of those. My heart aches with a yearn for pajamas and comfort and relaxation.

Why have I let myself become this study machine?

Anger bubbles in my belly. Anger at myself for letting someone rob me of... well, me.

"No more," I whisper, lifting my chin and walking into the room.

Asher must sense the movement and swivels to spot me, his shocked expression kind of adorable. I could seriously dive right into those eyes of his. They're gorgeous.

As is the rest of him, all shirtless and smoking hot, sitting there on the couch in his basketball shorts with his sexy bare feet and drool-worthy six-pack.

My brain threatens to shut itself down as I walk around the couch and get a full view of him.

Holy shit, he's so beautiful!

He gazes up at me, his expression a mix of confusion... and maybe amusement?

Say something. Anything! Right now!

"Hi." I lift my hand in an awkward wave.

"Hi, there." He draws out the words, obviously pleased by the fact that I'm even here.

I tut and shake my head, my brain giving me absolutely nothing in response. Instead, my eyes dart around his man cave, drinking in the neatly lined bookshelves and the framed posters on the walls. He's even got a mini fridge and a big-ass TV with all the PlayStation thingies and holy shit, look at that collection of hardbacks! My fingers itch to trail along their spines. I want to pull them out and palm the covers, then carefully open them and sniff the pages like I'm addicted to ink on paper.

"So... nice to see you." Asher's obviously choosing his tone carefully. "I think. I guess it depends what you came here to say."

I turn back to study him, doing my best to keep my eyes on his face and not the shape of his muscular pecs and torso.

Inching farther around the couch, I find a spot by the coffee table and rush out what I rehearsed on the way over. "I just wanted to pop by and smooth things over and tell you that I enjoyed talking books with you the other day and the coffee was great and conversation with you ignites me, too, and it might have been a tad rude of me to take off so fast."

I think I managed to get all of that out in about ten seconds flat, and it takes him a little minute to register everything before a wide grin splits his lips. "At least you didn't slap me this time."

He winks, and there goes my mushy heart again.

I let out a soft snicker, looking away from him and finding safety in the wall hangings.

"Gretzky." I point at the framed hockey shirt. "I've heard of him."

"Only the greatest hockey player of all time." Asher stands, proudly pointing out the signature. "My uncle got me this for Christmas my first year at Nolan U."

"It must be worth a pretty penny."

"Oh yeah." He raises his eyebrows, looking all stoked.

"So, a prized possession?"

"It's right up there."

I point my thumb over my shoulder. "I think mine would be that collection of hardbacks over there." I spin and walk over to the bookshelf, studying the spines.

"Yeah, I've been collecting those since I was about sixteen, maybe?"

"It's so impressive," I murmur, wanting to touch and pull them off the shelf, but also wanting to preserve their perfection. "Have you read any of them?"

He scoffs. "Only the e-books."

I grin. "Never crack the spine, right?"

"It's probably stupid." He shrugs. "I just like them to be in mint condition. If I really want to read the paper-back, I'll get it out of the library. Might as well keep my collection pristine, you know?"

"I totally know." I'm sure I'm blushing as I turn to look at him. I kind of love the way he's so particular. It makes me feel less like a neat freak. Or that being a neat freak is totally normal and acceptable. "I like this room. I like the way you keep it."

"Yeah, well, it's my only space in the house that isn't overrun by slobs, so I'm probably a little anal about it. I think if the whole house was mine and the tidy scale was a little higher, I wouldn't be quite so... precious... about this room."

"I get it. I live with Caroline." I bulge my eyes at him. "I don't think that girl would put away a single item of clothing if she didn't room with me."

Asher tips back his head with a groan. "Can you imagine the chaos in their house if Caroline and Casey ever live together?"

I snort and laugh, shaking my head as I picture it. You'd have to be prepared to run the gauntlet every time you stepped in the front door.

"There's just something about a made bed that makes me feel better about life, you know?"

"I do." I nod, and we share a smile that buzzes with this connection I can't keep denying myself.

My throat gets thick, my tongue all clammy as I wrestle my heart back into place.

"Actually, I've got something in my room I think you might like." He points to the door off the man cave. "Do you wanna see?"

I swallow, my brain jumping to images of rumpled sheets and naked bodies.

My lady parts start to tingle as this excited anticipation fights for position against the frenzied nerves that are begging me to run out the door.

It takes a second for me to realize that the look on his face is pure innocence and he's not asking me into his room so we can strip each other naked and have hot, passionate sex.

He just wants to show me something.

"Oh, um... yeah." I force a smile and follow him through that door, my heart pounding like a bass drum as I step out of Asher's man cave and into his inner sanctum.

CHAPTER 18
ASHER

I'm still kind of reeling that Lani's even here. Playing it cool when she walked into my room and then basically *apologized* was fucking hard. I couldn't believe it.

She's here.

Of her own volition.

She wanted to hang with me again. She came all the way to Hockey House to initiate this connection.

And now she's walking into my room. When I first suggested it, she went kind of pale, and for a second, I thought she was about to bolt again. But my little flight risk surprised me yet again, and now she's hovering next to my neatly made bed while I proudly point out a smaller bookshelf dedicated to my Harry Potter obsession.

Is it lame that I'm so into this magical world?

Probably.

But those books got me through some shitty years in

boarding school, and I will forever be grateful to J. K. Rowling.

Lani's lips rise into a wide grin as she moves around my bed and crouches down beside the shelf.

"Wow." She fingers my Harry, Hermione, and Ron Pop! Figures, then picks up my wand, casts a little spell, and laughs at herself while I drink her in like she's the most beautiful thing in this world.

Because she is.

That smile.

Her playful laughter as she picks up my Goblet of Fire replica.

I want to tell her that I've been gifted most of this stuff, but it'd be a lie. I've been buying myself a couple things a year, hiding them away in my room so the guys won't hassle me for my obsession. All of the stuff that I deem to be the coolest is in my man cave—comic books, video games, my signed Gretzky jersey. But my trivia board games, my Lord of the Rings figurines, and my coveted Harry Potter collection—yeah, that stuff stays in here with me. And now she's seeing it. I'm letting her into my inner sanctum.

"Oh wow! You're collecting the illustrated editions!" She carefully pulls out *Chamber of Secrets* and thumbs through the pages. "Aren't these stunning!" Her eyes bulge. "I'd love these on my shelf." She lets out a snort laugh. "I'd love a shelf! There's just no room in our dorm for extra things like this. My books are stored in a box under my bed, which is very sad." She puts on a pout, and I feel like I'm seeing a real version of Lani that she doesn't even realize she's showing me.

No wonder Caroline always goes on about how great she is.

This woman crouching by my bookshelf is unchecked, unhindered... carefree. I saw glimpses of her at the quiz night and once or twice in Denver. I like it.

Shit, I really like her.

A lot.

I just stand there watching her admire my stuff. She slides the book back onto the shelf, then notices something behind me.

"A piano." She pops up with a grin. "You've got your own piano!"

"Well, it's not mine. My aunt and uncle asked me to store it for them, and I didn't want it getting damaged, so I keep it in here."

"And you never play it?"

She brushes past me, her luscious curves setting my arm on fire as she squeezes past. It takes everything in me not to snatch her wrist and drag her back against me. I want to feel her lips again. I want to kiss a trail down her chin, licking a path from her collarbone to that valley between her tits.

She's got a great rack. It's full and luscious. Those fun bags could find a happy home in my hands. Or my hands would be fucking happy, anyway. My whole body would.

She is one fine woman.

And she's sitting on my piano stool right now, her

fingers tentatively touching the keys. She plays a few chords like she's reminding herself.

"How long's it been since you played?" I move to stand behind her.

"A few years. We have a piano at home, but my younger brother always hogs it. He's going to be a concert pianist, apparently."

I snicker. "You think he's good enough?"

She turns to look at me and winces. "No. But no one can tell him that."

With a soft laugh, I move in beside her, perching on the edge of the stool, then start up the bass line for "Heart and Soul."

She grins at me, then kicks in with the melody, and we play a few rounds before she launches into "Für Elise," and I quickly join in with the bottom hand. We find our rhythm easily enough and don't fuck up the song too badly. We muddle our way to the end, both laughing by the time we're done, and then I try to find the chords to play the opening for Beethoven's Fifth, because I know she likes it.

I screw it up and she laughs, correcting me.

Our hands brush, and there goes that electrical charge again.

It fires right up my arm, and maybe it has an effect on her, too, because she goes still and looks right at me. She's searching my face, and I think I'm reading her right. There's a look of heated desire in her eyes that I can feel pulsing through my body as well.

Unable to help myself, I lean in, giving her a chance to respond.

And she does.

She fucking does.

I can hear the angels singing as she shifts on the seat, her boob squishing into my arm just before her lips touch mine. I let out a soft moan of approval before swiveling for a better angle. My elbow hits the piano keys and a disjointed chord fills the air, making us both snicker, but we can't part our lips for long enough to let the laughter last.

Her fingers curl around my neck, pulling me close as she angles her head to deepen the kiss. Our tongues lash together, my hands curving around her waist so I can pull her tight against me.

She comes willingly, and I take advantage while I can. Who knows how long it'll take her to pull back this time.

The thought makes a knot form in my stomach.

I try to ignore it, letting my hands wander up her back, then taking a risk and brushing my fingers up her side. I curve one of those luscious boobs and give it a gentle squeeze, testing the waters.

She doesn't jerk back with a gasp.

She doesn't gape at me, then slap me across the face.

Instead, she groans like she wants more, so I brush my thumb over her nipple and get another sizzling response.

Fuck yeah!

My elbow hits the keys again, a jarring sound coming

out of the piano that doesn't make either of us laugh this time.

"Should we move to the...?" I can't even finish my sentence, too caught up in kissing her to bother.

"Yeah," she pants into my mouth, and we stumble off the stool.

As soon as we stand, she starts kissing a trail down my neck, her hands roaming my naked torso as she licks and nibbles her way to my pecs. She sucks my nipple, then draws a circle around it with the tip of her tongue. Fuck, that feels good. My hands scramble for a feel of her skin, my fingers wriggling beneath her shirt.

She pulls back and I tense for a second, but then she raises her arms, silently telling me to pull her shirt off.

Not a problem.

I whip the fabric off, throwing it over my shoulder and smiling down at that beautiful body. Her boobs are tucked away in a sexy, lacy bra that has my mouth watering.

Reaching for her tits, I cup them both, one per hand, rubbing my thumb over the lace and watching her nipples protrude in response.

"Hello, ladies," I murmur with a grin before diving for that valley and licking a path between them.

She groans, cupping the back of my head as I suck her nipples through the lace.

My hands weave around her back, unclasping her bra with practiced efficiency. Standing tall, I glide the straps off her shoulders. She bites her lip for a second before whipping the bra off and laying it on my piano stool. I want to stand there and take a mental picture of these world-class assets, but she launches herself at me before I can.

Our chests mold together, and that skin-on-skin action is fucking fantastic. I want her so badly, my love stick is standing to attention, poking into her while her nipples brush against my naked chest.

Holy fuck, she's awesome!

I shuffle us a little closer to the bed, bending down to pick her up and wrap those sexy legs around me. She kisses my shoulder, nibbling a path up my neck and sucking my earlobe as I climb onto the bed and lay her back down.

Her boobs jiggle and I capture her right nipple between my lips, sucking her like she's my favorite popsicle. Which she is. Fuck, she tastes good.

A soft breath pops out of her, followed by an appreciative moan, and then she's scrambling to pull down my shorts.

I help her out, letting my cock out of his cage. He's one happy guy right now, eagerly seeking out a dip in the love pool.

Her fingers wrap around me and I groan, sucking a little harder on her nipple while she breathily asks me, "Got a condom?"

"Yeah, yeah." I reach into the top drawer of my nightstand while she shimmies out of her jeans and underwear.

By the time I'm suited up, she's naked on my bed and I'm kneeling between her legs. I would usually draw this out a little, play with her pussy until she's a wet mess, but she seems keen to get on with it, snatching my arms and pulling me down on top of her.

"You want this?" I quickly check, although I probably don't need to bother because she's grabbing my dick and lining us up already.

I kiss her cheek, then pepper little kisses to her ear as she parts her folds and nudges my head into her entrance.

She's already kind of wet, and I can't help a soft grunt of pleasure as I push into her.

She closes her eyes, biting her lip and tipping her head back as I go a little deeper, then pull back and sink into her again.

Fuuuuuccccckkkkk. This feels so damn good.

I bury my cock in her warm oasis while she digs her fingers into my hair, clasping a handful and fisting my locks. I find us a rhythm, her slick heat making it easy as I trail my hand down her body and hook my fingers under her ass.

This almost feels too good to be true. To get to this point. The last two times we kissed, she pulled away and took off. I don't know what changed for her this week, but I'm now buried balls deep inside her, and I feel like the luckiest guy on the fucking planet!

"So good," I whisper in her ear. "You're so fucking good."

Licking her lobe, I kiss a trail back to her mouth and am about to slide my tongue between her lips when she breathes out a soft command.

"Stop."

I don't compute at first and complete another thrust before I hear it loud and clear.

"Stop. Please. Stop."

Jerking up, I look down at her face. "What?"

"I need you to stop." Her voice pitches, her face buckling like she's about to lose it. But then she whimpers and covers her eyes with trembling fingers. "Please. Just... get out."

I immediately do as she asks, my pulsing dick whining at me, then going into the five stages of grief as I try to figure out what's wrong.

"Are you okay?" I softly ask, brushing my fingers down her thigh.

She flinches away from me, curling into the fetal position.

"Did I hurt you?"

Her hair rustles on the pillow as she shakes her head.

She's still covering her face like she's embarrassed to look at me.

I resist the urge to touch her again and shuffle back on the bed. "It's okay." I try to comfort her, but I'm not exactly sure what to say.

"Really?" Her words are muffled by her hands.

"Of course." I frown, desperate to see her face so we can actually talk about this. Do I reach for her? Do I...?

Fuck, I don't know what to do.

This has never happened to me before, and a small part of me is frustrated that yet again she's pulling away from me. But a much bigger part of me is worried, because that look on her face when she asked me to stop was...

She was scared.

I reach for a tissue, getting rid of the condom. She peeks out from behind her hands and watches me throw the balled-up tissue in the trash.

Rolling over, she eyes me, like she's worried about what I might say next, so I keep my mouth shut. I glance at her and try for a reassuring smile, but I don't know what the hell crosses my face.

This is awkward as fuck.

Shit, why did I even start this? I should have known better. Of course she was going to pull away. It's like she's letting me have her in small increments, but never the whole way.

I don't get what is going on in that brain of hers. I—

"You stopped," she finally whispers, sucking in a breath.

I look back at her, running a hand through my hair. "You told me to."

Her eyes start to glass over, and I can feel my eyebrows dipping.

"Wait, did you not want me to stop? I... I'm very confused right now."

She lets out a shuddering breath and wriggles to the

head of my bed. Sitting up against the headboard, she curls herself into a little ball, wrapping her arms around her knees like she's trying to hide from me. She stares at my bedroom wall, falling into some kind of catatonic trance. She's shaking.

And it's freaking me out.

I don't know what I'm supposed to do or say right now, so I keep my movements slow, shuffling off the bed and finding my shorts on the floor. Pulling them on, I adjust my disappointed cock, then gaze down at her.

She's still staring at the wall, refusing to look at me. I frown, scratching my whiskers and then reaching for the blanket at the end of my bed. Draping it around her, I step back and try to catch her eye.

"I'm not going to touch you unless you want me to, okay? You're safe here."

Her eyes dart to mine and she grips the edge of the blanket, tucking it under her chin, which is now trembling as well.

Fuck. What is going on in her head right now?

I crouch down, resting my hands on the edge of the bed and softly asking, "Did something...?" I lose my question and let out a sigh. "I really want to understand what's going on. I don't know how to help you. I don't even know if you want my help. I just..." Another sigh pops out of me, and I'm running my hand through my hair again, then scrubbing it down my face.

She sniffs and shakes her head, but then her expression buckles like she's about to start ugly crying on my bed.

Oh shit. I'm not cut out for this!

My brain starts scrambling for excuses to escape— *Can I get you a drink? Something to eat?* Anything that will take me out of this room and away from whatever is brewing.

But what kind of asshole leaves a girl to cry on her own?

So I force myself to stay, to stew in this uncomfortable silence.

My knees start to ache, so I change position, resting on the edge of the bed and making sure I'm not touching her.

After what feels like a freaking eternity, she sucks in a breath and opens her mouth. Nothing comes out at first, until a slow tear starts to trickle down her nose. "When you have sex and, um..." She sniffs. "If things have already started, and then something feels off, so you ask him to stop..." Her jaw starts to tremble, her voice turning into a squeak. "And he doesn't. What is that?"

Understanding works through me, followed quickly by a rage as hot as a firestorm. I clench my jaw and struggle to get out the words. "It's rape."

Her expression crumples. "I thought so. That's what it felt like." She starts to cry and then whimpers, "He didn't stop." She lets out a choking sob. "He raped me." She covers her face and screams into her hands. "He raped me!"

CHAPTER 19
LEILANI

I thought I could do it.

My body wanted Asher so badly, and I had a point to prove.

I wasn't going to go sexless for the rest of my life because of some asshole at a frat party, so I made myself keep going.

And it was good.

It was so good.

Asher's hands, his lips, his magical tongue...

I didn't want to stop. I wanted those thrusts, that sense of being filled completely. I wanted his chest rubbing against my nipples, igniting me in all the right ways. I wanted to feel him come inside me, to share that moment of ecstasy with him.

But then... the word just popped out of me, and as soon as I whispered it, I knew I needed him to get off me, out of me... give me some space!

And he did.

He did what I asked. Then he stayed and tried to understand what the hell was going on with me.

I couldn't leave him hanging in all that confusion.

So, I said it.

I finally said it.

And now I'm screaming into my hands because, for the first time since it happened, I've actually admitted the truth to myself.

I'm finally acknowledging the R-word.

I was raped.

Raped.

"Lani, I'm..." Asher's voice is all choked up. "I'm so sorry."

He sounds broken, and it makes my hands fall away. I look at his face and see the anguish, like my news is tormenting him somehow.

"I'm so fucking sorry that happened to you."

Tears fill my eyes again and I lean forward, resting my head against his shoulder. His arm comes around me, arranging the blanket so I'm covered, and I curl into his embrace. He kisses the top of my head and whispers, "Is it okay if I hold you like this?"

"Yes."

We go quiet for a minute, and I close my eyes, soaking in the feel of his sheltering embrace. It's strong and safe. Secure in ways that nothing else has been since that night. It's almost like the world can't touch me if I stay leaning against him like this. If he holds me close and doesn't let go.

"Have you, uh... have you told anyone about this?"

I shake my head and sniff, my belly rumbling with a fresh sob. I try to clamp it down but can't stop the tears rolling out of my eyes. "I couldn't. The words just haven't come."

He squeezes me a little tighter, his lips brushing across my forehead this time.

"Who was it?"

Okay, so we're gonna talk about this?

My stomach clenches and I don't know if I can, but then my mouth opens and words come out.

Words I've been too ashamed to admit.

"I don't know. I was drunk, and we were strangers. I can't remember his name." My voice wobbles as self-loathing slathers me in its stench. "I don't even know if I asked for it. We were just dancing and then making out and then—" The words catch in my throat.

"Where were you?"

"At a party on campus." I slash the tears off my face and readjust my head on his shoulder. He loosens his grip on me, but I quickly snatch his hand, pulling it back around my body.

"It's okay. I'm not going anywhere," he murmurs, adjusting the blanket again so I'm cocooned within it.

"Do you think...?" He takes a breath, obviously choosing each of his words carefully. "Was it a frat party, or..."

"It was at the football frat." I wince. "I mean, I know they're not officially a frat, but that's what everyone calls their place, you know?"

"Yeah, I know. I've been there." His voice has dropped to something husky. Something low and dangerous. "Do you think it was one of them?"

I shake my head. "I don't know. I don't think he was a football player." I close my eyes as a shudder runs through me.

"Okay," he croaks.

"Thankfully, I haven't seen him around on campus or anything, but to be honest... I can't even really picture his face. It's like my memory has turned him into this blurry entity. And that's good, right? I never want to see him again anyway."

"But no guy's approached you since? You haven't felt someone watching you or..."

"No," I croak, the thought making me tremble. "I think I was just a quick fuck to him. He left the room as soon as he was done. He probably doesn't remember my face either. It's not like we stared into each other's eyes. I couldn't even tell you what color they are. We didn't exchange names. We just..." I close my eyes, bile burning my throat. I swallow it back down and manage to rasp, "We'll never interact again and that's... that's what I want."

Asher lets out a grunt of disgust. "I wouldn't mind finding him. I'd happily cut his dick off for you."

I let out a shallow laugh. It's hollow and raw—humorless.

"You didn't talk to anyone after? Tell them what happened? Report his ass?"

"It's not like he dragged me into a room," I murmur. "I went willingly."

"But he made you stay," Asher growls.

I curl closer to his side and he tuts, pulling me onto his lap so I can sit more comfortably against him. His hand starts running circles on my back, and I nestle my nose into the crook of his neck.

"After he was done, I... I was frozen. I couldn't move off the bed. I just... I felt... so gross."

Asher's jaw clenches. I can feel the muscles moving. He probably doesn't want to hear all of this, but I can't seem to make myself stop.

"I should have chased after him and screamed the house down, telling everyone what he did to me, but I was... I was... ashamed. Embarrassed that I'd done something so reckless. I don't go to parties and hook up with strangers, but I was in a foul mood and I drank too much. When he came up behind me on the dance floor, I sent him all the signals, you know? We started making out, and I was holding nothing back. I wanted it."

"And then you didn't." Asher's voice is gruff. "You're allowed to change your mind. This is not your fault."

"But I led him on. I was the one who undid his belt buckle. I was giggling and into it, until he spun me around and pulled up my dress. There was just a sudden roughness about him that I wasn't expecting. I tried to get past it, but..." I shudder again. "Something just felt off. I sobered up in an instant and knew I couldn't go through with it, but he'd already started and... and..."

"And that asshole showed no self-control," Asher barks. "This is *not* your fault." He leans back, taking my face in his hands so I'm forced to look at him. It's easy enough to do; his eyes are bright with assurance. "You asked him to stop, and don't try to tell me that he didn't hear you. You did nothing wrong."

My expression crumples. I can feel my face scrunching as my stomach trembles. "He heard me... and then he went really hard and... and... it hurt, and I... I..." My entire body starts shaking, my belly jerking as a surge of vomit fires into my throat.

Covering my mouth, I can't control my gagging as my physical reaction to that moment rears its ugly head again.

I'm gonna puke.

I'm gonna puke in Asher's lap.

CHAPTER 20
ASHER

I stand with a jerk and race to the bathroom. Flipping up the toilet lid, I place Lani on the ground in the nick of time. She's throwing up as she drops to her knees, hurling into the toilet bowl with these aching sobs that are killing me.

It's torture watching her go through this. Hearing what that fucker did to her turned my insides to ash.

No wonder she kept pulling away from me.

Scooping her hair back, I hold it away from her face while she leans forward and heaves into the toilet again.

I grimace, aching for her, raging for her, wanting to smash my fist through the bathroom tiles, then leave this house on the manhunt of the century. I want to find that motherfucker and end him.

How dare he.

How dare he take a woman that way.

How dare he use Lani like she was his sex toy to do what he wanted with.

That fucker!

I want to kill him!

Lani lets out a shuddering groan, pulling my attention back to her.

"You done?" I ask gently.

"I think so," she rasps. "I hate it when that happens." She wipes her mouth with the back of her hand, and I quickly stand to wet a washcloth for her.

She stays on the floor, leaning back against the bathtub. Ringing out the cloth, I hand it over, then stand there helplessly while she wipes her face down.

Once she's done, I crouch in front of her again and ask, "What do you need?"

Licking her lips, she gives me a weak smile and whispers, "Clothes."

"Do you want to go home? I can take you back to Huxley Hall if you—"

"Is it okay if I stay?"

"Of course." My voice has never been this tender before. Probably because I've never felt like this before.

I mean, I'm nice to girls. I treat them right. I'm a gentleman, but I've never felt like *this* before. Because I've never been with someone so vulnerable.

I like to play the shallow game. Keep it fun and light. Impress them, feed them fancy food, make them come— whatever they're in the mood for.

But girls don't open up to me like this.

Maybe because they figure I'm not deep enough. Maybe because I've never shown any of them who I really am.

But I showed Lani. I couldn't help it. She drew me out without me even noticing.

And now she's let me in.

And I will do fucking anything for her.

Scooping her back into my arms, I carry her to the bed, laying her down and rummaging in my drawers for the softest T-shirt I can find.

"Do you want your underwear or...?"

"Yeah, just the—" She points to her jeans, and I pull her bright orange panties out of them, grinning as I hand them over. "These are cute."

She gives me a weak smile, putting them on while keeping the blanket wrapped around her. I pass over the T-shirt, then turn to give her some privacy.

"Thank you." Her voice is wobbling again, and I spin back to check on her.

She's crawling under my covers, looking at me with those big brown eyes.

"Can I join you? Not for sexy times, just... wanna hold ya."

"Okay." She smiles again, and this one has a little more strength.

I slip in beside her, stretching my arm out so she can snuggle against me. "Want to watch a movie or something?"

I figure she's all talked out.

"I don't know." She shrugs, then lets out a shuddering sigh and wraps her arm around my waist.

I take charge, grabbing the remote and turning on the TV, which is mounted to the wall. I pull up *Harry Potter and the Sorcerer's Stone*. If she's seen it as many times as I have, she won't have to put much effort into concentrating. That magical music starts to play, and I feel her relax against me.

Since we both know the movie so well, I talk over the dialogue, telling her all these inane facts about the movie and books. I've watched so many behind-the-scenes documentaries and read so many articles about this franchise, I am filled with useless facts.

She lets out soft murmurs and sounds of interest... until she goes really quiet.

Harry has only just arrived at Hogwarts when I finally move to check her face.

She's asleep.

All that talking and crying must have really taken it out of her. I get it. I feel like I've been smashed by a freight train.

Hearing that shit was fucking hard.

Watching her throw up like that... seeing the effect that asshole has had on her... it was like taking a beating.

Rage rumbles through me again. It's hot and overpowering. My brain torments me, playing out images of Lani on that bed. Did she cry while he finished? Did she try to fight back at first, and he just held her down so all she could do was take it?

I feel sick.

Bile burns my throat as I snap my eyes shut, begging the torturous images to leave me alone.

I need to move. I can't be still in this bed right now.

Gently sliding Lani off my chest, I arrange her limp body against my pillows, lightly caressing her cheek with my knuckles, then brushing her hair off her face, before slipping out of the bed.

I'll be back soon. I just need to…

I don't know what the fuck I need to do. Punch a hole through a wall, maybe?

Stalking out the door and through my man cave, I walk into the main area and notice the TV playing. Rachel and Liam are snuggled up on the couch watching some rom-com while Ethan and Mick play chess at the dining table.

"That's not how you—" Ethan dips his chin, letting out a frustrated grunt. "You can't just move the pieces wherever you want. There are rules."

"Boring rules." Mick pulls a face.

"You were the one who wanted to play this." His voice pitches as he points at the board.

"Could you two keep it down, please?" Liam calls over his shoulder. "Why don't you just come watch with us?"

"Ugh." Mick pokes out her tongue. "That girly shit? No way."

"Oh, shut up, you." Rachel laughs at her, throwing a piece of popcorn at the table.

Ethan plucks it out of the air, shoving it in his mouth.

"Okay, fine, lil' mouse, let's play pool." He gets up from the table and spots me hovering near the kitchen. "Hey, man. You good?" His eyebrows dip, his face puckering with confusion.

Shit. What do I look like right now?

I don't know.

All I do know is that I can't stand here taking in all this domestic bliss when there's a girl in my bed who was sobbing against my chest less than an hour ago.

"Do you want to join?" Mick asks, her smile turning playful. "I'd happily take your money if you want to make this interesting." Her eyebrows wiggle, and then she glances up at her boyfriend with an impish grin. "Or we could play darts. Ethan loves darts, don't you, baby?"

He gives her a dry side-eye, crossing his arms with a warning growl.

She starts laughing like she's hilarious, and I can't take it.

She wants to bet on pool? She wants to play like it's the most normal thing in the world.

What's fucking normal?

Nothing, now.

My simple world is never going to be the same again.

"Nah, I'm good," I mutter, stumbling away from them all and heading for the front door.

I just need a walk. Some fresh air. A place where I can yell at the sky and let out some of this... this blinding rage.

Shoving my sneakers on, I walk into the cool night air.

The sun set while Lani was telling me her big secret. Seems appropriate somehow, you know? Like, how can there be light in a world filled with so much fucking darkness?

"Argh!" I shout, punching the air. "You fucker!" I scream to the sky, wishing that asshole was here so I could pummel him black and blue.

I let out another shout, my chest heaving as I lean over, bracing my hands on my knees.

"Uh... you okay?" someone softly asks behind me.

I spin around and spot Casey and Caroline standing on the path outside our house. Little Fezzik is on his lead, sniffing the grass around him. They're holding hands and gaping at me like I'm a crazy person.

I dip my head, closing my eyes and not answering them. What the fuck can I say?

I'm not okay.

I'm torn up and shredded.

"What's...?" Caroline approaches me with her hand held up, like she's attempting to tame a wild dragon. "What's up with you?"

I stand tall with a heavy sigh and take in her sweet expression. She's worried about me, but I'm not the person she should be spending that kind of energy on.

Do I tell her?

It's not my story to tell.

But as Lani's best friend, shouldn't she know?

My insides quake, and the second Caroline's hand touches my arm, the words slip out. "It's Lani."

"What?" Caroline's head tips back, fear stark on her face. "Is she okay?"

I shake my head and notice Caroline's skin go even paler in the glow of the porch light.

"I mean, yes and no." I wince. Scraping my fingers through my hair, I huff. "She's in my room. She's okay, but... she just told me something, and..." My throat constricts. "It's not great."

Caroline's lips part. "What?"

I work my jaw to the side. "It's not my place to tell you."

"You'd better tell me something." She hits my arm. "What did you do to her?"

"Nothing." I shake my head. "*I* didn't do anything to her."

Caroline immediately picks up on my tone and goes still, studying my face. "Someone hurt her?" Her voice shakes. "She won't tell me anything, but did she tell you? Do you know why she's been acting so differently?"

"Yes," I croak.

"And it's bad?"

I clench my jaw and nod, finding it hard to swallow.

"What is it?" she shouts, slapping my arm again.

"It happened at a party," I whisper, hoping she can read between the lines. "With a guy who... He wouldn't stop." I wince, hearing her voice in my head again. "I don't know when it happened, but—"

Caroline gasps. "I do." Her blue eyes bulge, her fingers trembling as she sprints for the front door.

"No, wait. She's sleeping." I chase after her, snatching her arm before she can open the door.

"Where?"

"In my bed."

"What?" Caroline spins around to frown at me.

I point at her, ignoring her incredulous look. "Don't you fucking wake her."

Caroline's frown deepens into an intense scowl as she shakes my hand off and shoulders the door open.

Turning to Casey for a little backup, I find nothing but another angry face. "What?" I snap.

"Don't grab my woman like that, man. Shit."

"I'm sorry," I mutter, slumping onto the front step. "But Lani needs sleep. She needs to switch off and..." I sigh. "She needs peace." Shaking my head, I lick my lips and stare out at the front yard. "You should have seen her face, man."

Casey still doesn't know exactly what happened, but maybe he can guess. The thing I love about the guy is that he doesn't need to know all the details. Squeezing my shoulder, he gives me a sympathetic wince while the puppy sniffs around our feet. We don't say anything as Fezzik snuffles the stairs, his little snorts and frantic movements entrancing me.

It's good. I don't want to look at Casey right now.

I don't want to try and make conversation.

Because there's nothing to say.

That fuckhead wouldn't stop.

And now Lani's paying the price.

CHAPTER 21
LEILANI

My eyes creep open to a gentle light. It must be coming from a lamp behind me, because it doesn't hurt my eyes too much to open them.

Asher's on the bed. I can feel him shuffling around. I kind of want to reach back and pull his arm over me, or maybe snuggle into his chest again.

I'm done talking. I've woken up feeling drained but maybe a touch lighter. I'm not sure. Just because I've told him doesn't mean the weight of what happened suddenly goes away. I'll still be tormented by it. But maybe I can start to move on somehow. Maybe I won't be caught in this trap forever.

Rolling over with a tentative smile, I'm about to shuffle against Asher's side when I suddenly realize that he's not the one beside me.

It's Caroline.

She's lying with her arm tucked under her head, her big blue eyes red-rimmed and puffy.

"Are you okay? What happened?" I sit up on my elbow, gazing down at her with a worried frown.

"It's not me." She shakes her head. "I'm fine, but..." Tears fill her eyes, her voice dropping to a soft whisper. "Why didn't you tell me? How could you carry that on your own all this time?" Her voice shudders. "It kills me that I wasn't there for you."

I go still, my heart rate dropping to nonexistent as I slump back down on the pillow and stare up at the ceiling. "Asher told you?"

"Not exactly," she mumbles. "I caught him yelling at the sky, and he was really cut up. I asked what was wrong, and he hinted that you'd told him something bad."

Tension coils my muscles, and I grip my fingers together.

"Lani, were you... did you...?"

"I was raped." Huh. Saying it was easier that time. My voice didn't waver. It's just a fact now—a permanent record in my history.

Caroline whimpers, covering her mouth with her hand while she struggles to speak.

I wait her out, staring at the ceiling, realizing she's gonna need a sec, just like Asher did. This truth isn't my wound alone. I didn't think about how it would hurt other people too.

Or maybe I did.

And that's why I held on to it for so long.

"I'm sorry," Caroline whispers. "I'm sorry I didn't know."

"That's not on you. I just couldn't get the words out."

"But I care about you so much. I love you, Lani. I want to help you, and I haven't been able to because I didn't know." Fat tears roll down her cheeks, and she slashes them off her face. "And now I'm making it all about me, and I'm sorry. I don't know what to say. I just... I want to take this away from you. I want to make it all better."

I roll to my side, reaching for her hand with a soft smile. "You can't. It's my journey. It's my experience that I have to deal with."

"But you don't have to do it alone." She touches my cheek, her thumb gently rubbing my skin, and I realize she's right.

I've been trying to carry this weight, and maybe if I'd let her in sooner, I could have coped better. I don't know.

But it's not like I could have told her that night.

"Why didn't you say something when it first happened?" Caroline gives me a pained frown. "We usually tell each other everything."

"I was going to." The memory comes back to me. I was. I had every intention of walking into our dorm room and falling apart, but then... "I got back to our room, and you were sitting on your bed with all these positive pregnancy tests and totally freaking out. You needed me... and I didn't want you feeling bad for bailing on the party when you were going through your own crisis."

Caroline's expression buckles, and I quickly wipe at the frown lines forming on her forehead.

"It's okay. Don't feel bad. It was my choice to keep it to myself."

"That's such a heavy burden to carry." She sniffs, blinking at me, then rolls over to snatch a few tissues from the box. She hands me two, and I bunch them into my eyes, forcing the tears back.

I don't want to cry right now.

"You can't carry this all on your own. You need to talk to a therapist or something. Student services will be able to help. I can take you there."

Her voice is so hopeful, her eyes bright with this "perfect" solution.

I don't know if she's right, but... maybe she is.

Maybe talking to someone impartial will be helpful. Maybe they can give me some ideas for how to work through this intense regret. This sense of filth and shame that's clinging to me.

"It's okay to lean on people for support," Caroline murmurs. "You let me lean on you through all my shit. Now it's your turn to lean on me. I love you, Lani. You're my favorite wahine in the whole world."

I can't help a watery smile. "You're my favorite too."

She lets out a whimpering laugh and pulls me into a tight embrace. I squeeze back just as fiercely and, once again, am surprised by how okay this feels.

I thought telling people would be the end of me. I didn't want to face their reactions.

But maybe this is what I've been needing all along. Maybe this is the start of my recovery.

CHAPTER 22
ASHER

Caroline took Lani back to Huxley Hall on Saturday night. As much as I wanted to beg her to stay, it's not my place. She needs to do what she needs to do. This isn't about me and my shit. I'll do whatever it takes to help her.

Apparently, she spent most of Sunday sleeping.

Having pushed herself to the limit trying to escape this thing, Lani has finally hit a wall. Obviously, letting the truth out has released some kind of plug, and now her body and soul are detoxing.

I wish I could help.

It's been impossible to sleep, to study, to concentrate. Even hockey practice this afternoon was a write-off. We were doing simple drills that I can pull off in my fucking sleep...and I was screwing up every shot.

"Make me work for it, man!" Baxter taunted me while I snarled at him and slapped the puck with my stick.

Of course I missed the goal by a mile and then skated into the wall, crashing against the boards with a flurry of curses. Coach told me off for being a dick, and I spent the rest of practice doing sprints while my team gave me looks that made me feel like a freak. Casey was the only one who got it, because he's the only one who knows.

He understands that all I want to do is be near Lani. To make sure she's okay, that she's coping. That she's able to process this shit and move on. But I can't force my way in. I have to let her come to me when she's ready.

But it's been three torturous days now, and I'm losing my fucking mind!

Rolling over with a huff, I check the time on my clock.

1:34 a.m.

I thump the mattress with a growl and wonder if I should just get dressed and go do a workout at the gym. I've got a card, so I can get into the arena and pump some iron or run on the treadmill until my legs are jelly.

Coach will be pissed—"Sleep is just as vital as any other part of your training!" He says that a lot. But it's offseason and I—

My phone vibrates, then starts to softly ring.

I frown, picking it up and not recognizing the number.

At first I think it might be some asshole from another country with a scammy offer, but it's a US number, and what the hell, I can't sleep anyway.

"Hello?" I mumble, sitting up and switching my light on.

"Hey. It's Lani."

My insides jump with pleasure until I realize the fucking time, and then worry floods me. "Are you okay? Where are you?"

"In my bed," she whispers. "I'm sorry to call you so late, but I figured your phone would be on Do Not Disturb and I could just hear your voice before leaving a message." She softly tuts. "Actually, I probably wouldn't have left a message."

I grin. "How'd you get my number?"

"I stole it off Caroline's phone. She's sleeping." Although Lani's speaking softly, her voice has a brightness to it that it was lacking on Saturday.

She sounds like she's doing okay, so the worry in my chest drops to a simmer as I sink back against my pillows and ask, "And why did you want to hear my voice?"

I picture her smile as she goes quiet for a moment.

"Did you miss my dulcet tones? That's it, right? You needed a little hit of the sexy Ash-Man's voice before drifting off to sleep."

Her laughter is soft and wispy. "I can't sleep. That's why I'm calling you." She sighs. "The truth is, I was hoping you'd answer, because you're the only person I know who can fill my head with inane facts that are boring enough to fall asleep to."

"O-kay." I frown. "Now I'm trying to decide whether to be insulted or take that as a compliment. You just inferred that I'm knowledgeable and boring in the same sentence."

She giggles. It's a light, sweet sound that makes my chest tingle.

I grin, drinking in this moment. Wishing I could see her, touch her... hold her again.

"Just tell me something. *Anything.* So I don't have to think. My brain is going nuts."

My lips dip with concern. "Do you want me to come over?"

"We shouldn't wake Caroline."

"We won't. We can go for a walk in the moonlight or something."

"But it's the middle of the night. I can't ask you to do that for me."

"You're not. I'm offering. If you want me to come over, I'll be there in a heartbeat."

There's a pause before she softly replies, "Really?"

"Yes." I say it emphatically, then throw in an extra mouthful of truth to really sell it. "I like you, remember? You're the girl I can't stop thinking about."

"I'm still having that effect on you, huh?"

"Uh... yup!" I exaggerate the word, and she laughs again.

But then a serious edge creeps into her voice. "Even after everything I told you?"

I take a breath, making sure my voice rings true. "Even more so than before. I'm here for you, in any way you need me. And if that means walks in the middle of the night, then bring it the fuck on, beautiful." I fling the covers off and jump up, grabbing a clean shirt out of my drawer and snatching a pair of sweats out of my closet. "Stay in your room until I get there, and I'll text you when I pull up outside."

"Okay. I'll see you soon."

I've never gotten dressed so fast in my life. Hopping around on one foot, I wrestle my socks on, then bolt for the front door.

Four minutes later, I'm pulling up outside Huxley Hall and grabbing my phone to text Lani.

But she pulls the door open and runs out before I can even get her number up.

"You were supposed to wait in your room," I grumble. "I was gonna come get you."

"I can run from the dorm to your truck." She rolls her eyes, then smiles at me, tucking a lock of thick black hair behind her ear. She's dressed in sweats and a big hoodie, her little feet tucked into a white pair of Adidas. This sporty-casual look is kind of adorable on her. "Thanks for coming."

"Anytime." I put my truck in gear, and we pull away from Huxley Hall.

"I thought we were going for a walk," she murmurs, glancing at me, then out the window.

"We can, if you want, but there's also this cool spot up on the hill where we can see the stars for miles. We could park up there and take a walk..." I check her expression. "Or we could just walk the streets around here if you prefer. Whatever you want."

"Wow." Her lips quirk into a grin. "You're so agreeable

tonight. Is everything okay? I don't think I've ever heard you say '*you want*' so many times before."

I snicker and shake my head. Damn, she notices everything, and she's never afraid to call me out either. It both excites and infuriates me.

Biting my tongue, I keep my eyes on the road ahead and wait for her answer.

She lets out a little huff, then leans back in her seat. "I know my news changes things, but... I don't want you to be different around me. It just makes me feel like there's something wrong with me, you know?"

"There's nothing wrong with you," I quickly assure her. "I just... I want to help you and take this away from you. And—"

"You can't take it away. Neither of us can change it." She pulls her sleeves over her hands and crosses her arms, like she's creating a shield to protect herself.

"So, what do I do? How do I make this better for you?" My voice is taking on a desperate edge. I can hear it, but I can't seem to stop it either.

"You can't fix it."

"I know," I huff. "And it's fucking killing me. I want time travel to be a thing. I want to walk into that party and find you and pull you away from that fucknugget before he can even look at you!"

She snorts, then lets out a surprisingly loud laugh.

I glance at her, annoyed that she's mocking my tirade.

"Sorry." She laughs. "It's just... fucknugget's a good one. I like that."

My laugh is shallow and humorless as I shake my head.

"Look, I know it's hard, and this is probably why I didn't want to tell people. I don't want them tiptoeing around me or treating me like some weak, helpless victim. I don't want to be that. I don't ever want to feel so powerless again. I'm strong. I don't *need* you to wrap me in bubble wrap."

"So, what do you need, then?"

"Just..." She shrugs. "Treat me like you did when you thought you hated me."

I roll my eyes. "I never hated you."

"I drove you crazy." She shoots me an incredulous look. "You called me a shrutebag."

"And you called me a lumpatious asshole." I glance at her and can't help grinning. "That was a good one, actually. And it's things like that that made it impossible to hate you." I raise my eyebrows at her. "You infuriate me sometimes. And you've pissed me off plenty. But you've also..." My words trail off as I feel the weight of what I'm about to say.

"I've also what?" Her question is quiet and cautious, like she's bracing herself for some kind of insult, formulating a quick rebuttal to slam me down.

I soften my voice to a gentle lilt. "You've also made me feel things I've never felt before. I've never wanted to be with someone more. And I've never been kept awake at night by thoughts of a woman. I've never woken up thinking about the same person every day."

She's gone eerily quiet, and I shift in my seat, waiting for her to respond.

I'm still driving toward the hill, but I've slowed my speed to a midnight amble. It's not like there are many other cars around.

"You know what," she finally murmurs. "The hill sounds good. Let's go stargazing."

It wasn't the exact response I was looking for. My gaping heart is now lying open on the operating table, and she's changing the subject.

But I've got no other choice but to take it. It's not like I can pull over and demand some kind of romantic response.

The hill's a gesture, right?

I try to let that thought settle over me as I nod, then resist the urge to rest my hand on her leg as if she's my girlfriend.

I don't know what she is.

What we are.

I've just told her how I feel, and she said nothing back. We've made out a couple times with an intense heat that neither of us could hide. And we've had sex... or at least started to.

We obviously like each other (at least I think she likes me. She's sitting in my truck right now, isn't she?). But I don't know if she's up for anything more than friendship.

After everything she's been through, I have to let her take the lead on this one. Even though she's told me not to treat her differently, it can't work like that. I'll do my best not to treat her as a victim, but I know shit now, and nothing can change that.

I'm gonna have to get over myself if she doesn't want the same things I do.

I can't expect her to get all mushy and tell me I'm the guy for her just because I was fool enough to give myself open-heart surgery at two in the fucking morning.

But she's asked to go to the hill, so I'm gonna drive us there and see what unfolds in the back of my truck. Whether it's an hour or two of inane facts so she can get some rest or some whispered words of affection, I'll take whatever she gives me, because just being with her is better than lying in bed on my own.

CHAPTER 23
LEILANI

Asher must have brought girls here before, because the bed of his truck is stuffed with pillows and blankets. When he lifted the cover and I saw them all piled there, I had to ask, "Do you do this often?"

His moonlit blush tells me enough, and I throw him a little side-eye before jumping into the back. He goes to help me but isn't fast enough, and I manage to scramble up to my knees and waddle to the back of the truck.

Throwing pillows and blankets down, we get set up. Asher lies back, casually resting against the cab, and I can't resist finding a home against his chest. He's comfortable and warm.

Tucking the blanket around my shoulders, he shifts so my head's at a better angle, and I can't help a soft smile.

All that stuff he said to me in the truck was unbelievably sweet and vulnerable. I wanted to tell him that he's my first thought every morning, too, but my throat had swelled so thick with emotion that I couldn't get one word out.

He went quiet after that, and I worried that I'd ruined everything, but he's letting me snuggle against him, so it can't be all that bad.

"So... inane facts..." He points up at the sky while I stifle a giggle. "Did you know that Orion is that constellation up there?"

I spot it immediately because I already know what it looks like. My dad is an avid stargazer, and I've lost count of the number of times we had to trundle out after dark to look through his telescope.

"It was named after a supernaturally gifted hunter. He was a bit of an arrogant douche, claiming that he was the greatest hunter in the world." Asher shakes his head. "See, it's okay to be confident, but don't go saying shit like you're the best, you know? Not only does it make you incredibly unlikable, but then fate proves you wrong. The guy got killed by a scorpion."

"Which is also honored," I continue for him, "with the constellation Scorpius. Which will be easier to find over the summer."

Asher turns to look at me. "How do you know that?"

I grin. "My dad. I've done a lot of stargazing in my time."

"Right." His voice goes dry as he shakes his head. "So me trying to impress you with my awesome constellation knowledge has gone down like a lead balloon."

I laugh at his expression. "No, it hasn't it. I love that you know all this stuff."

"Knowledgeable and boring," he mutters.

It's hard not to snort at his tone. "Don't be like that. It's nice to hang with someone who's as dorky as me."

"Who are you calling a dork?"

Oh crap, I've just gone and offended him again. I seriously should just stop talking.

"Why do I like you so much?" he murmurs, shaking his head.

I shift so I can see his face more easily. Resting my arm across his chest, I gaze into his eyes, my lips twitching. "I've asked myself that so many times." Running my finger from his bottom lip to his chin, I whisper, "There's just something about you that I can't resist. It's like this cosmic energy. I can't seem to fight it."

My words soften his expression, his lips curling up at the edges.

I smile back, then lean close, brushing my lips against his. He lets out a pleasant moan, cupping the back of my head when I deepen the kiss. I can't help myself. My body won't let me behave any other way.

He tastes so good, smells so amazing... and his hands on my body do things to me that feel new and exciting.

Pulling back with a soft breath, I stare into his eyes. He's searching my expression, obviously preparing for me to pull away. He won't get mad because he understands why now. I can see that he'll do anything for me, play it any way so I'll feel safe and secure.

But that's the thing.

I *do* feel safe and secure with him.

I felt it in his bedroom the other night. I just...

"Can I tell you something?" I reach for his face again, brushing my fingers down his cheek this time. His stubble is just long enough to be scratchy. I glide the pads of my fingers over his whiskers and feel the tingles run right down to my elbow.

"Anything." His voice is husky, the deep sound sending tendrils of desire flittering through me.

"Okay, well..." I lick my lips. "The other day, when we were in your room..."

"Yeah." His hand runs up my arm—a feather-soft touch that tickles in the best way.

I swallow past the lump in my throat. "I, uh... I didn't actually want you to stop." Biting my bottom lip, I wince. "I just needed to know that you would."

His lips part, his face the picture of such sweet sincerity that I have to take a mental picture of it. "I'll always stop if you need me to. I'd never push you into something like that if you didn't want to."

"I know. And I knew it then, too, but once I said it, I got hit with this flashback... and then you looked so worried, I had to tell you."

"Thank you," he croaks, then works his jaw to the side, obviously still feeling some of the emotion from that moment. "Thank you for letting me in."

"I'm glad I did." I take a breath, feeling myself relax a

little, which gives me the courage to ask... "So, do you think we could try again?"

His eyebrows rise like he wasn't expecting me to say that.

I fidget with the collar of his T-shirt. "I really want you. My body is desperate to finish what we started, and I... I want to try. Can we try?"

"Here?" He looks around us. "Now?"

I nod, anticipation quaking my stomach... until he winces and shakes his head.

"I didn't bring any rubbers. I mean, I might have some in the truck, but—"

"That's okay." I grin, reaching into my purse, which of course I brought into the back with me. I had to hope for the best, right? The zipper sounds loud in the cool night air as I whip it open and pull out the condoms I stole from Caroline's nightstand. What? It's not like I left her none. I'll replace them this week, and she'll totally understand.

If anything, she'll be stoked for me, because it means I'm making it over this hurdle.

If I can.

Dammit, you can! You can do this! You want this!

Sucking in a breath, I bite the edge of the condom wrapper with my teeth and reach for Asher's waistband.

Any delays are not going to help me. I just need to—

"Wait." Asher grabs my wrists, stopping my frantic movements to pull his pants down.

"What?" My shoulders deflate. "You don't want to do this?"

"Of course I do." He grins, pulling the condom packet from between my teeth. "I just don't want to rush it." Lightly cupping my cheek, he pulls me toward him, skimming his lips over mine before trailing a sweet path across my cheek. "If it's all right with you, I want to draw this thing out. I want to taste every inch of you. I want to make you come. I want to give you all the pleasure I can, because this right here needs to be the best sex you've ever had."

CHAPTER 24
ASHER

Her soft breath against my skin makes my insides tremble. Her skin prickles with goose bumps as I lightly suck her earlobe, then glide my tongue down her neck. She lifts her head back, giving me easy access to her luscious skin.

I take my time, painting pictures while I slowly take off her jacket.

"Is this okay?" I whisper.

"Yeah," she breathes.

"I don't want you getting cold."

"My skin's on fire right now." She grips the back of my hair, ending any conversation with a searing kiss that has my meat rod standing to attention, like a fucking general of the US Army has just marched up this hill, shouting orders at his troops, who scramble to salute him.

Desire burns swift and hot from my core to my

extremities as I fight the urge to rip her clothes off and plunge into her.

I said I'd take this slow, and I meant it.

This isn't about me. It's about her pleasure, which is actually my pleasure, too, because making her pant and writhe and come in the back of my truck is going to be fucking fantastic.

Peeling off another layer, I caress the pads of my fingers down her soft skin, marveling at the curve of her tits and how smooth they feel. I unhook her bra, capturing the strap with my teeth and pulling it away from her body. Her melons bounce free. They're so full and lush. I take them in my hands, pushing them together and licking the crease with the tip of my tongue before peppering kisses across them.

She lets out a soft snicker, running her hands along my shoulders and tipping back so I can have easier access to her body.

Sucking a nipple into my mouth, I lick and play, enjoying her sweet gasps and moans. Her fingers grip my shirt when I pinch the other, and I glance up to check on her. When her eyes capture mine, she gives me a fiery look that is all things sexy before whipping off my shirt and diving for me with her lips. It's my turn to be licked and sucked as she explores my torso. My sweatpants are tenting big-time, but before she can reach for them, I stop her once more.

"Not yet," I whisper, smiling at her as I tip her backward, angling her body so she's resting on the pillows.

Skimming my fingers into the waistband of her sweat-pants, I check her face. "This okay?"

She nods, brushing her teeth over her bottom lip and sending my cock into a frenzy. He's busting to get out of his cage, but he's just gonna have to fucking wait.

Hooking my fingers into both her sweats and her panties, I pull them off together, exposing her bronze skin to the moonlight. She's fucking beautiful, her island curves and the mound of black spirals protecting what I'm about to taste.

I lightly run my fingers through it and she shivers, but her lips are toying with a smile, so I take that as permission and lie between her legs.

It's not the most comfortable in the back of the truck, but as I part those hairs and find myself that hot, sweet center, all thoughts of comfort disappear. She becomes my everything, her wet folds beckoning me as I lick and taste her most intimate spots.

"My whiskers aren't scratching you, are they?" I murmur between licks.

"Uh-uh." Her breathy reply and urgent headshake give me permission to keep going.

And then her breaths grow even quicker, her fingers skimming my hair, then brushing over my shoulder, like she can't decide where to settle.

"Oh my..." Her words trail off in a high-pitched whimper as I massage her clit, swirling my tongue around it. Her low groan has a guttural quality to it—an uncontrolled, pleasure-filled sound that makes me feel like a fucking king. "Ash." She cries my name, fisting a chunk of my hair as her legs begin to tremble. "Holy shit, holy shit!" Her scream is soft and sensual, her hips arching as the orgasm rides through.

I swap my tongue for my thumb so I can quickly work my lips back up her body, sucking her nipple into my mouth as another wave travels over her. She cries out again, then clamps her legs together, squishing my hand in the process. "Stop moving! Stop moving!" she cries, then lets out a few more shuddering breaths before squeezing my hand even harder, then slowly going limp.

I sit back with a satisfied grin, watching her recover.

It takes her a minute, and when her head pops back up to look at me, I have to wonder if this is it. And if it is, that's okay, because that was one hell of an orgasm, and I got to enjoy it right along with her.

I'm about to ask her if we're done, but then she's scrambling for that condom packet, ripping it open with the ferocity of a wolverine. "Take your pants off. Right now."

I do as I'm told, fighting a grin as I flick them off the end of my feet and sit back so she can suit me up.

Resting my hands on her hips, I gaze up at her, loving the shape of her face and the way the moonlight is capturing her features. She's fucking gorgeous. My Hawaiian Hottie. I feel like the luckiest guy on Earth right now.

Once the condom is in place, she sits back, a hint of hesitation flittering across her face.

I go for a gentle smile. "How do you want to do this? Do you have a favorite position?"

"As long as you're not taking me from behind, we're all good."

I clench my jaw for a second, ugly pictures of what happened to her slapping me before I manage to get them under control.

Shuffling back, I fight my stupid brain while I lean against the cab of the truck, then beckon her with my fingers. "C'mere."

She walks on her knees toward me, and I cup her hips, pulling her over my pulsing cock and smiling up at her.

"You set the pace," I whisper. "And if you need to stop, you can just jump right off me."

Her eyes light with an appreciative smile before she looks down, rearranging herself over me. My head touches her wet center, which is practically dripping and feels so fucking good as she lowers herself onto me.

"Fuuuucccck yeah," I murmur.

She laughs, then tips her head back with a groan. "You feel good." She raises her hips, rising over me and then sinking back down with this slow, languid move that is sweet torture.

Her hot, wet oasis is holding me tight, gliding over me with a sensation so thick and strong, I'm seeing stars.

Squeezing her hips, I resist the urge to force her to pump a little harder and faster. I fight the request to pick up the pace. My dick's happy no matter what, and if she wants to take this slow, then—

Her hips jerk, moving a little faster over me.

Thank fuck!

It feels so good, I can hardly stand it. Her boobs bounce in front of me and I capture them in my hands, lightly massaging them while she rides me. Her pace is increasing again, breaths punching out of her, peppered with sweet moans that make my heart pump out of time.

Leaning forward, I capture her mouth, and she sits on me for a second, sinking so low that the head of my cock is touching her... I don't even know what the fuck it's called. My brain can't think of scientific words when I'm so deep inside this woman, I feel like I'm becoming a part of her.

She groans into my mouth, then sits back, bracing her hands on my shoulders and setting a heady pace of fast, quick jerks over my cock that have him twitching in antic-ipation.

I hiss as soon as the build starts to hit me, running my hands around the back of her ass and squeezing those cheeks harder than I probably should.

She doesn't seem to mind, though. Her pussy is only getting wetter, and then it starts to spasm, clenching my cock and forcing it to explode without warning.

"Ahhhh," I cry out, the unexpected pleasure blinding me as I pump her over me a few more times.

She milks me dry before sinking right down on me again, her body flopping against mine.

Trying to catch my breath, I trail my fingers up her naked back, lightly kissing her shoulder and then smiling big when she makes my fucking century.

"As much as I hate to admit this... you're right." She turns to puff against my neck. "That was the best sex I've ever had."

CHAPTER 25
LEILANI

My body is still warm and electrified as we drive back to Huxley Hall. I did it. I crossed that barrier I'd been worried I wouldn't be able to overcome, and it was so good.

Lightning bugs swarm my stomach and I fight yet another grin, resting my head back against the seat and gazing out the window as small-town Nolan rolls by. We amble down Main Street, the lack of human traffic eerie. It's usually bustling, but not at 3:30 a.m. I can't decide if I like this quiet stillness or not. I guess I'm just not used to it.

Asher indicates left, the blinker sounding loud and intrusive.

He turns to grin at me, and I feel those bugs surge and dive. This is ridiculous. I don't want a man to have this kind of effect on me, but he's so freaking hot and gorgeous—I've never been this attracted to someone before. My body betrays me every time I'm around him.

But he's also smart and sweet. In the back of his truck, he wanted to make me feel good. He gave me control, and I knew I could trust him to stop if I asked him to, so I let myself go, and it was better than I could have imagined.

His truck slows outside Huxley Hall, and I feel this weird sensation ride through me. What now? Was this just a onetime thing to prove I could have sex again? Or do I want something more with this lumpatious asshole?

My lips twitch with a grin and I stare down at my hands while he parks the truck and taps his finger on the steering wheel.

"So..." He clears his throat. "I feel like I should probably take you out on a date now."

I glance across at him. The streetlamp nearby casts a soft glow over his handsome face. I love the contours of his nose and chin. He's chiseled and... wait. Why did he just say it like that?

I should probably *take you out...*

My eyebrows dip together. I can feel my face tightening. He doesn't have to take me anywhere. Like I'm this big drag on his time. Tonight was an obligation-free encounter, and I don't want him to feel like he's now got to take me on a date. What a load of bullshit. I'm not some girl who needs pampering!

Anger simmers through me, making my voice terse. "Why?"

"Huh?" He looks at me like I'm stupid. "Because we just slept together."

"So?" I cross my arms and glare at him. The bugs are still flittering through my belly, but they're sparking now and I cling to that sense of indignation. "It's not like you owe me anything. I wanted it just as much as you."

He's still staring at me like he's trying to figure out what my problem is, but then his lips start to curl up at the edges. "Good. I'm glad you enjoyed it."

"I did, but you don't have to take me out now. Tonight wasn't some services rendered kind of deal."

"Of course it wasn't, which is why I'm so confused by why you're turning it into that." His voice is tightening now, too, a touch of annoyance creeping into his tone.

"I'm not turning it into that. *You're* turning it into that."

"I just want to take you out to dinner because I like your company!" he snaps, throwing his hands up in the air. "Why is that so hard for you to grasp?"

His outburst shuts me up, and I stare at his incredulous expression until a soft laugh bursts out of me.

"What!"

"Sorry," I giggle. "You've just got a really cute angry face."

"Don't," he growls.

I clamp my lips together but can't help my shoulders shaking with amusement.

"You are so annoying," he mutters.

"Yet you love my company."

"I know!" He flicks his hands up again. "You make me lose my fucking mind, woman! I should be running for the hills, but all I can think about is hanging out with you. So, just fucking say yes to the date, okay?"

His angry look dissolves, replaced with a frown of sweet desperation that I understand completely. I'm becoming obsessed with thoughts of him, too, and I swear it's a form of torture.

"Okay." I finally nod. "I'll go on a date with you. But I'm paying."

"No." He shakes his head. "Forget it, then."

"Excuse me?"

"You've paid the last two times we've eaten together. I'm not taking you out unless you let me pay."

I blink and gape at him for a second. "Are you that much of a chauvinist pig that you won't let a woman pay?"

"I let you pay twice!" He holds up two fingers. "And you probably have zero idea how hard that was for me." Swiveling in his seat, he angles his body toward me and reaches for my hands. "I want to take you out and show you how much I enjoy your company by buying you dinner and treating you like a fucking queen. Why won't you let me do that?"

It's tempting to rip my hands out of his grasp and bolt from this truck, but that would be so rude, and I need to try and explain this or his brain might explode.

With a little frown, I finally admit, "I don't need you to look after me. I'm not some helpless woman who needs saving. I don't want to be treated like a high-maintenance drama queen."

He gives me a long, hard stare, then huffs, letting my hands go and spinning back to look out the front.

"Fine. We can split the bill," he mutters. "But can I just say that I think it's really unfair that men get criticized for wanting to be a gentleman or chivalrous—which has nothing to do with helplessness, by the way—but women are allowed to be as feministic as they like and we just have to lump it."

Interesting. My lips fight a grin as I try to argue his point. "You have no idea how many men assume you owe them something if you let them pay for a meal." I scoff. "Do you honestly not get how hard women have had to fight over the years? How hard some of them are still fighting just to be seen as equals?"

"Yes, I'm well aware of the power struggle. But there isn't one between us." He turns back to face me, his tone lightening like a soft breeze. "At least I don't want there to be. And you don't owe me anything. It will never be like that between us." His gentle words embrace me. "I just want to take you out for dinner. I want to show you that you actually mean something to me."

My heart spasms, this foreign sensation spreading through my chest as he looks away, running a hand through his hair with a sigh.

I mean something to him.

Even though I make him lose his mind.

My lips start twitching again, and I let them relax into

a smile as I reach for his wrist and curl my fingers around it. "I guess I did pay the last two times."

He gives me a cautious side-eye.

"So... I'll let you pay. I'll let you take me out to dinner..."

He harrumphs like he doesn't believe me, and I can't help laughing.

He's still pissed, but I can feel him thawing out pretty rapidly, so I throw in another comment to lighten the mood. "And it better be a fancy-ass dinner, because from what Caroline's told me, you're one rich MOFO, and I'd kind of like to see what you're made of."

He snorts and shakes his head. "You drive me crazy."

"Thank you." I give him the sweetest smile I can muster.

A breathy laugh pops out of him as he reaches for my face, cupping my cheeks the way I love so much and planting his lips on mine. I fist his shirt, keeping him close to deepen the kiss into something rich and passionate.

We let our tongues linger, playing and teasing until we're out of breath.

Finally pulling away, he brushes his nose against mine and whispers, "Good night, my little Hawaiian Hottie."

"Good night, Mr. Chivalrous."

"Careful," he warns me. "Saying shit like that might have me jumping out of the car and opening the door for you."

"Well, we wouldn't want that." I give him one quick peck on the lips, then pop my door open and jump down to the curb. Gripping the frame, I turn back to give him a look that I hope is meaningful enough. My throat swells with emotion as I rasp, "Thank you for tonight."

His smile is beautiful as he nods. "Anytime."

With a grin, I shut the door and head for my dorm. I hear the window go down behind me, and I glance over my shoulder. He's still sitting there behind the wheel, watching me walk away.

"I'm fine!" I shoo him off with my hand. "I can get to my dorm without a protection detail! You don't need to watch me get inside."

"I'm just enjoying the view!" he calls back.

I can see his smile even in this dim light and can't help a laugh.

Turning away, I feel his gaze from my shoulders to my toes... and it feels good. As I swipe my card and step into the building, I refuse to let myself look back.

My insides are reeling.

I never thought I could feel this way about someone I thought I should hate forever, but that Mr. Bensen is full of surprises, and I can't deny myself the giddy jitters that burst through me as I think ahead to our fancy-ass date night.

CHAPTER 26
ASHER

Lani tried to bail on our date twice, but I wouldn't let her.

She wants a fancy dinner with me. I don't care that she has an assignment due and she wants to get in some extra studying for an upcoming test. Tough shit. She said she was giving me a date night, and so she shall.

I'll definitely make it worth her while. I am delivering so fucking hard, she'll be speechless.

It took me a week to get everything booked, to pull the right strings and make sure this date is nothing but perfect.

By the time I walk up to her dorm room in my black tux with a bouquet of tropical flowers, I feel in charge and on my game.

Until she opens the door and gapes at me with the hungriest look I've ever seen. Obviously, me in a suit does it for her, because I can practically see the drool pooling on the edge of her lips.

I would respond with something cocky to ruffle her feathers if I wasn't struck dumb by the sight of her as well.

She's wearing this glittery bronze dress that hugs her hips and accentuates her boobs. The plunging neckline goes right down between them, and it's hard to swallow as I drink her in, from those spaghetti straps to the tips of her painted toenails. The heels she's wearing match the dress perfectly, winding up around her ankles and lower calves. I swear shoes have never been so sexy. Ever. They also make her about three inches taller, and holy shit, she's so fucking gorgeous, I can barely breathe.

"Are you two just gonna stand there gaping at each other all night?" Caroline's red curls appear and then her blue gaze drinks me in, and I've gotta say... she looks impressed too. "Wowzers. You scrub up good, Ash-Man."

I smirk at her.

"And Lani here is looking hot enough to fry a steak on."

"She most definitely is," I finally manage.

Lani rolls her eyes but is fighting a grin.

"You look like some kind of celebrity couple. Seriously." Caroline shakes her head, grinning between us as she whips out her phone and forces us to pose for various photographs.

Lani finally takes the flowers from me, smelling them with an appreciative smile before passing them off to Caroline.

"I'll put these in water for you, sweets." Caroline grins. "Now you two kids go have fun."

Her playful wink makes Lani laugh, and she kisses her friend before finally stepping out into the hallway.

I give her my elbow and she takes it, brushing her hand down my arm and finally speaking to me. "Okay, so you're gorgeous in a suit."

"Why thank you, milady." I wink and she smiles, and I'm pretty sure I just started floating.

Leading her out to my uncle's Porsche, which he kindly let me borrow, I enjoy her impressed smile as I open the door for her. By some miracle, she lets me treat her like a princess, and we drive to a hotel in downtown Denver, listening to classical music and talking like a night in the big city is nothing new for us.

The two-hour trip flies by in a heartbeat, and we're soon riding the elevator to the top floor of The Grand Palais.

"This place is nice," she murmurs, nestling into me when I rest my hand on her lower back.

"Yeah, my parents bought it nearly three years ago. When I started at Nolan."

"Your parents own this hotel?" She blinks at me.

"They own a lot of places," I murmur, wishing I hadn't mentioned it. I'd rather choke on a turkey leg than spend this date night talking about my parents.

"What do they do?"

Clenching my jaw, I mutter my usual spiel. "They own an acquisitions and merger company. They look for dying businesses and buy them for a steal, then either pour money into reviving them or make the decision to dissolve them."

"So, this fancy-pants hotel was on the out-and-out?"

Lani looks like she doesn't believe me when I nod, and her skepticism only grows when I walk her through to the five-star French restaurant just below the penthouse suite.

Her lips part as she drinks in the view. The hostess seats us by the window, just as I requested.

"How are you tonight, Mr. Bensen?" She smiles at me, and I enter into some polite conversation while Lani continues to stare out the floor-to-ceiling window. The lights of Denver sparkle below us—magical glitter that obviously has her mesmerized.

As much as I want to order champagne, Caroline gave me a heads-up that Lani's not drinking thanks to what happened, so I settle for sparkling water, then acknowledge one of the regular waiters who seems to be here every time I come.

If my parents ever want a catch-up, they'll fly into Denver and meet me here. I'm, of course, expected to drive down from Nolan, because why would they drag their pristine butts to my backwater college? Forget that it's an elite university with a first-class hockey program. It's certainly no Harvard, so I guess it doesn't count.

"Wow." Lani finally turns to look at me, shaking her head in obvious awe. "This is classy."

She looks impressed, and I'm quietly relieved. I was

half expecting her to be one of those people who's snobby against the rich. I knew I was taking a risk going all out to impress her, but she did ask for it. I'm sure she was half joking, though, so I'm relieved she isn't judging me for having easy access to this kind of lifestyle.

"I'm glad your parents wanted to save this one."

I nod, drinking in the candlelit tables around us and the soft clink of silver on china, the quiet conversations, and the piano music wafting above it all.

"It was the twins, actually. This was the first project my father gave away full control of. My brothers found it, envisioned a plan for it, and then made it happen. My mother was all over it, and I think that's why Dad relented. On paper, this place probably would have gone on the chopping block, which is no doubt why he gave my brothers such a tight budget. But they made it work, marketed it really well, and now it's like the 'go-to' place in Denver if you're wanting something high-class."

"Well, it's definitely that."

She smiles when the waiter returns with our sparkling water and a detailed list of the specials. We peruse the menu, and she settles on the duck while I order the lamb.

And then time disappears again.

We talk about everything and nothing.

I tell her more about my family but cut those stories as short as I can so we can focus back on her. By the sounds of it, she grew up in a jungle while I grew up in a reptile enclosure. It's a miracle we have anything in common, but the more I listen, the more I understand that she never felt like she really fit. She would have been a lot happier in my ordered, scheduled, neat and tidy world.

But it could be so suffocating. Her upbringing sounds loud and fun and spontaneous.

Maybe there's a happy middle ground between the two. Maybe if Lani became my girl, we'd create something just like that.

My insides aren't even rattled by the thought. As I watch her spoon crème brûlée into her mouth, then drink in her pretty eyes, I'm actually excited by the idea of what we could become.

I'm jumping the gun here. We barely know each other.

But we do. All this talking... I've probably found out more about her over this one meal than I know about half the guys on my team, and we've been playing together for three full seasons.

Placing her teaspoon back in the ramekin, Lani licks her lips and murmurs, "Delicious." Then her eyes land on me, and I feel that heat like a fresh lick of flame. "So delicious."

Oh, she wants me.

She probably has no idea how much she's been doing it, but her hungry eyes have been drinking me in all night. Every time I've been talking, she's been eyeing me up like a piece of candy, and I've got to say... those stares are good for the ego.

And I'm sure I'm giving them back as good as I'm getting them.

By the time I've paid and we're heading for the elevator again, the heat between us is thermonuclear... which is why I guide her to the private penthouse elevator. My all-access pass can get me in anywhere in this hotel, and I swipe my card and step back when the doors open so she can enter first.

"Where does this elevator go?"

"Down to the parking garage," I assure her when her face flickers with concern. "It's just that this one is for penthouse guests only."

"Are we...?" She frowns again. "Are we penthouse guests?"

"Only if you want to be." I slide my hands into my pockets, trying to look unaffected as I wait for her answer.

She bites her lip and looks around, then shakes her head. "I need to get back for a study group I have tomorrow morning."

"No problem." I smile, ignoring my disappointment and pressing the down button. I figured it'd be a stretch for her, which is why I hadn't mentioned it.

I'm still hyperaware of what she's been through, and I don't want to do anything that will make her feel unsafe or forced.

But those eyes.

She's still looking at me like she wants to devour me... or wishes she could have said yes to a night of pure luxury. Oh, the things we could do on those silky sheets.

As we descend a little farther, I can feel the tension building around us. It's not filled with anger but definitely unrest. We need to unleash. To let off some of this steam or we'll both combust.

Slapping my hand on the emergency stop button, I force the elevator to a halt.

"What are you doing?" Lani whips her head to look at me.

"Do you want me in this elevator?"

A tendon in her neck pings and she blinks, obviously trying to look appalled but finding it hard to pull off. "No. Of course I don't."

"You sure?" My lips toy with a smirk as I step into her space. "Your fuck-me eyes are in full bloom, baby."

She glances to the floor between us, but there's hardly any space there right now, so her gaze lands on my chest. Her tongue darts out of her mouth, and her swallow is thick and audible before she murmurs, "I'm not doing it with you in this elevator."

"Okay." I nod, trying to sound casual as I take a small step back and hover my finger near the control panel. "So, you want me to press this button here and get us moving again? I'll do it if you want me to. I'll press this button and we'll glide down to the parking garage and I'll drive you home."

She licks her lips again, her eyes darting from the panel to my face, then back.

"Or... you can tell me what you *really* want, and I'll lift you up against this wall and take you the way your eyes are screaming at me to. It'll be the sexiest, most erotic thing you've ever done, and I can practically hear your pussy purring. But I'll never force you to do anything you don't want to do, so…" I lean a little closer to that red button. Her eyes dart back to mine, and I hold her gaze. "Tell me what you want, Lani."

She swallows and lightly shakes her head, obviously fighting for control.

I give her ten more seconds to change her mind, but she doesn't budge. "Okay. Just don't want you to have any regrets."

The pad of my finger hits the button, but I haven't even compressed it when she fists my jacket and pulls me back.

"I want you to take me in this ele—" Her last word gets swallowed by my kiss as I walk her backward until her perfect ass hits the plush wall of the elevator.

CHAPTER 27
LEILANI

Asher can read me like a book. I both love and hate that about him.

I've been eyeing him up all night, my traitorous brain ripping off his suit so I can have my way with him. No, not even ripping it off. I just want to expose one vital part of his anatomy and he can take me fully clothed, because holy shit...

Asher in a tux should be illegal.

He's so freaking sexy. I barely managed to contain myself when he showed up at my door looking like James Bond and holding a bouquet of tropical flowers. He didn't even go for red roses because he wanted to stand out. He wanted to show me that he actually thought about what kinds of flowers I might like. Acknowledging my Hawaiian heritage meant more to me than I can put into words.

Add that very smooth beginning to the Porsche and

the fancy food and my pussy has been weeping from the get-go. After hours of conversation with this man, who is growing more intelligent and likable by the minute, I am hornier than I have ever been, which made his tempting offer impossible to resist.

"Slow down, baby," he murmurs against my skin while his lips trail my neck.

"No, I can't wait anymore." I wrestle his zipper down and shove his boxers out of the way. Wrapping my fingers around his hard cock, I let out a groan, already imagining it inside me. "I've got to have you now." My words are breathy and hard to understand, but that doesn't seem to matter.

Hitching up my dress, his deft fingers pull my thong aside, and then he nudges his index finger inside me.

"So fucking wet," he murmurs between kisses.

"I want your cock, not your finger." My voice is urgent, and I whimper with relief when he finally picks me up and holds me against the wall.

My legs wrap around his hips as he lines himself up, then parts my folds with his smooth head.

I groan again, the pleasure enough to blind me as he adjusts position and eases himself all the way inside me.

"Holy fuck," he moans against my neck. "Is this okay?"

"Yes." I fist the back of his hair with one hand and grip his shoulder with another as he starts pumping.

It's hot and frenetic, our moans blending into one as we get caught in this moment of pure passion.

My body is getting the release it so desperately needed, and I can barely think straight as he plunges into me again, filling me all the way with his naked dick.

Oh shit.

My eyes pop open.

His naked dick.

I blink, going stiff for a second.

He notices immediately and stops, our puffing breaths mingling together as we stare at each other.

"You okay? Do you need me to stop?" He starts pulling out of me, and I dig my fingers into his shoulders to stop him.

"You're not wrapped," I manage.

He gapes at me, shock coursing across his face before he winces. "Fuck. Sorry. Got caught in the moment and—"

"No, it's okay, just... don't get me pregnant," I warn him. "I will kill you if you get me pregnant."

He goes to leave me, but I pinch his shoulders again, moving my hips and forcing him to stay.

"What are you...?" He frowns at me.

I bite my lip, unable to explain myself. A logical woman would be demanding he get out immediately, but the thought of him leaving is abhorrent. He feels so damn good right now.

He sighs. "Baby, I don't want to get you pregnant, and I swear I'm clean, but..." His voice trails off like he can't bring himself to a place of rationality either.

I didn't even think about that whole clean thing and nod my appreciation. "Me too."

We keep staring at each other, puffing the same air as we try to figure out what to do.

"I should... get a condom, right?" His voice is strangled, and he obviously can't help but move his hips a little.

I stifle a groan as that one gentle thrust sends a wave of pleasure through me. "Do you have one?"

He lets me go enough to pat his pockets, then nods.

I nod, too, but now my impatient body is moving. My muscles are humming, my V-jay unable to control itself as I sink my hips down on his shaft.

His breath catches. "You do that a few more times and I'm gonna come before I can get that condom on."

"The thought of you leaving me is a killer," I finally admit.

"It'll only be for a second." His voice breaks over the last word as I pump my hips again and create that friction. "Fuck, woman. What you do to me." He shakes his head, gripping my hips. His fingers dig into my flesh, a perfect pressure that gives away the effect I'm having on him.

A soft laugh whistles through me, shaking my belly as I grind my hips again and he lets out a whimper.

His breath is ragged as he lifts me a little higher, ready to exit the building, but my insane body fights him, creating a few quick thrusts of friction before he's gasping and whipping out of me like I've burned him.

Grabbing his cock, he pumps it a couple times, letting out a series of strangled gasps as the orgasm takes him full force. I slide down the wall of the elevator, hitting my butt on the handrail and watching in fascination as white cream spurts from his head. It shoots onto my thigh—one, two, three bursts of pleasure—then dribbles down toward my knee.

Slapping my hand over it, I rub his juices into my skin, and he looks like he wants to take me all over again. The heat in his gaze is searing, and I drink it in, silently beckoning him toward me.

Grabbing my face, he scorches me with the hottest kiss I've ever experienced, pressing me back against the wall before letting his hands roam. Squeezing my breasts, he then glides down my curves, tucking his hand under my knee and lifting my leg. His other hand finds a home between my thighs, and his magic touch sends sparks of pleasure firing through me. He massages my clit, starting with teasing, gentle tickles that soon become frantic circles as I bite the shoulder of his pristine suit and mewl for more.

It doesn't take long before I'm splintering with lusty cries that vibrate my entire body. Cupping my pussy, he holds me steady while I shudder against the wall, struggling to find my breath.

"Fuck," I softly rasp as I rest my forehead on his shoulder. "What you do to me."

His throaty chuckle vibrates against my cheek, and I close my eyes, not even trying to fight my grin.

As my heart finds its regular beat once more, I ease away from him and look up to catch him smiling down at me.

"Well, I've never done that before."

"Really?"

"Why does that surprise you?" He frowns.

"I don't know." I shrug, my lips curling at the corners. "You just look very James Bond tonight. It's hard to believe you haven't taken another girl in this elevator before."

His gaze softens as he lightly pecks my nose. "You're the only woman I know who can make me crazy enough to do something like this."

CHAPTER 28
LEILANI

So, I've been low-key dating Asher for a couple weeks now. After our lust-fest in the elevator, I nearly bailed on the idea of seeing him again, because I was maybe a little appalled at myself for behaving that way. My physical reaction to him is overpowering sometimes, and I kind of hate that I wanted him so badly that I threw all inhibitions to the wind. He wasn't even wearing a condom and only just got out of me before he came. What the hell was I thinking?

I wasn't thinking. Pure and simple.

My lips twitch with a grin as I relive the heady encounter yet again.

Ugh! Memories are a bitch... or a blessing. I can't decide.

Whatever they are, I've found myself saying yes to Asher over and over again. Every time he texts or invites me out, I make a way to be there. I even went and sat in on one of his hockey practices the other day. He got special permission for Caroline and me to be there, and since it's offseason and the training is less intense, the coaches agreed.

It was freaking freezing in the arena, but watching Asher on that ice, the way his body moves like lightning, his skills with the puck... it was a whole new level of sexy.

It's fair to say that things are going surprisingly well—the sex is fire, and hanging out with him makes me feel safe and happy in a way that nothing else ever has before. Yet I'm unsettled by it all. After what happened at that party, I was determined not be the kind of girl who needed a man in her life. But I find myself wishing for Asher's company all the time. I freaking pine for it some days, and I don't want to be that girl. But it doesn't take much for me to be rushing out of my dorm room to meet up with the sexy guy I'm coming to think of as my boyfriend. We've never actually had that discussion, but I heard Asher refer to me as his girlfriend the other day, and the biggest, goofiest smile spread across my face. I know this because I saw my reflection in the glass and nearly died.

He's making me goofy!

That should be a big red flag right there, but do you think I'm listening to the warning signs?

Nope!

Which is why I'm sitting in Hockey House right now, working on an essay at the dining table. We're all working... and getting caught up in distracting conversations...

but the thought of parking it in the library so I can study in solitude is too depressing. I *want* to be here. I *want* to be a part of this thing.

And the therapist at the student center, who I've now seen twice, said that hanging out with friends I trust is good for me. Shutting myself away like I did has potentially elongated this whole thing. Letting people in can be scary, but it's also healthy. And maybe she's right. I have felt lighter since talking about the rape. I do feel like I'm slowly making my way back to the Leilani I love. I don't know if I'll ever be the same again. In fact, the therapist told me I wouldn't be. But I can create a new version of myself. And Leilani 2.0 is going to be freaking amazing.

The thought makes me smile as I flip a page of the biography I've been using as one of my reference books and try to find that epic quote that will back up my point perfectly.

Casey is tapping out a drumbeat with his pencil, obviously struggling to concentrate on his studies and feeling the need to distract everyone around him. He leans in toward Caroline with a sexy smirk, and I can't help myself.

"If you kiss her neck one more time, I'm going to throw this book at your head." I narrow my eyes at him, and he jerks away from his girlfriend.

"Killjoy." He makes a face at me.

"You guys promised me that I could get my assignment done if I came and worked here, and so far I've managed one measly paragraph because you won't stop talking and kissing and playing pencil drums."

Asher snickers, sliding his hand down my leg and winking at me when I glance his way. "You knew the risks, boo."

I huff and shake my head, loving and hating the way he calls me that. It's so cutesy and... and adorably sweet. I feel like it doesn't fit me, but then... I know I'll be gutted if he stops calling me that. I'll never admit in a million years how much I love being Asher's boo.

"I can take you to the library if you want. Or we can study in my office."

Casey snickers. "There will be no studying in your man cave. You know you can't resist the Hawaiian Hottie. Her clothes will be on the floor before she even gets her laptop open."

I open my mouth to protest, but Caroline's grin tells me he's right.

I roll my eyes and don't bother arguing. Asher's irresistible.

He lightly squeezes my thigh, then trails his fingers up toward my lady parts, which are already starting to dance. I smirk at him, biting my lip and feeling like a sex siren when his eyes heat with desire.

He seriously makes me feel like a queen in the bedroom. The man knows just what to say, just where his lips are most effective, where his hands can create the most pleasure. I can't get enough of him.

And don't even get me started on the feeling of being

wrapped in his strong arms afterward. The guy knows how to be stone and cotton candy all in the same heartbeat. His muscles are firm and secure while the pads of his fingers whisper over my skin like fairy dust.

My insides tremble as I quickly relive our session last night and hope we can do a repeat tonight. It's the weekend, after all. No classes tomorrow. We could spend the night making love and—

Asher's phone rings, jolting me away from my sexy memories.

I catch Caroline's eye across the table and she's fighting a laugh as I blush up a storm and try to get back to my essay. But Asher's sigh distracts me.

"Olds?" Casey asks him.

"You know it," Asher murmurs, rising from his chair with a frown. I watch his back as he turns away from us and answers the call. "Hey, Dad, how's it going?... Yeah... Pretty good... I'm studying right now, actually." He spins on his heel and rolls his eyes at Casey, who starts to snicker and shake his head.

Asher hasn't actually told me too much about his parents. I mean, I know the facts, but not any of those intimate details... like how he feels about them. I pick up a little tension in his voice when they come up in conversation, but maybe there's more there than I realize.

Mostly, he talks about his cousins and aunt and uncle. He's obviously closer to them, and not just location wise. His voice softens, and there's always a smile in his eyes when he's talking about holidays with Harvey and Halsey.

I've yet to meet any of them. The way things are going between us, I'm bound to soon enough.

"I'm doing that!" Asher's voice rises with irritation.

I glance over my shoulder to watch him run his hand through his hair, then sigh again.

"I will, Dad. You know that." His eyes land on me, his smile kind of sad as he nods and scuffs his socked foot on the floor. "Yep... Thanks for that... Yeah, it'll be, uh... great. Thanks." He's saying words of gratitude and not meaning a one of them.

Turning back to Casey with a questioning frown, he kind of shrugs then winces at me. "His parents are hard work."

"I can tell. What is he 'thanking' them for?" I use air quotes, and Casey snickers.

"Who knows, but it's bound to be something about the business."

"Dad, I gotta go. This assignment's not going to write itself." Asher's wandering back to the table, cringing at whatever his father's response is, before saying a quick goodbye and dropping his phone with an agitated huff.

He plunks back into his chair with a thud and looks up to find three sets of eyes staring him down.

He sighs and mutters, "The usual bullshit. Am I working hard enough? How are business studies going? Because apparently they're the only classes worth asking about. And he's gone ahead and lined up a summer internship for me with a company in New York that's supposedly the best of the best and will be perfect training for when I join the family business. The twins had a great time there!" He snarls the last part, and I'm taken aback by his venom.

It must show on my face, because the second Asher glances at me, his shoulders deflate and he's reaching for my hand with an apology. "Sorry." He plays with my fingers, kissing the ends of them before threading our hands together, like he needs the support.

"If you don't want to do the internship, you should just tell him."

He lets out a hard laugh like I've just said something ridiculous.

"What?" I frown.

"Bensens don't say no to opportunities like that. They go, they comply, they join the family business." The dark way he mutters those words does nothing to hide his feelings on this issue.

I squeeze his fingers. "Baby, you don't have to do that. I can guarantee that there is no law in this land that says Asher Bensen must join his family business."

His eyebrows dip together.

"You're making it sound like a life sentence. I don't want that for you."

The way his expression softens with a smile makes my insides melt. I've obviously just said something to make him go mushy, and he swivels to face me, his voice silky sweet when he asks, "What *do* you want for me?"

"Well, I...want you to be happy. I want you to live a life that's gonna make you want to get out of bed in the morning. Everybody deserves that. If you want to play hockey or go pro or whatever, then screw the family business. You should be doing that."

His eyes light with a brighter smile, but then he's shaking his head. "I'm not good enough to go pro."

"I call bullshit," Casey mutters.

Asher glances at him. "Okay, fine, I'm not sure I *want* to go pro. I mean, don't get me wrong, I love hockey. I fucking love it. But do I want the kind of life where I'm traveling all the time? Playing away games? Working my ass off?"

"Well, what *do* you want to do, then?" Casey throws a pen at him.

Asher catches it with a lightning-fast move that makes my insides sizzle. So damn sexy. He twirls it between his thumb and forefinger, then shrugs. "I'm not sure." That answer obviously unnerves him a little, so I lean across with a comforting kiss.

"You'll figure it out. Something is going to come up that will make your heart jump out of your chest with excitement." I tap his pec with my finger. "It's in there right now, just waiting to wake up."

"Maybe that's you." He wiggles his eyebrows at me, and I laugh.

"I can't be your career." I bite my lip and join him in the eyebrow wiggling. "I can be other things, but not your career."

He chuckles and leans in for a kiss. I go for it, not caring that Caroline and Casey are no doubt watching us.

"And she yells at me for kissing you," Casey grumbles.

"She's kind of distracted right now if you want to take advantage." Caroline giggles.

And that is how Mikayla and Ethan find the four of us when they walk in with their overnight bags and dump them on the floor.

"Well, I see you guys are working hard." Ethan crosses his arms and grins down at us.

Caroline laughs. "How was the wedding?"

"Ugh!" Mikayla tips her head back with a dramatic groan. "May my mother never get married again. It was freaking painful!"

"It wasn't that bad." Ethan threads his arm around her shoulders as she comes to stand beside him.

"Are you kidding me? You *liked* that monstrosity?"

"I didn't say I liked it, I said it wasn't that bad."

"It was a pink nightmare." Mikayla bulges her eyes. "I swear, she hired the designers of the *Barbie* movie or something."

"There was a little pink," Ethan murmurs.

She slaps him on the chest. "Would you let me tell the story?"

He laughs, capturing her hand and sucking her index finger lightly before teasing her. "Baby, you're not telling the story, you're standing here bitching and moaning about colors. Yes, the bridesmaids were wearing pink.

Yes, the napkins had pink edges, and yes, there was pink glitter on the white tablecloths."

"The flowers were also pink."

"Is that why you didn't go up and try to catch the bouquet?" He smirks and winks down at her.

She rolls her eyes and turns back to us. "The only good thing about the entire event was that I wasn't one of the bridesmaids."

"Plus, the drinks were free." Ethan grins.

Mikayla laughs. "That was kind of essential, to be honest. I don't think I could have gotten through that thing if I hadn't been a little tipsy."

Ethan nods and turns to explain. "Mikayla's sister and stepsister—"

"Ugh!" Mikayla pokes out of her tongue.

"—were perfect bitches," Ethan finishes. "But..." He grins down at his girlfriend. "Your mom gave you a hug at the end of the night."

Mikayla's smile turns wicked. "And I thanked her for all the bitchy things she did, because it led me to reuniting with Dad."

Ethan cracks up laughing. "She went so pale. It was fucking epic." He wiggles his eyebrows, then turns to look at us again. "As were the jealous glares Mick got from Megan's friends."

Mikayla rolls her eyes, although she's fighting a grin when she admits, "My little sister's buddies want my boyfriend." She wraps her arms around his waist while he kisses the top of her head.

"And they can't have him, because I am all yours, lil' mouse."

She looks up with a gooey smile and mouths, "I love you." He replies with a tender grin and a kiss to her lips. "Thank you so much for coming with me."

The sincerity on her face is beautiful. For all their teasing banter, it's plain to see how much these two love each other.

From what I'd picked up, Mikayla was dreading going to her mother's wedding. Her complaints were endless, and Ethan's patient responses came on the back of every one of them.

"Who gets married on a Friday?"

"Your mother does."

"I have to skip my afternoon classes for this!"

"Why are you complaining about that? We'll be spending the night at a luxury ski resort."

"Do we really have to stay the night?"

"Yes. It's gonna be fine. The place is fucking six stars, Mick. We'll be treated like royalty. That's gonna be fun."

"I don't want to go to the breakfast thing the next morning. Can't you make up an excuse to get us out of this?"

"No! Your mother invited you. Take the olive branch, like your dad said. You can do this. I'll be right there beside you."

And he was.

And I can see how much it meant to her.

I glance at Asher, who's turned back to his laptop, knowing without a doubt that he'd probably do the same thing for me. Hell, any of the Hockey House men would step up for their ladies, because they're good guys.

There goes my heart again, getting all mushy.

I frown, turning back to face my own laptop. I start to reread the paragraph I was working on but get distracted by the man beside me. His eyes are focused on the screen in front of him, but I can see the tension in his face, and I wonder if he's still feeling the effects of his father's phone call.

It's obvious he doesn't want to do that summer internship, but I guess right now he has no real excuse to get out of it. If only he could figure out what he really wants to do with his life. I want to see him happy. He deserves to pursue a job that fires him up. Everybody does.

CHAPTER 29
ASHER

Rachel places the mammoth bowl of roast potatoes on the table and blows the bangs off her forehead.

"Is that everything? I think that's everything."

"*Mi amor*, this looks amazing." Liam squeezes the back of her neck, kissing her forehead and looking all proud of his woman. "You are the queen of the kitchen."

"Hell yeah!" Casey raises his fork with a cheer that fires breadcrumbs out of his mouth and across the table.

Caroline laughs, wrinkling her nose. "And you are the king of disgusting. The food's supposed to stay in your mouth."

With a wolfish grin, he grabs her pigtail and lightly tugs her toward him. "Let me share it with you, baby."

"No, ew!" Caroline's laughing and wriggling away, but he clamps his hand on the back of her head, holding her still and claiming her mouth until she melts against him.

I don't know how he gets away with that shit. For one,

I would never force Lani to kiss me because it's just plain rude, and two, she'd probably use my balls as a squeeze toy if I tried. At least I hope she would, because I never want her to feel like she's under my command. Like I have more power than she does.

From what I can gather, reading between the lines, that's the thing that kills her more than anything about the rape. She felt powerless.

Well, she'll never feel that way around me. Ever.

Which is why I can't force the whole "go to the police" issue. I've wanted to raise it a few times, but the moments I've found an opening, I couldn't bring myself to say it. I want her to go to the police and have that asshole arrested, but she doesn't even know who it is. I want to suggest we launch a full-blown investigation, question everyone who was at the party that night, but I doubt she'd agree, and I'm not about to pull that "what if he does it to someone else" card because she doesn't deserve that kind of guilt piled on top of her. I just hope these therapy sessions will help her move on, and if one day she feels like she can do something more, then I'll be there to support her.

"Would you guys stop making out so we can eat already." Mick throws a bread roll at Casey's head. "I'm starving!"

Fezzik yaps, wagging his little tail as he obviously agrees with Mikayla.

"Oh, shut up, you." She pokes her tongue out at the dog. "You've already had your dinner."

"Yeah, hangry girl over here." Ethan points at her. "Do me a favor and let my lil' mouse eat."

She shakes her head with a grin, grabbing the bowl of potatoes and scooping a couple onto her plate before piling his high.

I sit back and soak it all in. I don't know where the hell it comes from, but I'm suddenly struck with this surge of emotion. Listening to the banter firing between my friends fills me with such deep gratitude that I feel my eyes start to burn. I love these guys... and their girls. I love what we've created in the house, and I'm kind of gutted that we've only got a year and a bit left.

This house brought us together. I mean, sure, the team bonded us, too, but we wouldn't be this close if we didn't live in the same house. I'm lucky that my aunt and uncle let us use it this way. Without it, I sometimes worry that I'd just be the rich MOFO on the hockey team who no one really wants to hang with. But they live in my house, so they're forced to be my friends, and I'll take it, you know?

I just hope I can keep it after graduation. If my dad has his way, I'll be living back in New York, miles away from all the people who actually mean anything to me. I'd rather eat slugs than do this fucking summer internship, but I don't know how I'm gonna get out of it. My parents are already pissed enough that I chose Nolan U over Harvard. If I don't agree to this summer internship, they might cut my funding for my final year. I mean, that's a pretty asshat thing to do, but I wouldn't put it past them. Mikayla's mother and stepfather did it, so we all know that kind of shit happens.

Dad's pride and joy are the twins and how they've followed in his footsteps. It's never been about choice. Bensens join the family business. If I'm gonna break that tradition, I have to have a fucking good reason to do it.

And I don't know what that reason is, dammit.

Maybe I could try and sweet-talk Uncle Hayes into letting me join his real estate business. Would my parents swallow that?

Probably not.

They already resent the guy for pulling you away from the East Coast. Maybe it's best to leave him out of it.

"You want gravy?" Lani holds up the boat to me, and I take it with a smile. Her eyes narrow like she's worried about me. She's been giving me that look ever since my phone call, which tells me I'm doing a shit job at hiding my angst.

Sitting up a little straighter, I brighten my smile and smother my peas in the rich brown sauce before diving into this roast like a hungry bear.

Baxter joins us about halfway through—late, as usual. He saunters up to the table, eyes up the goodies, and makes himself a plate before wandering off again. Fezzik chases after him, his little nails tapping on the tiles while Casey shakes his head.

"That asshole's gonna give him scraps off his plate. No wonder the pup loves him the most."

Lani tracks Baxter with a look over her shoulder, then

shakes her head at me. "Does he not like you guys or something?"

"I have no idea. The man's a mystery." I shrug.

"How'd he get a spot in this house?"

Ethan starts laughing. "He was the first one Asher invited."

"Hey, he overheard my phone call and asked if I'd managed to secure some accommodation. I was so excited, everything just came out, and then he outright asked, 'Got room for me?' I couldn't exactly tell him no."

"Actually, you could have," Liam murmurs. "But I'm glad you didn't. Baxter might be quiet and likes to keep to himself, but he's a good guy."

"He's a weirdo, but we love him." Casey shrugs, shoveling in a massive bite that spurts gravy out the side of his mouth.

I cut my food into normal-sized bites and continue to eat like the gentleman I was taught to be. Some habits never die, I guess. The guys hassle me for being this way sometimes, but we were raised in completely different worlds. I'm the odd one out, but somehow I fit. Most likely because of Hockey House. If they lose me, they lose their home too.

Grabbing my beer, I take a swig from the bottle and relax back in my chair, letting my food settle while Caroline tells the story of how Lani is the worst snowboarder in the world.

It's pretty funny, and everyone is laughing by the end... including Lani.

Seeing this other side of her is a thing of beauty. She's been lighting up more and more over the past two weeks, and it's like watching a flower unfurl. She seems to be moving past what happened to her, and I'm glimpsing the girl Caroline always talked about. The fun-loving boss bitch who isn't afraid of anything.

Skimming my fingers across her shoulder, I play with the ends of her hair, wanting her to never be afraid of anything again. Wanting her to be completely liberated from what happened to her.

In every way.

My throat grows thick as an idea that's been brewing for a few days flitters through my head again. Would she hate me if I suggested it?

Does she trust me enough?

Will she understand what I'm trying to do?

I bite my lips together, wondering how I'll even raise the thought as Liam clears the plates and we head into the kitchen to do the dishes. The girls play *Just Dance* while the guys wash, dry, and stack everything.

Continual banter is called out between the sexes, but I can't seem to get into it. It's actually a relief when Rachel ends the game and asks if Liam wants to walk her home and stay the night. It takes him all of one microsecond to agree, and that prompts Mikayla to ask if she can stay in Ethan's bed. Casey then tells Caroline she's staying, and she bites back with a "You're so bossy," then jumps into his arms with a laugh.

He's nuzzling her neck as he carries her upstairs, Fezzik trotting after them with a few little yaps.

I rest my hands on the kitchen counter and look to Lani. She's straightening couch cushions and avoiding my gaze.

"What do you want to do?"

She glances up, tapping the remote against her finger before placing it on the coffee table.

"Do you want to stay? Or should I drive you home?"

"Um..." She licks her bottom lip.

"I want you to stay, but I'm not a bossy turd bandit like Casey, so..."

She laughs, the sound sweet and quiet. "I don't have my stuff here. Toothbrush. Pajamas..."

"Well, I've got a spare toothbrush, and as for the PJ thing... who needs 'em?" I wink. "Or you can borrow one of my T-shirts."

My look must be pretty damn hopeful, because she lets out a soft sigh and murmurs, "I'll stay for a little while."

"Okay." That's not what I wanted her to say, but I'll take it. Holding out my hand, I wait for her to walk around the couch, then thread our fingers together and walk her through to my bedroom.

My dick starts twitching with anticipation, the thought I had earlier rising in my brain like a hot air balloon. I don't want to scare her off, but I don't want her being held back either.

I should just fucking say it.

"So, you said something about a T-shirt?" She tucks her hair behind her ear. "Maybe we can snuggle up and watch a movie or something."

I nod, grabbing it out of my drawer. She slips out of her jeans and sweater, throwing my T-shirt on over her underwear. It falls to her upper thighs, and my mouth pools with water. She's so fucking sexy, and I want to experience her body in all the ways.

And I think she does, too, which is why I have to ask.

Her smile is sweet and oblivious as she brushes past me and walks into the bathroom.

I listen to her pee, then flush... and as she's washing her hands, I tap my knuckle on the door.

"Can I come in for a sec?"

"Sure."

The first thing I see is her pretty reflection in the mirror. She smiles at me, then asks if she can use my spare toothbrush. I grab one out of the cupboard, tearing open the packaging for her, then standing behind her as she brushes her teeth. Every time she bends over, her ass bumps into my hip, and the burning question grows bigger in my mind.

If I don't ask now, my brain is going to explode.

"Hey, um, can I ask you something that could potentially lead to an awkward conversation?"

She frowns into the mirror, then spits out her mouthful of toothpaste and eyes up my reflection. "O-kay."

"Do you trust me?" I rest my hand on the side of her waist while she wipes her mouth with the hand towel.

The toothbrush rattles as she places it in the cup holding mine, then nods. "Yeah, I do."

Fucking best answer in the world.

I smile, lightly kissing her neck before threading my arm around her waist. "What's your favorite position for sex?"

"Oh, a sex conversation. Right. Those can be awkward." She narrows her eyes at me, her lips rising up on the left. I love the way they do that. It's a playful smirk that makes my heart squeeze like it never has before. "Um... I'm not sure. Why, did you have something you wanted to try?"

She swallows, and my throat is getting thick, too, but I've started this now, so...

"I just noticed that you've been avoiding sex from behind, which is totally okay after what you went through."

She stiffens, her nostrils flaring like she wants to bail on this thing immediately. And I have to accept it if she does, but...

"Did you used to enjoy it?"

Her lips purse, then drop into a frown, her forehead wrinkling as she lines up my soap dispenser perfectly with the faucet.

"You don't have to answer if this is too much. I just... I've been thinking about it because I know that some women really like it. It feels different and good and... and

221

if you never want to do that... it's totally fine. I just don't want you being robbed of something that's enjoyable. You deserve all kinds of pleasure, and I want to give that to you."

She blinks a few times, then looks up, studying my reflection in the mirror. I catch her eye, holding her gaze while my heart beats in triple time.

"Do you like that position?"

I can't help a smirking grin. "Baby, I like all positions. I will enjoy your body any way you'll let me."

She smiles, running her fingers through the hair on my forearms.

I nestle my chin on her shoulder. "I'm just saying, if you ever want to try it with me... I'll make sure it's good and fun and safe."

Nuzzling my nose into her neck, I brush my lips across her soft skin, then step back to let her go. That conversation went well. She stayed calm, and I've given her something to think about.

My hand is just gliding across her stomach when she snatches my wrist and whispers, "Okay."

I pause, checking her face in the mirror. "Okay?"

"Yeah, let's try it."

My eyebrows pop high. "Like now?"

She swallows and nods again. "I trust you."

And there it is again, that sense of warmth that runs right through my chest when she says that to me. It's like the most precious gift she could hand me—her trust. And I'm gonna honor that as best I can.

CHAPTER 30
LEILANI

Asher's hand skims back across my waist as he moves in behind me again. Nerves skitter through me, but I want to try this. Because I don't want to be held back by anything. I won't let what happened to me deny me of a good time.

We'll start, and if I don't like it, I know he'll stop.

He's proved his self-control before, and I do trust him.

And I want the pleasure he can offer me. I want the pleasure I can offer him.

The pads of his fingers whisper over my thighs as he nestles his chest against my back. He's watching me carefully in the mirror, and it's then I realize that he has every intention of taking me right here so he can see my face.

Talk about being vulnerable with someone, but I guess I can watch his face, too, and there's something very sensual about that.

I raise my arm, wrapping my hand around his neck and giving it a light squeeze.

"If at any point this gets too much...," he murmurs against my skin.

"I know," I whisper, tipping my head back and kissing him as he wriggles his fingers under my shirt and glides his perfect hands over my body.

Squeezing both breasts, he pinches my nipples through the fabric of my bra, teasing with a rub that sends tendrils of excitement shooting down between my legs. I tip my head back, resting it against his shoulder and closing my eyes as he runs his finger along the top of my panties.

"Is this okay?" he whispers.

"Uh-huh." I swallow and let out a soft breath.

His hand dips beneath the fabric, trailing down to my sweet spot and drawing delicate circles over my clit. The pressure is so soft—a light tickle that's just firm enough to get my heart racing.

It feels so good. My teeth sink into my bottom lip as I meld back into him and let the pleasure curl through me.

He brushes my hair to the side, sucking my neck while still stroking my clit. It's hard not to pant and whimper when he pushes his hips forward, grinding his hard shaft between my butt checks. He's still in his jeans, his cock wrapped up tight in the clothing. I want to set it free. As this pleasure builds within me, I find myself wanting to lean forward and let him take me in a way I thought I'd never be able to handle again, but he's making it possible.

The bathroom lights are shining over me, the mirror just there. I pop my eyes open and watch his tongue glide down my shoulder, nudging the fabric aside. The muscles in his forearm ripple as he keeps working my pussy, and I'm mesmerized by him.

There's nothing dark and sinister in this bathroom.

Nothing feels off, which is why I can reach under the shirt for my panties and slide them down my hips.

"You sure?" he murmurs.

"Yes," I breathe, shimmying my hips and practically purring as the denim of his jeans brushes against my naked butt cheeks.

His eyes smile at me in the mirror, and I hold his gaze as the tip of his tongue trails up my neck, then nips my soft earlobe.

The energy running through me is building at a steady rate, his magical fingers adjusting pressure and speed until my clit is basically weeping.

"Yes," I groan, starting to pant, my chest heaving as the orgasm builds to an eruption that rips right through me. An embarrassing scream pops out of my mouth. It's short but high, and it makes Asher laugh against my skin as my knees go weak.

He cinches me around the waist, holding me steady and waiting for me to stop writhing. The pleasure pulsing through me is almost too much, but I soak in it, reveling in the buzz traveling through my body.

I flop my head forward with a moan, then listen to the sound of his zipper coming down.

I tense, my pleasure senses cutting off for a moment as the sound triggers something ugly in the pit of my stomach. Gripping the edge of the basin, I can feel myself on the verge of bailing. He promised me that would be okay. I'm in control this time. I can stop this whenever I like.

The drawer flicks open, and he pulls out a condom. I bite my bottom lip as he unwraps it, wondering if I should be saying something now.

Why am I not opening my mouth?

It's better to say it now than after he's started, right?

"Hey." He catches my attention, and I glance up. His warm gaze stares at my reflection in the mirror, and there's something about the calm smile in his eyes that stills me. His gentle hands round my hips as he nestles his chin on my shoulder. "You okay for this? You still want to try?"

"Yes." The word pops out with surprising swiftness, and my butt nudges backward of its own accord.

I feel his wrapped shaft skim my naked skin, and for some reason, I smile.

I'm doing this.

I *want* to do this.

Licking my bottom lip, I then scrape my teeth over the moisture and spread my legs.

He keeps his eyes on me, grabbing his cock and gliding it down my butt crack. It makes me shiver... in all the right ways... and I lean a little farther forward, giving him easier access.

"Keep your eyes on me, boo. I want to see your pretty face."

I look back into the mirror, watching him as he glances down to line himself up.

His deft fingers part my folds, his head nudging into my wet core. And then he's looking into my eyes, slowly pushing himself into me while studying my reflection.

My lips part, a soft breath punching out of me as he stretches me in that familiar way, filling me completely.

"You good?" he checks again.

"I'm good." A smile starts to curve my lips, and then my mouth drops open again as he pulls back, then gently glides back into me.

"Feel okay?"

"Yeah." I nod, my words coming out like breaths. "Do it again."

He holds my hips, pulling back and thrusting in once more, this time a little deeper, and I cry out as pleasure crashes through me. Holy shit, this angle is fucking amazing!

"Good?"

"Yeah, yeah, yes! You can stop asking now. You feel good. You feel so good," I whimper.

"So do you, boo. Fucking fantastic." He drives a little harder, and I enjoy the thrust, moving my butt back to take more of it.

His fingers float over my lower back, trailing a path of

delicious sensations until he's rounding my sides and cupping my breasts. He squeezes them for a while, then sails back down to my hips, gripping them as he picks up his pace.

I close my eyes for a second, and he gently coaxes them back open with soft murmurs. "Let me see that gaze of yours, boo."

I find his eyes again, drinking him in as I watch his face contort with pleasure. My body is owning him right now, and there's something so beautiful and empowering about that feeling. His lids snap shut and I nearly tease him, goading him to open them back up, but he's caught in a moment of abandon. I see the way the orgasm builds inside him, marveling at his gratification. His mouth forms a perfect O as his body starts to jerk inside me. He lets out a moan, followed by an uncontrolled thrust that buries his cock deep.

I can't help crying out as well. The tingles firing down my legs and through my torso are intense and wonderful.

He thrusts again, wrapping his arms around my waist and murmuring in my ear, "Fuck, you're so good. You're so good, baby."

I sink back against him, our bodies trembling in time as I close my eyes and soak in this gift he just gave me.

His eyes slide back open, and we stare at each other in the mirror. We're connected physically, as close as we can possibly be, and maybe now on a spiritual level, too, because right in this moment, I feel like I'm looking into his soul.

And I can't help loving what I see.

Which, for some reason, is just a little bit terrifying.

Shit, have I gone and fallen in love with Asher Bensen?

CHAPTER 31
ASHER

Her face has never been more beautiful. My Hawaiian Hottie, my queen. I'm in awe that she trusted me enough to let me do that. I'm honored by it. I'm stoked that it fucking worked. At one point, I thought she was about to bail on me. And that would have been fine. Disappointing, sure, but totally understandable.

"You're so strong," I murmur, feathering my fingers through her hair and wanting to stay inside her forever.

But my body's relaxing, and I can feel her pushing me out as we come down from our highs together.

"You wanna shower?" I whisper, and she nods, obviously struggling to find her voice.

I kind of need her to say something soon, because Lani not having a voice freaks me out a little. She usually has plenty to say, and if she's going through some kind of silent torture right now, I need to know.

"Boo, are you—"

"Please don't ask me if I'm okay." She grins into the mirror, then turns to face me. Resting her hands on my shoulders, she rises to her tiptoes to peck my lips. "Thank you." She murmurs the words against my mouth and ends up kissing my smile.

I can't help it.

It worked. It fucking worked.

Holding her face in my hands, I study her bright eyes and perfect nose and that silky skin of hers. She's the most stunning woman. I love her color, her smell, her taste, her shape.

I love... her.

I love her.

The thought rises in my chest like it's just been waiting for me to figure this shit out.

I love her... and I want to tell her, but I'm not sure where we're at on this whole thing, and if I whisper it now, will I just freak her out and send her packing?

She's still got an element of unpredictability about her. She's constantly surprising me, and I don't want to fuck up what's just happened by going too far.

So, I swallow those three words and turn for the shower instead.

As easy as it would be to make this another chance for sexy times, we both seem content to just soak under the hot spray. We stand sideways to the showerhead, the water running down our bodies while I hold her against me. I make sure the spray isn't hitting her directly in the face, and eventually we pull apart for a quick wash.

I offer to soap her down, but she shakes her head.

"No way. My body is still buzzing from before. I think another round will kill me." She laughs. "Your fingers are dangerous."

"Good dangerous?" I wiggle them.

"Oh yeah." She grins before turning her back to me and quickly soaping herself. Before I can follow suit, she's stepping out of the shower and reaching for a towel.

Wrapping it around herself, she walks out of my bathroom, and I stay under that hot spray, still reeling over how things have unfolded since that first time I drove her home from Denver.

I seriously thought she'd be my enemy forever. Her sharp tongue and snippy comebacks still drive me crazy, but they also ignite me in ways that no one else can. She's got depth and soul beauty that I've never found before. I didn't even know I wanted that, but I obviously do. She lets me be myself. I never have to check myself when I'm with her. Seriously, the shit that comes out of my mouth sometimes, it's a miracle she sticks around.

But this woman seems to be full of miracles.

She's got me falling faster than I thought possible, and holy fuck if it doesn't feel amazing.

"I love her," I whisper, laughing into the shower spray and shaking my head.

I'm not sure when I'm going to tell her, but a sudden urgency to be next to her again fires through me. I slap off the shower and jump out, grabbing my towel and quickly drying myself. I can't wait to slip into bed with her, wrap my arms around that lush body, and hopefully fall asleep together. I want to wake up with her beside me for once.

I know she said she'll stay for a while, but after what we just did, surely she'll be happy to stay the night. I don't want to drive her back to Huxley Hall or have to say goodbye. I want her here. With me.

Wrapping the towel around my waist, I head back into my room, expecting to find her standing there in my T-shirt or slipping between my sheets, but instead she's hovering by the door, lifting her bag onto her shoulder and waiting for me.

"What are you doing?" I grip the towel at my waist.

She points behind her like it's obvious. "It's probably time for me to head back to my own bed. I can call an Uber if you don't want to drive me."

Seriously?

All those happy, giddy, light feels from the shower disintegrate in a heartbeat as I rest my hands on my hips and frown at her.

I thought tonight was going to be this perfect, magical thing... but obviously not.

CHAPTER 32
LEILANI

Okay, so I've said the wrong thing. Again. I seem to be the queen of doing that around Asher, but was he honestly expecting me to stay?

I've never slept over before.

I know he invited me and everything, but I don't see why tonight should be any different.

You don't? my brain taunts. *Wow, you really are a moron.*

I close my eyes so I don't have to look at him. Or think about the fact that I am being the world's biggest coward right now.

What we did in the bathroom was not only mind-blowing but soul-awakening. I should be snuggled up in his bed right now, curled against his side and falling into a contented sleep. But instead I'm attempting a midnight flee so I don't have to face how strong my feelings are.

"Do you really have to go?" He sighs, obviously battling to stay cool and unaffected.

Oh, he's affected. He's downright pissed that I'm bailing after what we just experienced together.

"Yes." I nod, while my insides shake an emphatic *No!*

"You don't have to go," he mutters. "You just don't want to stay... for some reason." His arm flicks out. "Why are you doing this? I want you to stay. Stay with me. Please."

Aw, man, he's practically begging. I can hear that slight note of desperation in his voice, and it's so freaking endearing.

But I can't face this avalanche in my chest right now.

It's all too much. Too overpowering.

I want to run and hide from whatever the hell is going on inside my soul.

"I think it's better if I go." I rest my fingers on the door handle—a physical sign that I'm serious.

"I don't want you to," he grumbles.

"Fine, I'll order an Uber, then."

"No," he snaps. "Of course I'm going to fucking drive you. I just don't want to!" He huffs. "I don't understand why you're doing this. We've been having the best day together, and we just had a fucking epic session in there." He points to the bathroom. "And now you're bailing." His expression buckles. "Did I do something wrong? Did I say something? Did I...?" His eyes round. "Were you lying before? Was doing that in the bathroom too much for you?"

"I..." I shake my head, closing my eyes against the plethora of questions. I wish I could answer every one of them and take that look off his face. I'm hurting him. I don't want to do that, but... how do I admit what I'm feeling?

That's huge and terrifying.

I don't know if I ever want to fall in love, yet I'm allowing it to happen so easily.

Shaking my head again, I attempt a somewhat lame explanation. "The bathroom was great. It's not that. You're great. I just want my own bed."

"Bullshit!" he growls. "Why are you leaving?"

"Because I don't want this kind of relationship!" I suddenly shout.

His head jolts back. "What kind of relationship?"

"You know, where you *have* to be together all the time. It's pathetic."

Running a hand through his wet hair, he looks away from me, clenching his jaw and sort of nodding. "So, you want to be in a relationship where you *don't* want to be with your partner?" He shakes his head, turning back to face me with a confused frown. "Lani, that's not a relationship."

"I just don't want to need you," I retort.

And there it is. My big ol' fear rising to the surface. The thought of relying on someone else in that way kills me. Relying on people can get you hurt. Trusting people can kill you.

But you trusted Asher before. You let him in.

Because I was trying to prove a point that I can handle anything!

But maybe I can't handle this.

Maybe being in love is all too much for me.

"You don't need me." Asher's deep voice cuts through my thoughts, and I blink, looking up at him in surprise.

What did he just say?

"You are a strong, amazing woman. You're fuckin' fire. If anyone could make it on their own, it's you." He raises his hand with this hopeless frown. As it drops against his leg, he looks me right in the eye, and I swear he's gonna break my heart wide open. "I just want you to want me. To hang with me. To enjoy my company."

My heart starts to swell and pulse—a special beat just for him.

"I want you to sleep next to me. With no goal other than to rest and feel safe enough to drift off. I want to wake up beside you so we can start our day together. And I'm not asking for that every single night. I just..." He shakes his head, looking adorably sad as he murmurs, "I want you to want me."

My eyes start to burn, the emotion clogging my throat making it damn near impossible to speak. "Fuck you, Bensen," I finally manage to squeak. "I do want you." My bag drops to the floor. "I love spending time with you, annoyingly enough. You're... you're turning into everything I love about any given day!"

My outburst is followed by a thick beat of silence. He's staring at me, his eyes wide with hope as he whispers, "You love me?"

"I didn't say that." I cross my arms and scowl at him.

"You didn't have to." The grin that's stretching across his face right now is beautiful. His eyes are practically glowing as he does a little hip dip, then saunters across the room.

I roll my eyes. "Don't swagger."

"Oh, I'm swaggering." He raises his eyebrows, his smile growing even wider. "You love me."

"I didn't say that," I mutter again, but he acts as though he hasn't heard me.

Reaching my side, he lightly grabs my hips and tugs me toward him. Planting a sweet kiss on my nose, he smiles down at me, lightly touching my hair. "I love you too."

And there goes my heart. I can feel it pulling apart—right down the middle—gaping open to suck him right in.

I never thought I wanted to hear those words, but they're like water for my soul.

It's impossible to speak, so I rise to my tiptoes and curl my fingers around the back of his neck. Kissing his lips, I sink against him, and when he lifts me off the ground, my legs automatically wrap around him.

He carries me to his bed, climbing onto it with me still in his arms. When he lightly drops me against his pillows, I let out a soft laugh and don't mind one bit as he slowly undresses me until I'm wearing nothing.

Wrestling out the covers from under me, he rolls me onto my side and snuggles in behind me, wrapping his arm around my waist and kissing my shoulder before softly whispering, "Good night, my love."

A smile curves my lips as I run my fingers down his arm and shuffle back into the curve of his body. My eyes drift closed in the safety of his embrace, and for the first time ever that phrase *two become one* kind of makes sense to me.

CHAPTER 33
ASHER

I wake with her still in my arms. The one tucked beneath her is now totally asleep, and though I don't want to wake her, my bladder is calling—and I also wouldn't mind surprising her with breakfast in bed.

Very gently sliding my arm out from under her neck, I wince when she lets out a soft moan, but then she relaxes back into sleep, and it's maybe a little creepy—like Edward Cullen creepy—but I watch her sleeping for a minute.

No, do not ask me how I know about Edward Cullen and his stalker tendencies.

Okay, fine, I read the books.

But Halsey made me. And then I had to sit through the movies too!

All right, fine, it wasn't torture. I kind of enjoyed them, although I couldn't shut up about how fucked-up their relationship was. Edward was a possessive jackass, and Bella had basically no self-esteem. It bugged me that so many girls swooned over that. I may like being a gentleman, but I'd never lie to my woman in order to protect her. He just took everything too far.

When I told Halsey that, she got all pissy with me, threw a pillow at my head, and told me I was the least romantic guy she knew.

Screw her.

I can do romance.

A smile curves my lips as I shift away from Lani and think about her perpetual need to not let me be romantic. Jeez, she'll fight me at every turn.

She doesn't want to need me.

As much as her independent streak drives me crazy, it's also one of the things I love about her. She's strong and isn't afraid to speak her mind. She'll call me out on my bullshit, and last night, she let me call her out too.

And then she stayed.

She fucking stayed!

I throw on some boxer shorts and creep out of the room, using the bathroom upstairs so I don't disturb her. It's such a frickin' mess, which means Casey must have been on bathroom detail this week. The guy does bare minimum when it comes to housework. If it weren't for me, he'd live in pure filth, I just know he would.

Trundling back downstairs, I walk into the kitchen, humming under my breath, because like hell Casey's gonna ruin my day. I hardly ever use the upstairs bathroom, so the wet towels on the floor and pee spots around the toilet are not my problem.

No wonder Mick and Ray wanted to move out of here. I would have, too, if I had to live upstairs. Thank God for my man cave, bedroom, and en suite.

Pulling the fridge open, I scan the contents and decide a veggie omelet will be perfect for breakfast in bed. I get the coffee machine going and start chopping up an array of colorful vegetables.

"What are you so happy about?" Casey croaks as he wanders into the kitchen. His hair is mussed, and his pajama bottoms are only just clinging to his hips. He looks tired and grumpy.

I grin at him. "Why are you up?"

A small puppy yaps behind him, and he gives me a dry look before shuffling to the sliding door and letting Fezzik out for a pee.

"Parenthood getting the better of you, huh?" I try not to laugh while Casey yawns and gives me the finger.

"If you fucking tell me you knew it'd be harder than I thought, I'm going to punch you in the ball sack."

I chuckle, grabbing out the cheese and grating a pile onto the chopping board.

"Seriously, why are you so happy? And why the fuck are you going to so much effort on a Sunday morning?"

"I'm doing breakfast in bed." I pinch some cheese and pop it in my mouth.

Casey wanders back to the kitchen with a knowing

smirk. "I take it you've still got the Hawaiian Hottie in your bed, then."

"Yep!" I grin. "She stayed."

"Nice." Casey nods, his eyes sparkling with a tired smile.

"She loves me." I keep grinning like a happy chimp.

Casey's eyebrows pop high. "She told you that?"

"Basically." I nod.

His eyes narrow, and I can tell he's about to ask for deets, but he's interrupted by Baxter, who walks into the kitchen with a scoff.

"Love," he mutters, rolling his eyes as he fills up his water bottle. "You guys are all so whipped."

Casey snickers and shakes his head. "Just wait, man. Someone's gonna catch you by the balls one day, and you'll be powerless to stop it."

Baxter's unimpressed frown flatlines, and a flicker of something—holy shit, is that emotion?—scampers over his face before quickly disappearing.

I blink at him, but he just gives me a cautious side-eye before muttering something about a run and shoving earbuds in.

The front door thuds shut, and I turn to Casey with a mystified frown. "Did you see that?"

"Yeah." He yawns again. "Maybe? I don't know. I'm still half asleep."

"He's definitely been in love before... or he's in love with someone now but maybe can't have her... or him?"

Casey shrugs again, then whistles. "Fezz, come. Come on, boy."

Scampering paws pad back into the living area and he races up to Casey, his little tail going a mile a minute.

I turn away from the cuteness because I don't want to like that puppy who probably shouldn't be here. And when he does shit like putting his little paws up on Casey's leg and looking at him with those big doe eyes, it's hard to not fall hard for the guy.

"Well, enjoy your breakfast, Romeo," Casey mumbles, picking up the pup and patting his head while walking for the staircase.

"I will," I tell myself, a giddy smile busting over my face again. "She loves me."

As the toast is cooking, I race outside and manage to pluck a flower off one of the bushes running along the side of the house. We do the worst job of maintaining these, but it's early spring now, and even though we neglect most of the plant life on the property, this hedge just keeps on giving.

Arranging the tray, I place the flower on the edge of it, then neatly set it with cutlery, a mug of steaming coffee, and the best fucking omelet I've ever made. It looks awesome. Even Rachel would be proud.

I strut back to my room. It's impossible not to. I'm feeling on top of the world right now. Nudging open the door with my toe, I'm struck still for a moment, taken by the beautiful picture before me.

Lani is sitting up in my bed, the sheet wrapped

around her boobs. Her black hair is tumbling over her shoulder, and a small smile is tugging at her lips as she thumbs through an old photo album.

Aunt Carla gave it to me for my twelfth birthday, and it's always been a treasured keepsake. The album is filled with pictures of me and my cousins—Halsey and Harvey—growing up together. They're only vacation pics, since they lived here and I grew up on the East Coast, but I would always spend a large chunk of time with them during every break. Sometimes my parents would send me out here, just to give themselves some space from the active toddler who then became the whiny five-year-old who went on to become the argumentative eight-year-old who wouldn't shut up. I was the pain-in-the-ass (let's face it) unplanned son they never really asked for.

But Uncle Hayes and Aunt Carla welcomed me with open arms. They basically made me one of their own, and I always used to wish I'd grown up with them instead. I wanted them to be my parents. I wanted Harvey and Halsey to be my brother and sister.

Lani glances up and notices me standing there, a smile stretching across her face the second she sees me. "You made me breakfast?"

"Hope you like eggs."

"I do." She nods, and I walk the tray over with a proud smile.

She lets out a soft laugh and pats the bed. I place the tray down where she told me to and nestle in beside her, resting my chin on her shoulder.

"Holy shit, look at that horrific haircut." I point at a picture of my seven-year-old self, giving the camera a toothless smile as I strike a pose with Harvey. We'd dressed up as WWE wrestlers and look fucking ridiculous.

Lani giggles. "I'd be more worried about that latex."

"They're both an abomination." I groan. "Quick, turn the page already."

She laughs and flicks to the next page, but it's just as bad. Honestly, who the fuck dressed me? It was my mother, obvi, but what the hell was she thinking?

The problem with being raised in a house like mine, where appearance matters and first impressions count, is that you've always got to be wearing the latest trends... and that shit does not always last.

I snort when I spot the pic of Harvey and Halsey dressed up as Thing One and Thing Two for Halloween. My mom forgot to get me a costume, so Aunt Carla threw together the sheet with the eyeholes cut out. I was not impressed. And I can't remember why I was spending Halloween with them when I should have been at school.

I've got vague memories of a trip around Europe that apparently I was too young to enjoy, so I got shipped off for eight weeks with my aunt and uncle. That's right, I went to school with Harvey. He's a year older than me, but the school let me sit in on his classes, and I was able to keep up without any problems.

"These are your cousins, right?" Lani taps a picture of the three of us. "You guys look so close."

"Yeah. We were."

"Is it still that way?"

"Yeah, of course. They all live in Colorado, so I get to see them quite a bit. Harvey goes to Lennox, which is only an hour away."

"Oh, nice."

"Yeah, sometimes he pops down or I'll travel up. Maybe you should come with me next time." I tuck her hair over her shoulder and lightly kiss that delicious skin of hers. "I'd love for you to meet him."

She gives me a closed-mouth smile and nods. "That'd be nice."

Fuck yeah!

Maybe the smallest part of me was worried that when she woke up, she'd have another *don't want to need you* moment and bail out the door. But she's still here. Still sitting naked on my bed, looking through my childhood memories with interest... while her eggs get cold.

I nudge the tray a little closer, and she puts down the photo album while we eat, sharing the omelet. She thanks me for the sweet gesture, then sips her coffee, looking like a sex siren as she licks her lips and laughs at my stories of growing up around two brothers with sticks so far up their asses, they coughed out wood chips.

She then tells me stories of growing up in her "tribe." It was noisy and chaotic and drove her nuts half the time. "But I'd do anything for my ohana."

"Me too." I nod. "Especially my cousins."

Her smile turns gooey, her eyes soaking me in as she

sets her coffee aside and then lets the sheet fall off those luscious tits of hers.

I release a yearning sigh as I stare at them, memorizing their shape and beauty, reaching for them like they're calling to me. I rub my thumbs over her nipples and smile at the way they pucker at my touch. "They seem happy to say good morning," I murmur, leaning down and kissing each one with tender affection.

She runs her fingers through my hair, letting out a soft moan before fisting a handful and pulling me back.

Straddling me, she starts peppering my face and lips with hungry kisses before working her way down my body. Her tongue paints trails that spark my desire and have my rod harder than granite by the time she reaches my tented boxer shorts.

She glances up with a playful smirk before gliding her finger into the waistband of my boxers and yanking them down to let my cock spring free.

"He's happy to see you too." I grin. "Very happy."

With a sweet laugh, she curls her fingers around the base, licking up to the tip with her sultry tongue and then sending me to heaven with a blow job that is the best fucking way to start my day.

I knew it was going to be a good one, but holy fuck!

This woman has me all the way.

Baxter's right.

I'm whipped.

And I'm more than happy to be.

CHAPTER 34
LEILANI

Asher drops me back at my dorm after lunch. It's been a relaxed morning, and I saunter up the stairs with a smile on my face. Who am I kidding? Relaxing? It was mind-blowing! After sucking Asher off, he returned the favor, going down on me with that expert tongue of his. The orgasm that shot through me was explosive. I swear I've never had one so intense before, and I just lay there panting for who knows how long afterward.

He gathered me into his arms, and we lay on the bed together, talking, kissing, then watching the first Lord of the Rings movie. Asher's got the extended editions, so it took like three hours. But that was the relaxing part, I guess.

I unlock my dorm room door and step into the lonely, quiet space, kind of wishing I'd stayed at the house a little longer. As much as I love solitude, being in Hockey House is fun. At lunchtime, we all sat around the table eating and laughing and... it reminded me of the good times at home.

Taking out my phone, I quickly bring up my mother's number and see if she's free for a video chat. The screen beeps and blips while I wait for her to answer, and then Lehua's sweet face is filling the screen.

"Hi, Leilani!" she chirps, then smiles at me. Honestly, my ten-year-old sister has the sweetest face on the planet. Those big brown eyes are always so gentle, and my heart melts just a little bit as I smile back at her.

"Hey, beautiful. How are you?"

"I'm good." She licks a spot of something off the edge of her mouth. "Mom's letting us eat ice cream before Dad gets home!"

"You'd better hurry up! He'll be home any minute!" Mom calls. "Who are you talking to?"

"Lani!"

"Oh, my girl!" Mom's voice brightens, and she bustles into the room, her wide smile taking over my screen when she grabs the phone off Lehua. "Kaikamahine." Mom beams at me. "How are you, my daughter?"

"I'm good." I nod and actually mean it this time. I haven't been calling as much this year because I haven't wanted to fall apart and spill the truth. I just can't. Dad will never get over it. He'd be devastated to know something like that happened to one of his precious children. And there's no way Mom couldn't not tell him that his daughter had been raped.

I don't want to do that to them, so I've just avoided them instead.

But I'm feeling stronger today. And after talking to Asher about our families all morning, I'm kind of in the mood to speak to mine.

"How are the studies going?" Mom asks all the usual questions, and we chat about school.

Dad arrives home in the middle of it and blows kisses at the camera before noticing ice cream on Lehua's face.

"What have you been eating?" His mock roar makes Lehua squeal, then giggle. She runs away while he chases her like a bear, and then Keala and Rangi have to get in on the action too. I listen to the laughing commotion in the background and wave at the camera when little Melika crawls onto Mom's lap.

"Hey, baby girl," I croon.

She grabs the air, wriggling her fingers in a sweet toddler wave, while blinking slowly at the camera.

"She's due for her nap." Mom kisses her head. "I'd better go in a minute."

"Okay." I nod. "Nice to see you guys."

It's always so brief and chaotic. Dad lumbers back into the room with children clinging to his every limb.

"Hi, Leilani!" Makana shouts, and I wave to him in the background. He's dashing through the house with who knows what in his backpack. That kid is always up to something.

Dad will sort it while Mom puts Melika down, and

the rest of the kids will start crashing from their sugar highs in a minute. I'm kind of glad I'm not there for that.

But I do miss them.

Not the chaos, just the love.

Emotion swells in my chest as I wave to my siblings. "Love you guys!" I blow kisses at the camera and get a smattering of distracted waves and endearments.

"Love you, beautiful girl." Dad's face fills the camera.

"You, too, makua."

He grins, and we blow a kiss to each other before I hang up.

The quiet swamps me, and it's a nice, peaceful feeling, yet I'm still unsettled, which is why when Caroline walks through the door fifteen minutes later, I ask if she wants to go to the student gym and see if there are any classes on.

She's up for it, and we quickly change and head down there, happy to join in the second half of a Zumba class. We have some fun working up a sweat, then buy ourselves iced lattes on the way home.

"You seem happy today." Caroline grins at me.

I nudge her with my shoulder, feeling my face warm as she reads me with a narrow-eyed look.

"Falling hard for the rich MOFO, huh?"

"You know it," I have to admit.

She lets out a little squeal and wraps her arm around my shoulders. "I'm so happy for you!"

"Me too." I smile, then stop and grab her wrist. Turning her to face me, I stand in the late-afternoon sunshine and hope she can see how much I mean this. "Thank you."

"For what?" Her nose wrinkles.

"For being here. For taking me to my first therapy session. For just... being the world's best friend. I wouldn't be in this place if you hadn't kept nudging me and trying to get my butt out the door. Thanks for not giving up on me."

Her eyes glass with tears as she steps into my space and gives me the hardest squeeze. I hug her back, and we both sniff and have a gentle cry for a moment.

Pulling back, she wipes at her eyes with a laugh.

"I love you so damn much, bestie," she blubbers. "And I'm so happy that you're healing and finding your joy again."

"I love you too." I smile, kissing her cheek before starting to walk again. "And I love Asher."

Caroline gasps, and I can't help wincing when she starts bouncing on her toes and shouting, "I knew it!"

I give her a side-eye. "Wait a second... you *did* know it!" I nudge her with my elbow. "There's no way Casey didn't tell you today. Asher said he wants the whole fucking world to know. He didn't understand what my problem was when I got annoyed with him for blabbing about my slipup last night."

Caroline cracks up laughing. "Yeah, Casey told me this morning. Asher made you breakfast in bed?" She swoons. "How adorable is that?"

"I know." I bite my lip. "There was a flower on the tray and everything."

"I can't believe how sweet he is with you."

I give her a simpering smile. "He loves me."

"I know!" She tips her head back with a gushing smile, and I revel in this feeling.

With the sun on my face and my heart full to bursting —it's cheesy, but it's true—I've never felt so light before.

Asher loves me, and I love him.

It's like I'm stepping into this whole new era of my life, and I'm not afraid to embrace it.

I'm healing.

I'm falling in love.

And nothing's going to steal this joy away from me.

CHAPTER 35
ASHER

After my epic weekend with Lani, I'm starting Monday in a fucking good mood. It's hard not to smile and grin my way through the morning. Even Dad's reminder text about calling this guy for my summer internship hasn't put me off. I've just ignored it. I'll deal with that shit later.

Right now, I've got a lunch date to arrange.

I fight a grin as I text Lani to find out where she is. I can picture her walking about campus, her black curls bouncing against her shoulders as she moves with purpose. I wonder what she's wearing today. I can't wait to see her, wrap my arm around her waist, and pull her against me.

She's mine.

She loves me.

Fuck yeah!

"Dude, where the hell did that smile come from?"

I glance up at the sound of a familiar voice and laugh. "What are you doing here?"

Harvey grins at me, slapping my hand and pulling me into a hug. We pound each other's shoulders, then step back.

He's looking slick in black pants and a faded denim jacket. He perches his shades on top of his styled hair, oozing the kind of cool that makes most girls look twice.

Which one does as she glides past us. He smirks at her, lifting his chin and winking. She blushes with a coy smile, and he watches her walk away, his eyes firmly on her ass.

I snap my fingers to get his attention. "You just come down here to check out Nolan girls or what?"

He laughs. "Pretty much. I heard about a sorority party that's supposed to be lit tonight."

"On a Monday?" I frown.

"Some chick's birthday party, apparently. They're going big. Thought it was worth coming down for."

"What about class?"

"No one's gonna die if I miss the afternoon. I'm on top of my coursework, and I need to blow off some steam." He wiggles his eyebrows. "You want to come with?"

"Not tonight, man. I've got a date with my girl."

He bulges his eyes at me. "You've got a girl?"

"I do." It's hard not to give him a smug grin. I can feel my peacock feathers blooming, but I don't give a shit. My girl is hot and smart, and I'm the luckiest guy on the planet. What's not to be proud of?

"No fucking way," Harvey mutters, shaking his head with a teasing frown. "How you gonna go tying yourself to *one* woman. Talk about boring."

I roll my eyes. "You don't know what you're saying, dude. It's awesome. I wouldn't have it any other way."

My phone dings with a text from Lani.

I'll wait for you in the Judson Hall cafeteria.

I heart-emoji the message, because I do that kinda shit now, and turn to my cousin. "Come on, I'll introduce you."

His face flickers with a frown, but then he shrugs. "Okay, fine. Let's meet this woman who's gotten her hooks into you."

I laugh and slap him on the shoulder. "No hooks. And you'll understand when you meet her. She's seriously amazing."

He shrugs and saunters along beside me, sliding his hands into his pockets and telling me about school. He's seriously not into it. Studies are going okay, but he's bored. Athletics has started up again—he's a kick-ass middle-distance runner—and he's got some meets coming up soon, but even those don't seem to fire him up that much.

I wonder what his problem is. He was so excited to go off to college, but the last couple years, he's seemed restless and unsatisfied. It makes it hard to talk to him about stuff, but I muscle through his complaints, resisting the urge to tell him to stop whining. Hopefully he's not like this in front of Lani.

Walking through the entrance of Judson Hall, I turn right and start scanning for my girl. This is one of the older buildings on campus, and the brickwork and architecture are pretty cool. That's why Lani likes eating in here. I guess it's the closest she can get to the great hall at Hogwarts.

Damn, I love that she's a Potterhead.

My heart starts to dance as my eyes track along the outer tables near the windows. I spot her at the end of a long one. She's smiling at the girl she's talking to, and I can't wait to come up behind her and wrap my arm around her waist. Claiming her in front of all these people is a privilege.

"There she is," I murmur, pointing across the room.

"Black hair or blonde?" Harvey asks.

"The Hawaiian Hottie." I grin.

"That she is." He nods, obviously impressed. And so he should be. Lani is stunning. "She must be one fine fuck."

I slap the back of my hand against his chest and stop us walking. Turning to him with a warning glare, I whisper-bark, "Don't be a douche. That's my woman."

"Yeah, yeah. Chill, man." He raises his hand like I'm overacting, but what the hell?

A fine fuck.

She is, but I don't need to hear him say that. And you know what? I don't care if it sounds old-fashioned, but you don't fuck a girl like Lani. You make love to her, you pleasure her, you share a piece of your soul.

Fine fuck. I shake my head with a soft growl. Harvey can be such an asshole sometimes.

For a second, it makes me hesitant to introduce them, but then he mumbles an apology.

I keep walking and round the tables.

"Hello, beautiful." I make sure she can hear my voice before I touch her, and she sinks back into me when my arm threads around her waist.

"Hey, sexy." Tipping her head back, she kisses me, giggling against my lips when I cinch her a little tighter and dip my tongue into her mouth. Turning into me, she lets the kiss go a little further before the throat clearing behind me pulls us apart.

I ease back, brushing my nose against hers and murmuring, "Lani, I'd like you to meet my cousin."

"Which one?"

"Harvey. He popped down to visit."

"Oh, cool." She grins and looks around me.

Harvey steps into view, extending his hand with a smile.

But she doesn't move.

If anything, she goes stiff beside me. That warmth I was feeling only seconds ago has disappeared. And I have no idea why.

CHAPTER 36
LEILANI

I can't move.

I can barely breathe.

Thinking logically is impossible right now because all I can see is his face.

In front of me.

And in my memory.

There's no more drunken fuzz or darkness. No more blurry entity.

I'm reliving that party like it happened only yesterday.

And it's him.

He's the guy.

It's his face, his hand that he's holding out and expecting me to shake right now.

"Uh... hi." He smiles at me like he doesn't know who I am. Like we didn't dance at a party and make out in the hallway while we giggled and stumbled our way to an empty bedroom. He's looking at me like he didn't ignore my plea for him to stop. "It's nice to meet you."

That voice.

No. I can't hear that voice again.

"I'm not done with you yet."

The words scream through my brain, flashbacks hitting me on all sides as my world is destroyed all over again.

CHAPTER 37
ASHER

Lani is staring at Harvey like she's afraid to touch him. Her skin is pale, her brown eyes still and unmoving while Harvey stands there, holding out his hand for a shake.

He glances at me, silently asking what's wrong with my girl.

I dip my head, whispering against her ear, "You okay, boo? What's the matter?"

She flinches like she's coming out of a trance and starts blinking. "I'm... You know, I..." Covering her mouth with the back of her hand, she glances at me and her vision seems to clear completely. "I would shake hands, but I'm actually not feeling very well. I don't want to spread my germs."

She winces.

Harvey's still frowning at her like she's weird, and I'm standing there trying to figure out why she's lying.

Rising on her tiptoes, she leans into my ear and whispers, "Truth is, I think I just got my period, and this is the worst timing ever, but I've got a tidal wave situation going on and I have to bail, like right now."

I bulge my eyes at her, sympathy rushing through me. Being a woman seriously sucks sometimes. Resting my hand on her lower back, I step around her so Harvey can't see her face. She's no doubt fighting humiliation, and I don't want to make it worse for her.

"Do you need my jacket or something?" I glide my hand down her arm. "You could tie it around your waist."

"S-Sure." She nods. "Thanks."

I slip it off, securing it for her and giving her a gentle smile. "Do you want me to walk you back?"

"No." She shakes her head. "You hang out with... your cousin." Her voice squeaks, and now she looks like she's fighting tears.

"Hey, it's okay. I'll help you do the laundry when I come over later." I wink at her, and she bites her lips together, forcing a weak smile. Kissing her forehead, I gently nudge her away. "You go take care of yourself. I'll call you later, okay?"

She bobs her head, her lips trembling as she glances past my shoulder at Harvey, then dips her head and practically sprints out of the cafeteria.

"What the fuck was that about?" Harvey watches her go.

I let out an awkward laugh. "She's having a bad day."

"So, it wasn't something I did?" Harvey points at himself, looking mildly worried.

"No, man. Of course not." I slap his shoulder. "It's just... she needed to go change." I wince, wondering how much I should or shouldn't say.

Harvey's eyebrows rise in understanding. He's got a sister. He gets it.

"Right." Nodding, he lets out a soft laugh, then turns toward the food. "Let's go eat, man."

His voice trails off as we walk past a table of girls. They glance at us, and Harvey makes a point to wink and grin at the one on the end. She sends him a simpering smile before being nudged by her friend.

I roll my eyes and snicker. "You're such a Casanova."

"Wonder if any of them will be at the party tonight." He wiggles his eyebrows, poking out his tongue and looking damn gleeful at the idea of getting some later.

I have no doubt he will. The guy's a player—about as bad as Casey used to be. I wonder which woman is gonna make him fall one day. Surely one of them will. Women are powerful beings.

A smile works across my face as I think about Lani and the power she has over me. I never had any intentions of letting a woman see all of me so easily, but I've let her into my world, and it's the best fucking thing that's ever happened to me.

But I'm not sure I'll ever be able to explain it to a guy like Harvey, who's only after fun and flings. He's gonna have to experience true love for himself one day and see how it can take you out at the knees... and he'll go down happily because it's that fucking good.

CHAPTER 38
LEILANI

My knees nearly give out twice on my sprint back to Huxley Hall. I stumble on the path and nearly twist my ankle going up the wide steps.

Breaths are shaking me as my stomach trembles and spasm, trying to hold down sobs... or maybe it's bile.

The urge to throw up is overwhelming, and I fight it the entire way up to my floor.

This can't be happening. The man I love is related to the man I hate.

How can the universe be so fucking cruel?

Why? The word screams inside me—a raw, desperate cry.

I want to beat the ground and yell until my throat is hoarse.

This is so fucking unfair!

Panic claws at me, my heart thumping so hard, I feel

as though it might pop out of my mouth along with the entire contents of my stomach.

I run down the hallway, my boots echoing on the floor. Swiping my keycard, I push the door open and hear a surprised gasp.

"Oh shit." Casey scrambles for his boxers while Caroline wraps a sheet around her.

I see his dick, her boobs, and I can't even shut my eyes and apologize.

I just stand there in the doorway—mute and frozen.

"Lani?" Caroline frowns at me. "Are you okay?"

Sucking in a shaky breath, I manage to rasp, "I'm gonna be sick," before lunging toward the bathroom.

My legs wobble and I bang my hip on the edge of her desk, nearly tumbling to the floor. Casey catches me around the waist, helping me into the bathroom. I barely get the lid up in time before puke is spewing out of me. I drop to my knees, heaving into the toilet, then letting out a scream that sounds like a feral war cry.

Casey jolts away from me like I've lost my mind.

Maybe I have.

Or I'm in the process of losing it.

"What do I do?" I hear his shaky whisper. It sounds as if this is freaking him out more than Caroline's pregnancy announcement a few months back.

Another surge of vomit lurches out of me, and I spit into the toilet before leaning my forehead against my arm and starting to cry in earnest.

The faucet comes on and I hear shuffling and drips,

and then a cool washcloth is being pressed against my cheek.

"C'mere," Caroline murmurs, helping me sit up so she can wash the rest of my face. She wipes away my snot and tears while I whimper and tremble beneath her touch.

Once she's done, she holds my face, her tender gaze causing more tears to leak out of my eyes.

"What happened?"

I open my mouth, wondering if I can even find the words to explain this nightmare. Caroline takes a seat beside me, pulling Casey's T-shirt around her hips while he stands there shirtless, his arms crossed and a worried frown crinkling his expression.

Gazing across the room, I find a spot on the shower door and stare at it.

Caroline's patiently waiting for an explanation, lightly running her fingers through my hair until I can manage to mumble, "It's him."

"Who's him?" She perks up, obviously relieved that I've found my voice. Her blue gaze is so expectant, like if I tell her, she can help me. But she can't. No one can make this situation better.

No one.

I lick my lips, my jaw shaking when I whisper, "I just met Asher's cousin."

"Okay." Caroline nods.

Casey's bare feet shuffle on the bathroom floor. I watch them for a second, his broad soles taking up two whole bathroom tiles.

"Um... Lani, what's up with Asher's cousin?" Caroline prompts me.

I let out a shuddering breath. "He's the guy from the party. The one who—"

Caroline gasps, slapping a hand over her mouth while Casey gapes at me. "Harvey raped you?"

I nod, and then my stomach starts heaving again. Lurching to my knees, I choke into the toilet, my empty stomach hurting as my body jerks up a small mouthful of bile. I cry into the bowl, shuddering as Caroline's hand lightly rubs my back.

"I can't believe this," Casey mutters. "That little fucker! Asher's gonna kill him."

"No!" I jolt back, wiping my mouth with trembling fingers and staring up at Casey. "He can't know."

"What?" Casey balks at me. "He needs to know."

I shake my head. "This will kill him. Harvey's like a brother to him."

"Yeah, but he—"

"I have to break up with him." I can barely choke out the words. "It's over. It has to be over."

"No," Caroline whispers, sounding just as heart-broken as I feel. "Lani, you can't. You love him."

"You love each other," Casey clarifies with a pointed look.

"Which is why I have to end it." My voice starts to pitch and squeak again. "It won't work anymore." I slash the tears off my cheeks. "I can't make him choose between me and his own flesh and blood. It's over."

CHAPTER 39
ASHER

Lunch with Harvey was pretty good, although he kept getting distracted by girls walking past the table, and then when a brunette with blue eyes and rosebud lips took a seat beside me, he just outright ignored me. In the end, I left him to it. As much as I wanted to call Lani and check in, I had a class to get to, so I settled for a text.

She didn't respond.

It niggled for reasons I can't explain.

She had classes all afternoon, and she would have been busy concentrating, so I don't know what my problem is.

I just hope she's not suffering with bad period pain or anything. My mom used to get the worst periods. She'd sometimes be holed up in bed for a day with headaches and cramping.

Is Lani like that?

We've been dating long enough that she's probably had one period already and I didn't notice anything. Although, maybe some are good while others are heinous. I should ask. I want to know this stuff about her. I want to be the guy she can be herself around, even when she's having a shitty day.

Concentrating on my afternoon classes turns into a mission, and I'm more than relieved when they're over.

As much as I want to skip hockey practice and get straight to Lani, Coach will kick my ass if I'm not there. Thankfully, practices are light drills just to keep our fitness and skills up. We run through it efficiently and even have a few laughs when we end with a friendly game. I manage to get two past Baxter, who is silently fuming as we head to the showers. He never lets it show, but the clench of his jaw as he rips off his sweaty gear tells us enough.

"Don't sweat it, Bax." Casey slaps him on the shoulder with a grin. "Soon this place will be in your rearview mirror, and Mr. Second String over there will be hugging the post." His smile is met with a marked frown as Baxter glances at Donovan, the guy he's been helping to train up throughout the year, then shuffles off to the showers.

"Dude." I shake my head at Casey.

"What? I was trying to make him feel better." He flicks his arms wide, and I just shake my head again, snickering at his pathetic attempt. Ethan and Liam back me up, razzing him about how clueless he is.

Like any guy here wants to be reminded that they're

leaving the team and will soon be replaced by someone younger and potentially faster than they are.

I won't admit this to Baxter in a hundred million years, but Donovan is already showing huge potential and will no doubt be a superior goalie to our steadfast Baxter Brown. We're gonna miss the guy, but Donovan will make the loss easier to get over.

I rush through my shower and get dressed as fast as possible. I'm more than ready to go see my girl.

In case she's sleeping, I text first, asking if I can come over.

I hear back before I reach my truck, but rather than a text, she's calling me.

It's not hard to answer with a smile. "Aloha, beautiful."

"It's over." Her voice sounds rusty and raw, and I don't know what she's talking about.

With a confused frown, I jump into my truck and dump my bag on the passenger seat. "What's over?"

"You and me."

My insides go cold. "What?"

"I can't do this anymore." She sniffs. "It's not working." Her voice is going tight and rigid, her words clipping off at the ends.

What the hell is she doing?

Is someone holding a gun to her head or something?

She doesn't want to say this shit to me, so I call her on it.

"Wait, wait, wait. You don't want to do this."

"I do."

"I thought we were vibing. What's happened? What's changed?"

She goes quiet and I raise my eyebrows, a mix of emotions I can't even identify crowding my chest. Gripping the wheel, I run my tongue over my bottom teeth, willing this panicky feeling away.

"I just…" She sighs, then sucks in a shaky breath. "I can't be in a relationship right now. You haven't done anything wrong. I'm just not in a good place, okay?"

"Lani, come on, you—"

"I'm sorry." She hangs up on me before I can say anything else.

Holding the phone away from me, I scowl at the screen and mutter, "What the fuck?" as I call her back.

She doesn't answer.

So I try again.

It goes straight to voicemail.

I slap my phone down on the dashboard and shout, "What the actual fuck!"

Liam and Casey just happen to be walking past my truck, and they both jerk to a stop, blinking at me like I've lost my mind.

Well, I fucking have!

Slamming the wheel, I yell out a few more profanities until my door pops open and Liam calmly asks, "What's up?"

"Lani just dumped me!" I spit, turning to my friends like they can somehow help me understand this shit.

But how can they possibly?

No one can because it's fucking insane!

Yesterday, we were telling each other "I love you," and today she can't be in a relationship because she's not in a good place? I know she can be unpredictable at times, but this is like fucking whiplash. She does *not* want to break up with me. I know she doesn't, so why the fuck is she?

What did I do?

What changed?

"Did I pressure her?" I whisper. "Did I move too fast?"

I can feel my insides crumbling at Liam's hopeless frown, but then I just happen to look Casey's way, and his guilty face makes me snap.

Jumping out of my car, I step up to him, poking my finger into his chest as I try to read his mind. "You know why, don't you?"

He shakes his head but then looks to the ground.

"Casey," I growl. I was going for calm, but that is so far beyond me right now. "What's going on?" I bark the question at him.

He shakes his head again and I let out a roar, fisting his shirt and swinging him around. Smashing him against my truck, I yell in his face, "Tell me!"

"Dude, calm down." He shoves me away, but I rebound right back to him, fisting his shirt again.

"Don't tell me to calm down! Now start talking, you fuckhead!"

"Whoa, whoa, whoa." Liam tries to get between us, but I stick out my elbow, catching him in the throat. He coughs and splutters, backing away from me while another arm wraps tightly around my shoulders and hauls me back.

"What the fuck is your problem!" Ethan shouts in my ear. "Calm down! Right now!"

Liam rubs his throat with a sad frown while I look at Casey with... I don't even know how the hell I look, but my struggle against Ethan's hold on me loses some of its power, and there must be a desperate stench wafting off me, because all of a sudden, Casey shouts something that ends my world.

"It was Harvey!"

"What?" I snap.

Casey closes his eyes, looking sick as he scrubs a hand down his face and softly explains, "Harvey's the guy from the party. The one who raped her. That's why she's breaking up with you."

Even with his gentle tone, his words are bullets, hitting my flesh with a shocking pain that burns me.

"Harvey did fuckin' *what*?" Ethan barks.

I slump against him, ignoring his question as his hold on me immediately loosens. He lets me lean against him for a second while I try to wrap my brain around this bullshit.

"You guys all right? What's going on?" someone calls from the other side of the parking lot.

"None of your fucking business!" Ethan shouts, his tone a friendly warning.

"Whatever, dude!"

An engine starts and then another. Cars drive away, but we stay there—a circle of four shell-shocked guys trying to absorb this.

It can't be true. I shake my head. *It can't be.*

Casey sags against my truck with a heavy sigh. "She didn't want me to tell you, but when she saw him today, she knew right away. It's him."

"No." I keep shaking my head. "She said she didn't know who it was and... and Harvey wouldn't do something like that."

"She was raped?" Liam whispers, his expression wounded. "When?"

"Back in February." Casey winces. "It was at a party at the football frat..." He shakes his head.

My ears start buzzing as I picture the scene, Harvey's face appearing in my mind as he spun Lani around and roughly entered her.

Snapping my eyes closed, I choke out the words, "No, it can't be him."

"She was puking in the bathroom, man. She was crying and screaming and having a breakdown." His voice kind of shakes, like witnessing that was harrowing for him.

As much as that picture burns me, my stupid brain still can't compute. "You're lying. She had her period. She..." Agony rips through me like a sword blade. "He didn't even recognize her. They hadn't met before."

"That might be genuine," Liam murmurs, stepping into my line of sight. "Doesn't he sleep around a lot?"

I close my eyes, fisting the back of my hair and fighting to contain the roar rattling inside me.

"This can't be true. It can't be—"

"I'm sorry, man, but I think it is." Casey's voice is a low rumble.

"Oh shit," Ethan murmurs, obviously still struggling to absorb all of this. "I don't even know what to say. I mean, it's—"

"Shut up," I rasp, my fingers curling into fists as I stumble to my truck and smash the hood. "Fuck!" I smash it again, one hit for each profane word. "Fuck! Fuck! Fuuuuccck!"

The guys stand around me, letting me lose my shit, quietly supporting me with their hands in their pockets and their heads hung low.

Their expressions tell me that the foreboding in my gut is probably right.

Lani's telling the truth, and my cousin, the guy I've looked up to and loved for most of my life, is a fucking asshole.

"Shit." I seethe the word, shoving Casey away from my door and jumping behind the wheel.

"Where are you going?" He tries to stop me, but I flick the lock before he can open the door.

Starting up the engine with a high rev, I screech away from them. They're forced to step back so I don't run them over. I'm being an asshole, but my brain's on fire, and I can't tell them where I'm going. Because I'm not exactly sure yet.

Do I pound on Lani's door, asking for every detail?

Or do I track down my cousin and beat the shit out of him?

CHAPTER 40
LEILANI

The only sound in this room is my gentle sniffing as I try to deny myself even more tears. I can't cry again. My eyes are so swollen and sore. I've been dabbing them with tissues, but they're puffy and so tender that even the gentlest pressure hurts.

I sobbed on that bathroom floor.

Threw up more bile until my stomach and throat were aching.

Casey left at some point. I don't know where he went, and all I can hope is that it wasn't anywhere near Asher. I told him not to say anything, but will he ignore me and just do it anyway? Surely he's not that cruel. This will kill Asher. He can never know.

Caroline's stuck with me most of the afternoon. She helped me off the floor and made me take a shower. I cried under the hot spray, plunking down on my bare ass and weeping on the tiles. She ended up having to dry and dress me. Honestly, I just couldn't function. I couldn't make my brain work properly...

Until Asher's text came through.

Hey, boo. Is it all right if I come over?

I couldn't let that happen.

So I did it. I broke up with him the way I knew I had to. And it's the most painful thing I've ever done. Telling the guy you love that you don't want to be with him anymore is a torture I wouldn't wish on anybody.

Because it was lie.

I do want him.

I want him so badly my soul is flailing in my chest. My body aches and burns... and there's nothing I can do to ease this pain.

I'd give anything to have him walk through my door right now and hold me, kiss my tears away, and spoon me through the night.

But that's a romantic fantasy that will never happen.

Because his cousin raped me.

And I can't ever be in the same room with that man again. Which means I can never be with Asher because he and Harvey are blood. They're practically brothers.

Family first.

That's the way it's got to be.

A shudder runs through me again as I battle another

sob. It quakes my belly, and I whimper into my balled-up tissue.

This pain is immense. It's a soul ache that burns my entire body. I don't know how to handle it. And I hate myself for falling apart like this, but—

There's a knock on my door.

I flinch and turn to gape at the wood, because it's not a polite knock, it's a hard pound that's turning into a series of urgent whacks. The door handle jiggles, and I lean closer to the wall, starting to freak out that some-one's trying to break into my room.

What the hell has become of me?

The old Lani would have told this person to fuck off and stop being so rude.

But this Lani—this wretched, weeping wreck—can't even find her voice.

"Lani, are you there? Open up, it's me."

Casey?

With a confused frown, I jump off the bed. I've never heard him sound so worried before.

I pull the door back and take in his expression. Yep, he's definitely worried.

"Hey, are you okay?" His eyes scan my face with a panicky look. "Is Asher here?"

"No," I rasp. Ugh, even hearing his name hurts.

I grip the edge of the door as Casey visibly relaxes. "Okay." He breathes the word with relief.

"Caroline's not here either."

"That's all right. I was here to see you anyway."

My head jolts back. "Why? What's going on?" My voice is starting to shake... along with the rest of me. "Why are you acting weird?"

His relief is fleeting, his expression scrunching into a wince as he softly whispers, "Please don't hate me."

My insides revolt, clenching tight as I close my eyes. "You told him."

"I had to." Casey nudges his way into the room. I step aside to let him pass, and he glances around before turning back to me with a pained frown. "He was freaking out that you dumped him like that. He needed an explanation."

"But..." I suck in a breath that then comes out as a pitiful whimper. "He's gonna be devastated."

"Yeah, he really didn't take it well." Casey runs a hand through his hair, making it stick up at funny angles as he cringes and looks over his shoulder. "He took off like a crazed man, and I was worried he came here to... I don't know..." Spinning back, he takes me in with a sad smile, his voice dropping to a soft lilt. "I just wanted to make sure you were okay."

That's so sweet.

I try to smile my thanks, but tears blur my vision, and those sobs I've been fighting for the last hour start to jerk my body again. Plunking onto the edge of my bed, I snatch a few tissues out of the box and bunch them into my eyes, catching the tears before they can fall.

Casey lets out a soft sigh and takes a seat beside me. "Where's Caroline?"

"She went to get emergency ice cream," I blubber.

He lets out a soft laugh, his voice warm with affection. "Of course she did."

I sniff, my belly trembling when I glance up at him. "Ice cream's not going to fix this, Case."

"I know." His face buckles with empathy and he puts his arm around me, pulling me to his side so I can rest my head on his shoulder and cry for real.

I stop fighting and let the sobs punch out of me— these low, aching noises that I'd usually be humiliated by, but I'm in too much pain to care.

Casey squeezes my shoulder, resting his cheek against the top of my head and not saying anything.

At some point Caroline returns, the door popping open, then softly shutting behind her. She doesn't say anything, just shares a worried frown with her boyfriend before placing the ice cream on the floor and shuffling around to my left side.

The bed dips just a little as she takes a seat and curves her arm around my waist. Kissing my shoulder, she then rests her head against it, and we all sit there in debilitating silence.

Because there's nothing we can say to make this better.

Nothing is going to fix this shitty situation.

CHAPTER 41
ASHER

It didn't take long to find the party Harvey was attending. It was the only one happening on Greek Row. Even so, by the time I got there, the rage and anger building inside me was like a freaking hurricane, and when I spotted him, I couldn't contain myself.

He was leaning over a girl, her back pressed against the wall while he flirted with her, his hand resting on the wall while his fingers curled around the ends of her hair. She was looking smitten and proud that a guy like Harvey would notice her.

And all I could see was Lani on her knees, begging him to get the hell out of her while he held her hips and pounded on her.

I'm not sure if I roared, but the people around me seemed to gasp and flinch away from me as I charged at Harvey and fisted the back of his jacket.

Now he's pressed against the wall where that girl used to be standing and frowning at me like I've lost my mind.

"Asher? What the fuck, man?"

His shocked expression somehow stops my brain from short-circuiting, and I suddenly come out of my raging fog to notice more movement around me. Whispers scurry around us as phones are being held in my direction, pictures being snapped and sent. Fuck, they're probably taking videos, thinking this will be a fight worth posting on social media.

Dammit!

Calm the fuck down, Bensen!

"We have to talk," I growl, tipping my head to the side and stalking toward the front door.

Harvey mutters something behind my back, and I turn to make sure he's following me. He's giving the girl he was flirting with an apologetic smile, gently touching her face. "I'll just be a few minutes, okay?"

She nods, her expression adoring before she flicks me an acidic look.

I spin for the door, my insides churning. It's hard to imagine Harvey turning from Mr. Sweet into a guy who rapes a woman.

But Lani said he did.

Fuck. I want to believe her, but Harvey's not like that.

Sure, he's a flirt and sleeps around as much as Casey used to, but that's because he's popular. He appreciates women, enjoys them. Does he really rape them?

Shoving my hands in my jacket pockets, I stop in the

front yard, moving all the way to the tree so we're hidden by the black shadows its branches are casting over the lawn.

Laughter and music from the party float out of the house, masking our conversation.

"Dude." Harvey shakes his head at me. "What is going on with you?"

"Did you rape my girlfriend?" I don't have time for bullshit, so I get straight to the point.

There's a beat of thick, painful silence before Harvey chokes out his disbelief. "What?"

"Lani. Did you ra—"

"No!" He cuts me off before I can say it again. "I only just met her today. Did she say that I tracked her down later or something? What the fuck? I was with you all of lunch, then this afternoon, I hung out with that girl I met, and then I came here." He points behind him. "Did she say I did something to her?"

I clench my jaw, my throat so thick, it's hard to swallow. "It wasn't today. It was at a party... a few months back."

He shakes his head. "I can't believe this. I swear to you, man. I only met her today for the first time. I did not touch her or rape her or... shit, man! You honestly think I'd rape someone?" His voice pitches, and then he lets out this sigh like I've hurt his feelings. No, not hurt them, crushed them to dust. "You're my brother. How could you think that about me?"

Working my jaw to the side, I can't even look at him as

I squeeze the back of my neck and try to figure out what I'm supposed to do.

Lani said it was him.

But maybe she was wrong?

Maybe the guy who raped her is just really similar to Harvey.

The thought actually gives me a small spark of hope.

Harvey's a good-looking college athlete with brown hair that's cut short at the sides and styled into purposely messy spikes on top. There's a bunch of guys out there who look just like him. Lani did say she was drunk and things were fuzzy. Maybe the guy who did that to her had a Harvey essence.

The thought sits ugly in my chest.

I don't want to doubt her. I want to respect what she feels and believes.

But what if she's wrong?

I could fuck up everything if I go accusing my cousin of something he didn't do.

Squeezing my eyes shut, I mumble a few curses as I rub my temples.

"So, she was raped, huh?" Harvey's voice is soft with sympathy. "Man, that's... so wrong." The way his voice is trembling with emotion has a wave of shame washing through me. "I'm sorry that happened to her."

I open my eyes and stare at his face. The dim light makes it hard to see the detail, but I can see his eyes glittering in the darkness, and he sounds so genuine. So honest.

"I'm guessing she doesn't know who the guy is? If she thought it was me."

"Yeah," I mumble. "You must look like him or something."

"Well, if you ever find him, let me know. I'll come and help you pound his flesh." He lightly squeezes my shoulder.

I nod, silently thanking him for the support.

"You know I can bail on this party if you need me to—"

"No, it's okay," I croak. "I'm gonna go see Lani."

"Okay." He nods. "If there's anything I can do to help, I mean... I'm guessing she never wants to see me if I remind her so much of this guy, but... Please, if there's anything I can do."

"Thanks, man." My mind is reeling as I say goodbye to my cousin and shuffle back to my truck.

I don't know what to think.

All I know is that Harvey was telling me the truth just then. I'm no lie detector, but everything about his tone and posture seemed honest. He's my cousin, and I want to believe him.

But I want to believe Lani too.

She wouldn't make up something like this. In her mind, Harvey is the guy who raped her.

I guess I just need to help her see that it wasn't him.

But how do I do that without hurting her?

CHAPTER 42
LEILANI

Caroline and Casey stayed with me, even after I told them they should go out and do something fun. They refused, so we sat on the floor nibbling on melted ice cream. I ate a few spoonfuls but quickly gave up. My stomach feels like it's been put through a blender.

I sniff again, curling my legs against my chest as we watch a movie on Caroline's laptop. She chose the most unromantic thing she could find, but I'm still struggling to watch it. My brain is mush.

And as much as I hate this about myself, all I want is Asher.

Which is probably why, when there's a gentle knock at the door and I hear his soft voice say, "It's Asher. Can I come in?" my heart almost leaps out of my chest.

I sit up with a gasp, then hold my breath, my chest burning as Casey gets off the bed and opens the door for us.

"Hey, man."

"Is she here? Is she okay?" The worry in his voice makes my heart hurt.

I still can't believe this is happening.

I can't believe how unfair this all is.

"Yeah, bro. She's here."

Casey opens the door a little wider, and I spot Asher's face. He's pale and cut up, barely able to look me in the eye as he walks into the room and finds a perch against my desk. Gripping the edge of the wood, he drinks me in, and his voice sends tendrils firing through me when he asks, "You holding up okay?"

I nod, my lips trembling as I try to smile at him.

His expression is wounded and raw. And I have to ask, "Are you?"

"No." He shakes his head, dipping his chin with a heavy sigh. "My girlfriend was raped, and I want to kill the guy who did that to her."

I let out a quivering breath.

"But part of my problem is... is..." He works his jaw to the side.

"It's your cousin," Caroline finishes for him.

"That's the thing." Asher looks up with a frown. "I just went and confronted him, and he swears he never did that to you... or anyone."

My chest constricts, ice flooding my veins.

Caroline glances at me, then back to Asher. "Well, he must be lying."

"He looked so genuine," Asher croaks. "He wasn't

defensive. He was horrified that I would accuse him of something like that... and I'm torn in half over this, because I want to believe you." His eyes land on me. "I love you and want to back up whatever you say. But... what if it wasn't him?"

I curl in on myself, hugging my knees and blinking.

It would fix it, right?

If it wasn't Harvey, I could be with Asher and... and...

It's not that simple, though, is it?

Even if it wasn't him, Harvey is just like the guy who did that to me. Which means I can never be around him. I'm not strong enough to handle it, which means I can't be with his cousin. A cousin who adores him and loves him... and is completely wrecked over the idea that he'd do something like that to me.

I shake my head, softly trying to make him feel better. "Maybe it wasn't him."

"No." Caroline shoots off the bed, frowning at Asher, then spinning to face me. "Don't second-guess yourself. You had a gut feeling today, and it was right. Your physical reaction to seeing him was overpowering."

"But maybe he just reminded me of the guy. And I can't go accusing an innocent person." I shake my head, and Asher's shoulders dip.

A relieved sigh punches out of him, a trembling smile cresting his lips as he pushes off the desk and walks toward me.

I hold up my hand to stop him. "It still doesn't change anything between us."

"What?" His face goes ashen, the broken look in his eyes enough to slaughter me.

But I have to hold strong. My reasoning is sound.

"We can't be together anymore. Every time I look at Harvey, whether it was him or not, I'm going to be reminded of what happened."

"So don't see him!" Asher flicks his hands wide, but we both know as soon as the words are out there that his suggestion is unrealistic.

If we love each other, we'll want to carve out a life together, and we can't just exclude an important chunk of his.

"I'm not going to do that to you," I whisper. "I won't be the girlfriend who alienates you from your family. They're too important to you."

"*You're* important to me." He drops to his knees beside my bed, reaching for my hands and begging. "Please, don't do this. We can work through it. I want to be with you. I love you."

I sniff, licking my lips and trying not to fall apart in front of him. "I love you, too, but it's too hard. I'm sorry. I don't want to hurt you, but ending things now will be less painful in the long run."

He's shaking his head, but he knows I'm right.

I can see it in his eyes.

Caroline and Casey have gone painfully quiet, though I can sense them in the room still, watching us with heartbroken frowns. They get it. Everyone in this room is hurting.

Because they all know I'm right.

Leaning forward, I take Asher's face and lightly kiss him. His lips are soft and beautiful, pressing against mine as both comfort and loss swirl through me.

I pull away while I still have the willpower to hold strong on my resolve.

Rubbing my thumb along his cheek, I try to smile and silently let him know how much he means to me.

"Thank you," I whisper. "Thank you for everything you gave me. I'm really gonna miss you."

CHAPTER 43
ASHER

I don't know how I left Lani's room on Monday night. I don't actually remember it. I think Casey took me away, held my arm as we shuffled out of Huxley Hall together.

My brain has been in a fog ever since.

The week somehow passed me by, and now I'm standing in Uncle Hayes and Aunt Carla's house wearing a suit and tie while I mingle with the rest of my extended family. My parents have flown in from New York, and my twin brothers are loitering near the fireplace, talking in hushed tones and looking bored out of their minds. I should go talk to them. We haven't spoken in months, but I can't make myself move away from the window.

I don't want to be here.

I miss Lani.

She's gone cold turkey and cut me off. I guess it's easier for both of us that way.

Doesn't make it less painful necessarily, but apparently time's a healer, whatever the fuck that means.

The guys at Hockey House have been giving me a wide berth, probably because every time they talk to me, I growl at them like an angry bear. Shit, I must be so fucking painful to live with right now. They're probably all relieved I had to leave the house for the day to come down to this... what are we even celebrating?

Ugh, like I give a shit.

Sipping my whiskey, I stand on the edge of the room, listening to my mother go on about how amazing my brothers are. "They're really taking the business in a wonderful direction. Austin's given them two new projects to work on, and they're both booming." Her laughter is loud, proud, and fucking irritating.

I glance across the room, glaring at the perfect twins with their smug smiles and bored expressions. They've spent their life soaking in Mom's praise to the point where they don't even appreciate it anymore.

"And did you hear Austin's lined up an internship for Asher this summer?" She spins to beam at me. "Like the twins, he'll need to earn his stripes. He's got some big learning to do before he can work for Bensens & Co."

"I think it's so great you encourage that, Annabeth." Aunt Carla gives her a tight smile. She's waxing eloquent, but I know for a fact that Carla thinks my mom's a plastic Barbie doll. And she hates the way my parents continue to pressure me and control my life.

She's always let her children express themselves and pursue their dreams.

No wonder I like her better.

No wonder I wanted to be a Carmichael and not a Bensen.

No wonder Lani didn't want to come between us all.

Fuck! I hate this.

I get why she made that decision. If Harvey looks like the guy who hurt her, then I shouldn't expect her to be around him. It's too complicated, right?

Logically, I need to let her go and move on.

But I can't.

She's all-consuming, and I miss her with an ache so deep, it's killing me.

Gulping back my glass, I stalk out of the room, nearly running into Harvey and Halsey.

"Hey, man. You good?" He looks at me with a friendly smile, and all I can do is scowl at him. "Whoa." He laughs. "What's your problem?"

Stalking away from him, I feel my shoulders tensing as he follows me.

"I know you hate these things, dude. But make the most of it."

I walk around the bar and find the bottle of whiskey, refilling my glass while he leans there trying to sell this to me.

"You get free booze, plus the privilege of hanging with Zee and me for the day. That's not a bad payoff to spend a little time with your olds, right?"

Halsey throws me a weak smile, darting her eyes at Harvey before looking over her shoulder. I'm waiting for her to lean in with a conspiratorial whisper and say some shit like "Let's brainstorm. How are we going to torture the twins today?"

But she doesn't.

Maybe my foul mood is throwing her off. She can obviously read me better than my oblivious cousin can.

"Dude, seriously. You're killing my buzz here. Would you smile already?"

I slam the bottle down with a huff and glare at him. "I just broke up with my girlfriend, and you want me to smile and laugh like nothing's wrong?"

"Oh yeah, that's right." He winces. "Forgot about that."

I narrow my eyes at him, a growl rumbling in my throat. "Considering you're the reason it ended, I'm surprised you could dismiss it so easily."

He scoffs and touches his chest. "Dude, we've been through this. *I* am not the reason this ended. It's not my fault I look like him," he finishes with a grumble, sipping his vodka and shooting his sister a sour frown. "I told you this guy's fucking delusional." He tips his head at me, then gives me a sharp glare. "You can't go blaming me for this shit. Now get over yourself and let's turn this snore-fest into something interesting. Or you can fuck off and go sulk in the pool house."

Clenching my jaw, I feel my nostrils flaring as I snatch

my drink and mutter, "Fine," before stalking out the side door and heading for the pool.

Unsympathetic asshole!

I wrench the pool house door open and storm inside, pacing the room and downing my drink in one big gulp. It burns my throat, and I welcome it. Maybe I should get totally shit-faced. That can dull the pain and make this afternoon bearable, right?

I'll need at least three more tumblers to really have any effect. Two small glasses is hardly enough.

I walk over to the cabinets, pulling them open and seeing if there are any leftover bottles around when the door pops open.

"I'm not in the mood, Harv!" I shout over my shoulder.

"It's Zee." Halsey's soft voice makes me pause.

I let out a heavy sigh and turn to face her.

Her smile is sad, reflecting the ache in my chest, so I let her stay, because I think she gets it. She must have had some girl dump her in high school or something. I know she was dating some Vanessa chick for over half a year.

Shit, I was with Lani for less than two and my heart is shattered.

"So, Harvey told us about your girlfriend and the rape thing. Said he reminds her of the guy, and it's put this huge strain on your relationship."

I grunt, spinning my glass between my fingers and wishing there was still some liquor in there. "It ended it."

"That sucks."

"Yep." I pop the P and look away from her.

"Do you love her?"

My shoulders slump, that familiar sadness swamping me yet again. "Yeah." My voice sounds rough and raw, doing nothing to hide the pain riding through me. "But it's all too complicated for her."

"Yeah, I get it. She can't be around Harvey, even if he's not lying. It's too traumatic for her."

I nod.

"And if he was lying, well..." Her voice trails off, and I glance up, frowning at her.

She clears her throat, her movements stilted as she edges farther into the room. Glancing over her shoulder, she spins back to face me with a look I've never seen before. "We're not having this conversation."

"Huh?"

Her eyes take on a worrying sheen and she blinks, looking down at her hands while she fidgets with the ring on her pointer finger. "One of my friends in high school accused Harvey of raping her. It never stuck, because according to what everyone else said, she was making out with him, and no one believed that the sex wasn't consensual. But she swore that when he started taking things too far and she tried to stop him that he wouldn't listen. She told me he was rough and just wouldn't let up. She felt violated and..." Halsey blinks, wrapping her fingers around her arm and wincing. "I, of course, sided with my brother because he's fun and sweet, and he would never do something like that, right? He was so cut up that she would accuse him that way. You should have seen him." She glances up at me, her expression buckling even more. "But that isn't the only time I've heard stories like this. And now... I can't help wondering if maybe he did it. Because I'm pretty sure if you asked around at Lennox..." Her voice wobbles while my stomach writhes. "You might find some other girls who..." She shakes her head, her body snapping to attention when the pool room door opens.

She bulges her eyes at me before quickly turning to spot her father.

"Oh, hey." I can tell she's putting on a smile. Her voice is overly bright and breezy.

"Hey, cutie." Uncle Hayes winks at his daughter. "Mind if I have a quick chat with Asher?"

"Sure." She glances over her shoulder, her face folding with concern before she forces a smile and walks out of the room.

I watch her go, my heart pounding so hard, I nearly miss the fact that my uncle is talking.

"...find it hard, and I completely understand. Parents can be difficult."

I blink and try to catch up to what he's saying.

"But family is important, son. Even when we don't always like each other, we have to be loyal and true. We fight for each other, no matter what."

My head bobs automatically because I know that's what it's supposed to do.

And it's only then that I notice the hard gleam in my

uncle's eyes. I've never seen him like this before, and my gut twists into a painful knot as he stops mere feet from me and looks me right in the eye. No, not looks—he's fucking glaring at me.

"How dare you accuse my son of raping your girlfriend."

"I... I didn't." I shake my head. "I simply asked him if he did."

"Do you not see how abhorrent that is? That you would even think for a second that Harvey was capable of such filth!" He lets out a disgusted scoff. "I'm ashamed of you."

I blink, struggling to reconcile this man with the fun-loving uncle I grew up adoring. Struggling to wrap my head around this shit when Halsey just told me her secret.

"You know..." Uncle Hayes bites his bottom lip, shaking his head with a disappointed frown. "I've always thought of you like my son. I've spoken up for you, pulled strings for you. I've provided *free* housing for you. I even got that apartment for your little friends—Rachel and..." He flicks his fingers in the air.

"Mikayla," I croak.

"That's it." He clicks his fingers, then slides his hands into his pockets, all smooth businessman, like ruffling even one of his feathers would be an impossible task.

"So, when you accuse my actual flesh and blood of something so disgusting, it actually hurts me, Asher." He bores into me with an admonishing stare that's hard to counter. "You hurt me."

I end up dipping my chin, hating myself for it, wishing I didn't feel like a ten-year-old kid being reprimanded. His disappointment is like a tsunami wave trying to take me out.

"How am I supposed to stand up for you when you'd willingly betray the family this way?"

"I haven't betrayed anyone," I mutter.

"You bought into some woman's lie without hesitation. You came at Harvey with nothing but your anger and your bullshit."

My eyebrows rise as I let out a surprised breath. "I've gotta stand up for my girl. You get that, don't you?"

His eyes narrow as I find the strength to look right into them.

"She was raped. Violated by some asshole. And she thought it was him. I couldn't just turn my back on that, ignore how she was feeling. I had to make sure."

"Hmmm." He nods, his tongue skimming over his top teeth. "I'd be very careful if I were you."

His soft warning gets my back up, an eerie chill running down my spine.

"You have a lot to lose if you don't play your cards right here. As I already mentioned, we provide... *so much* for you." His voice grows soft and steely. "We don't have to do that, you know? We're under no obligation to take care of you. You're not our son."

My lips part, his words wrapping around me like poisonous barbs.

"And all of those generous, kind-hearted gestures could so easily be taken away. In an instant." He snaps his fingers. "You know what I mean?"

And that's when it hits me.

Like a fucking sledgehammer to the side of my head. I get it.

He's not calmly throwing out these threats because of some miscommunication. He's warning me off because he knows Lani might be right.

Well, fuck me.

The truth is like a punch to the gut.

It's impossible to respond as Uncle Hayes points at me. "All I'm saying is that you need to put your family first. We've looked after you, and now you return the favor. Don't go spreading shitty rumors about Harvey. You stay loyal to him, no matter what. You feel me?"

My only response is a soft breath, which my uncle must take as consent, because a broad smile crosses his face.

"Excellent. I'm glad we understand each other." Holding out his arm like he wants to hug me or something, he tips his head toward the door. "Come on, buddy. Let's go eat."

When I don't move, he starts walking for the door.

And I can't follow him.

I'm too numb to move.

I can't fucking believe this.

I can't fucking believe—

A breath catches in my throat.

Lani. I have to get to Lani.

"You coming?" Uncle Hayes turns to check on me, his friendly smile faltering when I slam my glass down on the bench.

"I'm not hungry," I seethe.

His eyes flash. "Don't make a mistake now, son."

"I'm not your son. Remember?" I grit the words out, relieved that I didn't have time to find another drink. I'm still sober enough to fully grasp this shitty conversation. I'm still sober enough to drive.

Hurrying past my uncle, I head straight for my truck and Nolan U. I don't bother saying goodbye to any of my relatives. I can't stand in a room with those fucking people playing pretend. Not after what I just heard in the pool house!

"Fuck," I whisper under my breath, cranking the engine and tearing away from their lush mansion as fast as I can.

I've got to see my girl.

I've gotta make this right.

CHAPTER 44
LEILANI

It's stating the obvious to say that I'm miserable.

Everyone can see it, and no one seems to be doing anything to change that fact. Even my therapist just had to sit there while I numbly stared at the wall for an hour. She was really good about my inability to talk. I mean, I gave her the very brief rundown, firing out my explanation as fast as I could, and then my energy was zapped.

All I could do was sit.

And she sat with me in silence... and it was honestly all I could manage.

Lack of sleep isn't helping.

Nights are long and painful as I toss and turn, questioning myself over if I made the right decision and driving myself crazy over my reaction to Harvey. Why did I think he was the one? Why did I have such a physical recoil when I met him? He sent me into a spiral, and he might not even be the one who raped me.

I still can't make my brain 100 percent believe he didn't.

But then the thought of Asher's cousin raping me makes me want to curl into a ball. I've lost the man I love either way, but I really don't want that for him. He'd be so cut up if he knew someone he loves had done something so abhorrent.

Asher.

My nose starts to tingle, my eyes burning as I stare at my laptop and try not to think about him.

I miss him so much.

Not seeing him is the main reason for my misery. I just don't want to admit it to anyone, because I never wanted to be that girl who needed a guy. I want to be independent and strong on my own, but...

He's left a gaping hole in my life.

I mean, I can survive without the guy, so maybe I don't *need* him. Maybe I just want him because surviving isn't the same as living.

We weren't together for that long, but even in that short time, I fell hard. Because he gets me. He's sweet and caring, and he put a flower on my breakfast tray. The way his face lights up when we discover yet another thing we have in common. The way I can nerd out with him over Harry Potter and trivia... and classical music.

It's like we were destined for each other, which is a romantic notion that I can't buy into, because if we were meant to be, then this thing with Harvey wouldn't be happening. I have to take it as a sign and just accept the fact that Asher will never be mine.

But that thought is a killer. My chest aches, my stomach writhes, my brain burns for him.

I miss him.

I want him back.

But it's too complicated. Too difficult. Too—

My thoughts cut off, my body going still when I glance up and spot him walking through the library toward me.

How did he know where I was?

Why is he here?

Why... does he look so cut up?

My heart cracks wide open when he stops by my table, his expression wretched as he drinks me in and looks on the verge of tears.

I sit forward, worry coursing through me. Pushing my laptop aside, I give him my full attention. "Are you okay?" I manage to whisper, my resolve to not see or talk to him again completely disintegrating.

I thought going cold turkey would make it easier, but screw that. He needs me. I can sense it.

The chair beside me scrapes against the wooden floor as he pulls it out and plunks into it.

"Asher?" I want to touch his hand, curl my fingers around his arm... something! But I'm scared that any physical connection will be my undoing.

That was the first thing I succumbed to—his sexy arms and lips and... that one kiss after the quiz night was something I couldn't control. And let's not even think about the elevator sex.

Curling my fingers, I take it a step further and sit on my hands.

He rests his elbow on the table and stares at me. He's wrecked, shaky breaths punching out of him. His eyes are glistening like he's about to start crying.

I've never seen him like this before.

"What is it?" My voice is a gentle coo, because I will do anything to find out what the hell is bothering him so much.

He shakes his head, swallows, then lets out a shuddering sigh.

"Asher, come on. You can't just walk in here and not say anything. It's freaking me out."

What happened to him? Was it one specific thing, or has he been like this all week?

Is his torment still over the breakup? Is he here to try and win me back?

Has he been hurting as deeply as I have?

Shit. Am I strong enough to withstand it if he starts begging?

He opens his mouth, his lips trembling before he manages to choke out, "Please forgive me."

"What?" My voice is barely above a whisper as confusion shimmers through me. "What do you mean?"

He swallows. "I made you doubt yourself." His breath hitches. "I didn't want to believe the truth, so I bought into his fucking lies, and I made you think you were wrong. And I'm so sorry."

It takes me a second to catch up, but when he finally looks me in the eye with nothing but pure agony, I get it.

"It was Harvey."

Asher clenches his jaw and nods.

"How do you know?"

His chin bunches, and then he lets out a breath and spills it. Every detail of his horrible family function, from the moment Harvey tried to get him drunk to Halsey's secret in the pool house to his uncle's ugly threats.

He's slashing tears off his cheeks by the time he's done, and my heart is hurting in new ways I've never experienced before.

I bulge my eyes, trying to process all of this and think of the right thing to say.

It's impossible. There is no right thing to say because... holy shit!

Glancing around, I struggle to breathe evenly, grateful that we're in a quiet pocket of the library. No one else is around, and that realization helps me find my voice.

"Do you think your uncle *knows* what Harvey's like... or does he just suspect it?"

"I don't know." Asher shrugs and sniffs. Swiping his finger under his nose, his eyes spark with a dark look of anger... and hurt.

This is killing him.

His nostrils flare as he bunches his fists. "I want to fucking kill Harvey. How could he lie so easily? He looked so innocent, but that ass-fuck is probably guilty of multiple rapes. Fuck!" he whisper-barks, his hair flopping over his forehead.

Thrusting his fingers through it, he lets out another string of whispered swear words.

I let him go for it because he obviously needs to let this all out.

I'm still in too much shock to find my anger. I don't even know what I'm feeling.

"I should have stuck around and beat the shit out of him before coming to see you," Asher seethes.

"No." I curl my fingers around his fist. It's an instinctual move. Thoughtless. Reckless, maybe.

It's first contact.

I rub my thumb over his knuckles and can't deny myself anymore. It feels so right to touch him.

His fingers unfurl and I slip my digits against his palm, squeezing tight and loving his instant warmth. It spreads through me in spite of this harrowing conversation.

He stares at our connection, his face bunching in agony as he raises my hand to his lips and holds a long kiss against my skin. Closing his eyes, he shudders before finally whispering, "I don't know what to do."

"Nothing," I tell him, my voice sounding steady and sure as I comfort him. "Asher, this isn't your fight. If I want to take this further, it's between me and Harvey. You don't have to get involved."

"I'm already involved." He looks me in the eye, and I can see new tears building on his lashes.

Is it possible to be more in love with him now than I was three minutes ago?

His agony over this is heart-wrenching and endearing... and speaks to how much this all means to him.

He's a good man with a soft heart, and... I love him. I love him so much.

Which is why I can't let him lose what's most important to him.

"You have to step back from this. Even though I know you hate what Harvey's done and what your uncle threatened..." I shake my head, scrambling for the right words to convince him. "I can't let you throw this all away for me. If you have to pick a side, you need to choose them. They're your family. And you stand to lose so much. Hockey House? I mean, you can't risk that. You could lose—"

"I can't lose you." His voice is raw with emotion as he takes my face in his hands. "I won't."

His eyes are wet with tears, and I can't help joining him as we stare at each other and I soak in those words.

I wrap my fingers around his wrists, loving the feel of his hands on my face. Hating the agony riding through him... and me.

But in spite of this pain, there's something else too.

Something I can't keep pretending I don't want.

"I can't lose you either," I finally blubber, giving in to my heart's desire and lurching for his lips.

He kisses me back and we sink into each other, his arms winding around me as much as they can at this awkward angle. I nudge my seat around so I can climb out of it and into his lap.

As my chest hits his, I wrap my arms around his shoulders and cling like I never want to let go.

Because I don't.

Ever.

And I know that means a shitstorm of trouble is coming our way, but if we're gonna have any chance of surviving it, we need to hold on to each other... just like this.

CHAPTER 45
ASHER

Lani sat on my knee until my legs went numb. I didn't complain. Holding her again was the best fucking feeling in the world.

She's mine. I didn't lose her. And it makes it easier to breathe.

She came home with me, and we ate dinner in my man cave, then curled up in my bed and watched Lord of the Rings until she couldn't keep her eyes open. There was no lovemaking, no more conversation. All we seemed capable of doing was holding each other and trying not to think.

The movies helped a little, transporting us into a world of hobbits and elves and orcs and the one ring, but...

Sleep is still eluding me.

Slipping out of bed, I make sure not to disturb her as I creep out of my room and head for the kitchen.

Maybe an herbal tea will calm me enough to help me switch off.

My brain won't stop tormenting me. Everything from Harvey's smug smile to Uncle Hayes's fiery glare is spinning nonstop, overlaid with my parents' demands and then harrowing thoughts of how they'll react if Lani presses charges against Harvey. She hasn't said if she definitely will or not yet, but if she decides to, I'm backing her all the way. It's her right, and if it can stop Harvey from treating women like his personal sex toys, then she should. She definitely should.

The weight in my stomach gets ten times heavier as I play out that scenario and everything it will mean for me.

And not just me.

All of the guys at Hockey House. And Mick. And sweet Rachel.

"Fuck!" I mutter, yanking open the fridge, then slamming it shut again when I can't see anything I want.

"Tough night, huh?"

Ethan's voice makes me jump a mile, and I turn with a growl.

"You scared the shit out of me."

He lets out a soft snicker.

"What are you doing down here? And why are you sitting in the dark?"

"Couldn't sleep." He stands from the table, shuffling toward the kitchen. "I come down here sometimes and just sit for ten minutes, do some deep breathing to try and relax. I'll go back up in a minute." He lifts his chin toward the stairs, then leans against the counter and crosses his arms. "What are you doing up?"

"Can't sleep. Obvi." I raise my eyebrows at him. I'm being a grumpy bastard, but Ethan doesn't hightail it to his room like I would.

He sticks around, quietly standing there watching me while I boil a mug of water in the microwave, then give up on tea and grab the whiskey bottle.

I only fill my tumbler with a little. I just need a small hit.

Ethan watches me intently and it's starting to piss me off, so I slap the glass down and glare at him. "Do you have something to say, because you're starting to creep me out."

His laughter is soft and throaty. "Just trying to figure out what's eating you up." He spins and rest his hands against the counter. "Liam said he saw you walk in with Lani earlier. Have you guys gotten back together or something?"

"Yeah." I sigh.

He frowns. "So, why aren't you happy about it? Why aren't you lying in your bed right now enjoying the feel of your woman beside you?"

I swallow and try to smile. I should be fucking ecstatic about it. And I am.

It's just all the other shit that's weighing me down.

Will Ethan even want to hear it?

It's usually Liam who sits there listening to our problems.

But he's staying the night with Rachel and... fuck, soon she'll be just as homeless as he is. I close my eyes with a heavy sigh.

"Today was shit," I murmur. "I got her back, which is great, and I am really happy about that," I assure him. "But... it's gonna come at a cost."

"What do you mean?" Ethan's voice is deep with concern.

So I tell him.

I tell him pretty much what I told Lani, but this rendition is peppered with a lot more profanity as I let my anger spark and flail. I had to keep that in check around Lani. I didn't want to scare her, but with Ethan I go for it, letting out my angst in growls and terse statements.

Ethan stands quietly through my rant, looking like a Navy SEAL as he calmly soaks it all in.

I end up slumping against the counter with a sigh. "And the worst part is that it doesn't just affect me. You guys would get caught up in this drama too. It won't just be me losing Hockey House."

"It's not about the house," Ethan growls, his eyes sparking with anger. "It's about Lani and doing what's right for her."

"I know that." I wince. "And of course I'll support her. She's everything. I just... I wish I didn't have to choose. I wish Harvey had never touched her. I wish—"

"That little fucker," Ethan spits.

"I know." I clench my jaw, shaking my head and staring out the kitchen window. The night is black, broken only by the soft glow of the streetlamps outside. "He deserves to go down hard, but it's complicated, you know? I stand to lose a lot. We all do."

"Not us." Ethan's sure voice makes me spin to face him. "You won't lose us."

I can't help a skeptical frown. "Come on, man. I know you only hang with me because we live in the same house. If I can't provide you with this anymore... are you seriously gonna want to know me? I drive you insane."

"Yet we'll be friends for life." His grin is broad, his eyes glittering with amusement.

My lips part in surprise. I was not expecting him to say that.

Moving around the counter, he comes to stand beside me, looking me right in the eye. "You're not my bro because of this house. Yes, you piss me off sometimes." He lets out a dry laugh. "But I wouldn't want to do life without you, man."

My throat swells with emotion, and if I fucking cry in front of him, I'm going to kick my own ass.

Blinking, I sniff and try to play it cool, like those words didn't punch me straight through the heart.

Ethan studies my expression, then lets out a soft "Aw. Did I get you in the feels?"

"Shut up." I sniff, slashing my finger under my nose, then flicking his hand away when he tries to poke my chest.

"I totally got you, dude."

"Fuck off," I grumble, annoyed that he can say something so meaningful, then shit all over it by hassling me.

Unless he didn't mean—

I quickly check his expression.

"I meant it." He gives me a sincere smile, which only grows a little wider when he says, "I love you, man."

A soft laugh punches out of me, and I have to give him the finger as he walks away or else my balls might shrink to unrecognizable raisins.

He glances over his shoulder and grins, flipping me off just before he disappears through the archway.

"Love you, too, bro," I murmur, his words sinking all the way into my core.

Looks like I'm not going to lose it all.

I stand to lose a whole fucking lot... but not the most important stuff.

Gazing into the dark living area and dining room, I picture hours of good times spent in this place. If this goes sour, all of that will go away.

But not my bros.

And not my girl.

I shuffle back to bed, slipping in beside Lani and draping my arm lightly around her waist. She lets out a pleasant moan and burrows back against me. I inhale the sweet scent of her shampoo and soak in the feel of her body pressed against mine, forcing my brain to focus on the things that matter most.

CHAPTER 46
LEILANI

"I'm telling you, it's the right thing to do." Mikayla puffs as she lifts her knee, then steps back into a lunge.

I do the same thing, trying to keep up with the instructor at the front of the room.

Stretching my arms in time with the music, I raise my right knee and continue the set, glancing at Caroline for backup.

Unfortunately, her red curls are bouncing as she nods in agreement with Mikayla.

"I know it's terrifying, but Mick's right. You really should report this."

I stop working out for a second, letting the class continue around me as I brace my hands on my knees and catch my breath.

I can't believe we're even having this discussion here. But the music is masking our words and we're at the very back of the class, so it's probably safe enough.

"Let's go, ladies!" the instructor shouts from the front. "We can do this!"

Her enthusiasm is grating, but I force my body back up, my mind running faster than my pulse as I try to figure out what I should do.

Asher and I told everyone at Hockey House what went down this weekend. We had to. This affects them all, and they have a right to know. I was dreading the conversation, but it ended up going way better than I thought it would. Ethan and Casey are ready to castrate Harvey, while Rachel and Mick seem more concerned about my mental health and well-being. The way they reacted was really sweet, actually.

The thing that surprised me most is the fact that none of them complained about the possibility of losing Hockey House. Even Baxter just shrugged and murmured, "We've gotta do what's right," before walking out of the room.

And now I'm at the student rec center trying to work out while Mikayla chirps in my ear about reporting Harvey to the police.

"This might be a totally shitty thing to say," she says between breaths, "but this isn't just about you."

I punch my arms, then let out a soft "Huh!" like the instructor is encouraging us to do. I'm sure she'd prefer I shouted it like a she-warrior, but I'm not feeling very warrior-like today.

Mikayla keeps glancing at me, her small fists punching the air until her arms drop with a sigh.

"I know you don't want to hear this, but... if you're not the only person this has happened to..." Her gaze is sad enough to make me stop. "You need to speak up for them and all the other girls who are gonna get caught in his trap."

"He needs to go down," Caroline says over my shoulder.

I blink, my throat too thick to even swallow. With a little sniff, I look between my two friends, then spin for the door and march out of the class. I didn't even feel like working out today anyway.

Wiping the back of my hand down my sweaty cheeks, I run to the cubby my stuff is stored in and wrench out my bag.

"Leilani."

I close my eyes. *Shit.* When Caroline uses my full name like that, I know she means business.

"I love you." She stands right behind me. "I'm not trying to hurt you, and I would never force you to do this. All I'm saying is that it's something worth thinking about." Her hand comes to rest on my sweaty shoulder, and I look behind me to check her expression.

She gives me a sad smile, but her eyes are filled with warmth. "I'll come with you."

"So will I." Mikayla crosses her arms, raising her chin and looking ready to get a little hellcat crazy on Harvey's ass.

I love how feisty and strong she is.

I used to be just like that.

And I've seen sparks of that in me, but Harvey took so much.

Only if you let him take it. Find your fire, girl.

Biting my lips together, I look between them. "It could screw up everything. Mick—" I turn to face her. "—you could be kicked out of your apartment."

Her expression goes dark, her tone is terse with venom as she seethes, "I know. Fucking asshole." She huffs. "But Ray and I have talked about it, and it's just an apartment. We'll find something else."

"But what about the guys?"

Taking my hand, she gives it a firm squeeze. "They'd walk out of that place in a heartbeat if it means you get the justice you deserve."

"That's right." Caroline nods. "I know this sucks ass. The whole situation is so fucked-up, but Harvey deserves to be reported. And you deserve closure."

"I've got closure," I murmur, my face puckering into a deep frown.

Caroline gives me a skeptical frown. "Knowing that fuckface is still walking around with zero consequences over what he did to you is closure?"

Snapping my eyes shut with a huff, I shake my head. "I'm just trying to work through this. I need to move on with my life. I need to be with Asher and make something of that. What's he gonna think if I go and report his cousin?"

"I'm pretty sure Asher's hating super hard on that crap-weasel right now, so the timing couldn't be better."

Mick raises her eyebrows. "You're his woman. And if I know anything about the hockey bros, they will do whatever it takes to keep us safe. They're very caveman when it comes to this kind of stuff." Her nose wrinkles like it should bother her, but I think the thing that really bothers her the most is that she loves it.

And if I'm honest, I kind of love it too.

The way Asher's been holding me the past couple days, the way he checks in and looks at me. He's so torn up over this whole thing, but he wants to make this right for me. For us.

He can't lose me.

The way he said that... the look on his face...

My heart expands like it's inhaling a deep breath. He fills me in ways no one else can.

Caroline's fingers curl around my arm as she gets my attention. "What happened to you was wrong. And you have the chance to try and make it just a little bit right. I know talking about it is repulsive for you. You don't want to go back to that night, but..."

"I'm strong enough to do it," I murmur for her, then run my hand down my ponytail with a sad sigh. "And if I don't speak up, Harvey might do this to someone else. And even though that's not my fault..." I shake my head. "It's gonna eat me alive if I don't at least try to stop him."

"That's right." Caroline smiles.

"Yes!" Mick punches the air, then jumps up and kisses my cheek. "Come on, hot stuff. Let's go take this asshole down!"

CHAPTER 47
LEILANI

Grabbing her bag, Mikayla flings it over her shoulder and practically drags me out of the building.

We arrive at the local police station fifteen minutes later—three little stink bombs who didn't even bother to shower before coming to file this report.

My insides are trembling as I take a seat and wait for an officer to come get us.

Mick rests her hand on my bobbing knee and gives it a squeeze. "Calm down," she whispers. "You can do this."

I nod and lightly sniff, then try to smile, but I'm sure what she sees is more of a grimace.

Caroline rests her hand on my lower back and gives it a light rub. Her smile is encouraging, and I soak up some of her bravery, yet still flinch when a tall officer with salt-and-pepper hair and a no-bullshit gaze strides out to greet us.

"Leilani I...Iona?" He struggles with my last name,

but I'm already standing, forcing my feet to follow him down the hallway.

Mick and Caroline flank me as my heart rate accelerates until I can hear it thumping between my ears.

"Take a seat." He points at the chairs opposite his desk, and I sit on the very edge, like my body needs to be ready to bolt if I have to. "I'm Officer McFadden. I'll be taking your statement today. So, you want to file a report?"

"Yes." I nod.

He raises his eyebrows at me, obviously drawing on the last of his dying patience. The guy must be having one of those days.

Maybe I should just bail... or ask to speak to someone else.

But then his look gets even more pointed as he clips, "What's the problem, then?"

"Well, I, um..." I swallow. "I was raped." My voice wobbles, and his expression flatlines.

The air in the room goes eerily still, and I'm thrown by the tension. Surely I'm not the first woman to walk in here with this, but the look he's giving me right now makes me feel like I'm more than an inconvenience on his hectic day. I'm a big fucking problem.

Mikayla jerks forward with a frown. "So, are you going to ask her about it or just sit there staring at her like a dumbass?"

His eyebrows dip with a silent look of reprimand before he clears his throat and shuffles in his seat.

"Go ahead. Please tell me about the incident." The way he accentuates the T is grating.

Caroline huffs. "Do we need to request a different officer? Maybe we need to talk to a female offi—"

"That won't be necessary. I've filed plenty of these reports. So, please—" He points at me. "—go on."

I share a dubious frown with Caroline, but she nods and I somehow spurt out what I can remember. Which is more than I wish I could. As I walk my brain back to that party, it returns with brutal clarity, and I'm able to tell him exactly which house I was in and what I was wearing. I tell him about the dancing and the kissing and how we found that spare room, and then my eyes start to burn with tears and my voice gets shaky as I explain the details of the rape, including what he said to me after I told him to stop.

"That arrogant fuck." Mick's small hands make two tight fists, and she looks ready to throttle something.

For some reason, her indignant rage spurs me on, and I make it through the rest of my statement without falling apart.

I glance at Caroline. Her cheeks are pale, and tears are slowly trailing over her freckles. I reach for her hand, and she grabs my fingers. "You're really brave, babe. I'm proud of you."

Her words mean more to me than I'm able to express, so I just give her a weak smile and hope it's enough.

The officer finishes typing into his computer, looking unaffected by the emotion in the room. Clearing his throat, he gives me a once-over, then nods. "And you know the person who did this to you?"

"Yes," I whisper. "His name's Harvey Carmichael. He's a student at Lennox College. He comes down here for parties sometimes."

"And you're sure it's him?"

I nod, but his stern gaze is unnerving me. "Pretty sure, yeah."

"Pretty sure? You know there's a difference, right?"

Mikayla huffs. "He raped her! What more do you want?"

The officer throws her a silent "shut up" before turning back to me. "You said in your statement that you were drunk, it was dark, and you didn't exactly converse much before going into the room with him. How can you be sure it was this Harvey person?"

"Well, I... When I bumped into him weeks later, I just knew. I recognized his face and voice and—"

"These are very serious accusations, Miss I...Io..." He huffs. "Miss. Do you know how many women come in here throwing out these statements like they don't cost anything?"

I frown at him, thrown by his sudden venom.

"Someone brought charges against my nephew, and he was put through hell trying to prove his innocence. And before you ask, yes, he *was* innocent. The girl was pissed off that he dumped her and was out for revenge. So, we'll need to know that you are sure, 100 percent, before we go after this Harvey guy."

A cold breath rushes out of me. "I'm not after any kind of revenge. I told him to stop, and he didn't. He raped me, and I don't want him doing that to anyone else."

The officer closes his eyes for a second, dipping his head with a sigh. "I'm very sorry about what happened to you. It shouldn't have happened, I'm not denying it for one second. I just know the detective investigating your case will need you to be sure. And the DA might not press charges if there isn't enough evidence."

Mikayla scoffs. "The least you could do is go talk to the asshole!" Firing out of her chair, she slaps her hands on his desk. "Do you have any idea how much courage it took for her to even walk in here today? She was raped, and that has been harrowing. Now she finally finds the guts to come down here, and you're telling her you don't want to go after this guy because it might not be him?"

"What if it's *not* him?" the officer bites back.

"Isn't it *your* job to investigate that?"

He huffs and leans back, wiping a hand over his mouth before giving her a pointed look. "I will do my job. This report will get passed on to a detective, who will contact you in due course. I'm just being realistic here. With the serious lack of evidence, the case will likely be thrown out before it gets any real traction. I've been doing this job long enough to know what any detective will say to you—witness statements from a party that happened months ago are hardly reliable, and there was no one in the room when this went down."

"So, it's my word against his." My shoulders slump.

The officer gives me a pained frown before muttering, "We'll do what we can."

It's hardly encouraging, but I nod and shuffle out of the police station, feeling numb and let down.

Mikayla is fuming, spitting out harsh insults as we walk away from the station. "I want to squeeze his balls to toothpaste. That asswipe doesn't deserve to sire children! Officer McFuckface with his arrogant smirk and '*I need more evidence!*' It's *his* job to find that shit!" She points at the station, her voice pitching in time with her eyebrows.

It's kind of a detective's job, actually, but I don't have the energy to correct her. All I can hope is that whichever detective gets assigned to my case will have a little more enthusiasm than that old-time cop who should have retired a few years ago.

"*The DA might not press charges.*" Mick scoffs. "That's a whole lot of bullshit right there!" She punches the air with her fists and lets out a roar.

I share a quick look with Caroline, who is blinking and squirming in her blue Converse with the sparkly laces.

"Have you ever seen her like this before?" I murmur out the side of my mouth.

"No."

"What should we do?"

"I think we just leave her to it and she'll get it out of her system."

"Do you think we should let her drive?"

"Definitely not." Caroline snatches the keys from Mikayla's flailing hands.

And I step into her space before she starts smashing her fists through car windows. "Mick, it's gonna be okay."

"Why the fuck are *you* comforting *me*?" she shouts up at me. "How are you not losing your shit right now?"

"I don't know." I shake my head, kind of perplexed myself. "You're doing a pretty good job for both of us, so maybe I'm letting you carry it."

"Oh." She nods, the thought seeming to calm her a little. "Okay. Do you need me to hit something or smash windows? I've got a bunch more insults I can scream at the station if that's helpful."

"You know what?" I find myself fighting a grin. "The 'squeezing his balls to toothpaste' thing kind of covers how I'm feeling."

Mikayla's lips twitch and she crosses her arms, kicking the ground with her scuffed-up sneakers.

"Unfortunately, I think the jackass may have already sired children." Caroline's shoulder hitches. "But I'd still love to see his ball sack as flat as a pancake."

"Ew." I make a face. "Now I'm picturing his ball sack."

Mick snorts and then lets out this watery laugh that soon turns into a miserable whine. "I'm sorry, Lani." She yanks me into a hug, her small arms surprisingly strong. "You don't deserve to be treated like that. It's not fair."

"It's also not over." Caroline wraps her arms around both of us. "I don't care what Officer McFuckface says.

We're not dropping this. We're gonna keep coming back until we're taken seriously."

"I just need some decent evidence," I mumble against Mikayla's shoulder.

"And we'll find some," she assures me.

I pull myself out of the group hug. "How?"

"I don't know." Caroline shrugs again. "I just know we will. This can't be over without some justice."

She brushes her hand down the back of my ponytail, her smile sad in spite of her fierce tone.

As the initial anger finally burns away, we're left standing in the parking lot, a pitiful silence settling over us as we try to reconcile with how badly that went.

And there's that doubt again. Niggling away.

What if it wasn't Harvey?

Just because his little sister thinks he might be guilty doesn't mean he is. Just because his father is worried enough to threaten Asher... it still doesn't mean Harvey was the one who raped me.

And Asher stands to lose so much if I pursue this.

Shit. This is such a fucking mess!

CHAPTER 48
ASHER

The house is a mess, and I hate it. I'm trying to study but can't concentrate, so I end up procrastinating by doing the dishes, then gathering up all the crap that people in this house seem to spread everywhere... all the time. I make a pile of Casey's stuff and leave it on the stairs, then fold Ethan's sweater, flicking it out with a growl as I try to shake off Mom's phone call.

She wouldn't shut up about the summer internship, which is annoying enough, but then just before signing off, she left one of those kick-you-in-the-balls comments that I didn't know how to reply to.

"You have such an amazing future ahead of you, sweetie. Keep your eye on the prize. You don't want to let someone come along and wreck your plans, you know?"

"Someone?" I gritted out between clenched teeth.

"Love is fickle. Family is forever. Just remember that."

I doubt Uncle Hayes outright said anything about

Harvey and his asshole ways, but I'm guessing he dropped a few little comments at the family function after I left.

"Might want to keep an eye on Asher. Think he might be going off track."

"I heard him mention a girl. Serious relationships in college probably aren't the best idea."

I can hear him saying that shit in my head, and I can't fucking believe I used to wish he was my dad. The only reason I did was because my dad and I have never gelled. I needed someone, and he was the best.

Until Saturday, when he made it blatantly clear that Harvey can be a total fuckwit, but I'd better keep my damn mouth shut.

And now he's got my mom in on it, too, and my dad won't be a hard sell.

It's all about business and success and being like the twins. They date strategically, going out with girls who will better their image, then flicking them off when it's inconvenient. They don't have friends to party with, because how will that get them more money?

They're fucking robots, and I don't want that life for me.

I never did!

Which is why I hung out with the Carmichaels so much. But after Saturday, I'm not sure I ever want to see them again.

The front door pops open, and I spin to see Rachel walking in with a bunch of shopping bags.

"Hey." I walk over to help her.

"Thanks." She smiles at me as I take the bags out of her hands.

"What's all this stuff?"

"Just some leftovers from the diner. Juniper was doing a big clear out and some of this stuff expires soon, so she let me have it. I thought I'd bake you up a storm and cook dinner."

"And this is why we love you." I wink at her, placing the bags down while she laughs and rolls up her sleeves.

"How are you doing?"

I shrug. "Just on a cleaning frenzy."

"Uh-oh." She tips her head with a frown. "What's up? Or is that like the stupidest question ever right now? I know you're going through a really hard time. I'm sorry."

I wince and grip the back of my neck. "You gonna hate me if you lose your apartment?"

"Of course not." She gives me a light kiss on the cheek and moves around me. "We have to do what's right for Lani."

I nod, sliding onto the stool to watch her. She secures Casey's joke Christmas present around her waist, and I grin at the apron with the large pecs, washboard abs, and huge penis on the front of it. I can't believe she actually wears it, but I think she's out to prove a point. Casey can't go giving her a prank Christmas gift. She will walk around with that cartoon penis on her front all damn day if she has to.

Fighting a smile, I look away from the dangling

manhood and shake my head. "What if Harvey didn't do it and this is all for nothing?"

She spins with a sigh. "What if he did?"

"Then I'd lose it all for her."

Rachel's face softens with a smile. "It's a big ask, isn't it?"

"I don't even know how it would all work." I flick my hands up. "I mean, sure, we'd probably get kicked out of Hockey House, and you and Mick would get the boot, too, but does that mean I'm disowning my whole family? Will I get shunned from Christmas and New Year's events? Will my parents cut off Hayes and Carla for treating me this way? Or am I the one on the chopping block?" I tap my chest. "Will they believe me or Harvey? Will they let Lani into their lives? Because they'll have to if they expect me to join the family business!" I'm getting all worked up and agitated. The stool wobbles as I jump off it so I can pace the floor.

Rachel calmly watches me, her eyes darting to the mixing bowl she's measuring flour into before coming back to rest on my face.

"Ash, can I ask you something?"

I give her a stiff nod and cross my arms.

"Do you even *want* to work for your family business?"

The air puffs out of me as I dip my head, then slowly shake it. "I don't fucking know. It's not like they've ever given me a choice. I've been raised with the expectation that I'll graduate from college and move back to New

York. They'll find a place for me at the company, and I'll lump it."

"Okay." She scoops some sugar and dumps it into the mixing bowl. "So, is the world going to fall apart if you don't do that?"

A shocked laugh punches out of me. "I'm pretty sure theirs will, and what the hell else am I gonna do?"

"Well, what do you like doing?" She sucks the end of her finger, then grabs a wooden spoon out of the utensil holder. "Have you ever let yourself think about your dream job?"

Scratching my head, I wander back to the counter and sit opposite her. "Have you?"

"Yes!" Her eyes light up. "I want to open a bakery and fill it with delicious food and hot coffee and all things warm and inviting. It'll be like a café where people can grab a quick bite or the place you stop at on your way to work. It'll have traditional bakery food like donuts and cinnamon rolls, but all of them will have a little Rachel flair thrown in." She grins, then spreads her hands across the air. "Sunshine and Cupcakes! Fill your heart with warmth and your belly with goodness."

I let out a soft laugh, loving her enthusiasm.

Her nose wrinkles. "I think the tagline needs some work, but you know what I'm going for, right?"

"Totally."

She sucks in a breath and nods a few times, turning her attention back to her baking. "I have no idea how it's going to happen yet, but it will. Somehow." She bites her bottom lip, then gives me a nervous wince. "To be honest, I don't even know where to begin. I mean, I've got the vision and the recipes, but... how do I turn that into a reality?"

"Well... you could get yourself a business partner, or a coach. Someone who understands how to get a business off the ground and can help you with marketing and strategizing. They can map out a plan for you and help you formulate the practical steps you need to take." I think of Desiree, my mom's best friend from high school. She was actually my first time, and the only people who know that are Ethan, Liam, and Casey. They hassled me for hanging out in Cougar Town, but it was just one time, and it was perfect. She was perfect.

I always admired her and what she did. Getting alongside people, helping them to get their businesses off the ground with practical help. It's kind of similar to what Bensens & Co is about, although there's no tearing down, only building up. And it's on a much smaller, more personal scale.

As her coaching business grew, she was also able to invest and offer financial support to the people she believed in most, and now she's a freaking money queen.

That'd be cool, doing what Desiree does. Shit, she'd probably be willing to coach me if I gave her a call.

All I'd need to do is find myself some clients and—

I glance up, my lips parting as the idea zings through my head. Is it completely stupid?

No! You're buzzing right now! Just say it!

"I could help." The words pop out, at first a little quiet, but then Ray registers what I said and her face lights up like the Rockefeller Center Christmas tree.

"Really?"

"Yeah, I mean..." I shrug. "I've got some learning to do, but I understand the basics of business, and I could help you put together a plan. Something to take to the bank so you can secure a loan."

"I do have some money already set aside... from my dad. It's in a trust, but I could access some for a business start-up. I just didn't want to do that unless I had something solid to work with." Her smile grows a little wider. "Do you really think you could help me?"

"Yeah. I'd love to."

"What's in it for you, though?" Her eyebrows dip into a worried frown.

I grin. "The learning opportunity. The chance to help make your vision come to life."

"Or you could be my partner. We could go in on this thing together, and you could help run the business and marketing side of things."

I nod, the idea sending another buzz of excitement through me.

"We can write up a contract and make it all legit and fair and..." She lets out a soft squeal. "Do you think this could work?"

"Yeah." I nod, then start to laugh as she jumps around the counter to wrap me in a hug.

"This is so exciting! I can't wait to tell Liam!"

"Can't wait to tell me what?" His deep voice pulls her away from me, and I raise my eyebrows at his assessing gaze.

Dumping his bag against the wall, he turns in time to catch Rachel, who's flying at him with animated babbling. I'm sure he's struggling to catch up as she talks faster than I have ever heard her talk before.

With a grin, he hugs her, throwing me a little side-eye over her shoulder.

I wonder how he'd feel about me working with his girl. Going into business together is a huge step, but Rachel's right about covering ourselves with a contract. Helping her realize this dream would be pretty freaking epic. And if it goes well, then maybe I wouldn't have to work for my parents.

They'll be so pissed and let down by my decision, but with everything else that's going on, it's kind of the least of my worries right now.

Having something that actually pumps me up about the future is... well, shit... I don't know if I've ever felt this way before.

I grin, feeling just a touch lighter as Rachel pulls Liam into the kitchen and keeps pitching him the idea. He watches her with an adoring grin, then glances at me, his quick wink telling me he's cool and this could actually become a thing.

Fuck yeah, that feels good.

And now I can't wait to tell Lani.

I stand up, hitching my pants, about to go call her, when I hear voices in the entranceway.

"I still say he's an asshole!" Mikayla gripes. "I'm getting pissed again! Picturing flattened ball sacks!"

What?

I shake my head with a perplexed little laugh... until I hear Lani's voice.

"He's got a point, though. I do need some solid evidence or this he said/she said thing will be a nightmare."

Concern rockets through me as I race out to the entryway. "What's going on?"

Caroline toes off her Converse with a sad smile. "Lani found the guts to go to the police today."

The air in my lungs turns frosty as I try to catch Lani's eye. She looks at the floor like she's feeling guilty or something.

"Good," I croak. "I'm proud of you."

She glances up, her eyes round with surprise, and I have to force myself to say it. "I am. I know that must have been really hard."

Her eyes glisten as she nods, and then Mikayla growls and starts snapping. "It was made worse by a cop who basically told her she can't go accusing guys of such a serious crime if she doesn't have the evidence to back it up."

"He said he'd pass my report on to a detective but warned us that it might not go anywhere," Lani murmurs, so obviously defeated by that feedback.

Mick scoffs. "He basically reminded her that she was drunk and her memory was probably fuzzy. Then he went on to say that it was too long ago for any witnesses to remember, so we really shouldn't get our hopes up!" She flicks her arm in the air. "He all but told us that this isn't even worth pursuing!"

As Mikayla's volume escalates, Lani seems to shrink further in on herself.

I don't like that look on her. It's not Lani. She's strong, not crushed.

Stepping around Mikayla, who's still snarling and ranting, I pull Lani against my chest and whisper, "What do you need?"

"Quiet," she rasps against my chest.

So, without a word, I pull her down the hallway and shut us inside my man cave—a safe little haven for as long as she needs it.

CHAPTER 49
LEILANI

As soon as the door clicks shut, I feel the tension start to drain out of me. It's not a fast drain, more like a slow leak, but it eases the pressure a little.

"So, the police, huh?" Asher glides his hands into his pockets, his expression kind of torn.

"I thought it'd be the right thing to do."

"It is." He nods, his forehead crinkling.

"I know. I've... started the countdown now, haven't I? The bomb's gonna go off soon, and it's all gonna turn to shit." My voice breaks, and I cover my face with hands.

"Hey, that's not on you."

Asher's arms come around me again. I lean into him, resting my weight on his solid chest. His hand cups the back of my head, and it feels so good. I'm protected here. Sheltered by this man who could so easily hate me.

I'm throwing his cousin into the firepit.

Where he deserves to burn!

But what if I'm wrong?

Or what if I'm right and he still gets away with it?

What if he walks free while his uncle boots Asher and his friends to the curb?

I shudder, and Asher's arms tighten around me.

"I know it sucks right now. It's shit." His deep voice washes over me. "But it's not always gonna be shit, and we'll be together." He leans back, taking my face in his hands. His eyes drink me in and I capture his gaze, transfixed by his affection. "We'll be together, and that's what I want."

"But they're your family." I say it yet again because I can't seem to get over that fact.

He shakes his head. "You think I want to be related to a rapist or a man who is willing to cover that up? You think I want to be connected to people who can't see past their own bullshit?"

I swallow, my lips parting at the look on his face.

"Boo, I want real. I want to be around people who are good and honest and will fight for the right things. I want to hang with people I respect. People like my hockey bros." His lips curl into a smile. "People like you."

My heart melts like a scoop of ice cream in the sunshine. The warmth traveling from my chest to my toes is comforting... and also sensual.

I love this man. I love the way he thinks and talks. I love the look in his eyes right now.

Brushing my thumb over the back of his hand, I tell

him without words, rising to my tiptoes and gently pressing my lips to his.

He breathes me in, wrapping his arm around my waist and suctioning me against him as we deepen the kiss. His tongue glides against mine, a slow dance that simmers and heats with each lap of his tongue.

My body starts to sizzle, and I know exactly what's going to break this tension inside me. I need release. And we need connection.

"I want you," I murmur against his mouth, fisting his shirt and sucking his tongue into my mouth. "I need you."

He smiles and starts trailing his lips across my cheek. "Thought you didn't need me, boo."

"Don't want to need you." I groan as his tongue finds the sweet spot beneath my ear. "But it turns out, on the very odd occasion..." I giggle when he lets out a soft growl, then tip my head back with a moan as his tongue glides a path down my neck. "I need you."

Gripping his shirt, I give it a firm tug, whipping the fabric over his head and flicking it to the floor. His body is hot and delicious. Running my fingers over his hard muscles, I kiss a trail down his body, dipping my tongue into the ridges of his abs while kneeling on the couch and unbuckling his belt.

"So sexy, boo." He digs his fingers into my hair, leaning down to kiss me again while sliding the jacket off my shoulders.

I have to let him go in order to slip my clothes off,

then raise my hands as he wrestles my shirt free and unclasps my bra. My breasts pop free on a sigh of liberation, but they're soon covered by his hands, then his lips and tongue. He sucks and nibbles until my body is on fire, sending my lady parts into a frenzy as his hands travel beneath my skirt.

It's soon bunched around my waist as I frantically shove his pants down, freeing his pulsing cock. It springs out of his boxers and I smile down at it, wrapping my fingers around the shaft and wiping the bead of moisture off his tip.

"So good," he groans into my mouth, sucking my bottom lip before owning me with his tongue.

I pump him while he kisses me, then lose concentration when his fingers part my folds and dance around my entrance. I'm wet and slippery, his fingers gliding into me easily before ducking out and searching for my clit.

As usual, he finds it without any effort. His panting breaths mingle with my sweet sighs as I rest my head against his shoulder and feel the electricity pulse down my legs.

We're both kneeling on his couch, pleasuring each other. His jeans are bunched around his knees while my skirt has become a cumbersome belt. But none of that matters as we're both transported to a higher plane.

My orgasm builds with surprising speed, and my nails are soon sinking into his shoulders as I cling to him and release a lusty cry. He groans with me. I'm still pumping his cock, my hand working in time with my racing heartbeat.

"I really want to come inside you," he moans. "Is that okay?"

"Of course." I wouldn't want it any other way.

I shudder once more, my body still zinging as he kisses my shoulder, then leaps off the couch. He nearly falls over as his jeans slip to his ankles, but he kicks them off, literally running out of them as he darts into his bedroom for a condom.

His naked butt is firm and gorgeous, and I can't help grinning that I'll soon be sinking my fingers into it.

I wriggle out of my skirt, dumping it on the floor and lying down just as he races back into the room, all sheathed and ready to go.

Raising my leg over the back of the couch, I boldly open myself right up to him, and he pauses, gazing down at me like I'm the most beautiful thing he's ever seen.

The depth of his intimate gaze stirs an emotion in me that's so strong and unexpected, I don't know what to do with it.

This man.

He's owning me right now.

Sitting forward, I snatch his wrist and pull him onto the couch. He kneels between my legs, skimming the pads of his fingers over my stomach. My body trembles in response, yearning for him in deep, soulful ways that should scare me, but they don't.

It's Asher.

My man.

I smile up at him, reaching for his face and trailing my fingers down his neck as he settles over me.

"I love you." His husky voice sends tendrils of pleasure curling through my body. Or maybe it's his words. Or the look that's still swimming in his eyes.

I nudge my hips toward him, reaching down to part my folds and guide him inside me.

Our eyes stay connected as he slides home, his rigid cock piercing me with a beauty that's indescribable.

Gripping his shoulders, I urge him with my hips, enjoying his second thrust, loving the way our bodies glide together. We find our rhythm easily and bask in it. My hands travel down to his butt, my fingers sinking into that firm ass as ecstasy glides through me, one wave after another.

His breathing hitches in my ear, his lips dropping kisses from my cheek to my shoulder as he gets lost in the feeling of us.

"Ahh," he groans, picking up his pace, his arms trembling as he shifts his weight from his elbows to his hands.

Rising above me, he changes the angle, stars scattering before my eyes as he thrusts even deeper, becoming a part of me as only he can.

I tip my head back, soft whimpers spurting from my mouth as he drives into me like a piston.

Yes, yes, yes!

"Asher," I cry out as I'm blinded by a thrill so fierce, it takes out my senses.

He spasms inside me, choking out a sound that's all pleasure as he takes his fill and thrusts into me two more times before splintering apart in my arms.

We couldn't move for a while after that session. I lay beneath him on the couch, our naked bodies relishing the skin-on-skin contact. There's seriously nothing better. We could have stayed there all night if someone didn't tap on the door, letting us know dinner was ready.

I couldn't bear to get fully dressed, so I borrowed a T-shirt and some sweats off Asher. The pants were way too big and kept sliding off my hips, but I held them when I walked, and once I was sitting at the table, they behaved themselves.

We, of course, got a chorus of wolf whistles and eyebrow wiggles as we entered the room.

"Whatcha been doing?" Casey laughed at us while Fezzik jumped and yipped around his ankles, wanting to know what the fuss was about.

Baxter scooped him up, giving him a kiss before settling him on his knee.

He really does love that dog.

I took the teasing with as much dignity as I could. It was made a little more challenging by the falling-pants situation, but Asher's grin was filled with pride, like I was the best prize at the table. As much as I hate the thought of being someone's prize, there's also something kind of nice about it.

He loves me. I'm his girl.

Dinner went well. We talked about everything but the ugly cloud of uncertainty hanging over all of us, so it was easy to pretend that life was grand and all was well. Asher and Rachel told us about their business idea, and Ethan put them through their paces like he was a judge on *Shark Tank* or something. But it was probably good for them. Asher rose to the challenge with a grace and dignity that completely turned me on. He's so smart and capable. He deserves every good thing to swing his way, which is why this situation with his family is killing me.

As nighttime took over and we slipped into bed, the whole thing started weighing on me again. I think it was bothering Asher, too, but we couldn't talk about it. Instead, we made slow, easy love in the darkness. It was a languid dance—soft and gentle. He came inside me with a murmured grunt, and I clung to his shoulders, never wanting to move from beneath his blanket of warmth and strength.

But that's not reality, is it?

We can't play pretend. We can't not talk about this.

Actions need to be taken.

Because Caroline and Mick are right. I need closure... and Harvey can't just get away with what he did to me.

Uncertainty rumbles in my chest again. What if it's not Harvey?

But what if it is?

There has to be a way to know for sure.

Asher's going through all this shit because of a hunch. I need concrete evidence, irrefutable proof.

As the early morning light dawns, I wake from my restless slumber with an idea that must have brewed in my dreams. As my eyes pop open, a question comes to life that I can't shake.

The police officer said witnesses won't remember that far back.

But what if they did?

What if someone saw who I was with that night?

It's a long shot, but it's worth taking, right?

I can't rely on a detective to follow this thing through with the same kind of determination I can throw at it. My foundations may have been shaken by what happened to me, but they didn't completely crumble. I'm nothing if not tenacious.

If Asher can put his future on the line for me, then I can most definitely find the courage to prove our fight isn't in vain.

I'm not going to know everyone who was at that party, but I do remember *where* the party was, and if that's not a good starting point, then I don't know what is.

Slipping from the bed as quietly as I can, I creep out of Asher's room and fumble my clothes on. My skirt is all creased from being bunched around my waist yesterday, but I flatten it out as best I can and tiptoe to the door.

I should probably take Asher with me, but I don't want to wake him. He's been under so much pressure, and I know he hasn't been sleeping well. I can do this without him and then report back as soon as I'm done.

Ordering an Uber, I pull my shoes on and slip outside, walking down the street to the meeting point I selected. Thankfully, I only have to wait at the corner for five minutes. It's hardly a busy Uber time, so drivers are readily available.

"Good morning." The driver's friendly voice is almost jarring.

I give him a polite smile and check to make sure he knows where to go.

He nods and thankfully picks up on my mood pretty quickly. We arrive at the football frat house without a word.

Slipping out of the car with a murmured thanks, I stare at the three-story Victorian-style house and shudder. Memories of strutting up the path in my skimpy black dress haunt me. I walked into that place with an angry determination. I was pissed off with Caroline for moping over Casey, and I didn't know she was worried that she might be pregnant. I stormed into that party looking for a good time and mindless pleasure... and two hours later, I shuffled out in shock, my mind barely functioning as I somehow made it back to Huxley Hall.

I honestly have no idea how I did. My memory of that part of the evening is a dark spot in my mind.

A nervous breath shudders out of me as I walk to the door.

About eight members of the Nolan U football team

live in this place. It's not actually a fraternity, but people call it the football frat anyway... maybe because of the alliteration? Or maybe this place used to be a fraternity house a really long time ago.

I don't know the history, but this house is kind of famous around campus. The team hangs here on a regular basis, they have frequent parties, and it's usually filled with members of Greek Row because this house is less than a block away from it.

I glance down the street, scratching my arm as nerves scatter through me.

"Get to it, Lani." I order myself forward, and five seconds later, I'm knocking on the old oak door.

It's only then that I notice the time and mutter under my breath. It's only just seven o'clock. That's way too early for a house call.

Social etiquette nearly has me turning away, but then the lock flicks and a handsome guy with a square face, swooshed-back hair, and a panty-melting smile appears.

"Hi, there." He takes me in, his eyes skimming my body from head to toe before giving me an appreciative grin. "How can I help you?"

"Uh... hi..."

Dammit, this is the worst idea ever! Just leave, Lani!

"Zan the Man!" someone calls from inside the house. "Who is it?"

"I'm not sure. All she's said is 'uh' and 'hi!'" The guy gives me a teasing smile as I tense at the sound of clomping feet approaching the door.

"Well, hey there, angel." A blond giant grins down at me, and I've never felt so small in my life.

"Don't go scaring her off, Wily. Come on, man." The shorter guy whacks the back of his hand against Wily's chest.

I swallow and try to ease my nerves by guessing which positions they play. Wily has got to be a lineman—he's too big to be anything else—whereas Mr. Smiles here looks more like a quarterback or wide receiver.

You know you still haven't said anything, right?

Talk or leave!

My urgent brain snaps me back to focus, and I suddenly blurt, "I was at a party here. Back in February and..." I pause and rally my courage. "Something... unpleasant... happened to me." I swallow and force the last of the words out. "I'm not sure if you can help me or not, but I'm trying to ID the guy. I mean, I think I know who it is, but I'm trying to find some kind of proof. A witness statement or..." My voice trails off as I finally take in their expressions.

Their flirty smiles have disappeared, both of them staring at me with a serious intensity that's unnerving.

The big guy looks like my news is causing him some kind of pain while this Zan the Man guy looks ready to throttle something.

"We don't tolerate that kind of fucked-up shit at our parties." His voice has dropped to deep and dangerous. "Was it a Cougar?"

I shake my head. "He doesn't go to Nolan U. If it's the person I suspect, he's a student at Lennox."

They both let out derisive snorts and shake their heads. "We hate those guys."

"All of them?" I raise my eyebrows.

"Yes," they growl in unison.

I bite my lips together, then try for a smile. "So, it's a long shot, but would you mind if I asked you a few questions? I just need to figure out a way to prove he was here that night. To prove I'm not losing my mind. That the person who... did that to me... is the one I think it is."

The shorter man takes in a long, slow breath, then nods. "I can do you one better." Stepping back, he beckons me in with a tip of his head. "Come on in."

CHAPTER 50
ASHER

My alarm beeps incessantly, forcing me out of a heavy sleep.

Man, I had no idea how desperately I needed it. I must have full-on blacked out, my body desperate for some recuperation after so many nights of stress and worry.

Not that the stress wasn't still lingering last night, but having Lani in my bed made all the difference. Doing it all slow and intimate like that before going to sleep probably helped too. I was as relaxed as I could have been, and my body took advantage of that and threw me into a nighttime coma.

Hitting the snooze button, I roll over with a sleepy yawn, about to pull Lani into my arms... except she's not there. When I find the empty mattress beside me, my eyes ping open and I sit up with a start.

"Lani?" I call toward the bathroom, but there's no response.

Scratching my bedhead, I shake off the last of my sleepiness and fling the covers off me. I'm still naked, so I throw on a pair of boxers before walking out to the man cave in search of her.

She's not there.

And she's not in the kitchen or the dining room.

She's not playing pool or darts. She's not watching TV or curled up on the patio with a book.

I even go upstairs to check the bathroom in case she didn't want to wake me with a shower, but when I get there, Liam is walking out the door, giving me his fresh-faced morning smile.

"Hey, man."

I grunt at him, running back downstairs to check my room for a note. But I don't see anything. The man cave is empty, with zero evidence of her even being here last night.

"Great," I mutter, trying not to let my annoyance get the better of me.

But what the fuck?

Why'd she just take off without saying goodbye?

Unplugging my phone, I press her name on my screen and figure a text can be ignored. But not a fucking phone call.

She makes me wait five rings before finally answering.

"Hey, babe."

She sounds nervous, which puts me on immediate alert and probably makes my words a lot snappier than I mean them to be. "Where are you?"

"Um…"

"Why'd you just take off?"

"I didn't want to wake you." I hear the catch in her voice, and my eyes narrow as I stalk to my closet and start pulling out my clothes for the day.

"Where are you right now?"

"Well, I…" She tuts. "The thing is…" She sighs again, and now my internal alarm system is going nuts, because Lani does not struggle to articulate herself. Ever.

"Boo," I grit out, struggling to keep my emotions in check. I have no idea why my insides are raging, but something is off. "I need you tell me what's going on."

"Okay, fine, but I'm safe."

"That's not helping." I shake my head. "Why do I need to worry about your safety right now?"

"You don't." Her tone gets sharp. "That's what I'm saying."

Snapping my eyes shut, I fist the shirt in my hand and squeeze the crap out of it. "You don't tell someone you're safe unless you're worried they think you might not be. Where are you?" It's impossible not to raise my voice.

She pauses, then clears her throat. "I'm at the football frat… trying to find some kind of evidence."

"You… What?" My eyebrows pop high. "You're there?"

"Yes."

"Right now?" My voice pitches as I put her on speakerphone and start throwing on my clothes with an urgency that no doubt looks comical.

"Yes. I just said I was here."

"With all those guys? By yourself!"

"Asher, seriously, I'm fine."

"If even one of them tries to touch you," I growl, wrestling with my belt buckle, which is being a stubborn ass and not finding the correct hole. "Put them on the phone!"

CHAPTER 51
LEILANI

Asher's indignant rage is maybe a little funny. If he wasn't so worried about me, I'd probably laugh, because he's seriously making a big deal out of nothing.

So far, these football players have been nothing but helpful and sweet. Right now, we're sitting at the dining room table, a laptop open in front of us as Wily types in his password.

With an apologetic wince, I pass my phone to Zander, who is the quarterback. I found that out a few minutes ago.

"What?" He stares at the phone.

"My boyfriend wants to have a quick word."

He gives me a dubious frown before taking the phone and pressing it against his ear. "Hello?" He flinches, his face going through a myriad of expressions—surprise, confusion, irritation. "Can you just take a breath for a second? You're gonna pop a blood vessel." He sighs and rolls his eyes. "We don't do that shit here." His irritation comes back in a flash. "Hey! It wasn't one of my guys... Yeah, well, that's why we're helping her!" He clenches his jaw, and I cringe as I hear Asher's muffled tone rise a few notches higher. "Fine... Yes... You have my word."

Hanging up with a definitive tap to my screen, he thrusts the phone back at me and mutters, "Your boyfriend's paranoid."

"Protective," I correct him, doing my best to stand up for Asher, who has not had the wake-up he was probably hoping for.

Poor guy. I didn't even think about that when I snuck out of the house. I should have left a note.

"You know, after what happened to you—" Wily turns with a gentle smile. "—I don't blame him. If I had myself a woman and she was violated, I'd be on the warpath."

"Thank you," I murmur, wondering what this gentle giant would look like if he actually got mad.

It's hard to picture, to be honest. Even though he's a tall beast of a man, his gaze is as sweet as his shy, dopey smile.

Zander crosses his arms and quietly agrees. "Yeah, me too." His eyebrows buckle. "And I hate that it happened here. There are usually a few of us on patrol, looking out for this kind of shit." He winces. "There was an incident or two at this place a few years back. Before we got here." He points between himself and Wily. "Anyway, the team was getting a rep, and it was pretty bad."

"Our new coach won't tolerate any bullshit." Wily raises his eyebrows. "We've got to be perfection on and off the field or we're gone."

Zander nods. "So, we're really vigilant at our parties. I hate the idea of chicks feeling like they can't come here and be safe, you know? We always have a guy manning the drinks area, checking for roofies, that kinda stuff."

"I wasn't roofied." I cringe, then have to tell the part of the story that I hate so much. "I went willingly. I thought I wanted..." My voice trails off as I shake my head. "But then I changed my mind." I work my jaw to the side. "Unfortunately, he didn't agree with my decision."

"He should have stopped." Zander's voice is low and dangerous again.

"Not to sound like some sicko, but it makes me wish we had cameras in the bedrooms, you know?" Wily looks to Zander, who is obviously still fuming over what happened to me.

"At least we have them in the main areas. We might be able to spot some footage of you with this guy."

"Yeah, we were dancing for a while." I point toward the living room, which is through the opposite archway on the other side of the house. Because of its age, the place is broken up into smaller rooms, although from memory, a few walls must have been taken out, because I'm sure there's a much larger area going out to the pool and patio.

"There's the hallway cameras too," Wily murmurs. "There might be a shot of you going in or coming out of one of the rooms. Do you remember which one you were in?"

I reluctantly scour my memories and come up empty-handed. There's a serious black patch between him walking out of the room and me getting back to my dorm.

"Thankfully, the system we got set up keeps footage for six months, so there'll definitely be something from the party." Wily starts typing, then tuts. "Hey, Grady!" His voice booms through the house. "Did you change the password on the security system thing?"

"Why you wanna know?" a voice from upstairs filters down to us.

"Because he wants to access it, dumbass!" Zander shouts back.

"Who you calling dumb, fuck-knuckle?"

Zander face splits with an instant grin, his shoulders shaking with laughter as feet come thundering down the stairs and a shirtless black guy with an eight-pack and biceps to die for strolls into the room.

"Who's this?" He points at me.

"Lani." I point at myself, feeling kind of awkward as he stares me down like he's trying to figure out if I'm trouble or a good time.

"Stop gawking at her, man." Zander lightly taps him with the back of his hand. "We're helping her out." His tone is clipped, and after a shared look that must be some kind of silent conversation, Grady accepts his vague answer without question.

Nudging Wily out of the way, he takes a seat at the table and taps something onto the keyboard. "What are we looking for here?" He glances up at Zander.

"A party back in February." Zander turns to me. "Remember the date?"

"Seventeenth." It'll be burned into my brain for the rest of eternity.

Grady nods and starts doing a search. I gnaw on my lip while I wait him out, then hold my breath as he nods, looking up to Zander again.

I rise from my seat, ready to move around the table for a closer look, but he holds up his hand to stop me.

"Your man-beast asked if we could please wait for him."

I snort and shake my head. "I doubt he said please."

Another smile flashes across his face, and he joins me in the whole headshaking thing.

And then someone's pounding on the door, barking to be let in.

"Ah, my love." I kind of laugh out the words, then cringe when Wily answers the door.

"Hi, there." His tone is warm and welcoming.

Asher's... not so much. "Let me the fuck in!"

"All right, all right, hockey boy, calm down."

"Wily!" he growls. "If you weren't friends with Ethan and Liam, I would smash your face in right now!"

Wily laughs. "I'd like to see you try, man."

"Move!" Asher booms.

"Okay, okay." The giant steps aside, giving Asher room to shove past him.

His steps are fast and agitated. "Where is she?"

"In the dining room."

"This way, jackass!" Zander calls out to him, and I cringe. Is the name-calling really necessary?

Asher storms in, his face mottled with anger as he takes in the scene. It's like he was expecting to find me tied to the table while the football team took turns with me or something.

"Baby, I'm fine," I reassure him.

His nostrils flare, and he lets out a huff through his nose before walking across to me, crouching down by my side and scanning my face like he's looking for a lie.

I raise my eyebrows and try to calm him down with a gentle smile. "They're helping me... because I asked them to."

He clenches his jaw and nods, lightly squeezing the back of my neck. "Please don't do this to me again," he whispers. "Waking up without you fucking sucks. Finding out you've gone *alone* to the... the place where it happened?" His expression crumples with a look of anguish that makes me feel bad.

I touch his cheek. "I wasn't sure if I'd even be able to find anything I could use." My face bunches. "And I wasn't sure if you wanted to hear it if I did. I mean, you know... if I'm right about who I think it is."

His swallow is thick and he blinks, resting his hand

on my knee as he slowly stands. "I'm in this with you, boo. All the way. No matter how fucked-up it is. No matter how much it hurts."

Giving his arm a grateful squeeze, I then turn to Grady and nod. "Okay, let's do this."

CHAPTER 52
ASHER

So, it's safe to say I lost my mind for a lil' minute there. I don't know what came over me. Raw fear, maybe? The thought of Lani being here unprotected sent me into a fucking spiral. Walking in to find her safe and sound was the biggest relief.

But now I'm tensing up again, agitation sizzling through me as I move behind Grady Newman, the best running back in Nolan U's history. The guy's gonna go far and fast. He's a bullet on the field. Not that I'm a huge football watcher, but I've heard about Grady, and I've checked out some clips online. He and Zander Donahue seem to work on the same frequency or something, because on the field, they're hard to beat.

I give the quarterback a little side-eye. He meets my gaze, and I nod at him. Just a minimal movement to say thanks. He raises his eyebrows at me, telling me I had nothing to worry about in the first place.

Okay, so I overreacted.

But with all the shit going down right now, I'm on edge.

I'm allowed to be protective of my woman!

Sliding my hand down her back, I find a home for it on the curve of her hip, curling my fingers around her and feeling like I need the support as Grady fast-forwards through footage of the party.

"There I am." Lani's voice is small but definitive.

She points at the screen, and I lean in to study her black-and-white image. She looks gorgeous, decked out in a little black dress that's sexy as sin, and smiling at someone. Shit, the quality of this footage is amazing.

"How much does this gear cost?" I murmur. "The quality is..."

"Yeah, it was installed last year when there was that prank war going on." Zander scoffs and shakes his head. "I don't know if you guys heard about it, but we had a few break-ins, and there's only so much whipped cream and slime on the walls that you can come home to, right? So, we got the best cameras we could find, and Grady here set it all up for us."

I nod, impressed. "You catch the bastards?"

"We did." Zander's smile is pure satisfaction, and Wily starts laughing.

"Oh, we got those frat boys good." He tucks a lock of blond hair behind his ear, looking all proud, until his smile drops.

I follow his line of sight, glancing at Lani's ashen face, then jerking my eyes back to the screen.

"That's him," she rasps. "See me dancing?" She points at the screen.

I watch her body gyrating on the floor and feel the earth shift beneath my feet when Harvey moves in behind her.

Fuck. She was right.

It's him.

She shudders, her shoulders twitching.

"You don't have to watch this," I murmur.

"Yeah, I do." She nods. "I need to see it."

So we keep going. The air in the room gets sucked into oblivion, the silence ominous as we stand around the laptop, watching Lani dance, laugh, and make out with Harvey. My stomach churns at the way his hands rove her body. I hate that he touched her, that his tongue was in her mouth, that—

"You don't have to watch this." Lani looks to me with a desperate frown.

I squeeze her side and mutter, "Yeah, I do."

And so I remain by her side and watch in pure torture as they stumble off the dance floor together and head down the hallway.

They disappear off camera for a second, but then Grady clicks a few buttons and pulls up a new screen. It's a shot of a hallway upstairs, and we get there in time to see Harvey opening a door and pulling Lani in behind him.

The door clicks shut, and we have to watch other people milling around for a while.

"How long were you in there?" Grady glances over his shoulder.

"I don't know," Lani whispers, her head shaking in short, jerky movements.

I pull her a little closer, and she closes her eyes—maybe reliving what happened to her? This is killing me.

Zander shifts uncomfortably, and I look at him. He's staring at Lani with an agonized frown before his eyes dart back to the screen. "Fast-forward a little, man."

Grady does as he's told, and nine minutes later Harvey's walking out of the room. He shuts the door behind him, running a hand through his hair and straightening his shirt. Moving away from the door, he walks down the hallway, raising his chin at someone off-screen. You wouldn't know he'd just raped someone. He doesn't even look guilty. How the fuck does he do that?

Lani squirms, and I wonder if she's worried that the guys won't believe her claims. This footage so far is not doing anything to help her cause.

But then the door creeps open again and she shuffles into view.

And it's so fucking obvious, I want to break Harvey's neck.

She looks traumatized. Even from this camera angle you can tell. Her eyes are huge, darting up and unwittingly looking straight at the camera. She's in shock, glancing around like she's not really seeing anything. She wobbles on her heels as she tries to walk down the hall-way, almost like she's drunk, but then she wraps her arms around herself and shrinks, shuffling toward the stairs with a desolate look on her face.

My jaw is shaking as I watch this shit.

He did it.

It was Harvey, and I'm so furious right now, I can't even speak.

No one seems to be able to. Lani is full-on trembling beside me. She's trying to control it, wrapping her arms around herself, just like she did in the video.

I shift, nestling her against me so she can lean into my chest. Cupping the back of her head, I hide her face from the guys as she buries herself in my chest and lets out a quaking sob. Her fingers curl into my shirt as she quietly shudders against me.

I glance to my left and spot Zander's face. He's raging. Wily's looking pretty dark, too, as they share a look, and finally Grady mutters, "Who is that thundercunt?"

Tapping the screen, he looks up to his friends.

"He was an out-of-towner." Zander's voice is low and heavy. "Grades, make a copy of that footage. Put it on a flash drive, plus upload it to my iCloud." He looks to me. "I'll send it you."

"Thanks," I croak.

"Is there anything else we can do?" Wily's expression buckles as his eyes skim over Lani.

I shake my head. "We'll, um... take this to the police and see what comes of it."

"Does she remember his name?" Grady leans around me, trying to look at Lani. "Do you remember his name?"

"I know who it is," I growl.

Wily's lips part as he points at the laptop. "You know the guy?"

"Yeah." I nod, panic sizzling through me. It's an effort to push it down. I'm trying to contain a lot right now—outright fury is mixing with panic-inducing dread. I know what I have to do. It's not going to be pretty... and a whole bunch of people who I really care about will be affected.

Grady jumps up from his chair, heading out of the room, and I stand there, holding my girl. I share a few awkward looks with Wily and Zander, then flinch when the front door pops open.

Wily walks to the hallway, popping his head out to see who it is. "Carson. Shit, man, are you just getting home?" There's a soft grunt, and Wily shakes his head. "Hungover again, I see." He starts laughing, then booms, "Good morning, good morning, good morning!" He's singing at the top of his lungs.

Zander snickers and then starts laughing when Carson swears up a storm.

"Shut the fuck up, you moron!"

"Moron?" Zander shouts toward the hallway. "That's the best you can do? How much did you drink last night?"

"I hate you all!" Carson yells, thumping up the stairs. "May you all die in a pit of fiery... I don't know...

some shit that's hot and will burn your asses to the ground!"

"Sleep well, dude!" Wily calls after him.

"Fuck you!" Carson shouts back.

Zander starts laughing again, just a soft one that dies away when Wily turns back with a frown. "He's going to get kicked off the team if he doesn't watch it."

"I know." Zander sighs. "I'll have a talk with him when he's not hungover."

"Good luck finding that window." Wily rolls his eyes.

Zander grunts and shakes his head, crossing his arms when Grady walks back into the room. "Did you know Darren's still here?"

"What?" Zander's worried frown changes to a pissed-off scowl.

"Yeah, he's in the kitchen eating all of our cereal."

"What the fuck is with that guy? Does he not know how to go home already?"

Grady shrugs. "I told him to get lost, but he just grinned at me and kept chowing down."

Zander huffs, storming out of the room, and then we hear muffled conversation coming from what I assume is the kitchen. I can tell by his tone that Zander's not impressed with their squatter.

Grady slips the flash drive into the laptop and starts creating a clip of the footage we need.

"None of your business!" Zander's voice rises. "We're just helping her out. Now would you go the fuck home, please?"

"I was invited here."

"Carson wasn't even home last night! I get that you guys were friends in grade school, but you need to let it go. This is a football house, meaning only team members live here."

"But you've let me crash on your couch before." The guy appears in the doorway, glancing into the dining room and eyeing us up before Zander nudges him toward the front door.

"What can I say, we're generous like that, but it only goes so far." There's a click as I assume Zander opens the door. "Now go home and stop treating this place like your crib."

"Fine, whatever. I'll see you at the next party."

Zander doesn't respond, and a few seconds later, the door slams shut.

Zander stalks back into the room, scratching his head and looking pissed. "No more parties," he mutters.

"You say it, but you don't mean it." Grady snickers.

Wily grins, then shakes his head when he catches my eye. "Maybe it's not the worst idea."

"Don't stop partying on my account." Lani pulls away from me and looks at the guys. Her eyes are rimmed red and she's still looking really pale, but her voice has its strength back.

Zander shakes his head. "I don't like this place being filled all the time with people I don't know. Maybe we should be screening it more. If I'd known what that fucker was going to do to you, I never would have let him through the door."

"You can't know these things." Lani sucks in a breath, brushing a finger across her cheek. "I didn't go into that room knowing what was going to happen to me."

I clench my jaw, my muscles vibrating.

Zander catches my eye, and I can tell he gets it.

"And I want to thank you guys for your help."

They all tell her not to worry about it, and if there's more they can do, we just have to let them know.

She gives them a weak yet grateful smile, and I kiss her forehead, still struggling to contain this emotion crashing through me. I need to get out of here. I need to find Harvey. Right now.

Grady holds out the flash drive and Lani takes it, wrapping her fingers around the stick.

"I can email you the file as well," Grady murmurs, his fingers poised over the keyboard. "I'll put it in Zander's DropBox and send you the link."

"Okay." Lani trips and stumbles through her email address, having to correct herself twice. She winces and shakes her head. "My brain is mush right now."

"That's all right," he murmurs, and then we hear the whoosh and know the email is heading to her inbox.

After that, it's awkward. We've got to go, and there are pleasantries to be said. I don't know how to do this shit when all I can think about is killing my cousin.

"I'm really sorry this happened to you." Zander's voice is deep and sincere as he looks at Lani.

She nods.

"And like we said before, *anything* we can do to help, you know?"

"Yeah." She nods again and tries for another smile. "Thank you."

"You guys take care." Zander pats my shoulder as I walk past.

Wily opens the door for us, and I usher Lani down to my car. I hold the door for her, and she doesn't even protest. No comments about her capability and how I don't need to be so chivalrous all the time. She just slips into the passenger seat with murmured thanks, and I walk around to the driver's door, wrestling with shock and grief and rage and...

Yeah, I really have to kill Harvey.

CHAPTER 53
LEILANI

The deathly silence in the car is suffocating, and I don't know what to say. I don't feel like myself as I fidget with the flash drive in my hands and try to shake off the memories that took me out while watching that security footage.

I should be happy about this.

I have the evidence I need—the proof that what I felt when I saw Harvey that day was 100 perfect accurate and real. I hadn't gotten it wrong.

But the fact that I got it right is awful.

So awful.

Glancing at my boyfriend's face, I watch the muscle in his jaw tic as he clenches and unclenches his teeth. He's furious. His white-knuckle grip on the wheel, the way his breaths are short and kind of shallow. There's a lethal vibration coming off him, and I... I don't know what to say to make this better.

There's nothing to say.

I need to take this to the police, and Asher... shit, he'll probably need to start packing boxes.

Unless I don't go to the police.

I stare down at that flash drive, letting the turmoil whip through me.

Do I fight for justice and cause Asher all this pain, or do I—

"I'll take you to the police station. There's just something I need to do first." His voice is terse, but when he looks at me, his expression softens for just a minute. "Is that cool?"

"Y-Yeah. I mean, you don't have to take me. This is a lot, and I don't want to torture you unnecessarily. I can go on my own."

"You're not going on your own." His tone leaves no room for argument. I'd usually ignore this fact and spit back a little venom, but I just don't have it in me.

I'm drained. Exhausted.

I need this to be over.

But it won't be anytime soon.

Squeezing the flash drive, I shuffle in my seat to face him. "When you said there's something you need to do first, are you... talking about morning classes or...?"

His response is a nostril flare that makes me nervous. "I can drop you wherever you need to go, and we can meet up later, go to the station."

"Asher, where are you going?"

His jaw works to the side as he pulls up outside

Huxley Hall. "I'll see you later. Call me when you're out of class."

"I'm not getting out of this car until you tell me what you're up to."

He huffs, a sharp, irritated sound. His finger taps on the steering wheel, and I bore him with a look that I hope is unrelenting enough.

"Asher, come on. What—"

"I have to go see Harvey."

My stomach sinks, and I can feel the blood draining from my face as I gape at him. "Why? What are you going to say?"

He turns to me with the most dangerous look I have ever seen. "Nothing."

I gape at him. "Asher, I—"

"Get out of the car, Leilani."

I stare at him for a moment longer, trying to come up with a valid argument to stop him, but my brain is dead. My mouth is void of any decent words, and even if I could say something... I don't think it'd be enough.

I can't stop him. The look on his face is kind of scary, so I slip out of the car. As soon as I shut my door, the tires squeal and he takes off down the road.

"Shit," I whisper. Why did I just let that happen? I never acquiesce without some kind of fight, and I let one lethal look push me out the door? "Fuck," I mutter, wrenching my phone out of my pocket and searching for any number I can call.

I start with Asher, because maybe I can talk him into

turning around, but he, of course, doesn't pick up. I should have known he wouldn't.

Turning my back to Huxley Hall, I start hustling down the sidewalk and turn left toward campus. I scour my phone in vain. I don't have contacts for any of the Hockey House guys, so I go for Mikayla's number. She doesn't pick up, so I try Caroline instead. She stayed with Casey last night, I think.

Her phone goes straight to voicemail, which probably means she's in class... where I should be.

I check my watch and swear again. I need to contact someone and tell them what Asher is up to. The way he was looking, I wouldn't put it past my boyfriend to end Harvey on the spot. I can't let him do that. As much as Harvey deserves a good swift kick in the balls... and maybe a little castration, I don't want my boyfriend getting in trouble.

Enough shit is gonna rain down on him as we pursue this matter with the police. I don't want Asher ending up in a jail cell with blood on his knuckles.

Picking up my pace, I start sprinting for Hockey House, hoping one of the guys will be there. I need Ethan. Or Liam. They can race after Asher and talk some sense into him, right? Maybe they can stop him before he does something insane.

I make it to Hockey House completely out of breath and ring the doorbell incessantly, trying the door handle and grunting in frustration when it won't budge.

"Is anyone home?" I shout, starting my doorbell routine again.

A dog starts yapping just as a voice calls from inside the house.

"I'm coming!" I think it's Rachel. "Calm down, Fezzi, it's all right. We've just got ourselves a visitor."

Her pretty face appears behind the wood. She's holding Fezzik, who's still barking up a storm and wriggling in her arms. She looks over his little head, her confusion turning to a smile that quickly drops to a frown.

"Are you okay?"

I walk past her, frantically moving into the dining/kitchen area and scoping out the place. "Are any of the guys home?"

"No, they're all in class." She puts Fezzik down and he scampers across the tiles, sniffing my ankles while his tail goes nuts. His little paws come up to my knees as he stretches to sniff my legs, but I'm too stressed out to appreciate how cute he's being.

"I need to find someone. Asher needs help."

"What's the matter?" Rachel's eyes round as she reaches for her phone.

"He's gone after Harvey." I show her the flash drive in my hand. "We now have proof that he was the guy at the party."

"Oh no." Her expression crumples. "He wouldn't have taken that well."

"Nope." I shake my head, my chest starting to heave

as panic tries to take me out. "We need to go after him and stop him before he does something that'll get him in trouble."

"Do you know where Asher's going? Or where Harvey is?" Rachel holds the phone up to her ear, then frowns and hangs up with a huff. "Liam's not answering. Everyone's in class right now."

"I know," I whine. "I'm supposed to be there, too, but I can't just—" I click my fingers and point at her. "Can I borrow one of their trucks or something? Maybe I can chase Asher down."

"Do you even know where he is?"

"He's probably gone to Lennox or—"

There's a knock at the door, and we both look toward the entryway, then back at each other.

Rachel's eyebrows dip together as she wanders to the door. It's probably a Jehovah's Witness or someone collecting money for charity. I hope it's the latter. I have some cash in my wallet, and we can get rid of them quickly and get back to the problem of finding Asher.

"Hi. Can I help you?" Rachel's always so polite, her sweet smile appearing automatically.

"Yeah, I'm looking for Asher. I need to talk to him."

My heart does a hard double tap, then lodges in my throat.

I know that voice.

Shit, it's Harvey.

I need to scream at Rachel to shut the door. Lock it! Bar it!

But her pleasant smile is still in place. "Uh, he's not home right now. Can I take a message?"

"Yeah, that's cool. Unless it's okay for me to come in and wait for him. I won't be any trouble." His voice is so cordial and sweet. So fake! "I can just read a book in his man cave or something."

Rachel hesitates and glances back through the archway to look at me. I shake my head, and she looks back to this unwelcome visitor and politely tells him, "I don't actually know you, so..."

"That's okay, sweetie." Harvey softens his tone, and my skin starts to crawl. "Man, you're beautiful. I bet people tell you that all the time." He sounds so fucking sincere. "What's your name?"

Rachel pauses, and I would rather slit my throat than have her answer that question.

A fury like nothing I've ever felt before rises inside me —an erupting volcano. He will not touch Rachel. He will never touch any innocent woman again!

Storming into the entranceway, I fire a glare at Harvey's flirtatious smile and warn Rachel, "Don't say a word."

Harvey's eyes bulge, and I know he recognizes me immediately.

As much as it terrifies me, I raise my chin and keep my glare in place. "Get out of here, Harvey."

Rachel gasps and tries to start closing the door, but he grabs the edge and forces it back open. She's not expecting it and lets out a little gasp as she trips backward. She finds her feet before falling over, but not in time to stop Harvey from charging at me with a spit-filled rant. "You are so out of line with everything you've started here!"

Fezzik starts barking, his little puppy growl sounding way too feeble against this big, mean man. Flicking out his foot, Harvey lightly kicks him aside and Fezzik yelps, scampering away to cower behind Rachel.

She picks him up, soothing him with soft words while Harvey decides to yell some more.

"I'm not going to let you get away with it! You can't just make up lies about me and drag my name through the mud!"

I shuffle back before he can touch me, fisting the flash drive in my hand and willing myself to stay strong. I need this healthy dose of rage to keep burning. I won't fall back into the pit of fear that's held me hostage for so long.

He's a liar... and a rapist! And a... a shit-eating fucknugget!

And he has no power over me. Not anymore.

Harvey wouldn't dare touch me in this place. I remind myself of that as I ping my shoulders back and tell it to him straight. "I've got evidence now. And I won't stop until you go down in a burning ball of flames, you arrogant piece of shit!"

CHAPTER 54
ASHER

I was halfway to Lennox when I got a call from Aunt Carla. She sounded worried and a little annoyed.

"You haven't spoken to Harvey since you stormed out of my house, have you?"

"No," I spit into the speakerphone, wishing I hadn't answered. My stupid brain went to autopilot, and I answered without thinking. I should hang up.

"Well, he told me he was going to see you today, and I can't reach him. Can you please get him to call me when he gets to your place?"

"Why is he coming to see me?" I bark, then pull to the side of the road and do a quick U-turn. Looks like I'll be getting blood on the floor at Hockey House, then.

Aunt Carla sighs. "Look, Asher, he's really cut up about what you're accusing him of. I don't think you've taken into consideration how awful this has been for all of us. You can't just go throwing around accusations like this. It's very damaging."

"So is raping someone!"

She goes quiet for a second, and then her voice trembles as she responds to me. "My son would never do that."

"Oh yeah, well, I've just seen security footage of him leading my girlfriend into a room, so we now know it *was* him at the party and she did get it right."

"Security footage?" Her voice goes light and wispy.

"Don't pretend like you don't know how he is with women. I'm sure this isn't the first accusation that's been thrown at him."

"None of them have stuck." Aunt Carla gives herself away. "He's just gotten into a bad habit of spending time with girls who want to take him down when he doesn't return their affections."

"Oh, you are so full of shit. How can you be so blind about him?"

"He's my son. And he's a good man!" Her voice cracks, and I feel the sadness wash through me.

"Yeah, I used to think so too."

"He wants to make this right with you. It's all just a big misunderstanding, I'm telling you. Give him a chance and listen to his side. Please."

I grit my teeth, making it hard to spit out the words. "There will be no explanation good enough for what he did to Lani."

"Please, Asher. I know he wants to talk to you. Don't

give in to your raging emotions. Just take a breath and give him a chance. And after that, can you get him to call me, please? I've left a message on his voicemail and texted him twice. I need him here for a family dinner tonight. We've got some potential clients who need charming, and he's always so good at that. They've got a daughter just a bit younger than you guys, and I know she'll love him. It could be—"

"You are so fucking delusional!" I shout, hanging up before I have to hear any more of this shit.

Pressing the gas, I speed back to Hockey House and hope Aunt Carla's right. If Harvey's waiting for me on the doorstep, I can haul him inside and give him a piece of my fist. Or better yet, I can do it on the lawn so we don't get blood on the walls.

Anger continues to rage through me like a toxic poison, and I make it back to Hockey House in record time.

The front door is open, which confuses me a little, but then I spot Baxter's car in the driveway.

I pull in behind it and am surprised to see Baxter's door pop open.

He lumbers out of the car, grabbing his bag and slinging it over his shoulder.

"What are you doing home?" I jump out of my truck. "And why is the door open?"

"I don't know." He shrugs. "Rachel was here when I left. Maybe she's airing out the place." He lopes up beside me. "And I'm home because I forgot my charger and my dying laptop can't even go an hour on battery anymore."

We walk across the front lawn, and as we reach the door, I hear a woman shout, "You can't scare me anymore! Now step back!"

"That's Lani," I whisper, jerking for the door and racing inside.

Just as I round the corner, I take in the scene—Rachel is standing there holding a squirming Fezzik, darting worried looks at my girlfriend, who has never looked so pissed off. She's shouting up at a guy in front of her and —oh fuck! That's Harvey!

"My parents have the best lawyers in Denver, you little bitch! You think some security footage is going to stick? You wanted me that night!"

I stifle a roar as I go to step forward and end this fucker, but Baxter snags my jacket before I can move.

Holding up his phone, he shows me he's recording, so against every instinct in my body, I play it smart and stay where I am.

But if he lays one fucking finger on her...

Rachel spots us over Harvey's shoulder and I can see her instantly relax, but my cousin is too busy ranting to even notice her relief.

"I may have gone willingly into that room, but I told you to stop, and I know you heard me, because you said, 'I'm not done with you yet.'"

My insides surge, and I can taste the acid in my throat. She didn't tell me that part.

"You can't prove that." Harvey snickers. "Face it, you wanted me to fuck you. You were begging for it."

He goads her, and I look to Baxter. *Can I kill him now?* I silently ask him, but he holds up his finger.

"So I did what you wanted." Harvey's tone is smug. Arrogant. So fucking punchable. I want to lodge my fist down his throat!

"You're so full of shit," Lani spits, and I can see her struggling to keep it together. This can't go on much longer. I don't care if Baxter's getting gold, I can't watch Harvey treating my woman this way.

"Girls never really know what they want, so I take charge and give them what they need. Your tight little ass deserved a good fucking, so I plowed you like the pro I am. If you want to call that rape, then you go right ahead, but bringing charges against me will turn into a living nightmare for you. Nothing sticks to me. I'm Teflon, baby."

Lani's eyes spark with determination, and I swear I've never loved her more. "I don't give a shit what you think you are. I'm not afraid to fight you on this. I will stand against you for as long as I have to. I'll do it for myself and all the other women you've violated. I'll do it for all the women who have yet to meet you."

A growl rumbles in his throat. "You fucking bitch! You wanted it!"

"I told you to stop!"

"You didn't mean it!" Harvey thunders, oblivious to

the thick pulse of shock that follows in the wake of his confession.

Lani lets out a soft gasp. "You admit it."

"I'm not admitting shit."

"But you just did." Lani's surprise is morphing into a triumphant smile, but it doesn't have time to form, as Harvey lets out a lethal growl and reaches for her throat.

"Now," Baxter snarls, and I release the roar that's been building inside me, lunging at my cousin with the full force of my rage.

Snatching his jacket, I pull him back, spinning him around and throwing him to the floor. He lands with a shocked "Oomph!" while Lani lets out a shaky breath, like she was keeping it together just long enough for me to step in.

Fezzik starts barking, and Rachel struggles to hold him while I check Lani's face.

She nods at me, resting her hand on her neck. "I'm fine."

As soon as I know she'll be okay, I turn back to my cousin, grabbing his shirt and hauling him to his feet.

"Let's go," I bark, yanking him out the door with a herculean strength that is born from pure, uncut fury.

CHAPTER 55
LEILANI

My knees give out and I sink against the back of the couch, forcing air into my lungs as Baxter shuffles toward me.

"I got it all." He holds up his phone.

I nod. "Thanks for that." I spotted him out of the corner of my eye when Harvey was telling me I needed a good fucking—asshole!—and it helped keep me grounded.

But now I feel like the floor is crumbling beneath me. I grip the edge of the couch and fight the urge to throw up.

"It'll be enough, right?" Rachel looks between us, stroking the top of Fezzik's head. The little pup has stopped squirming now that the bad man has been taken away. "I mean, he kind of buried himself with all that stuff he said to you. He basically confessed."

"I hope it's enough." I rest my hand on my forehead,

my insides trembling. It's still a case of he said/she said, because he could easily go back on his word, but surely this footage will only help my case. Pair that with what I got from the football frat house and there's no way the police can't take this further.

They wanted evidence, and now I have lots of it.

"Come on." Baxter tips his head toward the entryway. "Let's take you to the station. I'll drive you."

"You sure?" I glance up, thrown by the offer. It is Baxter I'm talking to, after all.

A small smile curves his lips. "I've got you, Lani. Can't let this kind of shit stand with the Hockey House girls. We've got to look after you guys."

His wink and shy smile are so unexpected, I blink, then cast a surprised look at Rachel.

She's grinning up at Baxter like she knew all along that he was made of shortbread and not sauerkraut.

With a shaky laugh, I force my body off the couch, walking to the door on slightly wobbly legs. But if I found the strength to face off with my rapist, I can find the strength to head to the police station and get this done right.

I can do this.

I can stop Harvey from hurting anyone else.

Unless Asher kills him before he can be arrested.

CHAPTER 56
ASHER

I threw Harvey into my car and am now driving him back to Denver. His mom wanted him home for dinner, well, she can fucking have him!

He hasn't said a word, and he must have been kind of shocked by my show of strength and anger, because after a very short scuffle in the driveway—which ended with my fist in his nose—he slumped into the passenger seat of my truck. He's been using his jacket sleeve to stanch the bleeding from his left nostril, but he hasn't said a damn thing. He hasn't even argued about leaving his car at Hockey House, and he hasn't tried to open the door and roll out either.

The farther we go, the thicker the tension in the car gets.

He keeps sniffing, then opening his mouth as if to talk before clenching his jaw again.

Little fucker probably doesn't even know what to say, and I'm too pissed off to even rant at him.

To be honest, I don't really know what I'm doing. As much as I want to haul this asshole straight to the police station, I'm not sure it'll do any good yet. I kind of want the cops to come and arrest him somewhere public because he deserves that humiliation. So instead, I'm dropping this douchenugget off to his parents, and they can figure out what to do with him.

Knowing them, they'll back him up, but this will be my chance to tell it to them straight.

They can't keep covering for him. I don't care who their lawyers are. They may be the best in Denver, but my parents have the best lawyers in New York. And all I can hope is that they'll back me and my girl when it comes down to it.

My insides are aching and swelling with this toxic feeling that makes me want to throw up, but I push a little harder on the gas and make it to the Carmichaels' home in record time.

It hurts to pull into the driveway. I used to love this place. Every time I drove in here, it felt like I was coming home.

But not anymore.

That sensation has evaporated now, and I'm left with a cold fury... and a sick dread.

This is it.

I'm about to lose Hockey House. I'm about to lose my

Denver family. I'm about to make a mess for the people I care about most.

But the woman I love needs me to do this.

And I want to.

For her.

And for all the other women who've been affected by this shitgibbon.

"Let's go," I spit, shouldering my door open.

Harvey gives me a cautious side-eye, but I hear his heavy sigh as I step out of the car, and he's soon following me into the house.

"Oh, good! You made it. Asher passed on my message, then." Aunt Carla's bright voice fades as she rounds the corner and spots us.

"Harvey?" She rushes toward him. "What happened?"

"Asher punched me," he spits.

I clench my jaw, my upper lip curling as I throw him the darkest look known to man.

My aunt spears me a sharp glare before wrapping her arm around Harvey's waist. "Let's get you some ice, sweetie."

I scoff and shake my head. "He doesn't deserve ice."

"What?" She spins, the word flying out of her mouth like a sharp slap. "You'd better check yourself, Asher Bensen."

I rise to her fierce look, my sneakers squeaking on the tiled floor as I slowly approach her. "I've got evidence now."

"Some security footage?" She scoffs at me like I'm pitiful. "That's not going to hold up."

My shoulder hitches. "Well, maybe the recording of Harvey yelling at my girlfriend, telling her she needed a good fuck and then admitting that he heard her say stop will help."

"I never said that!" Harvey snaps.

My scorn is potent as I shake my head at him. "You told her she didn't mean it when she said stop, which means you heard her fucking say it! You raped her, Harvey. You can lie to yourself as much as you want, but the truth is... you raped her."

Aunt Carla's cheeks pale, and she glances at her son before dipping her eyes to the floor.

Harvey's expression buckles with pain, but it doesn't last long. Uncle Hayes walks into the room. His clipped steps seem to echo off the marble, and I brace myself for battle.

"What's going on here?" He looks between us, his lips flatlining when he spots Harvey's red nose and the dried blood crusting on his upper lip. "I see you boys have had a disagreement."

I let out a harsh laugh. "I don't even know you guys anymore." Pain slices through me. "I used to adore you. I used to wish you were my parents and that Harvey was my brother. I used to beg my parents to let me stay here for longer."

Aunt Carla's expression softens for a moment, like she can't remember why she's mad at me, but then I remind her, because that's why I'm fucking here, right?

"But I can't be a part of this family anymore. Not if you're gonna keep covering for him." I point at Harvey. "He's a rapist. Why are you trying to protect him? Do you not care about the girls he's ruined? Do you not give a shit that the next party he goes to, another innocent woman is going to fall victim to him?"

"They don't all say no!" Harvey spits. "They don't all tell me to stop."

"Harvey, shut up." His father throws him a look of pure disgust before turning back to me. "It's loyalty, Asher. He's my son. I'll defend him no matter what."

"Well, you're not doing him any favors." My voice rises, echoing back to me off these cold, pristine walls. "He needs help!"

"And you need to get out." Uncle Hayes's glare is so hard and unrelenting.

I don't even know this man anymore.

How could it all change so quickly?

How could they do this?

I shake my head, a deep sadness sweeping through me as I frown at my family and realize how delusional I've been. It's like I've had blinders on or something.

They were so great. So perfect.

But they're assholes, thinking they're above it. Thinking the rules don't apply to them.

Fuck this.

I don't even want to be related to them anymore.

Shaking my head, I give them a pained frown and turn to walk away.

"Remember what I told you," Uncle Hayes calls after me. "Don't go doing anything stupid. You drop this nonsense, or you're out on your ass."

I slowly spin back to glare at him.

He gives me a pointed look, sliding his hands into his pockets. "You and all your little friends. Homeless." He almost looks smug, and my fingers curl into a fist before I can stop them.

The urge to beat his ass is so overpowering, but I fight my instincts. Hitting him won't do me or Lani any favors. I have to be aboveboard on this shit, right? Do everything in my power to ensure that Harvey does go down for what he did.

Licking my lips, I let out a short, disbelieving laugh and shake my head.

"I'm going to do this the right way," I assure my uncle.

He smiles at me, his eyes glittering like he knew I'd cave.

Little does his know the shitstorm that's coming.

Harvey snorts, standing a little taller and looking as smug as his father does.

Gone is the wounded victim in front of his mommy. He's back to being the arrogant fuck who raped my girlfriend.

The way he spoke to Lani rings through me again, and I let the anger swell and surge, stepping forward to deliver a final goodbye before walking out of this place for good.

My punch lands true, whipping Harvey's head back with a snap. He groans, grabbing for his nose again and tumbling onto this butt.

Aunt Carla lets out a horrified gasp as Uncle Hayes grabs the back of my jacket before I can hammer my fist into Harvey's face again.

"You are so done!" he yells at me. "This is over!"

"It was over the second he raped my woman." I shove him off me, turning on the man with venom. "He's not going to get away with it anymore. And that punch was the least of what he deserves!" I point at my cousin still writhing on the floor. "And you know the sickest part about all this?" I look between my aunt and uncle. "You know I'm right, but you won't do a fucking thing about it."

Straightening my jacket, I throw Harvey one more disgusted glare before shaking my head and walking out of that house, knowing I'll never step foot inside it again.

It kills me.

But I did the right thing.

And that's fucking liberating.

CHAPTER 57
LEILANI

With Baxter towering beside me like a silent guardian angel and the two lots of evidence I had, the police took me way more seriously. We spoke to a detective this time, which helped. He was kind and calm, listening carefully and writing notes while I spoke.

As I left the station with Baxter and Rachel flanking me, I felt lighter somehow.

Harvey's cutting words and vicious snarling have slipped away. Even talking about the rape this time was somehow easier. It wasn't pleasant, but I was able to recount that party in more detail than I ever had. I was able to talk about it without fighting the urge to puke all over the desk.

Detective Callahan assured me he would be following through on this, and I could leave it with him. Rachel insisted that he keep me updated, her usually mousy voice firm and unrelenting.

I guess people can surprise you.

Baxter holds the door for me, and I slip into his car. Rachel climbs in the back and buckles up, resting her head against the window with a tired sigh. I get it. I'm exhausted too.

"Thank you both," I croak, then clear my throat and try again. "I really appreciate you being there with me."

"Of course." Rachel leans forward to squeeze my shoulder. "You can always count on us."

I look over my shoulder with a watery smile, then glance at Baxter. "Do you think Asher's okay?"

He grunts, his left shoulder hitching. "I think he was about ready to kill his cousin, but I doubt he'll go that far." After reversing out of the parking space, he changes gears and spares me a glance. "He really loves you. Never seen the guy so protective before. I'm pretty sure he'd do anything for ya."

I wince. "That's partly what I'm afraid of. He's willing to give up *everything* for me, and I can't help feeling guilty about that."

"Don't waste your emotion on guilt. It's not your fault his cousin's a shithead."

"It's not his either," I mumble. "And his decision to stand by me affects everyone at Hockey House too." Rubbing my forehead with a shaky sigh, I feel the tension starting to build again.

"Look, at the end of the day, he wants you more than all of his family bullshit and... and so do we. Love can make people do crazy shit, but it also helps them figure out what's worth fighting for."

My lips part. I'm not sure I've ever heard Baxter say so many words in one go. I wonder if he's even aware of it.

Rachel shifts in the back seat, leaning forward as if transfixed by the marvel of what is happening right now.

"If Asher loves you, we all do. Hockey House is a family, and you're part of that now. If we get kicked out on our asses, we'll get up, brush ourselves off, and find someplace else to live."

I give him a weak smile. "I just don't want this to pull you guys apart."

He snickers and shakes his head. "We're stronger than that."

I blink, then glance in the back. Rachel looks like she's ready to cry. She has the biggest smile on her face as she gazes at Baxter in awe.

Seriously. This is like a phenomenon.

I wonder how far I can push it.

"Do you have a girlfriend who you'd do anything for?"

His jaw clenches, and he shakes his head.

Glancing at Rachel again, she gives me an eager nod, so I keep going. "I was just wondering if there's anybody you'll ever bring into the Hockey House family."

"Nope." He shakes his head more firmly this time.

"So, you want to stay a bachelor for the rest of your life?" Rachel's voice pitches with surprise.

He doesn't say anything, and I study the side of his face. "Is it that you... don't like... girls?"

He throws me a side-eye. "I like girls."

"Okay, so... what's with the look on your face, then? Why are you so determined to stay single?"

He clenches his jaw, his shoulder hitching.

"Oh, wait." My eyes round. "Have you been burned before? Is that it?"

His nostrils flare slightly, and I know I'm probing, so I try to throw the attention back on me for a moment.

"I get it. After what happened to me, I was determined to stay single for the rest of my life. I didn't want anybody, and I wasn't going to fall for some guy. I wouldn't let myself be that weak. But..." I let out a soft laugh. "Asher was meant to be mine, and every time I tried to fight it, I just felt worse. And then I finally let go... and it's been amazing."

"Same for me and Liam." Rachel grins, her smile dreamy. "When love comes a-knocking..."

"Do you girls have a point, or are you just trying to make me feel like shit?" Baxter grumbles.

"No." Rachel's eyes bulge. "That's not what we're trying to do at all. We just... If there's someone out there you want, well, we're just saying you should go for it." She looks to me for backup, and I clear my throat and angle my body to face him.

"She's right. We don't know what's happened to you in the past, but if there's any way we can help you get over it..." I leave the statement hanging, hoping he'll fill the space, but he doesn't, so I try for a different angle. "Or maybe there's a special person who you're too shy to connect with? I mean, could we help?"

He glances across at me, his shoulders deflating. "You're not gonna let up on this unless I spill, are you?"

I give him an apologetic smile, then shake my head. "You don't have to tell us. We just... want you to be happy."

"I am happy."

"Well, we want you to be even happier." Rachel beams from the back seat. "Come on, Bax. Let us in. We won't tell the guys if you don't want us to. We just want to know if the big, quiet goalie has himself a love interest."

She wiggles her eyebrows, looking adorably cute... enough to make Baxter's lips twitch. "No love interest, because..." His face washes with the saddest frown, his voice soft and broken when he finally admits, "I can't have the one I want. She's in love with someone else and they're married now, and..." He shrugs. "I'll never meet anyone else like her, so... I'll stay in my cave. I like my cave." His voice is getting gruff now, which makes it hard to believe him.

"What's her name?" Rachel whispers. "Does she go to Nolan?"

"No, she's from my hometown." He shakes his head, his expression turning gooey as he whispers, "And her name's Tamara Tan." The nostalgic smile on his face tells me he's walking back to a sweet time in his memory. I don't know if he had her once and lost her or if he loved her from afar and didn't act before she was taken by someone else.

I want to ask, but I don't want to push it. I just want to let Baxter hang out with his sweet memory for a while.

Sharing a look with Rachel, we settle back in our seats and drive the rest of the way home in silence. By the time we get back to the house, Baxter's gone into hiding again. He quietly gets out of the car and waits for us to shut our doors before locking it.

I trail in behind him and find the whole crew lingering in the lounge. The atmosphere is subdued, and Baxter takes his leave without a word, darting down to his room before I can thank him again for taking me. Fezzik scampers after him, his little nails clicking over the entryway as he chases his favorite person in the house.

Liam's the first to notice us and bolts out of his chair, coming over to wrap his arm around Rachel, and Caroline gasps when she sees me, running across to envelop me in a fierce hug that makes it hard to breathe.

"I just heard what happened," she wails in my ear.

"How?"

"I spoke to Asher," Ethan pipes up.

I gaze across the room at him. "Is he okay?"

"Should be home any minute."

Turning for the entryway, I'm tempted to wait for him outside, but the door clicks open before I reach it and Asher walks in looking wrecked.

"Baby," I whisper, launching myself against him.

He holds me tight, kissing the side of my head and murmuring into my ear, "Are you okay?"

"Yeah." I sniff and briefly update him.

He tells me I did good, rubbing my back and comforting me when I should be the one comforting him.

Wrapping my arm around his waist, I walk with him to the living area, where everyone's looking at him expectantly.

"It was shit," he tells us. "But I did get to punch him a couple times, so..." He holds up his hand, showing off his red knuckles, and Casey stands, giving him a serious look before starting a slow clap.

Asher closes his eyes with a pained frown. "Don't fucking slow clap, man. We're probably gonna get kicked out of Hockey House."

"I gotta do this," Casey argues. "You're a fucking legend, dude."

Asher's eyes pop open, and he glances around the room in surprise. I'm sure he was expecting disappointment and anger, but all I'm seeing are nods of understanding and approval.

Soon, Rachel gets in on the clapping, and then Liam joins in too.

"Is this the cheesiest moment we've ever experienced?" Mick asks the room before joining in on the clapping and then throwing in a whistle as well.

"Puck yeah!" Ethan laughs and starts whooping and clapping as well.

Asher shakes his head. "So fucking cheesy, you guys." But he looks ready to cry.

They love him, and I think he's starting to see just how much.

Reaching up on my tiptoes, I press my nose into his cheek, then kiss him when he turns his head. My fingers thread through his dark locks and I hold him against me, hoping he can feel how much I love him too.

CHAPTER 58
ASHER

I can't remember falling asleep, but when I wake up, Lani is lying beside me. Her long black hair is draped across my pillow, and her naked shoulder is calling me like a siren. I brush my lips across it, then nibble my way up to her ear.

She lets out a sleepy murmur and a soft giggle, rolling over to face me.

Her brown eyes drink me in like I matter, and I soak in her gaze before pressing my lips to hers, then meandering down her body and taking my time paying attention to all her most sensitive spots.

Her fingers dig into my hair as I lick her clit and send her spiraling with an orgasm that rocks her entire body. She cries out my name, reminding me how important she is... why I've turned my back on blood for the sake of this woman.

Grabbing my shoulders, she urges me back up her

body, sliding her tongue into my mouth and begging me to finish what I've started.

"I want you," she whispers, kissing my whiskers and licking a line down my neck while I scramble for a condom.

She wraps me, then easily guides me inside her.

I take her slowly at first, filling her core and drinking in her ecstasy until I start to lose the ability to focus. She feels so fucking good encasing me that soon all I can feel is her wet heat wrapping my cock like a glove. She draws me in, her heels digging into my ass cheeks as she urges me deeper.

Our pants mingle together and we kiss each other's breath, our rhythm picking up tempo. Her fingers draw deep lines on my shoulders as I suck her neck and she starts to gasp.

My pace quickens even more, and then I start to splinter. A choked groan oozes out of my mouth as I thrust into her and let myself go.

It's fucking amazing, and she clings to me when I thrust again and bury myself as deep as I can go.

"Love you, baby." She whispers the words repeatedly against my skin, and I revel in it.

She's my woman, and I would do anything for her.

And that's exactly what I say to my dad when I speak to him two hours later.

He called me as I was leaving a lecture, and as much as I wanted to ignore him, I figured, why delay the inevitable?

"They'll crucify you for this," Dad warns me. "Is she really worth it?"

"Dad," I huff. "Even if she wasn't mine and I'd found out what Harvey did… I still couldn't stay silent. He can't keep doing this. Someone has to stop him, and even if it means walking away from my Denver family, I'll do it." I hold my breath, almost afraid to ask the next part. "Will I, um… will I be walking away from my New York family too?"

Dad pauses, like he's surprised I'd even ask that. After a thick beat, he assures me, "Of course not. You're our son. And yes, it's awkward right now, but our loyalties lie with you."

I squeeze my eyes shut, still hating this great divide. Mom will be feeling it. Uncle Hayes is her brother. *Her* flesh and blood, and this whole thing will set them against each other.

Trudging down the stone steps, I find a bench in the sunshine and take a seat, ready to see just how far my father's loyalties will go.

Pressing the phone to my ear, I will my courage not to fail me and quickly blurt, "Will you still be loyal to me if I tell you I don't want to do the summer internship?" I wince and figure I might as well get it over with in one hit. "If I tell you, I don't really want to work for Bensens & Co?"

He goes deathly quiet for so long, I actually check my screen to make sure he's still on the line. "Dad?"

"I was worried that might be the case. You weren't

exactly excited about that internship, and..." He sighs. "Asher, your whole life, you've always been so determined to walk to the beat of your own drum. We had to make you go to that boarding school, and I had already bought you a Harvard jacket when you went and picked Nolan U. I thought you were doing it just to piss me off, but..."

"I wasn't, Dad. I didn't pick Nolan to spite you. I wanted to play hockey here, and they have a great—"

"Is that what you want to do? Go pro?" He sounds more than disappointed.

I ignore his tone and answer honestly.

"No. But I don't want to work for you either. I'm more interested in small start-up businesses. Kind of like what Mom's friend Desiree does. I want to build something from the ground up. I want to help people get started, working alongside them one-on-one. I don't want to spend my days in high-rise buildings, in constant meetings with boards and businessmen who have been around the block a dozen times already."

"You want to help people turn their dreams into realities."

"Yes." I nod. "And I know compared to what you do, that is so small-time and insignificant, but—"

"It's not insignificant."

I'm so surprised he's agreeing with me that I'm stunned silent for a moment.

"Look, I'm sorry if you felt like you couldn't tell me this. If you felt like I wouldn't support you. But it really disappoints me that you never thought to come forward with this."

My lips part, and I blink at the green grass in front of me. "You never asked me what I wanted to do with my life. It was just assumed that I'd join the business."

"Yeah, well, that's on me, I guess."

"Mom's gonna be pissed." I rub my forehead.

"She might surprise you." I think I hear a smile in his voice, and it cuts a little of my tension. "I'll talk to her."

"Thanks," I rasp.

"And as for the Harvey nightmare, just make sure all of your actions are aboveboard. Don't try and take matters into your own hands and do something stupid."

I wince. "I kinda punched him already."

"So I heard." He tuts. "But I've lined up my lawyers, and they'll be ready to step in with legal aid if it comes to that. And let your lady friend know that we can support her, too, if she needs it."

"Really?" I perk up.

"Son, if you love her enough to throw away free housing, then I'm guessing she's pretty special to you."

"She is."

"Well, then, we'd like to meet her. How about you two fly back for the weekend? It'll give us a chance to get to know her a little."

"That'd be... Wow, Dad. That'd be great. I was not expecting you to say that."

"Can you please stop sounding so surprised that I want to support you?" He kind of snaps the words, and I wince while also fighting a soft laugh. "You're my son. And you're an honorable man."

The words ring through me so loud and clear, I get a little choked up. Those words are the closest thing to an *I love you* that I've ever heard, and I sit in them for a minute, soaking them up like they're fucking gold.

"Now, I'm sure you have another class to get to, so I'll let you go for now, but we have some more conversations to have, young man. We need to figure out where you're going to live for the last year or so of college, and I'd like to look over whatever business plans you might have, make sure you're on track with your ideas. I'm not taking over... just supporting."

"Sure, Dad." I raise my eyebrows, fighting a grin. "I'll keep you posted on the housing thing."

"There's still some surplus left in your college fund."

"Yeah, I know, but I want to make sure everyone at Hockey House is taken care of."

"We're not a charity, Asher."

"I know that, but these guys are my brothers. I won't leave them high and dry."

He huffs, obviously not impressed by my answer.

"Don't worry about it. I'll think of something."

And I'd damn well better, because when I finally get home after my evening workout, I find a stack of flattened boxes resting against the wall in the living room.

I frown at them, then turn to find Liam giving me a glum smile. "Your uncle stopped by. We've got two weeks to get our asses out of here."

"What? I thought we'd get ninety days. That's the law, isn't it?" I pull out my phone, starting a quick search to confirm that.

"Yeah." Liam interrupts my frantic hunt. "But in two weeks, he's gonna start charging us rent, and dude..." He cringes. "It's astronomical."

My lips part as he hands me a sheet of paper and I gape at the figures. "Eight thousand a month? That's criminal!"

"Do you think he can get away with it?" Liam scratches the back of his head.

I work my jaw to the side, slapping the paper against my thigh. "I guess we could try fighting him, but by the time it all goes through, we'll be out of this place anyway."

"That's what we figured, so..." Liam buries his hands in his pockets and shrugs. "Time to start looking for new digs."

My frown is sad and desperate; I can feel it tugging my lips down and wrinkling my forehead.

"Don't really want to be here anyway, after all this shit, you know?"

Liam's murmured words ring true, and all I can do is nod my agreement.

CHAPTER 59
LEILANI

In less than a week, Hockey House needs to be empty. And so does Rachel and Mikayla's little apartment down the road. Hayes Carmichael was going to double their rent. No more special deals for friends of the family.

The Carmichaels have been hardline and unrelenting. It probably doesn't help that the police arrested their son a few days ago and charges have been pressed against him. Asher's parents have stepped up with their lawyers, and I'm so incredibly grateful.

I got to tell them that this weekend, when we flew to New York for a two-day visit.

At first, his mother was overly cautious of me, and I spent the first meal being grilled like she was searching for a chink in my armor. But I obviously said all the right things, because by the time dessert was served, she was telling me how brave I've been and that Asher was right to stand up for me the way he did.

After a day on their boat, sailing along the Hudson River, I was assured of their support, and Asher was being complimented on his fine taste in women. I didn't love being referred to like I was an aged bottle of wine, but his father just talks that way, and I can live with it for Asher's sake.

He's come from such an upper-class, structured life-style that I'm sure the chaos of my upbringing would be too much for him, but it was nice to catch a glimpse of the world Asher grew up in. It definitely helps me to understand him on a deeper level.

And I won't lie... there are serious perks to dating a rich man.

Not that I'm with him for his money, but it is a fine, fine life that I could quickly get used to.

Yeah, Asher's not interested in joining the family business, and although he'll probably get a chunk of start-up cash from his trust fund, he'll still be on his own, making his way in the world. But that doesn't mean we can't tag along when his parents take off to Europe... or we can't enjoy some fine dining or a free night in one of their hotels.

Making love on silk sheets... yeah, I could get used to that.

We flew late Sunday afternoon tired but happy... until we walked into his man cave and realized how much stuff Asher still had to pack. I've been helping him as best I can. He still doesn't know where he'll be living, and that sick uncertainty is vibrating throughout the entire house. They've been looking at rental properties in the area and trying to figure out how much they can afford.

It's not much, and their quest to stay together is looking futile.

The thought is bringing everyone down, and packing has kind of stopped as we all dribble into the dining room after class on Monday.

We sit at the table, nibbling on bowls of chips and popcorn as the late afternoon rolls around. No one's talking, and Baxter's probably reveling in it. He stares at his plate, his nose twitching while Fezzik sits at his feet whining. The puppy soon gives up and tries to beg for scraps from Casey, who's the softest touch of us all.

He breaks a chip in half and feeds it to the pup.

"So...," Ethan starts but then sighs and shakes his head.

Mikayla gives his forearm a squeeze, her smile sad until her phone starts ringing.

She jolts, snatching for her device and nearly dropping it in her haste. She reads the screen and her face lights up as she looks to Rachel. "This could be it!"

Her best friend lurches forward in her chair and then chases her out of the room as Mick disappears to answer the call.

"What's up with those two?" Asher asks.

Ethan and Liam share a perplexed frown, then shrug.

It's obviously bothering Liam more than Ethan. The guy scratches the back of his head, turning in his seat and straining to catch Rachel's eye as she hovers in the archway, watching Mikayla pace to the front door and back.

Her voice starts pitching with excitement, and then she lets out a squeal.

Ethan winces. "What the fuck was that?"

Rising from the table, he's about to go investigate when Mikayla shouts, "Thank you! I love you too!" then hangs up and starts happy dancing.

"What are you doing?" Ethan calls across the room.

She laughs, hugging Rachel and practically skipping into the room.

"What is with the squealing?" He crosses his arms and frowns at his girlfriend.

"What?" She gives him a coy smile. "I squeal."

"Not like that." He smirks, and her face blushes pink as she laughs at him. "This is a different kind of excitement, okay?"

"So, what's going on?" Liam looks to Rachel, and the smile that crosses her face is brighter than the sun, I swear.

"Well..."

CHAPTER 60
ASHER

"We've got a place for us to move into!" Mikayla finishes for her, then thrusts her hands into the air and shouts, "Puck yeah!"

No one joins her because we're all sitting here in shock.

"Fuckin' what?" Ethan blinks at her, looking more confused than ever.

"Okay, I didn't want to say anything until I was sure it'd come through, but I just spoke to my dad and..." She looks around the table with a huge grin. "How do you guys feel about doing a summer renovation?"

"Okay, back up a second." I flick my fingers through the air. "Fuckin' what?"

She laughs, the sound deep and throaty. "You know how my step-grandpa owns a bunch of restaurants and resorts and stuff?"

"Ye-ah."

"Well, I called my dad after your uncle came to visit and told him what was going on. I was just doing it to rant, really, but a couple days later, he called me back with an idea." She sits in her chair, pulling her knee up and hugging it while Rachel takes over for her.

"His father-in-law is always looking for ways to expand the business, so as a favor to us, he started looking for hotels close to Nolan."

My eyebrows rise.

"He didn't find anything suitable, but..." An excited smile blooms across Rachel's face, and Mikayla butts in to finish for her.

"He did see one place online that's a little outside the box, but he asked us to go look at it anyway!"

"Okay."

"So we did!" Mick's voice squeaks, and Ethan gives her an odd look before starting to fight a grin. He's never seen her like this before. None of us have. "It's this old villa about ten minutes outside town. It's got like eight bedrooms and two lounge areas, plus a parlor and a den. There's even an old billiards table in what I assume was like a smoking room!"

"There's a huge kitchen, which needs refitting, but the space is amazing." Rachel's face lights like a Christmas tree.

"It used to be a ranch, but the owners sold off the land piece by piece. The house and the few acres it sits on have fallen into disrepair, and no one has bothered with it since the owner passed away," Mikayla explains.

"Oh! There's also a two-bedroom pool house, which some of us can sleep in. It's pretty crappy at the moment, but we can do it up."

"And the rest of us can move into the main house. Which will still leave like five guest rooms. And they'll take a while to fill anyway, because the place needs serious work! But my dad thinks we can get the house open for business by springtime next year."

"Business?" Caroline murmurs.

"Yeah, we'll run like a legit bed-and-breakfast!"

We all gape at the girls. Their excitement is palpable, and it's impossible not to be affected by it. But I need some more deets before I truly lose my shit with relief.

"So, you found this old place, and your dad's father-in-law just agreed to buy it? Just like that?" I snap my fingers.

"Well, Dad's done all of the work for us, really. He pitched the idea, threw together a quick business plan, and flew out to see the villa a couple days ago. He loved it and had this epic vision for how it could all come together, so he put in an offer."

"Your dad was here and you didn't tell me?" Ethan frowns.

"I'm sorry, baby. I just didn't want to get anyone's hopes up unnecessarily."

"And that squeal that you did before... was that the offer being accepted?"

"Yes!" Mikayla beams. "He's stoked. He's getting it for a steal, which is great because they'll have to invest quite a bit to get it up to code. But it'll eventually turn a profit. I mean, Nolan's a pretty town, and there are some awesome hiking trails around this area. In the winter, we're not far from decent skiing, and he's confident a little bed-and-breakfast is a great investment. Plus, I volunteered us all as free labor if we get to live in the place. And Rachel's more than happy to manage guests and stuff. Plus, Dad will eventually hire someone to help run the legal and admin side of things once it's officially open for business."

"It means I can quit my job at the diner and look after guests full-time. I'll be the hostess with the mostest." Rachel bats her eyelashes.

Liam gives her an affectionate smile, running his hand down the back of her hair. "You'll be so good at that, cariño."

"But what about school? Our exams and study and hockey—"

Mikayla raises her hand to shut Lani up. "It's a summer project, and even though the sale was confirmed today, we can't move in until the paperwork is finalized, so we still have to find us some digs for a few weeks. We can focus on getting through exam week, and then our attention can turn to the house."

"I can see if my parents will splash out for a local motel or an Airbnb," I offer. "If it's only short term, they'll probably agree to it."

"But..." Lani's still shaking her head. "Who's going to run the place after we all graduate?"

Mikayla shrugs. "We'll help Dad find someone to take over if we don't stay in Nolan, but that's a problem for a few years away. I mean, I've got at least three more, and you've got two, right?"

"Yeah." Lani nods. "Although, I won't be living there."

"Well, you can if you want to." Mikayla shrugs again. "There's plenty of room. The only stipulation is that if you live there, you've got to pitch in. Once all the renovations are done, we'll be expected to run the place, meaning cleaning and maintenance and looking after the guests. So..." Mikayla looks around the table. "If any of you don't like that idea, then..." She trails off, obviously not wanting to say *don't come.*

There's a silent beat as she waits us out, and then...

"Yes!" Casey finally pipes up, punching his arm in the air. "Fuckin' yeah, bros! We can keep living together!"

His outburst makes Caroline jump, but then she starts laughing, and that sets us all off.

This is unbelievable.

Hockey House isn't going anywhere.

Sure, the new place is out of town, and we'll have to live in it while it's being renovated, but... Casey's right. We get to keep living together.

Our family stays intact.

"You guys wanna go see it?" Mikayla jumps up from her chair. "I'll give the real estate agent a call and ask her to meet us there."

It takes all of two seconds for us to agree, and as soon as Mikayla's spoken to the agent, we're piling out the front door and jumping into vehicles. Even Baxter comes along for the ride. We have to leave Fezzik behind, much to his heartbreak, and he puts his little paws on the fence and whines as we pull away.

"Sorry, lil dude," Casey murmurs.

"Back soon, baby!" Caroline calls out the window.

Following Ethan's truck, we head out of town to check out this villa.

As the laughter and enthusiasm bubbles around me, I can't help a grin. I'm kind of reeling over how fucking lucky I am.

CHAPTER 61
LEILANI

"Still feeling lucky?" I murmur, nudging Asher's arm with my shoulder as we stand in the old villa and gaze up at the water stains on the ceiling and the curling wallpaper.

He doesn't say anything at first and I wince, biting my lip. "You don't have to agree to this, you know. If it's not your thing, you can—"

"I love it." He turns to me with a grin.

"Really?" I laugh at his expression. "I thought you were having major doubts."

"No, I was just picturing the potential. Look out that window." He points west and I turn, drinking in the dark orange ball of sun that's sinking below the mountains in the distance. "And look at this floor." He points down at the scratched wood beneath our feet. "With a good sanding and polish, it's going to be stunning." He steps away from me, walking to the window seat and then doing a slow spin. "Can't you see new paper on the walls or a fresh coat of paint? Guests will come in here for drinks before dinner is served. We could turn this wall into a shelf stuffed with books. There could be a chess set here on a low coffee table with some plush chairs." His voice grows with excitement as he grabs my hand and drags me through a doorway and straight into the kitchen.

It's a dump, the equipment so outdated, I'm surprised it even works.

"Imagine this all kitted out with shiny new surfaces and equipment. Ray could cook up a storm in this place."

"I know!" She skips in from the other doorway with Liam in tow. Spreading her hands over the counter, she taps the wall. "I want to ask if this could be opened up so we could turn it into a serving station. Do you think we could knock a hole in this wall?"

Liam runs his hand over it like he knows shit about building, then shakes his head. "Not sure, but we could ask."

"You definitely can." Baxter appears behind Liam. "I was just looking at the other side. It's not load-bearing. You could turn that room into a dining area for guests, make it like a café style, even."

Rachel gasps. "You know, this doesn't just have to be a bed-and-breakfast. What if we made it a café as well?" She spins to look at Asher. "That could work, right? We could serve like a high tea kind of deal, and people could come out here for an afternoon, catching up with their friends over a cup of coffee."

"Isn't it a little too far out of town to be convenient?" I wrinkle my nose.

"It's only ten minutes... and that's kind of the point," Asher murmurs. "You're not just grabbing a coffee to go, you're meeting up for the pleasure of delicious food and a stunning view. We could maybe build a little playground area out in the yard for kids."

"Yes!" Rachel rises to her toes, then touches her cheeks, spinning to look up at Liam with a watery smile. "My bakery. I could make food so incredible that people will want to drive out of town just to experience it."

Liam's smile is wide and encouraging as he pulls Rachel into his arms and kisses her.

Asher throws his arm around my shoulders and smiles down at me. "I want to be a part of this. I want to get this place off the ground and make it a must-see place to visit in Nolan."

I rest my hand on his stomach. "If anyone can do it, you can." My heart swells with affection. "I don't know if I've ever seen you so excited about something."

"I am." He stares around in wonder. "Seriously, I'm so pumped for this."

Baxter catches his eye and nods. "It's gonna be awesome."

"Really? You're in?" Asher asks. "But you graduate this year."

Baxter shrugs. "I've got no place else to be for the summer. Might as well kick around here and help you guys out. I'm used to working construction jobs over the long breaks, so..."

"Oh yeah? That's handy."

He shrugs, like giving us details is too much effort, then spins out of the kitchen before we can ask for more.

I snicker and shake my head. The guy is a perpetual mystery. It's like he's only ever willing to expose a small corner of himself. But I'll keep picking away. Eventually, I'll understand how the guy ticks.

"So..." Asher takes my hand and pulls me out of the kitchen. We head back through the parlor and out to the entrance. There's a wooden staircase with a beautifully carved railing leading up to the bedrooms. "What do you think, Miss Iona. You like this place?"

I ascend the stairs and smile at the laughter above us. Sounds like Casey and Caroline.

"I like you in this place," I finally tell him. "I love the look in your eyes and the potential you see."

"Think you'd want live here?"

I jolt to a stop. He's two steps above me, and I gape up at him. "You want me to live here? With you?"

"Eventually." He shrugs, then walks back down to cup my face. "I know it's too soon right now, and I'm not trying to rush you. You love being at the dorm with Caroline, and you should totally stay there, but... I mean, this summer. Would you want to stick around?"

I hold his wrists, brushing my thumb across the hair on his arms. A smile grows within me, then starts to show on my face as I nod. "I'd like that."

"Yeah?" His laughter is thick with relief.

"Think you'll be able to stand it?" I tease him. "I can be a bossy bitch when it comes to projects like this. There's a strong chance everyone will hate me by the end."

"I could never hate you," he assures me.

"You used to."

He laughs and shakes his head, pulling me in for a firm kiss before looking me in the eye. "I never hated you."

My insides turn to mush as I bask in his affectionate gaze. "I never hated you either."

His grin grows a little wider. "Love you, my little shrutebag."

I laugh and slap his butt as he comes in for another kiss. I let him have it, deepening the kiss with a tongue sweep that makes him groan.

Pulling back, I smile against his mouth and murmur, "I love you, too, my lumpatious asshole."

CHAPTER 62
BAXTER

Slipping the hammer back into my tool belt, I step back, cross my arms, and then look to Rachel for approval.

"That gonna work?"

"Yes." She beams at the new shelves I've just installed in her walk-in pantry. "You're the best. Thanks, Bax."

"Not a problem." I give the bottom one a little shake to make sure it's secure. I already know it will be. I guess it's just a habit I picked up from my dad.

He's a builder. Not that I've ever worked for him... except when I was in high school.

Working on this house project over the summer has actually been way better than I thought. Dad even came down for a week to check in and help out. I wasn't expecting that, but I was grateful.

Everyone had so many fucking questions for him, but he's better at talking than I am, so I left them to it.

Since then, he's been calling to check in on how

things are going at the villa and said he might even make the trip over again to see what I've been up to. I've sent him pics to make him feel like he's part of it, and even though he'll never say it, I think he appreciates the gesture.

Mom always loved pics. She wanted every detail.

Not having her around anymore has cast a gray shadow over our lives, which is why getting out of one more summer in Gladstone was a relief. My small town has a population of around five hundred people, and everyone knows everybody else's business. You can't trim a toenail in that town without someone hearing about it, and I'm sure Dad got a whole bunch of sympathy about my decision to stay in Nolan for yet another summer break... and I got a whole bunch of scathing comments behind my back.

I don't give a shit.

If it weren't for Dad, I'd never set foot in that town again. I usually fly in for a few days over Thanksgiving and stay in the house as much as possible before shooting back to Nolan.

"So, I think that's all I need from you down here." Rachel interrupts my thoughts. "I'm gonna quickly put this stuff away, then head into town. Mick and I will have lunch together, and then I'll check out that thrift shop off Main Street." Rachel gives me an excited grin as she loads up the shelves with her newly acquired containers. Lani helped her label them all last night—white sugar, brown sugar, flour, etc. They used Lani's label maker and got way too much satisfaction out of such a simple task.

With the kitchen being brand-spanking new, Rachel wants to keep it as pristine and as organized as she can for as long as humanly possible. She and Lani seem to get off on tidiness and structure. And Rachel's beyond excited about making her dreams a reality.

She really was born for this role.

She's sweet and friendly with the workers who have been coming and going. She knew exactly what she wanted and fought for it with a smile. It's pretty easy to do anything she asks because she's so damn nice about it. She's even scored a few smiles from Vanessa, the woman who's been hired to tick all the boxes and make sure this place complies with every code, policy, and whatever other shit has to be signed off. Mick's dad hired her, and she's... well, she's Vanessa—or "Scary Hag," as Casey likes to call her.

Work on the place went way faster than we anticipated. I guess having so many volunteers really helped, and the six-month renovation only took four. I know. It's a miracle.

I mean, sure, there are still a few things to do. The place isn't ready to open to the public yet—Vanessa's a stickler for the rules—but all the main stuff is done. The builders have packed up and gone. And now it's up to me to finish up all the loose ends.

We're waiting on fittings for the upstairs bathrooms, which I can easily install, and some light shades haven't turned up yet. The third-floor bedrooms need painting and furnishing, and the girls have been on the hunt looking for knickknacks, which Mikayla rolled her eyes at.

"They're dustables. That's all they are! More things to clean!"

"Mick." Rachel gave her a soft look of reprimand. "They'll make the rooms look pretty. Guests will love it. And besides, if all you're having to do for the privilege of living here is dust a little, I wouldn't complain."

That shut her up.

Riccardo—Mikayla's step-grandfather, and the owner of this place—wants to go for an old-style modern feel, meaning it looks like you've stepped back into the 1800s but with all the mod-cons you could want.

The old man came to visit last week with Mikayla's father, and they're really impressed. They've decided to name this place Ponderosa Countryside Villa thanks to the massive Ponderosa pines that line the back edge of the property. A new sign was installed at the gate just this weekend with a big 'Opening Soon!' sticker across the edge.

They're already talking about soft launches and how to get this place humming. Asher muscled his way into those conversations—I still don't know how—but he's loving it and was beyond stoked when his suggestion to run a few weekend specials for exclusive guests was taken on board.

I think the plan is to open up the café while we finish

off the last of the rooms, then try for some exclusive two-night stays in November, then an official Christmas opening to see if we can attract some guests to spend a snowy winter break in this quaint homestead.

Some shit like that, anyway. These guys have got it all figured out. I'm just gonna go with the flow... and in my mind, I'm gonna keep calling it Hockey House, because no matter what kind of fancy-ass name this place gets, it's still filled with my hockey bros. So, Hockey House 2.0 it is.

I wave to Rachel, leaving her to finish organizing the kitchen.

The house is empty except for the two of us. Everyone else is off at school. Vanessa is in California this week—thank God—so things are quiet and relaxed. Hockey season has already started, so the guys are out the door at stupid o'clock to get their workouts in before classes start.

It's a busy hive of activity in the early mornings and evenings. People are constantly coming and going depending on work schedules, practices, and study groups.

Except for me.

I'm here all the time, because I haven't found it in me to start the dreaded job hunt yet. I scratch my beard, which has grown in over the summer. I couldn't be bothered shaving and now I think I'll feel naked without it. It's gotten a little wild and I'll need to tidy it up before I start going for job interviews but...

I don't even know what I want to do. I majored in

business studies, because I didn't know what the hell else to choose, and it bored me to tears. I went to college for the hockey, but I never wanted to go pro either. I just wanted to have some fun and figure it out as I went along.

The problem is...

I never figured it out.

Working on this old villa over the summer has been pretty fun. Maybe I should be going into construction.

Although, part of the fun was hanging with everyone. Yes, I'm a quiet guy, and everyone thinks I'm a hermit. But that's only because I don't want to talk about shit. If I can just sit there watching everyone, I'm happy. And people have been so busy doing jobs over the summer that I've been able to do just that. Work away in the background, listening to funny conversations and watching my friends laugh and be stupid together.

During the height of our busy season, we ended up all bunking in the pool house. We set up air mattresses on the floor and piled in there together. It was like being at a sleepover in high school. I think. I never got invited to them, so I wouldn't really know, but... I can imagine that they were awesome.

Clomping up the stairs, I head for the third floor, figuring I can get an undercoat down in the north-facing bedroom before I'm due at the local arena.

I've been roped into coaching Mini-Mite hockey this season. They were short a guy, and I just happened to be in the wrong place at the wrong time. The head of the arena pointed at me, recognized me as a Cougar, and asked how long I'd been playing hockey.

I stupidly responded, "Since I was four."

"Perfect! You're in."

I shouldn't complain. It's a little extra cash, and those five- and six-year-olds are damn cute. I'm only an assistant coach... unless the head guy doesn't show up. On those days, I also have to stick around for the Mite and Squirt practices. And occasionally, I'll run a Peewee session too.

The older those kids get, the faster they are on the ice, and I won't admit this to anyone, but I kinda love watching their progress. I almost hope I can keep the position for more than a year or two so I can watch my little Minis improve.

Which tells me I probably want to stay in Nolan for now.

I scratch my whiskers again, surprised by that. I always thought Nolan was a four-year stop, but where the hell else am I gonna go?

I'm not a big-city man, and I can't go back to Gladstone. I'd run out of oxygen by day three. And everywhere I turn, I'll just be reminded of her.

That town is too small to survive in.

And at least Nolan is filled with mostly good memories.

I reach the top floor and am just getting ready to lay out some drop cloth when I hear a voice downstairs.

"Hello? Anybody here?"

I wait for Rachel to respond, but she doesn't say anything.

"Hello?"

With a frown, I squeeze the back of my neck and wait out one more "Hello?" before giving up with a huff and clomping back downstairs.

Rachel must have left already. She probably went out the back, which means she wouldn't have seen whoever was coming in.

"We're not actually open yet," I call down the stairs, but my voice dies when I reach the landing and see the woman waiting in the foyer.

My breath hitches and I'm frozen in place, my heart thumping wildly as she turns around and spots me.

Her almond eyes crease at the corners, and I'm sucked back in time for a second. Back to that moment when I'm pretty sure I fell in love with her. It was the Fourth of July, and she was wearing red ribbons in her hair and a stars-and-stripes T-shirt. Her smile was radiant as she laughed at something her friend said, and then she looked right at me and winked.

And now she's standing here like an apparition. Her hair is shorter—cut to her shoulders—and she's got a kid perched on her hip.

I gape at the boy, my insides curdling as I force my legs to move down the final stairwell.

"Baxter Brown." She grins at me. Her smile is still the same. I could never get enough of those dimples.

Stopping on the final step, I grip the railing and try to play it cool. That's how I get through most things in life—aloof and unreadable.

"Hey, Tammy."

My little TT. That's what I used to call her.

Tamara Tan—the only girl I've ever loved—is standing just a few feet away from me.

And she's holding a kid.

Not my kid.

His kid.

It's gotta be. The boy looks like he's around four-ish, and that's when she was dating *him*. That's the reason they got married... or at least one of the reasons.

Working my jaw to the side, I beg my mouth to work as I step onto the wooden floor and close the space between us.

"And who's this guy?" I have to ask, right? I have to smile and pretend like it's not a knife through the chest.

"This is Kai." She lightly brushes her son's nose, her smile gentle and encouraging.

"Hey, buddy." I raise my hand in a wave, but he just bulges his eyes at me and buries his head in his mother's neck.

"He's shy." Her voice fades, her eyes instantly glassing with tears as she tries to explain. "It's been a rough couple days."

I frown, worry coursing through me, even though I don't want to feel anything around her anymore. I did that. I got burned. And then I swore off women for life.

"I'm sorry to just show up like this." Her voice wobbles. "I can't go home. You know what Gladstone's like." The soft curls bounce around her face as she shakes her head. "My parents won't understand, no matter what I say... and none of my friends will get it either."

"Tam, what's going on?"

"Hudson's having an affair." Her voice catches, instant tears lining her lashes.

That fucking shithead! I knew she was too good for him.

Clenching my jaw, I try to stop the dark emotion from showing on my face. I always hated that guy.

Yeah, only because he got the girl you wanted... then impregnated her.

They got special permission from their parents to get married, and the wedding bells were ringing before graduation day. Who the fuck gets married in high school?

A week later, my mom died in a car accident, and I left Gladstone in my rearview mirror. I couldn't stay in that backwater town anymore. I couldn't watch Tammy be married to that asshole, and I couldn't stay in my house when the thing that made it sunny was no longer there.

Dad understood, and we took off for a month-long road trip before I left for Nolan.

But then he went back... and I stayed as far away as possible.

"I just need somewhere to lie low for a few days while

I figure this out. You were my best friend in high school, and I know we..." Her eyes dip to the floor, and she worries her lip. "I mean, we... well, we lost touch...after..." She clears her throat, avoiding mention of the worst reason why.

My skin flares hot, and I bite my lips together and look to the floor as well.

"But... I don't know where else to go."

I glance up in time to see a lone tear slip from her left eye, tracking down to the edge of her mouth.

Without thinking, I shove the past aside and step forward, brushing that tear away. "It's okay," I whisper. "You can stay here for as long as you need. We'll find a space for you."

She gives me a watery smile, and my heart starts to hurt all over again. I've loved her since the fifth grade, and even after all this time, one look at her face and I'm a goner all over again.

And now she's finally single.

I mean, maybe.

I shouldn't get my hopes up.

She may have come running to me, but that doesn't mean she'll stay... unless I can finally find the right thing to say. Unless I can finally convince her that she deserves more than an arrogant prick who could never love her the way I do.

Baxter's friends-to-lovers, second-chance romance - THE ONLY GOAL - is releasing in August 2024.

Keep an eye on Katy's social media for the release announcement of this sweet and sexy V-card story.

NOTE FROM KATY

Dear reader,

Thank you for reading Lani and Asher's romance. I loved these two so much. She's such a strong, amazing character. I love her tenacity and fight. And Asher... oh man! He turned out way sweeter than I thought he'd be. He's a bit of an antagonist in *The Forbidden Freshman*, but the guy's got layers and I loved getting to know him and seeing his sweet, romantic side come out. The way he choose her... yeah, that melted me all the way through.

And do you know who else is gonna melt me?
Yep - you guessed it. *Baxter*.
Initially, I hadn't planned to write a book for him, but one of my lovely readers—Shae—messaged me, asking if there was a story coming. We chatted about it and within minutes had a cool idea and so you can thank this lovely

lady for her brilliant idea. *The Only Goal* is coming to be because of her, so thank you, Shae 🤍

Our mystery man, Baxter has got a great story brewing. I can't WAIT to watch him win Tammy's heart and finally get to be with her the way he's always wanted to. I'm so stoked to write his V-card story and I can't wait for you to read it.

If you enjoyed *The Love Penalty*, I would so appreciate you leaving an honest review on Goodreads. Even just a star rating is helpful. You don't have to write anything if you don't want to. But star ratings and even short reviews really help validate the book, letting readers know it's worth a shot. It also tells book retailers that this novel is worth shining a spotlight on. I know there are a bunch of readers out there who love college sports romance just as much as we do. If you can help me reach them, then that would be freaking fantastic. Thanks for the assist!

I'd also like to thank a few key people who have been instrumental in helping me prepare and release this book —Megan (superstar cover designer), Kristin (legendary proofreader), Beth (the best editor ever), Rachael (world's best assistant), Melissa (mentor and biggest cheerleader). I love each and every interaction I have with you guys. Thank you for your constant support. You help make my dreams come true.

My review team—Thank you for all the words of love for these books and characters. Thank you for the reviews and posts and teasers - they all mean the world to me.

My readers—I love you! Every email, every DM, every sale... every time I know someone out there is enjoying one of these books, it makes my day. You are so important to me and I appreciate you so much. Thank you!

Brenda—you are my truest, dearest, most steadfast friend. Thank you for always cheering me on and having my back no matter what.

Maggie—one of my favorite people and such an inspiration. Thank you for your constant support.

My beautiful boys—thanks for loving me, hugging me, playing cards and board games with me, watching movies with me, singing way too loud with me, making me laugh and celebrating every win with me. You guys are the best!

My God—thanks for being there through thick and thin. You love me always and so completely. You created me to be exactly who I am and I'm so grateful. I love you.

xoxo
Katy

BOOKS BY KATY ARCHER

NOLAN U HOCKEY

Hockey House V-cards (prequel)

The Forbidden Freshman

The Heart Stealer

The Game Changer

The Love Penalty

The Only Goal

The Forever Game (Epilogue novella)

NOLAN U FOOTBALL

Releasing in 2025...

The First Play

The Forever Play

and more...

NOLAN U BASKETBALL

In development

CONTACT KATY

I love to hear from my readers, so feel free to email me anytime. You can also find out more on my website.

EMAIL: katy@katyarcher.com

WEBSITE: www.katyarcher.com

And if you want to connect with me on social and see pretty reels and teasers from the books, you can find me Addicted to College Sports Romance on...

INSTAGRAM
@addictedtocollegesportsromance

FACEBOOK
@collegesportsromancebooks

TIKTOK

@katyarcherbooks